MW01243037

DARK TEMPTATIONS

An Amarah Rey, Fey Warrior Novel

Harmony A. Haun

Copyright © 2022 Harmony Haun

All rights reserved. No part of this book may be reproduced or used in any manner without written permission of the copyright owner except for the use of quotations in a book review.

ISBN: 978-1-7363432-7-2 Paperback
ISBN: 978-1-7363432-6-5 e-book
ISBN: 978-1-7363432-8-9 Hardback

First edition

Author Contact: harmonyhaunauthor@gmail.com

An Amarah Rey, Fey Warrior Books

AWAKEN

FEY BLOOD

DARK TEMPTATIONS

DEDICATION

This book is dedicated to everyone who's not perfect. For those of us who struggle with inner demons, no matter how big or small. For those of us with darkness in us. Dark thoughts. Dark desires. You're not alone. You can't have light without a little darkness. It is ok to embrace it! Embrace everything that makes you, YOU. However, if it gets to a point that's not healthy. That scares you and threatens you, please seek help. Again, you're not alone.

DARK
TEMPTATIONS
An Amarah Rey, Fey Warrior Novel

Word Definitions

All "The Unseen" words are English words translated into Estonian. Click on each hyperlinked (ebook) word to listen to the pronunciation from Google.

Alfa: Alpha

Ammune: Old

Beeta: Beta

Esimene: First

Kaitsja: Protector

Keerutaja: Trickster

Konsiilium: Council

Lapseealine: Young

Libahunt: Werewolf

Maa Family: Earth Fey

Müstik Family: Mystic, First Fey

Õhk Family: Air Fey

Rändaja: Traveller

Sigitis: Brood

Täiskuu: Full Moon

Täitjad: Enforcers

Tulekahju Family: Fire Fey

Ülim: Supreme

Valmistaja: Maker/manufacturer in Finnish

Valvur: Guardian

Vanemad: Elders

Vesi Family: Water Fey

Võitleja: Warrior

Võltsimatu: Pure

Amarah Rey Series Playlist

Listen to the entire series playlist here: Spotify

Logan: Control The Anger

Stay — JVP Remix by Adelita's Way

I make the hike to the Fire Fey's home in record time. My anger distracting me from my tired limbs, and my Wolf propelling me forward with the need to dominate.

The need to mate.

That last need burns hot in my veins, as I prowl down the long familiar castle hallways, and a frustrated growl escapes my throat. How many times have I made this trip? How many times have I wished that this time would be different? That this time I would *feel* something with my heart and not just with my dick?

I finally reach the large, fire-red door and change back into my human form effortlessly. I don't bother to knock. I storm in, a six-foot, naked, muscled body vibrating with anger. Anger that nothing and no one can damper. Anger that I hide well. Most of the time. She's waiting for me like I knew she would be.

So fucking predictable.

So fucking pathetic.

The Fire Fey Princess is lounging in a sea of black silk

pillows and sheets. She attempts to look relaxed, at ease, but everything about her, and this scene, is staged.

Propped and prepped.

A scene for my viewing pleasure. Her long, tan legs are stretched out in front of her. The red lingerie is a vibrant pop of color in all the black, hugging her curves, and presenting them up to me as a gift. A gift I'll certainly accept but not one I necessarily want.

I stand just inside the closed door, chest heaving, fists clenching, and cock stirring. She notices the stirring and slips off the bed. She'll come to me. She always does.

I don't beg.

I don't chase.

I don't have to.

She saunters toward me in her barely-there clothing, swaying her hips excessively. My eyes take all of her in, from her bare feet to the heated look in her eyes. She is stunning, and yet, she does *nothing* for me. Yes, I'm going to fuck her. A man has needs. But it's never more than that, and that truth sends another wave of anger through my body, causing me to shiver.

Hallana smirks, as if my shiver is because of *her*. I don't say shit. I let her think whatever the fuck she wants to think. I never lead her on with pretty words or promises because they would be a lie. I don't need to lie to her. She sees what she wants to see and makes up her own happy fucking story in her head. If she sees the truth, the giant red flags I wave loud and proud, she chooses to ignore them. Why do females fall in love with the *idea* of who men can be? Why do they hang on for dear life to our *potential* and not what's glaringly obvious?

"I've missed you," she says, as she slides her hands up my chest, leaning in to kiss me.

I grab her wrists, to stop the movement, and lead her hands down to my throbbing cock. "Show me how much you've missed me,"

I say, through gritted teeth, containing the anger just below the surface. When her hands grip my hard cock, I put pressure on her shoulders, pushing her down. "Show me on your knees, with your mouth."

She kneels in front of me with such heated passion in her eyes. Such need to please me. I watch as she takes my hard cock in her mouth. That first wet, hot touch of her mouth makes my cock twitch and she moans as she slowly works her mouth over me. She's watching me watch her and I know she's trying to be passionate. Trying to be sexy. I don't want, slow and soft. I don't want, *passionate*.

I grip the back of her head and push my cock in her mouth until I feel it hit the back of her throat. Again and again, I fuck her mouth, hard. She's still moaning, still enjoying it so, I push harder, further. I make her swallow my dick until I'm balls deep, down her fucking throat. I hold her head so she can't move until she's gagging and I know she can't breathe. I pull my dick all the way out until just the tip is in her mouth. I hear her take a gasping breath and then I force myself down her throat again. It isn't enough.

"Fuck," I growl in frustration, as I lift her off the floor and carry her to the bed.

The look on her face is clearly one of pride, as if my curse is a declaration of her amazing head skills. It isn't. I set her on her feet and turn her around before she can do or say anything else I don't want to hear. I grab what little fabric there is covering her ass and rip it off her body.

She looks back over her shoulder, "mmmm, I love when you're so eager to be with me."

I push her chest down onto the bed, leaving her standing on the side, her ass and pussy served up as an offering. An offering I'm about to take. I slide the tip inside of her and she starts to moan instantly. I grip both of her wrists, and hold her arms behind her back, as I slam everything I have into her. I'm not exactly small and she isn't ready for all of me in one furious push. She cries out and it isn't a cry of pleasure. I don't fucking care.

I pull almost all the way out before I slam into her again and then again. By the fourth push, her body is open and she's moaning her pleasure into the mattress. Her moans do nothing for me. I don't care if she's enjoying it or in pain. I'm cold and empty inside. Anger is the only emotion driving my body. That and a basic need for release. I just need a damn release. A release I'll get any way possible.

"Oh my God, Logan, you're going to make me cum," she pants beneath me.

I don't speed up or slow down, I keep the pace I'm doing, knowing this will bring her over the edge. I pump deep inside of her and feel her orgasm, as her pussy squeezes my dick, and soaks it with her pleasure. She cries out again and this time it *is* in pleasure. I still don't give a shit. Her screams just annoy me.

I growl my frustration as I pull out of her, pick her up, and throw her on the bed. I kneel behind her and lift her hips to me while I push her head down into the mattress. I don't want to see her and I don't want to hear her. I just want to fuck her, get my release, and be fucking done with her. I slide my hard cock in her again, and this time, there's no resistance as I move in and out of her in a steady rhythm.

Despite her head being lost in a sea of ridiculous pillows, I still manage to hear her stifled moans. I know she's close to another orgasm so, I let her have it. I'm not that fucked up. I won't touch her, or put my lips on her, but I won't deny her pleasure from my cock. How she can ever think we could be something more than this is beyond me. I've never given her any indication this will ever change. Yet, she still hopes.

Once she cums, screaming into the mattress, I just want it done. I squeeze her hips and start to pound into her, hard. Pulling almost all the way out in long, hard strokes. I close my eyes and focus on how tight and wet she is.

So eager to please.

So eager to get me to notice her.

To feel *anything* for her.

I growl at the thought and lose myself in the feeling of my cock inside of her. I let out a roar, trying to release the anger, and suddenly I'm sitting up in bed, panting and drenched in sweat.

It takes me a minute to remember I'm at Amarah's house and *not* with Hallana. It had only been a dream. No, a nightmare. A flashback to who I used to be. I can feel some of that anger I've carried with me for centuries starting to rise back up. Anger that was quenched in a *second* the night I found Amarah at that stupid club.

She didn't come back home last night. She left me.

She.

Left.

Me.

Just like my mother abandoned me when I needed her. Just like my Pack abandoned me when I needed them. This. This is the catalyst to my anger. Because it's so much easier being angry than it is to be lonely. Last night, Amarah used her power against me. Against *me,* of all people. A growl starts in my chest, but I silence it, as I get out of bed and head into the bathroom.

Turning on the faucet, I splash cold water on my face. I need to get a hold of myself. Amarah isn't acting like the Amarah I know. She just went through a traumatic experience, one she blames herself for, and she's letting the trauma control her. She just needs time and someone to be there for her. I can't be that person if I let my anger start to consume me again. Besides, I'm not really *angry* with her.

No, my feelings are hurt.

My heart feels like it's breaking apart in my chest, and

although I haven't felt this type of pain in centuries, it's exactly like I remember it. *Worse*. The spot where our connection usually sits comfortably in my chest is empty. I'm literally missing a piece of myself and I know she's feeling it too. Amarah is exactly where I've been, and where I'm trying desperately not to be again. She's allowing the anger to fill her up.

I won't let her. I won't let her become what I've been for the past three hundred-ish years. I won't let her become an empty vessel where her anger can ride and take over. It's just not an option for her. She is too... *good*. She's a freaking half Angel for fuck's sake. She can conquer this situation, these feelings, and I'm going to be there for her every step of the way, until she's back to being the Amarah I know.

The Amarah that my Wolf chose for life.

The Amarah that I am so in love with, that I don't know who I will become, if I lose her.

No. I won't let her. I *can't* let her. Not only for her sanity but for mine. Does that make me selfish? Perhaps. But my intentions are pure, and coming from a place of experience, love, and caring. It has to be enough. *I* have to be enough. I look at my reflection in the mirror, resolve and determination filling my eyes.

I just have to get through to her. I have to reach her and show her that she's not a bad person. She's not evil. I need to help her realize her truth, and what happened with Andre, is not her fault but a result of war.

I send a message through our bond.

Amarah, can you hear me? Where are you? I'm worried about you.

Silence.

Deafening silence that sits like an anchor in my chest. I have no way of knowing if she hears my voice in her mind or not so, I opt for the logical next step. I send her a text message.

Me: Amarah, where are you? I'm worried about you and I'm going crazy not knowing where you are or if you're even ok. Come home or let me come and get you. I need you here. With me. I need to feel you safe in my arms. Please, Angel, I love you.

Not knowing one single thing is driving me insane. I can't help the crazy thoughts flitting across my mind. Is she cutting our connection off on purpose still or is she just too far away to hear me? Is she unconscious somewhere? Is she hurt? My mind is racing with the worst possible scenarios of Amarah, lying somewhere cold and alone, bleeding out.

I shake my head, "I can't think this way. I just need to find her and talk to her."

I hastily get ready and throw on a pair of dark blue jeans, a red v-neck t-shirt, and black and red sneakers. I run some styling gel through my hair with my hands, brush my teeth, put on deodorant, and I'm ready to be out the door in less than ten minutes. This intense sense of urgency has me moving faster. I know I have to find her sooner rather than later.

As I walk out into the living room, I notice her dog, Griffin, trailing behind me, and the thought strikes me. I can just wait her out. She'd *never* leave Griffin without making sure he's taken care of. Knowing this, she'll be back soon, and I can just wait and be here when she comes back. The thought lingers for a second but the anxious pit in my stomach is having no part in it. I can't just sit here and wait. I need to act. I need to go to her. Now.

"Sorry, little buddy," I pick Griffin up and kiss him on his head. I make sure he has water and food before I sit him down on the couch. "I'm gonna go get your momma and we will be back soon."

I merge onto I-40, heading West, and cut across traffic to the far-left lane. I normally drive somewhere between grandpa and reckless, but today, I'm definitely leaning closer to reckless. My nerves are shot. I'm anxious to find Amarah, to get her back home, where I can protect her. Where I can help her. Where she'll be safe.

I park in the first available spot I find, and sprint down the sidewalk towards Headquarters, my heart racing with anticipation. Amarah doesn't have many places she can go. I doubt that she'd go to one of her human friends' houses at a time like this. That would mean she would have to explain what's wrong and everything that's happened. How exactly would she explain The Unseen, Fey power, demons, and war? No, Headquarters has to be where she is. She has a room here available any time she needs it. She's here. She has to be.

I head straight for her room and don't bother knocking as I storm in, bringing my dream, no nightmare, and those same feelings back to the surface. No. This is not the same situation. Not even close. I'm not the same person either. I shake my head and clear those thoughts away as I scan the room. It hasn't been touched. I check the bathroom and walk-in closet just to be sure, but there's no sign that she's been here. There's no trace of her scent either.

I run my hand through my hair in frustration, "Where else can she be?"

Maybe Queen Anaxo has heard from her or seen her. I leave the room behind and go to find the Queen. I find her in the library.

"Ana…" I rush into the library.

"Logan? What's wrong? What happened?"

She's on her feet and heading my way before I can say more. Ana knows me better than anyone else. I watched her grow up and become the Fey Queen. She, unfortunately, witnessed my anguish and anger first-hand. She knows what's at the very heart of me and why. When my Pack abandoned me, she took me in, gave me purpose. She gave me a place where I could channel my anger and direct myself towards doing something *good*. She's the closest thing I have to family. Until Amarah.

"Have you seen or heard from Amarah? She left last night and didn't come back. She's not in the right headspace after everything that's happened. I *need* to find her, Ana."

"No, I haven't," she sighs. "I was worried this might happen, but I knew she was with you so, I didn't worry as much as I should have. I should've reached out. What kind of an aunt am I if I don't even check-in?"

I shake my head, "I don't think it would have made a difference. And the fact that she didn't come here, to you, worries me that much more. She's not herself right now, Ana. She's letting the darkness get the best of her and she's acting like *she* is the dangerous one." I start pacing, because I can't stand still for even a second, not knowing where Amarah is. "Do you have any idea where she could be?"

"We've all been in her shoes, Logan. We've all had to overcome our own demons. She's strong and her heart is *good*. She will get through this." She puts her hand on my arm, for comfort, stopping my pacing. "Have you checked in with her sister, Iseta?"

"Oh my God, of course, Iseta! How did I not think about reaching out to her first?"

"You're worried about Amarah and not thinking clearly. That's normal too, but if you want to be there for her and help her, you've got to get a hold of yourself, Logan. I've known you for a long time. I know what you struggle with. You have to keep your anger in check if you want to help her."

"I know! I know. I'm trying." I say, through gritted teeth. "Thank you, Ana. I'm going to call Iseta and keep looking."

"Let me know when you find her, please. Keep me in the loop and let me know if there's anything at all I can do to help. She's my family too, Logan."

I nod and head back out to my truck. I dial Iseta as I walk. She picks up on the second ring.

"Hey, Logan. Everything ok?"

"I'm not sure. Have you heard from Amarah? Last night, she left the house talking about saving me by not being with me and a whole bunch of nonsense about her being evil and dangerous. She didn't come back and I'm worried about her. I need to find her, Iseta. Please tell me you've heard from her?"

She sighs heavily on the other end, "I thought this might happen. She hates hurting people and always puts the blame entirely on herself. She's always been this way, even when she was young. She lets her guilt consume her and this is definitely a drastic situation. Someone she cared about lost their life, even though it was *not* her fault, she feels like it is. I'm sorry Logan but I haven't heard from her."

I hold back a burst of curse words, "well, if you haven't heard from her, and she's not with Ana, where else could she be? Do you think she would have gone to one of her friends' houses?"

"No, I don't think she would involve them in anything like this. Especially if she is feeling like *she* is dangerous. She wouldn't put anyone in any kind of danger. There's only one other person I can think of that she might not worry about corrupting or hurting. I'll give you two guesses but you're only gonna need one."

The anger stirs inside of me and a growl escapes my throat, "Valmont."

2

Valmont: A Dangerous Game

The Man That I Am by James Otto

I feel her presence and smell her sweet, aromatic blood as she approaches my office door. Just the scent of her sends my heart racing faster in my chest. Well, it would if my heart were actually...*alive.* From the very first moment I was near her, she made me feel more alive than I've felt in centuries, and after drinking her blood, my reaction to her is a million times stronger. Just the memory of how she tastes makes my body shudder. It would be even better if I was buried deep inside her with more than just my fangs. I haven't felt this way since...*Viveka.* Back when I was a young, naive human. Bloody Hell, I barely remember my life back then, but one thing has never faded. My memories of...*her.* That was over two thousand years ago.

And now? You would think as old as I am that I'm a Master of my entire self. I am. In every way. Except when it comes to Amarah Rey. It takes all my strength and willpower not to touch her. Not to sink my fangs into that soft, sweet skin so I can taste that heavenly blood flowing just below the surface.

I want to be *her* Master.

I want her to hunger for me, to beg me, to crave me like no

---

other. To worship me. And yet, I want to be her slave. I want to drop to my knees before her and give her everything she's ever desired.

Everything I have.

Everything I am.

Everything I will become.

And that fucking terrifies me.

She's standing on the other side of the door, my body is tense and anxious, waiting for her to knock. Waiting for the next moment I can see her again. It's only been a couple of days since I saw her last but that's days too long. Why is she even here? I haven't the foggiest idea, but I selfishly hope it is for *me* and not because of our alliance. I wait patiently…

Ten seconds…

Twenty seconds…

Thirty seconds…

Until I can't wait any longer, I walk over to the door and open it. I'm my usual cocky and arrogant self when I answer the door. I even exaggerate my British accent because I know she likes it.

"Amarah Rey, couldn't stay aw…" the smirk on my face, and the teasing remark, vanish as soon as I see her. "Bloody Hell," I hold the door open for her and stand off to the side ushering her inside. "What on Earth has happened?"

She steps inside just enough for me to close the door and then I move to stand in front of her. She's wearing sweatpants, a long sleeve t-shirt, and, my Gods…*fuzzy* socks. Could she be any more *human* or more adorable? But her face. Her face breaks my heart.

"You've been crying. Why? What's happened?"

"I…" she struggles to speak. She starts to shake her head, too fast, too frantic. Her eyes are drowning in something painful and I can't stand to see it.

I take a step to close the distance between us, reach out, and gently cup her face in my hands. Her skin is shockingly cold, and her eyes are searching, searching, for something they can't find. Her pain is so deep I almost feel it in my soul just from looking at her.

"Aamrah Rey, talk to me. What has happened?" I ask, softly.

I see how hard she's fighting to remain strong. How hard she's fighting to keep all of the emotion, all of the pain threatening to spill down her cheeks, locked down tight. She's losing the fight and takes a step back, pulling out of my grasp, but the door is right behind her, and she has nowhere to go.

Nowhere to run.

Nowhere to hide.

She slides down the door until she's sitting on the floor. She hides her face in her hands, and then I hear the first sob escape her sweet little throat, and my heart feels like it drops to my stomach. I watch as she lays on the floor, curling up, and holding herself. I stand here, frozen, watching her suffer and I can't handle it. I'll do anything to take this pain away from her. I would gladly take it and shoulder it myself if I could. I'll find whoever caused this pain, and make them wish for death, but Amarah Rey doesn't need my fury right now. She needs my comfort and I'm more than happy to oblige.

I lower myself to the floor, with my back against the door, and lift her so her head rests in my lap. I still have no idea why she's here. I have no idea why she's breaking apart on my office floor. But if she's here with me, this broken, and not with Logan... well, I don't need to be a psychic to figure it out.

Something terrible has happened between them. That's the only thing that makes sense. The only thing that would drive her to *me*. As much as I hate seeing her in pain, a small part of me is thrilled and hopeful. I know I can never come between her and Logan. Their connection is, frustratingly, undeniable. It makes me sick to see it and admit it. So, I do my best to ignore it and play the ever-arrogant Vampire I'm so good at playing. But if something has happened between them...*I* have a chance to be everything she needs.

So, I sit here, on the floor in my Armani suit, and stroke her hair, whispering that everything is going to be alright. I have no idea if everything will be alright, but she needs words of comfort, so I lie. I hold her as her body shakes violently with her excruciating sobs. I can smell the salt of her tears as they soak through my pant leg. I don't know how long we stay like this, but the cries slowly subside, and her body finally rests and relaxes.

Amarah Rey is asleep in my lap. I've dreamt of a moment like this, but the dream had been far happier, and she had been exhausted from a night of pleasure, not pain. I don't want to move and risk waking her, but I won't let her sleep on the damn floor.

I slide out from under her and scoop her up in my arms. Gods, she is so small and so fragile. How is it that she is also one of the strongest and most determined... and stubborn, people I know? So much responsibility and duty rested on her beautiful shoulders. The last thing she needs is more loss. More heartbreak. I shake my head and sigh as I carry her to my private elevator. I feel slightly guilty that even in her depressing state, I'm hyper-aware of her body in my arms and relish in just how *good* it feels. How good *she* feels.

I enter my Penthouse and head straight for the bedroom. I gently lay her down in my bed, and again, I can't help thinking of how I've dreamt of her here with me so many times, but none of them were like this, and it's bittersweet. She shivers as I pull the covers over her but she never fully wakes up.

I sigh, "Oh, Amarah Rey, what am I going to do with you?" I take a few seconds to watch her settle into what I hope is a peaceful sleep.

I gently sweep aside her hair, caressing her cheek as I do, and then I lean over and lay the briefest kiss on her temple. No more than a mere brush of lips to skin but it sends a heatwave through my body.

Her scent.

The slightest taste of her skin that lingers on my lips.

Every ounce of my being wants to slide under the covers and feel every inch of her body pressed against mine. I'm not quite sure what to make of it, that I can feel this way, after all this time. I reluctantly pull away and head back to my office to make arrangements. The Penthouse is secure on its own, only accessible by one elevator, which needs a key and code that very few have access to. Still, Amarah Rey is far more precious than anything else in this world. She needs to be protected. Always. And if there's one thing I can give her, it's safety.

Back in my office, I pick up the hand-held, two-way radio off my desk. "Pierce, Emerson, to my office."

I walk over to my minibar and pour my favorite drink, honey mead over ice, before heading to the couch. Taking off my suit jacket first, I settle onto the couch as I wait for my security.

A few minutes later, I sense them approaching, followed by a knock on the door. Even though I've ordered them to come to my office, they still know to wait for my approval before entering.

"Come in!" I yell from the couch.

Emerson and Pierce, yin and yang. Emerson, just under six feet tall, with blonde hair and blue eyes, would look more like a surfer, if it wasn't for the muscles and cold, calculating stare. While Pierce is six-five, skin almost as dark as the night, with eyes to match. Pierce is also a Vampire but Emerson is human, and one of the only humans I trust, as one of my own. Both are extremely dangerous in their own ways yet they both come and stand with respect and attention before me.

I may be lax and flirtatious with Amarah Rey and others around me, but there's absolutely no room for niceties, when it comes to my employees and my business. Nice is too often mistaken for weakness. As a Virtuoso Vampire, Leader of my Territory, I can never show any sign of weakness. There's always some ambitious, young Vampire trying to make a name for themselves, and will quickly move to exploit any perceived weakness. This is exactly why my feelings for Amarah Rey, whatever they may be, terrify me. If anyone finds out how I truly feel about her, they'll use her to get to me. I can't...*won't*, put her in that kind of danger. Ever.

"Amarah Rey will be spending the night in my penthouse and she can stay as long as she likes. Since she's our ally, and the reason we no longer have to fear fire, I expect her to be treated with the utmost respect and be protected. Furthermore, any guest of mine, ally or otherwise, will always be safe under my care. As you are each, head of night and day security, you will ensure her safety while she's here at all times. Is that understood?"

In unison, "yes, sir."

"I will also require added security to the underground living quarters as that is where I shall retire for the upcoming day. Ensure that the master bedroom is suitable for my needs."

"Yes, sir."

"Of course, sir."

"I don't need to remind you what will happen if security fails and something...*unfortunate,* were to occur?" My voice remains calm and authoritative but the underlying threat is clear.

"No, sir."

I nod, "good. How is business tonight?" I ask, as I sip my drink, feeling satisfied that security measures are understood and will be sufficiently enforced for the last-minute changes.

"The casino floor is already busy, sir, and the VIP list for the nightclub is full. No incidents to report at this time." Pierce's deep voice suits his large frame and only adds to the intimidating factor. Not that anyone needs to hear his voice to be intimidated. There's no denying he's dangerous. Hell, even if he didn't have large muscles barely contained in his all-black suit, one look in his eyes and *anyone* would realize he's the threat in the room.

"That's all for now," I wave my hand dismissively, and my two right-hand men leave without another word.

The night is just getting started, and I have so much work to do, but I can't get my mind to focus on anything else except the woman asleep in my bed. My attraction to her was immediate, but mostly, she had intrigued me. Especially, when I found out I couldn't hypnotize her, which is one of my greatest abilities. Then, only a few days ago, I tasted her blood during the fight against Revna, Aralyn, Luke, and the demons. That's when it all made sense and everything changed. I found out she's part Angel and that's why I can't hypnotize her. That's why her blood always smells so damn delicious. That's why I've been drawn to her in a way that's so foreign to me. Her blood.

Delicious.

Intoxicating.

Powerful.

Dangerous.

Addicting.

But it's not just about her blood. No. She's beautiful, inside and out. She's genuinely a *good* person, with such a pure and naive heart, and always tries to do what's right. The poor girl is way out of her league in this world and yet, somehow, she's managed to inspire hope. Somehow, she's managed to fight and become a Leader in this war. Somehow, she's also captured my complete and undivided attention. Maybe it's her big, soft hazel eyes, that hypnotize me.

Ironic since she's not the one with that power, and yet, I'm in complete *awe* when she looks at me. Maybe it's her lips, so full, and they look so warm and soft. *Inviting*. I'm dying to feel them on mine. I scrape my fangs along my bottom lip, tasting her skin, from the kiss to her temple I gave her earlier. I'm getting excited and aroused at the mere thought of tasting her mouth. Feeling her tongue slide against mine.

That's why I did what I did.

A Vampire bite is pleasurable to any who receives one. The stronger the Vampire, the more pleasurable and intense the bite is. Getting bitten by a very powerful Vampire, say a Virtuoso Vampire such as myself, can be *very* addicting. Of course, I knew the power of my bite when I chose to bite her. I hadn't *planned* on biting her without her knowing the side effects, and getting her permission, but once I tasted her blood, I knew I was lost. I wanted her to want me as badly as I wanted...as much as I *want* her. If I was a better man, I would feel guilty about it. If I was a better man, I wouldn't have done it at all. But I'm not a better man. I don't regret it.

I've always been in the background when Amarah Rey is connected to Logan, but if she's no longer with him or gaining his strength from their connection, it opens her up to our mutual addiction for each other.

The blood in my veins feels like molten lava, I swear I can feel my heart beating, just *thinking* about tasting her blood again. Goosebumps erupt across my skin out of nowhere. My body is betraying me, making me feel things I shouldn't be able to feel. I have to keep this hidden. I have to keep her secret safe. I have to keep *her* safe, because this is a dangerous, dangerous game.

I slam the rest of my drink, rest my head on the back of the couch, close my eyes, and rub my aching cock.

"Bloody fucking Hell."

3

Amarah: More Questions Than Answers

The Stages Of Grief by Awaken I Am

It takes me a few minutes to realize I'm no longer in my dark dream, but awake, in a dark and unfamiliar room. Normally, I would've panicked a bit, not remembering where I am, but recent events have made me a bit more...*careless.* So, I stay content under the warm covers and recount my dream.

I sigh. How could I have been so foolish to believe Archangel Michael was visiting me? Maybe Revna had been on to something when she said as much. Angels don't visit you. They don't get involved. They stay up there, in the clouds or wherever, and let you *learn* from your mistakes. Meanwhile, the Prince of Lies, good 'ole Luci, is taking advantage of the competition-free playing field. Had I really agreed to his help? Had I taken his offered hand, as if it wasn't a snake in the grass, just waiting to strike?

I run my hands down my face and still feel the sensation of that warm, thick liquid coating them. No, not just thick liquid. Blood. Fey blood. On *my* hands. I bring my hands up to look at them but it's too dark to see anything. I literally can't see my hands in front of my face. Who needs a room this dark to sleep in? My mind slowly starts

---

piecing together the night before and my heart immediately starts to ache.

"Oh God, Logan," I mutter to myself. Not at all the way I usually say that phrase.

Logan has done everything right. He's so supportive and so accepting. He's everything I've always wanted and it is literally breaking my heart to pieces pushing him away but I *have* to do it. I *have* to keep him away from me to keep him safe. I double-check to make sure our connection is blocked off so he can't slip into my mind with his deep seductive voice and soft loving words that will undoubtedly undo me. I'm not strong enough to reject him again. It took all of my strength to leave him last night. I need to maintain this distance and space until I can fully accept this situation. They say time heals all wounds, right? How much time will it take me to get over Logan, when I'm so deep in love with him, I'm bound to reach China if I dig myself in any further?

As a newly matured Fey and half Angel, I'm practically immortal, I guess I have an eternity to figure it out. Time is on my side and I don't think the reality of this truth has ever hit me harder than it does right now.

There's an emptiness in my chest, in my soul, that I've lived with for thirty-four years. Until I met Logan. Our connection, as strange and mystical as it is, has filled me up. Completed me in a way I've never felt before. Even just blocking the connection now, barricading my heart and mind, I feel that gaping hole. I feel the loss of him immensely. It's a dull ache compared to what it had been before Logan, but that's even worse because I constantly feel the lingering connection buried deep inside of me, begging to be set free and make me whole. Now I have an eternity of missing him. Missing a piece of myself that's right beneath the surface, itching to break free. Along with a freshly broken heart. This is going to be impossible to overcome regardless of how much *time* I have.

I change the course of my thoughts, I remember stumbling into the casino last night, looking like a crazed woman. And then falling apart on the floor in front of Valmont. At least he didn't judge me. He allowed me to grieve my losses with a comforting presence and I'm grateful to him for that. Jesus, Amarah. What a way to make a mess of your life.

"How embarrassing," I sigh again, and throw the covers back, sliding my legs over the edge of the bed so I can sit up. I squint and try to see a hint of *anything* but this damn room is pitch black. Am I somewhere underground? It doesn't feel or smell like I'm underground. The Fey Headquarters is underground and I can always just sense it. Like I can feel the weight of the Earth all around me. No, this doesn't feel like that.

Standing up cautiously, I start shuffling around, my arms flailing wildly in front of me. I have to eventually touch something but I don't want to blindly ram into anything and hurt myself either. My hands find what feels like a lamp so, I start feeling around for a switch of some kind. I eventually find a little knob, twist it, and a soft white glow illuminates the room around me.

With the small amount of light, I'm able to walk over to what looks like curtains, if curtains come in twenty-foot lengths. Maybe they aren't curtains at all but some kind of drapes to hide something? I mean, can a window be *that* big? Reaching out, I take a hold of the thick and heavy, yet extremely soft and sleek material, and thankfully, it glides easily to the side.

Moving the material reveals that, it is indeed, a curtain. I'm left standing in front of a gigantic window, that provides me the best view I've ever seen, of the Sandia Mountains and the sunrise that is just starting over the mountain's peaks. I also notice a balcony off the bedroom, that is just as luxurious as the room is, with inviting couches and those fancy fire pits with the pretty fire glass. My mouth makes a silent...*wow*, as I watch the crisp blue sky come to life, as if

I'm watching a movie from the best seat in the theater. It's one of the most beautiful things I've ever seen and leaves me momentarily speechless. I'm so lost in watching the sunrise that I forget where I'm standing, where I am, and everything going completely wrong in my life.

A knock on the door startles me out of my awe-induced daze. I hurry over to the door but hesitate to open it. I know where I am, and I know I'm safe, but what if Logan found me? I can't face him right now. I open my mouth to ask who it is, but then it will confirm that I am, in fact, here. Then again, if it is Logan, he can hear my breathing and my too-loud thumping heart anyway. I hesitate long enough that another knock makes me jump.

"Amarah, it's Emerson."

I let out a relieved sigh and open the door, "hey, Emerson."

Emerson holds out a handful of clothes with a pair of sneakers on top. "Valmont left these for you last night and he wants me to make sure you get them and anything else you might need."

I realize I'm still in the sweats, a long-sleeve t-shirt, and fuzzy socks, that I had run out of my house in last night. Embarrassingly, I waltzed right through the casino like this. I take the offered clothes and inspect them. They look like they're actually *mine*. Like they were pulled straight from my closet at home. I shake my head, clearing any thought of how Valmont has clothes for me, and instead choose to focus on what Emerson said.

"Thank you. I do need these, especially the shoes," I laugh nervously. "I don't need anything else though. I just need to get back home."

Emerson nods, "I'll wait in the living room and escort you out."

"You really don't have to do that. I'm sure you have more important things to do than babysit me. Besides, I'm pretty sure I can find my way out of a casino I've been to a million times."

"I'm sure you can, however, the elevator to the Penthouse is restricted. You need a key and code to access it. Take your time, I'll be waiting." He turns to leave but stops short, turning back around, "oh, and Valmont also had this. I'm sure you'll be needing it."

Reaching out, I gingerly take my cell phone out of his outstretched hand. I've been so preoccupied with my thoughts and my surroundings that I completely forgot about my phone.

"Thanks," I smile weakly.

He nods and then I watch him walk off in the direction, I assume, will be the living room. Still stunned, I shut the door and lean against it, staring at the cell phone clutched in my hand. I know there will be messages from Logan, and a part of me is desperate to unlock the phone and read his words, while another part of me is terrified. My hand is shaking as I punch in my pin. Twelve missed calls and forty-three text messages. Two from Iseta and the rest from Logan. My heart is racing as I open his messages.

Logan: Amarah please come back. We'll work through this, together.

Logan: I know you're hurting but being alone isn't going to help. Let me be here for you.

Logan: Amarah, Angel, please don't do this to me, to us. You're the mate I chose, I need you and I know you need me too. I'm not going to just walk away. I won't just let you go. I can't.

Over and over his words seem to punch right through the tiny screen with a direct hit to my chest. My cheeks are wet, my heart is desperately trying to piece itself together, and I'm choking on sobs I refuse to unleash. I read the most recent text that came through minutes ago.

Logan: Amarah where are you? I'm worried about you and I'm going crazy not knowing where you are or if you're even ok. Come home or let me come and get you. I need you here. With me. I need to feel you safe in my arms. Please, Angel, I love you.

Locking the phone again, I rest my head against the door, and remind myself why I'm here. Why I'm doing this. Images of Valmont's body, cut up and bloodied, his body trying to heal and failing. Andre's eyes, so calm and so full of love as he held my gaze, while his body broke down and he took his last breath in my arms.

Blood.

Blood everywhere.

So much blood all I can see when I close my eyes is red. So much blood I'm literally swimming in it.

My dream.

Lucifer.

Bloody hands.

All my fault.

I push my love for Logan back down, I lock it up tight.

"I'm doing this to save him," I remind myself.

Saying the words out loud helps me believe it. I know I'm doing the right thing. The right thing is usually the hardest thing to do and this...this is excruciating! Therefore, it has to be right. Not for me. *For him.*

I pull a large breath into my lungs, hold it for a second, then slowly blow it out, opening my eyes and focusing on the present. Oh... yeah, I'm standing in a bedroom, in Valmont's Penthouse. Penthouse! With a private elevator! I'm not just in a nice hotel suite. No. That wouldn't do for Valmont at all. I shake my head at the excessive, boujee Vampire but I admit, it doesn't surprise me. It suits him actually and I can't help but smile at the ridiculousness of it.

I find the bathroom, if that's what you can call it, and hit the lights. It's got to be the size of my entire living room and kitchen at home. It's all white and grey marble with dark grey and soft blue accents. I place my small pile of clothes on the extra-large, his and hers, counter. My eyes are immediately drawn to the *ginormous* bathtub that looks more like a jacuzzi. I notice the same type of curtains hanging behind it and immediately walk over to them and pull them open.

"No fucking way," I whisper.

The bathroom, and more specifically the jacuzzi-sized *bathtub,* has the same view as the bedroom. You can literally relax in the bathtub and watch the sunrise or, just enjoy one of the best views I've ever seen. I take a mental note to amend my alliance with Valmont to include penthouse benefits. Although I'm far from boujee, and elegant stuff generally makes me a bit nervous, I'm definitely going to enjoy using this tub at least once!

Pulling myself away from the views, and my daydreaming, I get dressed. Valmont has managed to get me a pair of dark blue jeans, an extremely soft, black cashmere sweater that I immediately acknowledge is *not* from my closet, and a pair of all-black Nikes. Included in the pile is also underwear. Since Logan didn't seem concerned with them when he hastily dressed me after my shower incident, I appreciate them immensely, because how can anyone wear jeans without underwear? I grimace at the thought. As thankful as I am for them, I'm also deeply unnerved. Since they are *not* from my closet, I wonder where Valmont got them, and also how he seems to know my size since everything fits me perfectly. That's a question for another day.

I head out of the bedroom, which I still haven't had the chance to explore, and head in the direction Emerson had gone. I find the living room easily enough and Emerson, the ever-serious bodyguard, is standing alert by the elevator doors.

"Ready?"

"Yes, thank you for waiting."

I watch as Emerson takes out a tubular key and inserts it below the pin pad. He then proceeds to enter in a code and the elevator doors silently swish open. He removes his key and holds his arm across the door, gesturing for me to enter, as he follows close behind me. Once inside the elevator, the doors close but he still has to insert the key and enter a code on another pin pad before we begin moving.

"That's a bit excessive don't you think?"

"Not for the Virtuoso it isn't."

I think about those words before I answer. "I'm confused. By being Virtuoso, doesn't that make Valmont one of the most deadly and dangerous Vampires out there?"

"Yes."

"So why does he need so much protection? I mean, he doesn't have much protection when he's going about his daily...well, nightly, life. It's not like people are trying to kill him or anything," I snort.

Emerson doesn't respond and stays facing forward as if I'm not even here.

My mind is contemplating what I just said, and I realize, I have no idea if Valmont has enemies. He's always just helped me with mine. "Wait, are there people who would actually try to kill Valmont?"

Again, Emerson doesn't answer. The elevator doors open and I'm rushing after him as he hurries out. We're on the ground floor of the Casino by Valmont's office. I've never even noticed this elevator before.

"Emerson," I'm practically running to keep up with him at this point. "Are there people who want to kill Valmont? Does he have enemies? Am I even safe here?"

Emerson stops so quickly I bump into him. The look on his face makes me take a step back instinctively and swallow down the instant fear that crept up my throat. I know he'd never hurt me, he has no reason to, but this is definitely the Navy SEAL look I hadn't yet seen. The one that shows just how cold, calculating, and dangerous he truly is.

"One thing you never have to question is your safety while you're here and under Valmont's protection. Do you understand?"

I'm so shocked at his instant change of character, the tension in his body, his muscles seem to be bulging, and his eyes are so...cold, that all I can do is nod.

He seems satisfied and warms slightly, rolling his shoulders, "as far as your other questions, those are answers Valmont can give you if he chooses to do so. His business is his own and not for myself, or anyone else, to share. Understand?"

I quickly nod and then I'm hurrying after him again. He escorts me out to my car which is sitting right in front waiting for me. He opens the door, and I slide into the driver's seat, avoiding his hard gaze.

"Get home safely, Amarah," he shuts the door and walks off before I can wrap my mind around everything that's just happened.

Everything about this morning is blowing my mind, from the penthouse, to the crazy security precautions, to Emerson's instant change in demeanor about my safety. Was he personally offended or something more? And does Valmont have enemies of his own? Had I roped him into helping me with my problems while he had his own that he's dealing with? No, *he* approached me about the alliance. Maybe it's the opposite. Maybe it's *him* roping me into helping him with *his* threats, which is honestly, the last thing I need right now.

"What the fuck?" I ask myself, as I start my car and finally head back home.

Amarah: Calling In A Debt

Can't Go Back by The Drifted

My mind is racing a million miles a minute, say that five times fast, as I make my drive back home. There are too many thoughts fighting for attention. I know there are things that I can't ignore for long, like my training, the war against the demons, Aralyn still out there somewhere, scheming, and the fact that I've basically partnered with the war Leader himself.

What does this mean for the Fey? Where do I now stand in the war? Just because I want Lucifer's help with mastering my darkness, does *not* mean I agree to stand by and watch my people, or humans, die. How have things gotten so complicated? I have no idea what I've gotten myself into, and more importantly, how I'm going to get myself out.

All of these problems are high priority. I should be putting all of my personal opinions and *feelings* aside and running to the Queen to devise a plan, and yet, there's only one thing making its way to the forefront of my brain again and again.

Logan.

Logan.

Logan.

If I know anything about Logan, he won't just let me go. He said as much last night. And, God knows, I don't want him to! I don't want to lose the only thing that makes sense since my life has been turned upside down. Knowing how hard it was to leave him once, I know I can't do it again. Because I truly don't want to. The realization of the situation hits me. I can't do this on my own. I need help.

Instead of heading home, where Logan is probably waiting for me, waiting to wrap me up in his protecting arms, waiting to shower me with love and affection, and anything I need, I ignore the aching emptiness in my chest, exit the freeway, and head towards downtown. It's still early in the morning and the streets are deserted. The nightclubs have just shut down a couple of hours ago, and most of the other businesses, restaurants, and shops, aren't open yet.

I park directly in front of Nature's Magical Whispers & More. It's a nondescript two-story building that looks like all the other buildings along the street. The decals on the front windows read, tarot card readings inside, crystals, herbs & more, but the neon open sign is currently turned off, and the blinds are pulled shut. There are no bars on the windows or metal locking security gates, like other businesses in this area have, yet the security here is far superior to anything the other buildings have. *Magic.*

I feel it hanging heavily in the air as I climb the stairs and stand before the front door. My recent experience with Witches and magic has improved my detection of it. There's still so much I don't know but I'm starting to understand when I'm sensing magic in the air. It's like feeling a sudden warm or cold draft. Those moments when you get goosebumps for no apparent reason. Magic. It also feels heavy, and can easily be mistaken for humidity, but there is a difference. If you pay attention, you can feel a type of charge in the air, almost like an electric charge. And this magic I'm standing in now is powerful indeed, but still not as powerful as what I felt from Revna and Iseta.

I don't have to worry about either of them though. Revna is no longer an issue since Iseta killed her before she could kill me, in a recent battle, and Iseta is...well, *family.* Iseta is a Gray Witch which means she's on her own. She's chosen to be alone, instead of with a Coven, because she doesn't always agree with their beliefs and practices. Being a part of a Coven makes a Witch's magic more powerful, the whole, *stronger together* concept, and yet Iseta being stronger than this entire Coven, demonstrates just how powerful she is. I don't even think she realized it until recently.

Yet here I am, standing at the door to the Desert Rose Coven. The first and last time I was here, I almost had my brain turned to mush when the Ülim tried to force her way into my mind, to test how strong I am and pry into my every thought. Needless to say, she didn't succeed, and because she attacked me with no provocation, and regardless of the destruction I caused, she now owes me a debt. And it's time to collect.

I square my shoulders, take a deep breath, and ring the doorbell. It takes a few minutes before I see a face peek through the blinds. I recognize her high, round cheekbones and soft, dark brown eyes. A moment later, I hear the door unlock, and then it swings open, revealing a young girl standing in the doorway.

I give her a half-hearted smile, not feeling particularly cheery or talkative but there's no need to be rude. "Hello, Alisha."

Alisha returns a half-hearted smile, but hers is laced with confusion more than anti-socialism, like mine. "Hello, Amarah. I'm sorry but we weren't expecting you," she hesitates. "Were we?"

I shake my head, "no apologies needed. You're right, no one is expecting me, but I'm hoping the Supreme will be kind enough to see me anyway."

"Oh," she looks genuinely surprised. "I'm not sure. The Ülim doesn't usually see anyone without a scheduled appointment."

"I understand. Perhaps you can check with her and see if she's willing to make an exception?"

She starts to protest again but I interrupt her. I guess I'm being rude after all.

"It's regarding the debt she owes me," I say more firmly.

I suddenly feel the need to remind Alisha that *they* wronged me the last time I was here, and the least they can do now is make time for me. Not to mention, I levelled the entire Coven in my self defense and practically destroyed their shop. I'm betting they want to avoid a repeat of that disaster.

Alisha's suddenly paler skin and wide eyes tell me I'm right. She's either remembering their disgraceful act or understanding the threat in my tone. Either way, she steps aside and motions me inside.

"Please wait here and I'll let the Ülim know you're waiting." She rushes off before I can acknowledge her plan or thank her.

I shrug and busy myself with perusing the merchandise while I wait. It's amazing how all of this stuff, that was once considered *evil,* is now mainstream. Crystals of all varieties, raw stones and polished ones, necklaces, rings, and bracelets, different types of sage for burning and cleansing, incense, tarot cards, bags of black salt and sand, candles of all shapes, sizes, and colors, natural homemade soaps and fragrances, and of course, can't forget the tourist trinkets with *Albuquerque* and *New Mexico* plastered on them.

"Amarah?"

I jump and almost drop the ceramic, dragon incense holder I had been examining. I was so distracted by all the beautiful things around me, I hadn't heard Alisha come back.

"Shit! You scared me," I laugh, nervously.

"My apologies. The Ülim will see you downstairs. Would you like me to escort you?"

"No, that's not necessary. I remember how to get there.

Thank you."

I put the item down and head towards the back of the shop where there's only one door to go through. I split the bead curtain down the middle and am left with the delicate cracking sound behind me as the beads hit each other and settle back into place.

Rounding the corner at the back of the room, I descend the stairs that lead to the basement, where the Coven has their workspace and altar. The last time I was here I didn't know I could block my senses to the magic so it wouldn't overwhelm me. It's heavier and more alive, more powerful, as I get closer to their altar but this time, I know what to expect, and my block is already in place so the magic doesn't affect me as badly. I still feel it, and it still sends chills down my spine, but it isn't threatening to crawl down my throat and suffocate me. That's a bonus.

On the landing, at the bottom of the stairs, I can see most of the room laid out before me. However, the basement is huge and I have no idea what could be hidden down here. My imagination has fun with the idea though. Before I can become too nosey, a voice draws my attention.

"Amarah, it's good to see you again," her voice is the same as I remembered but not as cold.

The Supreme is standing at one of the tall workstations. Her shrewd brown eyes make contact with mine as she addresses me but quickly focuses back on her work. Her dark brown hair is lined with grey and combed in the same loose, messy bun I remember from last time.

I make my way toward her, "Ms. Delaney, thank you for seeing me. I apologize for coming unannounced. I wasn't really… thinking."

"I've been expecting you to come at any time, and please, call me Mae. We're far beyond any titles or formalities with each other, don't you agree?"

"Yes, I suppose we are," I say, hesitantly. I'm fairly confident I can protect myself against Mae if she decides to try and attack me again but I don't think she will. Still, I'm out of my comfort zone being here, alone, so I remain cautious.

She finally sets down her project. It looks like she was etching symbols of some kind into the sidewalls of black pillar candles. No doubt needed for a ritual of some sort. She wipes her hands on a towel and motions toward the nearby table.

"Let's have a seat and you can tell me what you need."

"How do you know I need anything?" I ask defensively.

Mae gives me an incredulous look, "why else would you be here? Besides," she waves her hand in the air as if shooing away my defensiveness, "Alisha told me you mentioned the debt."

"Oh, right," I say, quietly, as I sit across from her. I really need to get my head out of my ass and start thinking straight.

"I heard about what happened at the Air Fey village. I'm deeply sorry for you and everyone that lost someone. How are you holding up?"

I study Mae from across the table. She seems sincere in her sympathy and concern but she's no ally of mine, and for that reason, I don't trust her. Hell, she isn't an ally to *anyone*. Mae and the Desert Rose Coven refuse to get involved in the war and only fight when they need to protect themselves. I see the survival benefits in their approach but I don't agree with it. The war with the demons is going to affect everyone if they aren't stopped. Not to mention, I'm sure the Coven has made their own enemies along the way. Hell, they almost made one out of me.

It would make more sense for the Witches to join forces and fight with us. We have a better chance of winning, and just being overall successful in The Unseen, if we're all united and proactive. Instead, we're still divided and *reactive* to attacks and that isn't going well for anyone, but I can't force the Witches into fighting. There will come a time when the war hits them hard and they'll finally see reason. Until then, they'll continue to live in their little self-made, protected bubble of the world.

Not wanting to reveal any weakness, I respond with a half-truth, "thank you for your kind words. It hasn't been easy but we're all working through the losses and the continued war efforts. The Fey are strong and resilient. We'll survive and continue to fight." No need to reveal how badly I'm struggling with my guilt and darkness.

"No doubt about that," she studies me just as intensely as I'm studying her. No trust between us makes this awkward.

It doesn't help that I feel as if she can see right into my soul. Right into the deepest, darkest part of me and see my bloody hand reaching out for Lucifer. My heart starts to race and my hands become sweaty. I need to get out of my head and my guilt, because if I don't pull myself together, I'll give myself away by sheer lack of control over my feelings. Taking a steadying breath, I shut all the dark thoughts out, push all the emotion and guilt down, and instead, I focus on Logan. Not a better option honestly but he's the main reason I'm here.

"So, about this debt that you owe me," my voice comes out a little weak. I clear my throat and speak with more confidence, "I need to collect."

"Yes, yes, that's implied," she huffs with impatience. "What do you want?"

"I want protective wards placed around my property and my home. I want to be alerted when someone, or something, crosses onto my property and I don't want anyone, or any...*thing*, allowed to enter my home without my permission. Is that possible?"

Mae doesn't respond right away. She's still shrewdly studying me and I can't help but squirm just a bit in my chair. I try to hide it but no doubt she notices.

"Yes, that's possible. I owe you a great debt for my previous transgressions against you, Amarah. Of all the things I can do to you, or for you, you simply want protection wards?"

"Yes. That's all I want."

"You understand that you have the right to ask for much, much more?" She persists.

"Yes. This is what I want."

"And you understand that once I do this for you, we will sign the debt contract I have written up and it will be concluded explicitly and sealed with magic. There will be no more debt. No more favors. No more requests."

I'm the one getting impatient now, "I understand."

"This is something any Witch can do for you. I've heard about this Witch, Iseta, whom you seem to have a connection to. She helped you when even I couldn't, she is obviously very powerful. Why not ask her for the protection wards and leave your debt with me uncollected for, perhaps, a better future need?"

Whether it's the pressure of the magic in the air, or Mae's constant questioning and probing, my head starts throbbing right behind my eyes. I rub at them, tired and frustrated with not only this situation, but the situation I'm trying to avoid with Logan. "Mae, listen, I appreciate your concern, although I'm certain your concern is more for yourself and the reputation of you and your Coven. Can't let anyone think you settle your debts so cheaply or poorly, am I right?"

Mae inhales audibly and reacts as if I've reached across the table and struck her.

"Again, I understand, but our business is between us and us alone. No one will ever find out from me how the debt was created or how it was settled. So, unless you or one of your girls talks, no one will be the wiser. You trust your Coven, right? Plus, I want this taken care of now. Today."

She takes a second to compose herself. It seems I always have a way of offending her when we meet but I can't help it. It's not like I do it on purpose. She just works my patience and honestly, I'm still holding a grudge against her and her decision to stay out of the war, while the rest of us fight and die. Constantly losing people we love. Andre's vacant eyes stare up at me through my memory as real and terrifying as if he was in my arms again. Dead.

Mae's voice shakes me out of the horrible memory. "Well," she finally says, "once again, Amarah, you come into my home and presume to know me and act as if you're better than me. At least I've learned from my past mistakes and have the willpower to hold myself in check, unlike you it seems. Very well. You want wards, you shall get your wards, and I will be done with you and with this debt," she stands up, indicating we're done.

I swallow against the heaviness in my throat as I follow her lead and stand to leave. "Perfect." I ignore her jab at my perceived rudeness, "who should I expect to come and complete the wards?"

"I will be there shortly with a couple of girls. Leave your address with Alisha before you leave." And with nothing left to say, she waves me off like an annoying fly, buzzing around her head.

I gladly leave the basement and head back upstairs. Alisha is waiting patiently for me by the front door. I give her my address and can't leave fast enough. Once I'm back out on the street, I feel better, lighter, and I can finally take a deep, cleansing breath. Maybe this isn't the best way I can call in my debt, but it's what I need *now* and beggars can't be choosers, right?

Trying not to think too much more about it, I get back into my Camaro and finally head home. I start to pray, asking God to please not let Logan be there and that the wards would be in place before he came back. Maybe being half Angel means my prayers receive special attention? Thinking about how hard I prayed over Andre's dying body, how hard I begged for him to be saved, takes the words right out of my mouth. What good are prayers when they aren't heard? Or at least not answered. I drive the rest of the way home in utter silence, thinking about how the darkness is always there, waiting, listening, and eager to please. And I can't help but wonder how I can benefit from it now.

Amarah: Setting Boundaries

Every Little Thing by Carly Pearce

Thankfully, Logan's truck is gone when I open the garage door and pull in. A small part... oh, who am I kidding, a *big* part of my heart sinks because I want him to be here waiting for me, but the small part that knows this is for the best, is relieved. Fuck! Why are feelings so damn complicated?!

Griffin is here though, eager to greet me, so I scoop him up in my arms and soak in the comfort and peace his little soul always gives me. After a bit of inspection, I realize that Logan hasn't taken *any* of his things. That can only mean one thing...he plans on coming back. And I can't allow that to happen. For my sanity and his safety.

I make the hard decision to pack up his things and have them ready for him to take when he comes back. I start with the clothes hanging in the closet and I'm not sure if it's a mistake or not. None of this is easy, but I pull the first t-shirt off the hanger, and I do something extremely stupid. Something that makes this even more impossible than it already is. I bring his shirt up to my face, close my eyes, and inhale. I can smell the laundry detergent, but underneath that, I smell him.

I smell Logan.

I smell comfort.

I smell love. I smell...*home*.

And it's like a movie of all our memories and time together playing like a vivid reel behind my eyes.

My heart instantly starts to ache, and it feels like I have the biggest boulder sitting in my chest, threatening to crush my ribs and suffocate me. It's hard to breathe and I realize I'm choking on painful gulps of air in between ragged sobs. Why? Why do we do ridiculously dumb things that make shit harder on us and further add to our own torture?

The ring of the doorbell makes me jump and pulls me out of my devastating internal movie of memories. For a split second, I think it might be Logan, but then my thoughts clear, and I know it isn't him. He would have just used his key to come in. Yup, he has his own key. Thank God I'm having wards put up and won't have to deal with changing my locks. That feels like such a mundane thing to deal with amongst all the preternatural problems in my life. The doorbell rings again, and I realize it must be Mae coming to complete the wards, so I push myself up off the floor. The floor? When had I fallen to the floor? I seriously need to get a grip on myself.

"Coming!" I yell, as I make my way to the front door.

I hastily swipe at my face, trying to wipe away any evidence of the mess that clearly is *me*. I wipe away my weakness and take a small detour to look at myself in the hallway bathroom mirror. My eyes are just a touch red, but other than that, I look ok.

"Idiot," I mutter to myself, as I continue to the front door. I silently scold myself for letting this happen when I knew Mae would be coming soon.

Looking out the peephole, I recognize Mae right away, and she isn't alone. I take a deep breath, steel myself once again, then open the door. There are three other girls...Witches... standing behind Mae, but I don't recognize any of them. Alisha is the only other Witch of the Coven I'm familiar with, even though they had all come together to *attack* me the first time I had met with Mae, but that had all been a blur. I swear The Unseen and all this magical nonsense is going to kill me. If heartbreak doesn't do it first.

"Mae, thank you for coming so quickly," I say, with a smile I know doesn't reflect in my eyes.

At least I try! Mae doesn't even attempt niceties, "before we get started, tell me exactly what you want, and we'll get it done."

I let my fake smile go and think about my request. What exactly *do* I want? Does any woman ever truly know what she wants? The scene from, *The Notebook*, comes to mind. Do you want Logan? Do you not want Logan? It really *isn't* that simple! I almost respond with that quote and have to stop myself from chuckling. I don't think Mae will share my sense of humor in all of this.

"Well, I'm not exactly sure what's possible and what's not, but I would like to know when someone or some...*thing*, anything really, steps on my property, and I don't want anyone to be able to enter my home without my permission. Well, my human friends obviously don't count, but anything *not* human," I say, tentatively, not sure if I'm making a fool of myself or not.

Mae nods, "very well. We will get started with the boundary spell. How would you like to be alerted when the boundary is crossed?"

I stare at her cluelessly, "ummmm…"

Mae sighs heavily, "do you want a piece of jewelry that will glow or vibrate? Do you want an actual visual image in your mind? Do you want fireworks to erupt? Or bells to ring? The options are limited to your imagination."

"Ok, well...ummmm, I don't want anything noticeable, and I definitely don't want images popping into my head at random and inopportune moments," I laugh, nervously. "Can we do like a mark of some kind? A tattoo? But an...*invisible* mark? Maybe like a tingling or itching in my palm can alert me? Or...something like that?"

"Yes, that can be done. We will start on the boundary and once it's up we can link it to you. One of my girls will need access to your backyard. We need anchors facing North, South, East, and West."

"Sure. Yeah, no problem," I open the door wider and step aside so one of the Witches can come in and head out to the backyard. I point toward the sliding glass door, "you can go right through there."

The Witch that steps forward is tall and buxom, yet she seems to glide instead of stomp, as I would have assumed. As she passes by me, I feel her energy push against my skin. It's uncomfortable, but not unpleasant, and I don't feel threatened in any way. Her mahogany brown eyes hold mine for a moment and there's something there that I can't quite put a finger on. Intrigue? Curiosity? She gives me a small smile and nods her head in greeting before proceeding towards the backyard, leaving me staring after her.

Mae and the other Witches make their way to the front and each side of the house. I step outside to watch but stay close to the door. I don't want to get too close or interfere in any way but I can't help the curiosity of what I'm about to witness. Mae starts chanting and then the others join in meeting her words in unison. I can't make out what they're saying and I'm not even sure it's anything I would understand even if I could hear them. I stand still and watch eagerly, waiting for something magical to *wow* me. Unfortunately, magic isn't typically something that you see with your eyes, but even though I can't see anything happening, I know it is.

I can *feel* it.

The air suddenly has that electrical charge to it. The hair on my arms and neck stand at attention and I cross my arms in a protective gesture instinctively. I can feel the air around me getting heavier and it reminds me of the way the air feels in the Coven's basement. Thick with magic. I'm more sensitive to these feelings now because of my training with the Õhk Family. I've learned to feel the living, moving particles that float in the air all around us and how to control them. Granted, I'm far from being a Master of Air, but I know the basics, and part of my training is to keep practicing, keep getting better.

The air is pressing in on me, my skin is tingling all over, as if my entire body has gone numb and I'm trying to regain feeling. It's an intensely annoying and frustrating feeling. It doesn't hurt, exactly, but it doesn't feel good either. Just as I'm about to use my power to shield myself, there's a deafening boom and a huge gust of wind that hits me hard and makes me take a step backward to steady myself. Then, just as quickly as the wind came, it's gone, and the air is back to being light and fresh.

"Amarah."

I jerk my head toward the sound of my name and Mae is waving me over.

"The boundary is up. Humans will not be able to detect it and most preternatural beings won't be able to either. However, those that are sensitive to magic and of course, other Witches, will be able to feel the boundary. The lesser beings with only a slight sensitivity to magic may not even realize what they're feeling." She reaches out with her palm flat, as if she's touching an invisible wall, "it's here. Reach out and feel it, get a sense of it."

For once, I don't hesitate to comply and mirror her stance. I feel the outer edges of the boundary spell and for lack of a better word, it *does* feel like a wall. There's a barrier here, but unlike a solid wall, you can pass through it. I push my hand through the magic, feeling its warmth against my skin, and then I feel the cool, crisp air as my hand breaches the other side. The barrier feels about two inches thick and it feels so...*alive*.

"We need to link the barrier to you. Give me your hand."

Now, I hesitate, but only for a split second before I hold my hand out to the Ülim. She's only doing what I've asked her to do, and considering how we're even in this situation to begin with, I don't think she'll try anything to harm me again. Not without cause.

But when she produces a small blade, my mind can't help but think, maybe I'm wrong. Maybe she would take this opportunity to do something to me. I open my mouth to say something, but she deftly slices a small cut in the middle of my palm, and then the knife is gone just as quickly as it had appeared. It all happened so fast I never got a word out.

She lifts my bleeding palm to the magic and I immediately wince from the pain and try to jerk my hand back. Mae holds it firmly in place and starts chanting again. It feels like the magic is crawling into my hand from the open wound. I can feel it making its way *inside* me. And it *hurts*! It feels like Mae still has the knife to my palm, slowly pushing it into me, slicing me up as it cuts deeper and deeper. My jaw is clenched tightly to keep from crying out. I'm so focused on the pain that I barely hear some of the words Mae is saying.

Blood and magic bind
To keep this barrier in place
Let me not be blind
Help me to protect this space

When Mae finally finishes her spell, the pain subsides, and she lets go of my hand. I immediately cradle my injured hand and examine it. It's completely healed. There's no trace or scar to identify the cut that had been there mere seconds ago.

"Son of bitch," I exclaim. "That didn't feel very good."

Mae only raises her eyebrows but ignores my complaint. "Now, anyone can pass through this barrier. Like I said, most won't know it's here, some will." Mae takes a big step and is standing on the outer side of the ward. "You won't feel when people leave the barrier from inside, only when the barrier is breached from outside."

She then takes the step back across the barrier and my palm ignites, as if it's on fire, but the sensation is gone before it causes any significant pain.

"Son of a bitch!" I say again, with more feeling this time. I look down at my palm but it's just my normal palm. There's no indication of any kind that magic is attached to me. "So that's what I'm going to feel every time the barrier is breached?"

"Yes."

"Well, that fucking sucks! It's not a very good feeling!" I repeat in frustration.

"What did you expect? A nice gentle love tap?" Mae scoffs, "you need to know the difference between an alert and normal itch or tingle. If it was anything less than what it is, there's a chance you would mistake it or ignore it. A warning system needs to *warn* or else what's the point?"

I open my mouth to argue for argument's sake, but before I can say anything, she's walking off toward the house. She just leaves me standing here with my mouth gaping open like an idiot. I contemplate her words and I know she's right but I don't have to like it. I close my mouth, grumble to myself, and stomp off after her. Back inside, Mae and the other Witches are huddled in the kitchen, talking about the next spell.

"This next one is going to take a little more time and we will need a spot to set up a few things."

"Fine. Whatever you need, just get it done." I'm not ready to play nice after Mae left me standing there feeling stupid, but she doesn't even seem to notice my snarky attitude, which just makes me fume even more! The audacity of this Witch, Supreme or not, coming into *my* home and treating me like…oh. This must be exactly how she felt the two times I visited her and treated her like less than the powerful Ülim she is. Touché Mae. Touché.

Two of the other Witches go out to their vehicle and come back with armloads of...*things*. I watch them lay down a blanket and start arranging candles and incense on top of it. It's all very similar to what Iseta had done in the same spot just a month or so ago. Seriously, how has this become my life?

Mae takes a bowl that was placed on top of the blanket and walks over to me. "Let me guess, you need my blood?"

"I do. All magic is more powerful with the use of blood, and since this is a spell directly linked to your permission to pass it, I need your blood."

I sigh, "of course."

She produces her small knife again as I hold my arm out to her. Where is she hiding that thing and how does she get it so quickly? She makes a fairly deep cut across my forearm and I wince. I hadn't been expecting it to be that deep. When Iseta took my blood, it had only been a small, shallow cut. Mae places the bowl underneath my arm to catch the blood as it pours out of my body.

"That cut seems a bit deeper than necessary," I grumble.

"And what do you know is necessary? We need enough blood to cover every entry point into the house, doors, windows, vents. Any potential place that someone, or some*thing* as you put it, can enter. That is what you want to prevent, isn't it?"

Since we both know she's right, and it's a rhetorical question, I don't answer. Once again, I'm left feeling uneducated and inadequate in front of the Ülim and I don't like it. Hence the grumpy mood. Good ole insecurity at its finest. Add in a dash of the pity party I'm having and it's a jolly good time!

"You may as well have a seat. This is going to take a while," Mae says, as she walks off with a bowl full of my precious blood. I say a prayer that she won't be able to tell what I am just by using my blood in a spell, but without any way to change the situation, I listen to her advice. I walk over to the couch, sit down, and stay out of their way. Griffin, the smart boy that he is, jumps up and joins me. And so, we watch.

Mae isn't wrong. This spell takes a loooong time. The other three Witches sit on the floor, in a circle, holding hands and chanting, while Mae walks around my entire house placing my blood on practically everything, while keeping up the chant along with the other Witches.

With my blood
You're at an impasse
With my command
Only then shall you pass

Over and over again, they chant. I zone out until I realize I no longer hear the chanting. I sit up and look over to the Witches.

"Is it done?" I ask.

"It's done," Mae says, softly, as she walks back into the room with the empty bowl in her hands.

I can hear the weariness in her voice. Both of these spells, as easy and common as they are, still took a lot of her energy. I wonder if maybe Mae isn't quite as strong and powerful as she claims? I've seen Iseta, and Revna for that matter, do a whole lot of powerful magic and not be this worn out.

Mae walks toward me and is unfolding a piece of paper. "This is the contract that states the details, reasons, and fulfillment of our debt. I need you to sign it." She hands it over to me along with a pen.

I quickly glance through the document and read the events that happened which caused the debt in the first place. Everything looks correct and in order, so I sign my name to the bottom, underneath Mae's signature. As soon as I finish signing my name, both the pen and paper just disappear.

"Whoa! What happened? Did I do something wrong?"

"The contract is complete and will be stored with the others we've gathered throughout our Coven's history. Our debt to you has been fulfilled and our business is concluded. No offense, but I hope not to see you again any time soon."

"Trust me, no offense taken. The feeling's mutual."

Mae nods, "then we'll be on our way. Take care, Amarah."

"You too."

Once they're gone, I sit back down on the couch and sigh heavily. I was so tense and nervous the whole time they were here, now my body can finally relax. It's done. I'm safer now than I've ever been. No one can get inside my house unless *I* allow them in. It's a good feeling and yet, it's also a scary feeling. I can stay here forever and no one would ever be able to get to me. I can almost just...*disappear*, and after everything that's happened, Andre dying, losing Logan, disappearing sounds really appealing. But what if I get hurt somehow? No one will be able to save me if I can't let them in. Well, my normal friends can still get in, but if I'm hurt somehow, it probably won't be a human friend I need. Ugh. There's never an easy fix to a problem. There's always a downside.

My stomach takes this time to groan loudly and yell at me. It's already mid-afternoon and I haven't eaten all day. I'm starving! And exhausted, I realize. Even though I haven't been the one doing the spells, I still feel exhausted from it all. Pushing myself off the couch, I head to the kitchen.

"First food. Then sleep," I say to myself.

I open the fridge and rummage around to see what food I have and what I can make fairly easily when my palm ignites. That searing pain is so intense, there's no mistaking it for anything other than a warning, and then as quickly as it started, it's gone. My heart is racing as I realize the boundary has just been crossed. Then, Griffin starts barking like crazy, and I hear the garage door open.

"Logan," his name is like a delicious sin on my lips.

A forbidden apple dangling on a branch, tempting me to grab it, to sink my teeth into its crisp peel and feel the sweet juice explode in my mouth. Logan is everything I want and nothing that I can have. To keep him safe, I keep reminding myself. This is all to keep *him* safe.

A million different thoughts and feelings run through me and I have no idea how I'm going to handle this situation. One thing I do know though, there's no rest for the wicked.

Logan: Not Letting Go

Dear X, You Don't Own Me by Disciple

I let out a relieved sigh when I open the garage door and see Amarah's car parked inside. "Thank God."

I spent all day looking for her and fighting with Emerson. I knew she had been at the casino, I could smell her, but Emerson refused to give me *any* information. Until right now, I didn't know if she was still at the casino...with *him*, or not. Valmont is inaccessible during the day, and I know I was just spinning my wheels with his lackey, but my anger is making it hard to think straight. As much as I hate to admit it, Emerson is a damn good bodyguard, for being human. He held his own against me and that's saying something. Then again, I can't just *Wolf out* in the middle of the day in a casino full of innocent and ignorant humans. Still, Emerson will no doubt be bruised and sore. Not my finest moment.

I park the truck and quickly get out, heading to the front door. I just need to see her, make sure she's ok, and pull her in close to me. I want to hold her in my arms and never let go. Never let anything bad happen to her ever again. I put my key in the lock and push to open the door, but it won't budge. I turn the key back and hear the door lock. I twist it again and hear it unlock. I turn the handle and sure enough, it isn't locked anymore, but I can't get the door open.

"What in the hell?" I use my shoulder to push a little harder. Nothing.

Is the door stuck? Sometimes humidity makes wood swell, which then makes it hard to open. I try with a little more force but it just won't budge. A low growl threatens to escape my throat as I head back into the garage. I'll just enter from the laundry room door which is connected to the garage.

Denied.

The laundry room door is *never* locked. I wiggle the handle and again, the same thing. It isn't locked but I can't get it open. I have no idea what's going on and my frustration starts to build. Frustration that will quickly lead to anger if I'm not careful. Anger that won't settle until I see Amarah. Until I know that she's ok. That *we're* ok.

Back at the front door, I knock, "Amarah! I don't know what's going on but I can't get either of the doors open. Can you let me in?"

Silence.

I focus all my senses on the other side of the door. Our connection is still blocked but I have Wolf senses that I can use to my advantage. Closing my eyes, I listen. I can hear her heart beating rapidly. Then, I hear the quiet, stifled sob. She's crying, trying not to make any noise, but it's no use. I hear her. I hear her crying and it breaks my heart.

"Amarah, I know you're in there, I can hear you. I can hear your heartbeat and...and, you don't have to do this. Just let me in and we can talk all of this through. You weren't thinking straight last night and I'm not mad. Just really worried. Please, let me in, and let's figure this out. Together."

I hear her swallow hard and take a deep breath. She's walking toward the door now and I hear the gentle brush of her hands when she touches the door.

"I *was* thinking straight last night. I *am* thinking straight now, Logan. I'm doing the right thing. You're not safe around me. No one is. And you're never going to be able to open this door, or any door in the house, without my permission."

Magic. Of course. How else would she ever be able to keep me out? It dawns on me that even though I can't get in, that means no one else can either. She's safer than she's ever been, and that gives me some relief. She's trying to be strong, her words are firm and certain, but her voice betrays her. She's on the verge of breaking and I can stop that from happening. If she would just...

Let. Me. In.

"Amarah, I know you believe that's true because of what happened to Andre, but you're wrong. You're not dangerous. This world is dangerous with or without you in it. You're no more dangerous to me than I am to you. Don't you remember how close I came to Wolfing out on you? I mean, I bit you for Christ's sake! And it wasn't just a little love bite. Please, just open the door and we can talk about this."

"It's not just Andre. I'm a target and being close to me makes you one too. Look at what happened to Valmont. He almost died too! Vyla and the kids! Their home was attacked because of me! And Iseta..." I hear a sob escape and I desperately want to hold her. Comfort her. Keep her safe. "I won't survive if anything happens to you, Logan. I can't ever have that image in my mind. I can't ever hold onto you while I'm forced to watch you die! You need to stay far away from me."

I hear a soft, *thunk,* against the door as she leans her forehead against it. My hands ache to reach through the door and touch her. She's so close, just on the other side of the door, and yet, she's a million miles away from me, and I don't know how to reach her. Desperation and panic start to set in.

"Amarah, I'm not going to get hurt because of *you*. You are not responsible for this war. We can fight it together. We are stronger together! Amarah, please don't push me away." I beg. "I *need* you. You said I'd never be alone again. You said you'd be my family."

No response but I know she's still standing there, listening to me.

"I love you, Amarah, with all of my heart and everything that I am. Every fiber of my being is alive because of you."

Still no response.

"I know you're there. I know you're listening to me. I can hear you and...and, I know you're crying, and it's breaking me apart. This isn't right and you know it. You *feel* it! Or else you wouldn't be crying."

No response. More crying.

"Amarah, I know you love me too, and I know you think you're making the right choice. That somehow, you're keeping me safe, but you're not. You know what's more dangerous than you or any demon?"

Still, no response but I haven't heard her move, so I continue.

"I am. I'm more dangerous to myself than anyone or anything else will ever be, and you're the only one who can save me, Amarah. You're the only one who *has* saved me. Please, let me in."

Silence.

My anger starts to rise and I run my hands through my hair in frustration. Why isn't she listening to me? Why isn't she saying anything? I need to hear her voice. I need her to keep talking to me. I need her to let me in!

My hands are clenched in fists and I pound on the door making it groan with the force of the hit. My Wolf is rising and joining the action, and my voice is a growl as I yell, "open the fucking door, Amarah!"

I hear her scared, muffled scream and I hear her backing away from the door. I immediately regret my actions and force the anger and my Wolf back down. The last thing I ever want is for her to be afraid of me.

I sigh, "shit, I'm so sorry, Amarah. You know I would never hurt you. I'm just really frustrated and I don't want to lose you. Please, don't do this. You're causing us both unnecessary pain."

Her voice is steadier now and further away, "you need to leave. Now, Logan. I don't want to see you. I'll have someone from Headquarters come and pick up your things and take them to your room."

"There's nothing in there that I want except you," my voice comes out weak and cracks on the last word as my throat starts to constrict around the emotion.

This feeling, this heaviness in my chest, is so foreign but I know what it is. Heartbreak. But I refuse to give in to it so quickly. I refuse to just let Amarah make this decision to end us. My Wolf won't let her go either. He chose her, his mate, and that means for life. I refuse to give up this quickly. Or ever. Not when I know our love is powerful. Not when I know we're meant to be together. Always.

"I'll go," I finally say. "I'll leave you alone for now, but I will be back, Amarah. I'm fighting for this. For us. Whether you want to or not. I'll fight for both of us. And…" I shake my head, disappointed in myself, "I'm sorry."

As I turn to walk away, I hear her break. I hear her ragged breaths as she tries to breathe between her agonizing sobs. Her hold on the block to our connection falls for a moment. Just a split second when she loses control but she regains it quickly. That split second is enough to bring me to my knees. I feel her emotions and I fall to my knees with tears streaming down my face. She's in soooo much pain. How can any one person handle that much pain? How is she going to survive such devastating pain?

It takes me a few minutes to process the pain I felt and regain my composure. Now more than ever, I know I need to fight for her. I need to save her from herself. But how am I going to do that when she refuses to even see me? I don't know. But I *will* figure it out. Until then, I need an outlet of my own. I need to work through my anger, so that something like what happened earlier, doesn't happen again.

If I'm going to save Amarah, I need to be the best version of myself. Pulling out of the driveway, I stare at the house. I know what's happening behind those impenetrable walls and I just hope that I can get to her in time. Before it's too late. Before the darkness takes over and I lose her, forever.

As I drive away, my anger stirs again, I call someone I haven't called in a while. At least not for personal reasons.

"Hey man, what's up?" Ethan's deep voice rumbles on the other line.

"Hey, I'm calling for a personal favor."

"Alright, what is it?" He sounds hesitant.

"I was wondering if I could train with your Wolves sometimes. I need an outlet and somewhere where I can let go and everyone is still safe."

"You know you're always welcome as a guest in my Pack and you know the rules."

"Yes, I know the rules, and I understand. Like I said, I just need to let go of some frustrations from time to time, that's all."

Okay, so I'm downplaying the severity of my anger, but I hope to catch it before it gets out of hand. I'm more powerful than any of Ethan's Wolves, Hell, I'm more powerful than the Alpha himself. That's why I sit at the side of the Queen. The fact that Ethan is allowing me to physically fight amongst his Pack shows how much he trusts me. I can easily hurt or kill any one of them. Of course, that's not my intention. I respect Ethan. He's a good Alpha, a good Leader, and an ally. No, I just need to be able to fight someone who can at least attempt to fight back. Someone who can handle my supernatural strength and someone who can heal a few cuts and bruises.

"Alright. You know where to go."

"Thanks, Ethan. I appreciate it."

"You've never crossed a line with me or my Pack before. I have no reason not to trust you. Don't give me one. Neither one of us will like the results if you do." His voice is steady and it isn't necessarily a threat.

No, it's more like a plea. A reminder that he's the Alpha of the pack and I'm no one. A Lone Wolf with no pack of my own. No family to protect me if an infraction is made against him or his Pack. As a Lone Wolf, I shouldn't be more powerful than any Alpha, yet the Fey life-force in me changed that rule. It's a fine line for both Ethan and me to walk. For him to allow me to be a guest within his pack and for me to hold back my strength and not challenge his authority, even accidentally. It's only our mutual respect for one another, and the fact that we're both decent men with our egos in check, which allow us to walk this line.

"Understood."

"Then we'll be seeing you soon." With nothing else worth saying, Ethan ends the call.

This is far from a perfect plan but it's a step in the right direction at least. A precaution for my turmoil that boils just below the surface. As far as the rest? As far as saving Amarah? They say that love is the strongest force in the universe. Love conquers all and all of that. Our love should be enough. It should be enough to penetrate anything else she's feeling but…I felt her pain. Her love for me is being trampled on by her pain. By her fear. I have to figure out how to quench that pain and fear so the love can once again shine, and I don't think I can do it on my own. This is another war to fight. I lost

the battle today, but I'll recruit soldiers and we *will* win this war. At
least it's one we have a chance of winning.

A small chance. Like a one in a million chance. I can't help but feel like Lloyd from Dumb and Dumber, holding onto optimism and hope. There is a chance and I'll die before I stop fighting for her.

Music has become our thing. A way for us to speak words we can't quite put together ourselves. I text her a song to reiterate what I've already said.

Spotify Link: War for You by Jay Allen

Logan: I'm fighting for you, Amarah. For us. Even if the war I have to fight is you.

7

Logan: This Is All Insane

Withdrawals by Tyler Farr

I've been parked discreetly down the street, watching Amarah's house, for days. I'm on my third straight day to be exact. Not that I even need to be discreet at this point. Amarah hasn't so much as looked through the blinds much less walked outside to find me stalking her. She wouldn't notice if I was parked in her driveway much less down the street but...here I am. The inside of my truck is starting to look more and more like a dumpster by the hour with all the fast-food bags and containers pilling up. With all these convenient services now offering fast-food, and restaurants by delivery, it sure makes a stak out a whole lot easier. Of course, I don't just watch from afar.

No. I also text...a lot! And every day I drive up to the house and knock on the door. Every day I stand out there, banging on the door, begging her to talk to me. This is all so strange to me because I've *never* begged anyone for anything. But Amarah isn't just anyone.

So, I continue to make an ass out of myself and it's a miracle the neighbors haven't called the cops yet. But every day I'm met with silence. She refuses to answer my texts, even though I know she reads them, and she refuses to say one single word to me when I'm at her door.

No, I only get silence. Utter and complete, silence.

Cold.

Dark.

Deafening.

Silence.

And trust me when I say, it's the absolute worst! I would prefer to hear her yelling at me to go away, that she doesn't want to see me, versus the empty, nothingness I'm currently receiving. The only indication I have that she's alive in there is the fact that she leaves my ass on *read*.

Every.

Damn.

Time.

That doesn't stop me from sending yet another song.

Spotify Link: Wait For You by Elliott Yamin

Hell, the way I look, she probably doesn't want to see me right now anyway...or smell me, for that matter. Three days straight in here, with no shower, and the stench of fast-food clinging to me, my current state would probably just further her desire to not want to see me. Good thing it's early November and no longer ninety degrees outside or I'd have body odor to add to my recent list of appealing attributes. I take a quick sniff of my armpits just to make sure.

I scrunch my nose, "eh, not terrible...yet."

I run my hand through my long, messy hair and sigh. I just want to *see* her at this point. Just the tiniest glimpse to make sure she's ok. The tiniest glimpse to ease this ache in my heart. In my soul. I throw my head back against the headrest and settle in for another few hours of waiting.

"This is insane," I mutter to myself.

I'm starting to lose patience, and once that's gone, the anger will be there to replace it. But seriously, how long can she stay inside? If I can just wait her out, she has to leave at some point. Then I can follow her and finally be able to talk to her face to face.

"Just a few more hours and then I'll go get myself cleaned up," again, I'm stuck talking to myself, and worse, bargaining with myself. "This is definitely *not* healthy," I say, as I look around my truck. "None of this is healthy," I sigh and set my sights on the front of Amarah's house.

I jerk awake when the cab of my truck is illuminated with a brilliant light. Headlights to be exact. Headlights from a vehicle pulling into Amarah's driveway. This street doesn't have any lights on it, something I've *never* liked, and its currently pitch-black outside. Taking a glance at the clock, I can't believe it's just past 10:00 p.m.

"Shit!" I scold myself for falling asleep but quickly focus on the SUV now parked in Amarah's driveway.

I can't see a damn thing but I don't want to turn my headlights on and bring attention to myself. Luckily, I don't have to. I call on my Wolf and shift my eyes, something not very many Werewolves can do. A growl trickles out of my throat as I see who emerges from the SUV.

"Valmont," I spit the name out like it's the most disgusting thing to ever cross my tongue.

Leaning forward I grip the steering wheel, consciously

trying not to shred it to pieces with my claws, as I watch Valmont approach the front door. Considering the fact that Amarah hasn't even peeked out of a blind in three days, I don't expect Valmont to have any better luck at seeing her than I have. I feel frozen in place, staring, eyes narrowed, as he rings the doorbell and then adjusts his, no doubt designer suit, as he waits. First, his hands adjust his tie, then his jacket button, then his cufflinks, and then back to his tie. Is he...*fidgeting?* If I didn't know any better, I would say he looks nervous.

A part of me wonders if somehow, he can get through to her, when I can't. After all, it was *him* she had run to when she could have turned to several other people. *Anyone* else. I would be lying if I said the Vampire doesn't inspire jealousy in me. Especially after he *bit* her. Just the thought of his hands, his lips on her body, makes me want to jump out of this truck, walk up to him without saying a word, and rip his fucking throat out. Taking a deep breath, I continue watching as the seconds tick by into minutes, and she still hasn't made an appearance. She's going to ignore him too, thank fuck. Just as I'm about to sit back and relax, the door opens, and my heart stops.

My Wolf gaze zeros in on only her. Her hair is tied up in a messy ponytail leaving her face exposed. She has her arms crossed over her stomach and doesn't look happy to see the Vampire. I can't help but smirk. I've always loved her courage to stand up to anyone, speak her mind, and deal with the consequences later. But the smirk fades quickly. Her face doesn't have a trace of makeup on it and she's been crying. Her eyes are slightly puffy, her cheeks a little blotchy, and her nose a bit red. God, she's still the most beautiful woman I've ever seen. She takes my breath away just like she did the first time I ever saw her and every moment after that.

My chest aches where our link is empty and silent. I can't touch her. I can't hold her. I can't even feel her through our link. Our deeper connection to each other. I don't care if there's nothing but pain to feel. Any part of feeling her would be better than nothing. I would gladly share her pain if she would only let me in!

Amarah, let me in!

I send a desperate plea down our link, hoping and praying it will get through. And just then, her eyes look my way, and I stop breathing. I know she can't see me this far away, through the darkness of the night, but I swear her eyes lock on mine. Our connection has always allowed us to find each other. To know where the other person is at any moment, anywhere in a room, regardless of how many others are in it. She knows I'm here. She feels me, even without the link, even if she doesn't want to. She stays looking in my direction for what feels like forever and not long enough all at the same time.

The weight of her gaze holds me motionless. I want to get out of the truck and run to her! I want to take her in my arms and smell her sweet skin. I want to kiss her tears away and tell her everything will be ok. I want so many things, but I'm frozen in her stare. It holds me in rapture. It consumes me. Every part of me. Everything I am, everything I have, belongs to her. Why can't she see that?!

I finally snap out of my trance when she looks away and the door closes, hiding her away once more. I take a deep breath, blink, and the world seems to come slamming back around me. Valmont is no longer standing outside. She let him in.

SHE.

LET.

HIM.

IN.

Instant fury explodes through my body as I jump out of the

truck and charge down the street towards the house, thankful for the cover of darkness, and the late hour. Pierce and another Vampire I don't know are leaning against the SUV and look up as I approach.

Pierce steps in my way, "Logan, we don't want any trouble."

"Then save yourself some and get the fuck out of my way," I manage to calmly say through my anger.

Pierce shrugs, crosses his arms back over his chest, and goes back to leaning against the SUV, "good luck trying to get in."

I snarl at him as I pass by. He thinks I don't know about the wards. The wards. Shit. They *are* a problem, I have no idea what I'm going to do, but I know I can't just sit back and do nothing! Not knowing Valmont is inside with Amarah. *Alone.* With that thought leading the charge, as soon as I reach the door, I pound on it as if my body is a battering ram. If it wasn't for the magic protecting it. The door would be in pieces at my feet.

"Amarah!" I roar. "I'm not leaving until you open this door!"

My body is taut with anger. Every muscle in my body, every inch of my skin, feels like it's been hit by lightning. I feel like I'm going to physically explode at any second. As if that's not enough, my Wolf is pushing at me from under the surface. He's also trying to break through and attack any and all challenges.

She is *my* mate.

She is *mine* to protect.

She is *mine* to touch.

She is *mine* to fight for.

And I *will* fight for her.

I'm persistently banging on the door when it finally opens but my fists stay pressed against the invisible boundary. Valmont is standing just on the other side of the boundary with a smug smile on his face and his hands casually placed in his pockets. Everything about his demeanor says, *I win.* I growl and push as hard as I can against the boundary but it's no use.

"Logan, how nice of you to join us instead of acting like a psycho stalker watching from down the street," he tips his head in the direction of my truck. "Well, I guess, you can't *really* join us, can you? My apologies." His tone is nonchalant, but his eyes sparkle with humor.

"Why don't you join me outside so I can make you *really* sorry," I challenge. My fists are clenched at my sides, my chest heaving, the adrenaline is begging for an outlet. So is my anger. And my Wolf.

"You should try and get a hold of yourself, mate. You're acting like an animal. Ahhhh, once again, my apologies," he places a hand over his heart, mocking genuine sympathy.

"Yeah, you're real tough, hiding behind those wards. We both know what would happen if you came outside but that won't happen, will it, Valmont? Because you're a coward. Always have been. Always will be. Hiding away like always."

I watch the humor fade from his eyes, along with any spark of life, as the dead Vampire makes his appearance. "It's not wise for you to keep challenging me, mate. My patience is not limitless and I am beyond tired of hearing you run your mouth with idle threats."

I throw my arms out to the side, challenging him even more, "I'm right here, big, bad Vampire! What are you gonna do about it?" I let my claws emerge slowly and I know my eyes are now amber. My Wolf is ready for this fight.

"Both of you stop!" I hear Amarah's voice carry outside. It's filled with tears and pain. "Valmont, please don't make it worse. Just shut the door."

"Amarah! I just want to see you! I want to talk to you, please! Why does he get to see you and I don't? Just give me five minutes, Amarah, please!" I know I look weak, begging in front of Valmont, but I don't care. Nothing matters except Amarah. Nothing else. Not my ego. Not pride. Fuck all of that.

She's whispering now, but my Wolf hears her, "Valmont, I *can't* see him. I can't! Please, just shut the door and stop this." I hear her sobs through her words. She's crying...a lot.

"She doesn't want to see you, mate. You're only making things worse. Don't you see that?" There's no humor in his eyes now. It looks like a small ounce of the same pain I'm feeling. Neither one of us wants Amarah hurting.

My anger diffused instantly, but not because of what Valmont says, but because of Amarah. My anger and jealousy *are* making things worse, and I don't want to make this harder on her than it already is. Harder on both of us. I know Amarah better than anyone else and even more importantly, I trust her. She may be pushing me away, but that doesn't mean she doesn't love me. The type of love we have doesn't just disappear. No. All she needs is time. I'll give her time, and I'll wait, because she's worth waiting for.

"Fine," I run my hand through my hair. "I'll go for now. For *her*, not because of you, but I *will be* back. And Valmont, keep your hands off of her." I point an accusing finger at him but he just smirks again.

He puts his hands up in defense, "I'm just here to make sure she's ok. Don't worry, I'll take *really* good care of her," he says, as he slowly slides his tongue across his fangs and winks.

And just like that, my anger is back ten times as intense, as I charge the door again. It shuts in my face as I slam my fists against it. Blue sparks fly from my fists and send a shock wave rippling through the protection ward. I recognize my Fey power but I didn't mean to use it. It's never come out unprovoked and it sure as Hell has never done anything like *that* before. It's enough to sober my mind a bit and clear the haze caused by my anger. I slowly pull my fists away from the door and notice two indentations, covered in frost, embedded in the door.

I have no idea what's just happened. Confusion and anger

mixed together isn't the best combination for anyone, much less a Werewolf. I need to get out of here and somewhere safe. Somewhere where I can't hurt anyone...too badly.

"Son of a bitch!" I yell my frustration to the night sky and stalk back to my truck.

I don't see Pierce or the other Vampire as I leave. I don't even remember getting into my truck, starting it, or driving off. All I can see is red.

8

Logan: A New Distraction

Animal I Have Become by Three Days Grace

I don't remember driving Downtown, and I vaguely remember parking in the private employee parking lot of Knockouts, before I head towards the door. It's like I blink and I'm suddenly here. My vision is still hazed by red, I know I have to let go of my anger before it consumes me, and this is the only place I can do that somewhat safely.

The parking lot is cloaked in darkness. All of the lights in the tall light posts are burnt out and purposefully not replaced. Darkness tends to be a natural deterrent to most humans, and we preternatural creatures of The Unseen use this cover and fear of darkness to our advantage.

I use my Wolf senses to scan the parking lot. Even in my anger-induced state, I never let my guard down when it comes to my safety. I don't anticipate running into any trouble here, but strange things have been known to happen, and right now I'd eagerly welcome a fight. The parking lot is filled with several other vehicles, but there's no one, and nothing else, I can sense.

I reach the back door, yank it open, and make my way inside.

I knew it would be open because it always is. Sometimes, people just need to get inside and out of sight, quickly. I also know there's better security inside. The entire inside of the building is almost as dark as it is outside. This time, the haze in my vision is caused by black lights and fog, and I'm immediately hit by the booming base of music being blasted in the front room and reverberating throughout the building. I have to turn off my Wolf hearing or risk becoming deaf. I don't know how the others can handle this all the time. After the initial shock to my hearing, my other senses heightened. I can smell alcohol, and the sour undertone of drugs, but what permeates the air above all else, is arousal. Sex.

I don't need to see the front room to know what's happening. I know there will be at least three girls on stage and several more working the floor, looking for their next horny target. Not to mention what happens behind the closed doors I'm now passing by as I walk down the narrow hallway. According to the law and the human police, this is a respectable, adult entertainment establishment. But the truth is, a little excess drinking, drugs, and sex is discreetly encouraged. Why? It provides the best distractions to everything that happens right under their noses. That, in addition to the location being right in the heart of Downtown, on Central, where the crowd is a mix of homeless, thugs, rowdy, young, and drunk humans, which allows for the occasional...*unnatural* occurrence or sightings more freedom. They're often chalked up to hallucinations and imagination.

It's a perfect way to use humans' own desires and weaknesses to our advantage. To hide in plain sight. A strip club, a Casino and Nightclub, a tourist shop, a Church...all places where humans visit with a certain focus in mind.

Desires.

Gambling.

Addiction.

Devout religion.

Feigned safety and comfort.

Ignorance.

Selfishness.

Tunnel vision.

All forms of weakness that The Unseen take advantage of.

I come to the end of the hallway and another door. This one is guarded, but at a glance, no one would suspect the person standing in front of it to be a guard. The boy standing here is only about five-eight, with a small build. The only thing that helps his cause, and assists him in appearing his age, is the full beard and mustache, though he keeps it clean and short.

Still, it's hard to hide the babyface, even under all the facial hair. His black hair is shaved close on the sides and left to a tight curl on the top in a kind of small afro. Genetics I know he gets from his mother. I'm acknowledged right away with a beaming smile that only adds to his youth and innocence. Oh, how looks can be deceiving.

"Logan, it's good to see you, man! My dad told us to be expecting you." He says in a voice that is a bit deeper than you would expect. Genetics from his father.

I can't help but smile back as I take his offered hand and we do the typical male shoulder bump and tap, which is our version of a hug. Although, it's a bit awkward since he's quite a bit smaller than I am.

"Kaedon, it's good to see you, too. Man, look at you, all grown up. How old are you now, twenty-four?"

"Yeah, twenty-four, and I'm Valvur now. Worked hard to get here and work even harder to stay here, but it's worth it!" Kaedon gives me another ear-to-ear grin.

"Guardian, huh!?" I let out a whistle, impressed by the news. "I'm not surprised. You've always been the hardest and most determined worker in the room. You can work your way all the way up to Beta...Hell, Alpha one day if that's what you want."

"I've always been the one with the most to prove, you know that," he shrugs. "People still underestimate me."

"And I don't doubt they soon realize their mistake and you make them pay for it?"

He answers with another beaming smile. A smile that can disarm just about anyone or any situation, but if you pay attention, his dark brown eyes spark with fire. They say the eyes are the windows to the soul and Kaedon's soul is ten times the size of anyone else's. His eyes don't match the rest of his understated packaging. They're shrewd and focused. He notices and picks up things most people don't. Things that give him an advantage either in a fight or just in life.

As the runt of the litter, Kaedon was expected to be Omega, but his mother had always been his biggest fan. She encouraged him when everyone else thought she was crazy. She taught him how to be quiet and observant. She taught him how to utilize his size and ability to be underestimated to his advantage. His size also makes him extremely quick and agile, and as a Werewolf, you don't need to pack on all the muscle to have supernatural strength. His mother also taught him how to handle pain and not to show any signs of weakness. I know all of this because I've watched him grow up and have been in the training ring with him a time or two.

I place my hand on his shoulder, "I know your dad is very proud of you, and your mom would be too, if she was here to see how much you've accomplished. I know she's still rooting for you, and watching over you, always."

His Adam's apple bobs harshly but he refused to show the emotion in his eyes or on his face. Again, something his mother would have been proud of, if she were here to see him now. In his short life, he's learned more control than most people who have lived twice or even three-time his age.

Kaedon just nods and changes the subject, "so, you're here

for some training?"

I run my hand through my hair, my anger having slowly dissipated as I talked with Kaedon. "Yeah, I need to redirect my focus on training. I've been slacking lately and it's time to get back in shape and stay on point." Not a complete lie.

Kaedon chuckles, "I don't think you will ever *not* be on point, Logan." He leans in close and whispers, "you're the best fighter I've ever seen and with the most control over your Wolf, but I'll deny I ever said it in front of my dad."

"Well, I have lived quite a while, but I'm willing to bet that you will learn much quicker than I ever did."

He shakes his head, "I doubt that."

He finally steps aside so I can continue to their private underground Base, but before I'm through the door, he stops me.

"Hey, can I join you on the mat sometime? For some lessons? When I'm off duty, of course."

"Anytime, man. You're Valvur now. I'm excited to see what you've learned and what I might pick up from you." That earns me another genuine smile before the door closes between us and I head downstairs.

Ethan has an office upstairs, as the owner of the strip club, or rather the front to his actual base of operations for the Los Lobos Pack. At the bottom of the stairs is a simple storage room. Even as a front, this is a thriving business and therefore requires actual product and actual work. Not something I envy the Alpha. I pass by shelves and shelves of supplies, mostly beer and liquor, and head towards the industrial size walk-in freezer. The walk-in refrigerator and freezer are also necessary as they serve food along with the alcohol and skin show. Food helps sober the customers up which in turn, increases the alcohol sales, because they can drink more. Win-win.

No one ever wants to spend any additional time in a freezer than necessary, so it's the perfect spot to hide the entrance to the real underground base of operations for the Pack. I'm through the hidden door and on the other side before I see anyone else.

The place is buzzing with energy. Werewolves are more hot-blooded and, well...*alive,* than any other preternatural species. The Fey are the closest to nature, so their energy is very balanced and calm. The Witches are the closest to humans, their spells are what give them their energy. The Vampires are cold and dead creatures that don't give off *any* kind of energy. No, the Werewolves are definitely the liveliest of the bunch. Walking into the energy I realize how much I've missed it. How much I've missed being around a Pack. A family. Even though I'm not a part of this Pack, it eases something in me to be here, even as a guest.

There are some new faces I'm not familiar with, but for the most part, I recognize everyone I see, and they all know who I am, too. As the right-hand of the Queen and Kaitsja, everyone knows who I am, regardless of whether I know them or not. Not to mention my reputation precedes me everywhere I go. I'm known for my anger, ruthlessness in a fight, and my ability to control my Wolf. Not many Werewolves can partially change their body at will. It's a sign of power and strength.

I receive stares and head nods as I navigate my way to the weight room. A few others are working out, but this late hour means people are either hunkering down for the night and upcoming day or getting ready to hit the nightlife. Some Werewolves choose to live a somewhat normal life, working regular jobs, and trying to sustain regular relationships. Typically, the relationships don't last. At least not the ones with humans. Especially for the younger Wolves that are still fighting to learn control over their Wolf. Still, some try for a modicum of normalcy.

Most, however, work and live here at Base. They contribute to the Pack and pull their weight any way they can. Omegas clean and cook and watch over the pups, there are Healers, Hunters,

Guardians, Deltas, and Betas. A Pack is made up of several levels of strength, and with Werewolves, it *always* comes back to strength and its many forms.

I had been a Beta once upon a time. I had trusted my Pack and respected my Alpha. I had given him, and my Pack, everything I had. And how did they repay me? They turned their backs on me. It was a long time ago, and yet, it still weighs heavily in the back of my mind and heart. My Alpha had been old-school and set in his ways of thinking and running the Pack. At least that's what I've thought for a long-time. That's the logical excuse I've told myself. I had been so young and naive then, trying to justify his weakness. His cowardice. I feel my anger stirring again at remembering the day I was outlawed from my Pack. My family. Over three hundred years later, Gregory's cold words still haunt me.

"We've discussed your situation at length. It pains me to do this," Gregory lifts his chin defiantly, "but I have no choice. You're no longer võltsimatu, pure. Your Täiskuu Blood has been tainted. We cannot, and will not, allow your foul blood to contaminate the Full Moon Pack Bloodline."

The memory of my exile, the last time I had been a part of a Pack, the last time I had seen my mother's face, tears at my already bleeding heart. I haven't thought about this memory, or talked about it, since I told Amarah about it vaguely the night we camped on our way to the Fire Fey. Amarah has taken front and center in my mind and overshadowed my entire past. All of my anger and all of my pain, locked away in the shadow of *her*. And now, as her presence is fading, everything that had faded into the background is coming back with a vengeance.

"Ahhhhh!" I let out a frustrated yell, as the weights I'm lifting crash to the floor.

It's too easy to get lost in your own thoughts lifting weights. I need to do something that requires me to focus my thoughts on something, *anything* else. I rack my weights, ignoring the uneasy looks of the few others still in the weight room, and then I head out to the training mat. Again, there are just a handful of guys here as well. There are two sparring on the mat, one watching them, and one working a punching bag off to the side.

Walking up to the mat, I stand next to the guy watching. I recognize his face but can't remember his name, so I extend my hand, "Logan."

"Jack," his handshake is strong but doesn't linger. "And I know who you are," he looks at me nervously, from the corner of his eye.

I give him what I hope is a, *I'm not here to hurt you*, smile and nod, then turn my attention back to the sparring. I recognize Declan. He's one of the Delta Wolves and therefore, one of the training instructors. He's about the same height and build as me. His blonde hair is shaved on the sides, but long on top that he styles in a top-knot. His face is clean-shaven, sharp, and he appears to be in his late thirties but I know he's closer to a hundred and fifty than thirty.

He's working with someone I don't know, and judging by his fighting technique, I assume he's pretty young and in the early stages of learning. He's quite a bit smaller than Declan both in his height and his build. I can see that he isn't confident in himself yet. There's something a little...*ungrounded*, in his presence. Like he's still getting used to his body and strength. He also appears to be in his late twenties but my guess is he *is* in his late twenties. I focus on him and use my Wolf to smell his essence and confirm my initial thoughts. He's one of The Turned.

Declan has just laid him out pretty hard, and instead of getting back up quickly to his feet, he stays laying on the mat panting hard. His dark brown hair is plastered to his head with sweat, his bare chest and stomach are covered in varying shades of yellow, green, blue, and purple, telling me that Declan has been training with him for quite a while.

"I think we'll call it a day," Declan states, as he helps the young man to his feet. He's not even breathing hard, there's no trace of sweat on his skin. He's definitely training a newbie.

They walk over to where Jack and I are standing and Declan extends his hand toward me. I take it. It's just a handshake and no bro-hug like I had done with Kaedon earlier. Declan is more business than pleasure. He never crosses lines with anyone, especially on the training mat. He's a trainer first, and always, never a friend. I'm sure he has friends, I would hope, but I've never seen him be anything other than one hundred percent professional. He doesn't have a lot of emotion and that makes him one Hell of a fighter. He's all about black and white, following the rules, and making sure everyone else does too, when he's around. Me being here isn't something he necessarily agrees with, but he was told by his Alpha that I'm to be treated as a guest, and he'll follow the order without hesitation.

"Logan, welcome back. You know Jack," he motions to the man standing beside me. "This is Brandon."

I give all of my attention to Brandon and can't help but feel a bit bad for him. He looks wrecked. His eyes are a bit too wide and panicked, his thin lips are set in a slight frown, and his overall expression is very bleak. It's like he's going through the motions of everyday life through a haze of shock.

"Brandon, this is Logan Lewis. He is Kaitsja and right-hand to the Fey Queen. He's an instrumental part of keeping The Unseen safe and has been for a long time. He's not a part of our Pack but he is our guest and is always to be respected."

"Brandon, it's good to meet you," I shake his hand, it's a firm handshake, but I feel a slight nervous twitch, confirming my theory that he's brand new to all of this and completely overwhelmed. "And don't worry, you're in good hands. Declan is one of the best trainers and fighters I've ever known. He'll get you up to speed before you know it."

"Nice to meet you. I hope so, I don't know if I'll ever get used to it." His voice comes out steady but filled with hopelessness.

I think by *it*, he means all of it, not just the training. His entire life has been turned upside down and I can't imagine what that must be like for him. One day you're a normal human, going about your life, and the next thing you know every bone in your body is breaking and you become a Wolf once a month. That has to be mentally and physically traumatizing.

Declan steers the conversation away from Brandon and back to me, "you here to do some training?"

"Yeah, you know, I've been slacking and need to get back into it. I'm happy to see you're here this late. You up for some sparring?" I try to sound as nonchalant as I can.

Declan shakes his head, "count me out. I've been training all day and I'm spent. I can still hold my own against Brandon here, but I'm too worn out to get on the mat with you."

"Fair enough." I turn to Jack, "what about you?"

Jack shakes his head and puts his hands up in a defensive gesture, "sorry, but there's no way I'm getting on that mat with you, even if it is just practice. I've seen you practice and I don't want that many bruises."

I look around and notice the guy at the boxing bag has stopped and is watching us. "What about you? You wanna go a few rounds?" I yell across to him.

The guy's eyes widen and he shakes his head emphatically then returns his attention to the bag in front of him. Cowards. Here I am, offering training, in a sense, of my own. I'm better than Declan on my worst day and these men should be lining up and jumping at the chance to spar and learn from me.

Kaedon knows what an opportunity it would be and made sure to take advantage, and that's the difference between him and all these other guys. Kaedon isn't afraid of a challenge, especially one he knows will only make him better. He isn't afraid to get...*bruises*, I almost roll my eyes at the ridiculousness of it. A Werewolf afraid to get bruises. I can't help but think, what a weak Pack, but I keep that to myself. But not Kaedon. He's anything but weak physically or mentally and that's why the smallest Wolf of the Pack is now a Guardian. That's why he will make a good Alpha. His character, his determination, and his spirit, set him so far apart from everyone else but no one else seems to notice. They still treat him like he isn't good enough. Like he's still the little runt destined to be Omega. This Pack doesn't deserve him.

"Oh, come on," I plead. "I just want to practice a bit and shake off the cobwebs, nothing serious. I promise to go easy out there. I just need a partner. Seriously? No one?"

"I'll get on the mat with you."

I turn around to face the new voice. A woman is walking towards us and she exudes confidence. She's dressed in all-black, leggings and a tank top that accentuate her long legs, toned arms, and curves. She's wrangling her unruly, long, and naturally red hair into a ponytail, as she stops in front of me, exposing a strong jaw. She's tall, only a few inches shorter than me, and her piercing blue eyes sparkle with mischief as she holds my gaze. Her eyes and soft, full lips softened her otherwise strong features.

She offers me her hand. I'm a little slow to respond as I push through my shock but I finally manage to get my body moving as I take her hand in mine. It's a very firm handshake and I can feel the Wolf energy radiating off of her. She's a Natural Wolf. She's powerful. And she's gorgeous.

Her lips tip up at the corners in a sly smirk as her smooth voice slides across my skin, "I'm Atreya Stone."

9

Amarah: Taking Back Control

Devil Inside by CRMNL

I'm lying on the couch, Griffin cuddled next to me, watching a Lord of the Rings marathon that's playing on TV for the millionth time. I'm grateful for the repetitiveness of local TV because they tend to always play my favorites, Harry Potter, Lord of the Rings, and The Hobbit. The only reason I know it isn't Christmas yet, or close, is the fact that they haven't started playing classics like A Charlie Brown Christmas, another favorite, on repeat yet. But I'm grateful for the small miracle these magical stories give me no matter how many times I've seen them. Comfort.

I haven't moved much from the couch since I locked myself away from the world...what, days ago? Weeks? Months? I have no idea how much time has passed by. Hell, I can barely distinguish day from night anymore. All the blinds are drawn closed and I sleep...*a lot*. My energy is low due to the lack of movement and nutrition, so my body is going into preservation and survival mode. Not to mention, sleep allows peace. Well, most of the time. If I'm not having a nightmare or being visited by the Devil.

I tried sleeping in my bed my first night alone but that had been a disaster. I ended up in the fetal position, on Logan's side of the bed, hugging his pillow and crying uncontrollably until I passed out from exhaustion. All his things are still in the room and bathroom, so I avoid them at all costs. I even moved my necessities into the spare bathroom. Hell, if it wasn't for Valmont coming to check on me daily, or nightly rather, I probably wouldn't even shower. But damn that Vampire and his stubborn ass! Even though I hate to admit it, I need him. He and Griffin are the only things keeping me sane.

Don't get me wrong, people are constantly checking in on me. I never pick up the phone to talk to anyone, but I respond to worried texts. Well, I respond to everyone but Logan. I just can't bring myself to hit the send button on anything I type. I know if I respond, it's just going to reopen that connection, and everything I'm trying to avoid feeling. I can barely handle it when he sends me beautiful and heartfelt songs that I end up listening to on repeat, much less when he shows up, banging on my door and begging to see me. It causes my heart to break more and more every time. When he does show up, I have to go into the bathroom, shut the door, and drown him out with the shower on full-blast and my pathetic sobs. And that barely helps. But, to everyone else, I let them know that I'll be fine. I just need some time. A lie I think everyone believes and I try desperately to believe, too.

I'm standing by a river that I know well. It's a small river, not very wide, but it has a man-made dam and waterfall that manages to be quite thunderous for its small size. The river, this particular spot, hasn't been this clean and clear of overgrown weeds in years. That's how I know what I'm seeing isn't real, but I still take a moment to close my eyes, feel the fresh grass under my bare feet, and breathe in the fresh air of the country before I face reality. Or dream rather.

The hair on the back of my neck stands on end and alerts me to my host. I sigh heavily and speak without turning around to face him, "why here?"

"Well, hello to you too, Amarah," his Scottish accent is pleasing to my ears, his smooth voice seems to glide over and caress my skin. I shiver, even as the bright sun warms my skin. "You can at least pretend to be happy to see me instead of breaking my heart."

I roll my eyes and turn to face him. He's wearing a plain white t-shirt and light-blue jeans with rips and tears in them. Like me, he's also barefoot. I glance down and noticed that I'm wearing a simple white sundress adorned with light-blue flowers. Another dress. Always a dress in these dreams. The dress isn't overly tight but it hugs my body and highlights my curves. It doesn't escape me that we always seem to be matching. It's all just fun and teasing that Lucifer likes to have at my expense, so I ignore it.

"Why here?" I ask again.

"Because you require comfort and familiarity and this place provides you with both. It can also help you with your current... dilemma, if you're open to accepting the truth of this place."

I snort unattractively, "this place has shit to offer me."

"Doesn't it? Think about it." His sky-blue eyes hold mine and seem to see everything. All of my truth, my lies, my past, present, and future. I can't hide from those piercing blue eyes.

What does this place have to offer me? This is where I grew up. A small valley that doesn't even register on a map. A place where more animals live than people, and those who do choose to live here, often struggle with one thing or another. The only thing this town is known for is drugs, bad decisions, and stealing youth and innocence.

Standing in front of Lucifer, it dawns on me that this is a place full of sin. So much sin! And yet, I can't help but smile at the fond memories I have here too, a lot of them in this very spot. Even if the good memories are few and far between, they are there.

I have memories of being here with friends, running and jumping or pushing each other in the water, dunking, splashing, being loud with no one around to care. Memories of a trashcan fire, music, boys and silly crushes, heartbreaks, and too much alcohol at a young age. I also have memories of coming here with my mom and sisters, in the few times that we were all together as a happy family. This place is filled with so many memories! All of it, the good, the bad, and the ugly, all contributed to the foundation and building of *me*. Who I am at my core is because of how I grew up. I have been through a lot in my short life and this is a great reminder that I *am* a survivor. That thought sparks the dying fire in my chest. I'm a survivor, not a victim!

Lucifer's smile widens as he watches my face closely, "aye. You've just realized something. Anything you care to share?"

"I'm not a victim," my voice is barely above a whisper, as I say it more for myself to hear than for Lucifer.

"No, Amarah, you are not," Lucifer says, as he reaches out, his fingers sparking on my chin as he gently lifts my head so he can meet my eyes. "Look at everything you have endured, everything you have overcome. I know when you're in the moment, it can seem hopeless, but is it? Was any of it ever hopeless?"

"No," I say, with more conviction.

"So, what's holding you back? What is the one thing that's always made you weak?" His voice is calm and steady, soothing, and coaxing out my revelations.

"I am. My, my... *emotions*. My emotions always get the best of me when I'm in the moment, and then, I always look back at the situation and wish I had been stronger and not so...so, damn stupid!" Just thinking about some of my past experiences and how I let them cripple me unnecessarily adds fuel to my growing fire.

"Aye!" Lucifer agrees, excitedly. "Once you master your emotions and stop letting them master you, you will be in complete control. This is what I've been trying to get you to understand. Stop living for other people, Amarah. Stop trying to be what other people want you to be. What other people *expect* you to be. Who are they to demand anything of you?"

"No one!"

"When you were growing up here, in this vile, ignorant town, what did people expect of you?"

"Everyone expected me to follow the path that had been laid at my feet. Partying. Drugs. Abuse. A life stuck here and going nowhere. Becoming a victim."

"But you proved them all wrong, didn't you? You got out. You lived a better life and never looked back. So, why have you forgotten that you are in control of your life and no one else? Where is that girl who refused to take the easy road? Why are you letting your current circumstances make you a victim?"

I shake my head, "I don't know. It's just...you're right. It's easy. It's easy to let emotions take over. It's easier to lie down and surrender than it is to stand up and fight."

"But you have never laid down for long," his fiery gaze is locked on mine.

It's like I can feel his strength and determination entering my body and rousing my own. I let myself get defeated. I've been so caught up in this new world, this new role, that I've been trying too hard to be someone I'm not. I'm not perfect. I'm not *all* good. I'm not a savior.

"You've been so caught up in doing what everyone else wants you to do that you've lost all indication of what *you* want to do, Amarah. Stop thinking about what others want. Stop thinking about what others will think." He's speaking with so much passion and his words are so impactful, it's like he's stamping them directly onto my soul.

As if he's reading my mind, Lucifer continues coaxing me with my thoughts brought to life, solidifying them. "Who's stopping you from living the life you want, Amarah?"

"I am. Just me," I whisper.

"Here, I want you to take this."

I glance down to see him remove a ring off his finger and place it on mine. It fits snuggly on my middle finger. I lift my hand to examine it. At a distance, it looks like a solid black band but up close I can see flames etched into it. The flames catch the light and at certain angles, the black looks deep red.

"What's this for?" I ask.

"It's a reminder of what you remembered here today. Oftentimes, objects help us to make things more real, solidifying them, and you need a constant reminder right now. A reminder that you're not a victim, Amarah. When you find yourself struggling or forgetting, look at this ring and ask yourself. Who do *you* want to be? What do *you* want to do?"

"Why are you here, Lucifer? Why are you helping me? What's in the arrangement for you?"

"When I offered you my help, and my hand, did we make any kind of deal? Was there a stipulation to my offer? Did I ask you to eternally damn your soul and sign a contract? Forget everything you *think* you know about me." His eyes flash with indignation, his jaw tenses and he seems to be reliving something in his memories, somewhere far away. That only lasts a second before his eyes are back on mine.

"You're special. So special, and beautiful." He gently strokes my jaw and lifts my chin, demanding I see him. "Surely, I'm not the first one to tell you this. I'm here because I want to be here, Amarah, with you. I want to set you free!" He exclaims with fierce determination. "Do what *you* want to do! Live the life *you* want! Whatever your heart desires in any given moment, act on it! Stop living in fear of judgment and constantly worrying about doing the right thing. There is no good versus evil. There is no wrong or right. There is no darkness. Only *your* truth. Who you are inside. Why would you have urges if you weren't meant to act on them? And who decides which urges are a sin? Who has that right?"

I'm frantically searching his face for any signs of deception but all I see is genuine excitement. I hear the truth of his words but they're the opposite of everything I've ever been taught. The idea to act on whatever I want, at any given moment? I can't lie, it's enticing. Thrilling. Why can't I? Who's stopping me?

Lucifer's hands move up to cup my face and I love the feel of his body heat on my skin. I inhale sharply realizing how close we're standing. My immediate thought is to take a step back and move out of his reach, but a small voice in the back of my mind asks, *why*? My brain is fighting to make sense of everything. *He's the Devil!* He is the representation of everything bad in this world. But he's also an Angel. He can't be *all* bad just like I can't be *all* good, right? If I take all of the *good versus bad* talk out of the equation, and just listen to my desires, what do I want? At this moment, right here and now, what do I desire?

Lucifer notices my hesitation and takes the last step toward me, bringing our bodies a hair's breadth away from touching. I can smell his skin like the most intoxicating and treacherous wildfire. He's smoky and sweet and everything dangerous and exhilarating. Every sinful thing I've ever thought or desired is literally at the tip of my fingers. I imagine what it would be like to feel his lips on mine. That thought makes my blood race in my veins and my stomach turn at the same time.

"Amarah," his minty, clean breath is hot on my face, "look at me."

I don't realize I'm squeezing my eyes shut until I open them to obey him. His eyes are soooo blue. Crystal clear and mesmerizing and dangerous.

"You have a desire at this moment. Now is your chance to take back control. Now is your chance to take the first step toward living the life you want. What are you going to do? Are you going to be true to yourself, to your heart's desire? Or are you going to continue to strive for the acceptance of others?"

I can feel my heart pounding in my chest. The desire is a fire coursing through my veins, fuelled by his body heat combined with mine. His hands cup my face with a firm, almost demanding grip, forcing me in place and not letting me run away. My mind is being pulled in opposite directions, good vs evil, trying to make sense of what's happening. But trying to make sense of life and a world that is so much bigger than anyone can fathom is pointless. All anyone can do is live in the moment. Live in the moment and not just survive this life. Live!

He trails his thumb across my bottom lip leaving a trail of sparks in its wake and my lips part on a sigh. "Amarah," my name on his lips sends a thrill through me and feels like a new log being thrown into the fire in my belly. I close my eyes and bite my bottom lip, the sensation sending a moan up my throat and out of my mouth.

"You have to make the decision. I can't make it for you," he says, firmly.

I open my eyes and see the same heat I'm feeling inside of me reflected in his eyes. Other than the passion in his eyes, his face is completely blank. He isn't wearing the typical cocky smirk he usually wears. My eyes drop to his sensuous lips, so full and the perfect shade of pink. I desperately want to feel them against mine, so why shouldn't I?

Logan.

Always, Logan.

But I'm no good for Logan. I'm only going to cause him pain or worse, death. I've already broken up with him but he still thinks there's hope for us. For me. I need to do something to push him further away, to let him know I'm beyond saving. He's also one of those people who want me to be something I'm not. He's the one that's all good. He deserves better than me and I need him safe. I need him far away from me and my dangerous power. He just needs more incentive to leave, so I'll give it to him. I'm doing this to save Logan and not because I want to do it. A little white lie I tell myself to make this easier.

Without any more hesitation, I place my hands on Lucifer's stomach and feel the chiselled abs I've seen once before. I slowly make my way up his chest and end with my fingers slipping through the hair at the back of his head and then I slowly move my lips towards his. Right before they touch, right before I close my eyes, I see the corner of his lips pull up into that knowing, arrogant smirk, and I can't seem to care.

The moment our lips touch, they spark, and my breath catches in my throat. His lips are soft but all I feel is heat, and then his tongue caresses mine, and I ignite from within. The dream world fades away, and I'm left standing inside my own burning flame, kissing the Devil.

Amarah: A New Threat, A New Me

I'm Back by Royal Deluxe

I'm pulled out of my fiery dream when my palm ignites. Minutes later, there's a loud banging on the front door and Griffin starts barking like a wild animal. I reach for my phone and turn the screen on. I wince at the brightness and squint, focusing only on the clock display, 3:08 p.m., which means it's Logan out there and not Valmont.

I groan and pull the blanket over my head, "go away," I mumble.

The knocks continue and I realize they're just that...knocks. Not intense pounding, and typically, Logan is yelling at the top of his lungs when he's here. Then I hear a soft female voice.

"Rey? I know you're in there! Open the damn door!"

"Paula?!" I throw the blanket off me and hurry to the door.

I take a second to look through the peephole. I have to make sure it really is Paula out there, by herself, and not either my imagination or a trick somehow. When I'm completely sure she's alone, I open the door.

"Hey! What are you doing here?" I ask, holding the door open for her.

"Oh, I was in the area and thought I'd stop by," she says, as she comes in for a bear hug. "Ewwww, you're all sweaty! And it's freaking roasting in here. Are you trying to create a sauna in here or what?"

My dream. I had been burning up in my dream and felt like I was literally on fire. It must have been because I was burning up physically and it had translated to my dream. There's no way my dream affected my real world...right? A glance at my hand reveals I'm wearing a ring on my middle finger. Lucifer's ring. I can't help but swallow down the fear of what this means. How can anything that happens in my dream become real? My fingertips touch my lips, and they feel swollen, as if from kissing. The blood is pounding in my ears and I'm on the verge of freaking the fuck out!

"Rey, hey, are you ok?" Paula's voice pulls me back to the present.

"Hmmm? Oh, yeah, totally. My bad. I fell asleep earlier and the heater must be on pretty high, I'll turn it down and it should cool down pretty quick." I head into the hallway where the thermostat is and it's set at 68 degrees. No way it should feel this hot in here and definitely wouldn't cause me to sweat. Shit.

"Come sit down, I'll get you some ice water." I motion her to the island as I walk into the kitchen.

"And Jesus, Rey, open some blinds and let some light in. Feels like a damn tomb in here. What's going on with you?"

"What do you mean? I just happened to fall asleep and haven't really gotten going for the day. Nothing wrong or weird about that." I slide the glass across the counter and then proceed to open the blinds to the sliding glass door, letting the blazing light flood in.

"Rey," Paula says, in an accusatory tone.

"What?! I'm serious!" I argue, my voice is a little too high.

Paula raises her eyebrows at me, not believing a word I say. "Your sister messaged me on Facebook. She asked me to come and check on you because she's worried about you, and now I'm starting to worry too. What's going on?"

"Nothing is going on. My sister is just being my sister, you know how that goes," I laugh, trying to make light of the situation.

The last thing I want is another person worrying about me and I sure as Hell don't want or need a lecture. Besides, how am I going to explain *any* of what I've been dealing with to Paula? She has no clue about The Unseen. She has no clue who her best friend *really* is.

"I would normally agree with you, but have you seen yourself in a mirror lately? Rey, you've lost weight and the dark circles under your eyes say there is definitely something going on. So, don't tell me it's nothing. You don't have to tell me anything you don't want to, but don't lie to me either."

I sigh, "fine. Yea, things have been a little...*rough*, lately. Just a lot has happened. I've learned some family secrets, not everyone is who they said they were, and my world has just kinda been rocked."

"Awwww, I'm sorry. You know that I relate to that. Family can be shitty sometimes."

"Tell me about it," I sigh, again. "Then, on top of that, I met someone..."

"What?! You didn't tell me you met someone!" She leans over and playfully slaps me in the arm.

I can't help but smile, "well, I didn't say anything because it kind of ended before it began. I mean, we only dated a couple of months, but fuck, Paula, I fell *hard* and fast for this one. He's perfect. Absolutely perfect, and everything I've ever wanted." I look down at the glass I'm holding, trying not to cry as all the painful memories come flooding back.

"If he's perfect, then what the fuck happened? Why did you guys break up?"

"It's complicated," I shrug. "I really don't wanna get into all the details, they're too painful. I'll tell you about it sometime, just not right now, ok?"

She sighs in frustration but doesn't push, "alright. Well, for now, we're getting you some food, my treat. What do you want? Pizza? Burgers? Pizza and burgers with lots of fries?" She laughs, "we are going to put some meat back on your bones first and then get you back on your feet."

"I really am fine, I swear. I mean, I haven't been but I had a...a, ummmm...*realization* earlier. I know I need to live for *myself* and no one else."

She stops typing on her phone to look at me, "well, you don't stink."

I scoff, "what?"

"If you had stopped showering, I would have been more concerned, but I believe you. I know you're way too strong to let a man keep you down. We've both been there and done that and we're never letting that happen again, right?"

"Hell fucking no we're not! Now, order that damn pizza, I'm starving!"

"Yassss!"

My stomach agrees with a fierce grumble. Seems like once the mind is made up, the body is on board, just like that. Our minds are such strong forces but we tend to always be led by the heart instead. The heart is strong too, but too easily swayed and damaged. Time to shut it up and let my mind lead instead.

With windows open, the entire inside of my house is engulfed with daylight, and I've tidied up by the time the pizza is delivered. It's amazing what simple sunlight and fresh air can do for your soul. Add in some delicious comfort food, and someone who genuinely cares about you, and your whole world can change. Suddenly, you have a different outlook on life. Suddenly, there's more to life than just your own woes and self-pity. Suddenly, life is *alive* again.

"So, since you've been a hermit, literally living under a rock, I'm guessing you haven't seen the news lately?" Paula asks, as we sit on the couch fighting our food coma.

I shake my head, "I haven't. What's going on in the news?"

"Turn on your TV and see for yourself. It's crazy! Seriously, it's like something straight out of a movie...a *horror* movie," she shivers.

I laugh, "really? What could be that bad?"

"You'll see. It's been playing everywhere, local news, national news."

I find a news channel easily, the headline at the bottom of the TV reads, *a trail of bodies across the States*. I turn up the volume and listen to the newscasters. The FBI and the Canadian Security Intelligence Service, or CSIS, have been working together to investigate a trail of bodies and trying to locate the actual starting point to the slaughter.

So far, they have traced the gruesome murders from Alaska, down Yukon Territory and British Columbia, entering the United States in Washington and traveling through Oregon, Idaho, Nevada, Utah, and Arizona.

"They're not even talking about the bodies anymore but photos and information got leaked at some point. I was able to save some of the pictures before they were taken down," she hands me her phone.

At first, my eyes refuse to make sense of what I'm seeing. It's like my brain is trying to protect me from the grisly images that I know I'll never get out of my head once I see them. Slowly, I start to piece together the scene. Piece together the...*bodies*.

There are so many of them. Some are still intact, well, butchered, but still intact. Others are literally ripped apart, limb from limb. The bodies are barely bodies anymore, even the intact ones. There's a mix of jagged rips in the skin and clean cuts. As if someone used some kind of blade and someone else used...*claws*. It's all horrific but something doesn't look right. Not like I've ever seen anything like this exactly, but I have been in battle, and something is missing. But what? It takes me a minute to realize what's so strange.

"Blood," I whisper.

"What?" Paula asks.

"Where is all the blood? There should be way more blood than there is."

I zoom into the image as far as I can and that's when I noticed them. Bite marks. Vampire bite marks. The pizza I had just stuffed down my throat is threatening to come back up again. I close my eyes and take a steadying breath.

Paula just shakes her head, "No one knows what to think. Some people are saying serial killer, others are claiming it has to be some wild animal. I mean, look at those gashes and tears. I don't know any human that could make tears like that. I mean...it has to be an animal, right?"

"I don't know. Look at some of the other cuts though, they're clean and precise. Like from a sharp blade or weapon. An animal can't do that either."

My mind is racing with possibilities. Could it be more demon attacks? Demons have worked with humans before. I've seen them work with the Witch, Revna, and the traitor, Aralyn. Could it be Aralyn again? But why would she be leaving bodies across the US and Canada? That part doesn't make any sense. But then the Vampire bites? Is it possible a group of Vampires, demons, Fey, and Witches are all working together?

Again, this all makes no sense. Vampires are terrified of demons because of their ability to use fire. As far as I know, Valmont and his Vampires are the only ones that have magical protection against fire...thanks, mostly, to me. And even then, not all of his Vampires have the protection. Is it possible that other Vampires have something similar? It's possible but I highly doubt it. Then again, what do I really know about this world?

Too many thoughts and questions are flying around in my mind. I need to talk to both Queen Anaxo and Valmont. Paula's voice brings me back to the present moment.

"I told you, crazy, and is it just me or does that trail of bodies seem like it's headed straight for us next?"

I hand back her phone, "no, it definitely looks like they are going to hit us next. Hey, can you send those pictures to me?"

She shrugs, "sure."

"Thanks," I say, still distracted. "Speaking of, where is *my* damn phone?" I start moving blankets and checking in the cracks of the couch.

"Here it is," Paula hands it to me.

I turn on the screen to find eight missed calls and a million text messages. Everyone is trying to get a hold of me and I have a feeling they're not exactly the, *I'm just checking in to make sure you're alive,* messages.

I click to open the first message. It's just a coincidence that it happens to be from Logan. At least that's what I tell myself.

Logan: Amarah, please answer! There's been an attack at Headquarters. Ana is ok but you need to get here as soon as possible. Please, just put everything about us aside. You're Võitleja, you need to be here. You need to be here for your people. You need to be here for your family.

The adrenaline is instantly pumping through my veins, "Oh my God! I'm sorry but I have to go!" I say, as I jump up from the couch. "Something has happened with, ummmm…with one of my aunts. She was attacked…mugged!" I add quickly, "she was mugged and I need to go make sure she's ok."

"Oh my gosh, how scary. At least it was just that and not this," she lifts her cell up between us, indicating the slaughter.

"You're not wrong about that," I hug her as she stands up. "Seriously, thank you for everything today. It was just what I needed to get my ass moving again. I owe you!"

"That's what friends are for. I know you would do the same for me."

"Damn right I would! I've gotta get changed but I'll text you later, ok?" I wait for a head nod and then I'm down the hall and into the bedroom tearing off my clothes and putting on jeans, boots, and a tank top.

I run into the bathroom to brush my teeth and throw my hair into a ponytail. There's no time for makeup, so I just splash cold water on my face and wipe it down. When I finally hear the front door close and Paula's vehicle roar to life and pull away, I reach under the bed and pull out my weapons. I quickly tie on my thigh holsters, pull the sword over my head and adjust the strap. I slide the sword out of the scabbard and feel my warm power buzz through my hand and up my arm.

It's familiar.

It's comfort.

It's home.

It's *me*.

I feel more like myself than I have in a while. The news I've just heard about, those bodies and the attack at Headquarters are *not* a coincidence. I know it like I know the sky is blue and the grass is green. Aralyn has to be behind this. All other insignificant thoughts and feelings are pushed aside and forgotten as the Warrior takes center stage.

Aralyn has tried to have me killed on more than one occasion, and now my aunt, the Queen, is attacked in her home. This is personal and this needs to end...*now*! The sword glides into its sheath with a deadly *zing*. With a promise to slice through Aralyn's throat just as easily next.

I hear Lucifer's voice in my mind.

Who do you want to be? What do you want to do?

I can't help but look down at his ring, touching it again to make sure it's real and I'm not just seeing things. I let out a nervous breath and then I look into the mirror.

"I'm not a victim, but anyone who gets in my way, will be one," I say to my reflection. The fire ignites behind my eyes. With a newfound purpose and attitude, I leave for Headquarters and Aralyn's head.

Amarah: Time To Bring Sexy Back

Look What You Made Me Do by Taylor Swift

I'm rushing into Headquarters, already frustrated from not seeing the messages sooner, and then I couldn't find a damn parking spot to save my life! Event signs everywhere advertised, *Native American Heritage Day*. Just my luck that the area would be busier than usual when I'm in a rush. It's also a Blessing in disguise considering I'm wearing a sword across my back and daggers strapped to my thighs. People can assume I'm part of some show for the event. The sign also shows the date, Friday, November 27th, which means I've been locked away in my house for about three weeks. Somehow, it's felt so much longer and not long enough, all at the same time.

Then it dawns on me that I've missed one of my favorite Holidays. A pang of sorrow runs through me at the thought of everything I've missed, everything I had imagined this year's Thanksgiving would be with Logan by my side. I take a second to feel the sorrow, to feel sorry for myself before I squash it. I had my time. I had my pity party. It's no longer Amarah's time, it's Võitleja's time.

I enter the San Felipe de Neri Church and it feels like I've entered a different world. The Church is quiet and calm, in complete contrast to the loud, bustling energy right outside its doors and what's hidden underneath. The Church is like the eye of a Hurricane, always centered and calm while destruction and chaos rage around it. I instantly slow my rushing steps to match the environment around me and focus on steadying my breathing. I don't want to bring unnecessary attention to myself. Unfortunately, there's nothing I can do to ease the anxiety rushing through my veins.

I'm about to see Logan for the first time in almost a month. I keep telling myself that it'll be ok. That *I* will be ok. It's one thing to say it and another thing entirely for it to be true. I just have to keep reminding myself that now is *not* the time. Today is not about me. There has been an attack against our Queen and that takes priority above *everything* else. No matter what my stupid heart says.

I descend the hidden stairs quickly and stand in front of the closed door that leads to the Great Hall and Throne Room. I can already hear the commotion on the other side. I wish Valmont was here. He's been a steady companion and someone I've come to rely on in these past weeks. Hell, he's the only one, other than Lucifer, that I talk to and let in. Dare I say Valmont has become my...*friend?* I wish I had his comforting presence now, but I don't. I take a deep breath, make sure my connection to Logan is locked down tight, along with all of my emotions, and then I give myself a small pep talk.

"Alright, Amarah, you can do this. Stay focused on the task at hand. This is *not* about you. This is *not* about Logan. This is about business. Focus on Aralyn and hold onto your anger. No mushy shit, got it?" I breathe in deep, square my shoulders, and hold my head high. "Got it," I say to myself, as I push open the door.

There's a cluster of people standing around the large meeting table and more standing next to the dais. No one is calm enough to sit down it and everyone is talking at the same time creating loud, incoherent nonsense. How anyone can make out what anyone else is saying is beyond me. All I hear is what you hear when

Snoopy and Woodstock talk to each other. Noise. The air is charged with energy, kind of like how the air feels when magic is present, but on a lower scale. Still, the atmosphere around us is alive. The Fey are magical in their own way, as are Werewolves and Vampires, and the energy I feel is radiating off of their emotions. I feel frustration, concern, fear, confusion, and anxiety, but stronger than anything else, I feel anger.

No one seems to notice me approaching and I take the moment to find Logan. It's not hard. I'll always find Logan, connection or not, it's like I'm always just *drawn* to him. Like I've never even had a choice. He's leaning against the dais, and damn it to Hell, he looks so good! My heart seems to miss several beats before it starts pumping into overdrive. His hair has grown out a little more and hangs over his forehead, almost in his eyes, but it doesn't take away from his handsome face. He's wearing a burnt-orange v-neck t-shirt that looks perfect, as it strains against his muscled, caramel skin.

And he looks bigger, if that's possible, as if he's been hitting the weights harder. Sweet baby Jesus! I have the strongest urge to squeeze his impressive biceps and run my hands over his strong chest, down his stomach until my hands find the edge of his shirt and sneak beneath it to trace that treacherous V that insists on leading me south. I have no control as my feet slowly start to move towards him.

It takes me way too long to notice there's a woman, whom I don't know, standing next to him. *Too* close to him. Her hand is on his arm and she's leaning into him whispering in his ear, and she is...*gorgeous*. He's so focused on her and what she's saying that he hasn't even noticed me yet. I stop dead in my tracks. The air leaves my chest in a brutally painful rush as if I've just been hit in the chest with a baseball bat. I can't breathe, it feels like I'm suffocating, and it's déjà vu and pain all over again.

I have a flashback to the very first time I was in this room. I had been observing the crowd and secretly watching Logan. We had just met but there had been that undeniable connection and attraction. He had kissed me... *several* times, and I assumed he was available. Hell, he *told* me he was! Then, Princess Hallana of the Tulekahju Family, walked up to him, caressed his arm, and whispered in his ear, almost the exact way this new woman is doing. It had been Aralyn who informed me that Logan and Hallana were together. Maybe not in a committed relationship, but they did have a physical one, and the way this new girl seemed comfortable with Logan, *and his body*, I immediately put two and two together.

He's sleeping with her.

My mind seems to go blank.

...

...

...

Then it screams.

He's *sleeping* with her!

HE'S SLEEPING WITH HER!

When was the last time he had shown up at my house to fight for us? Thinking about it now, I realize it has been less and less frequent. Because of *her*. I still can't breathe and I can't take my eyes off of them. My first instinct is to run and hide, lock myself up in my room, and ball my eyes out like I did the first time this happened, but then I hear Lucifer's voice in my mind again.

Who do you want to be? What do you want to do?

I touch the ring on my finger. I'm not a victim, I remind myself. I refuse to be a victim. A victim to my circumstances. A victim to loss. A victim to heartache. And I sure as Hell am not going to be the other woman! It was that fact that gave me strength and resolve when I was dealing with him and Hallana, it will give me strength again. It has to.

I take a deep, searing breath into my lungs and stoke the fire inside of me. A fire that fills the void of where my emotions should be. They're long gone. Burnt away by the anger and fire. I pull that anger out and all around me. Anger is my new shield. I'm so far beyond anger I can't even describe it.

Fury?

Rage?

Wrath?

I hear gasps and whispers around me, Logan finally snaps his head in my direction, and then everything goes silent. I see Logan mouth my name, but I can't hear anything. He moves to take a step toward me but the hand on his arm stops him.

SHE.

STOPPED.

HIM.

I give her my full attention. Her hair is pulled back, revealing a beautiful and strong face. Her blue eyes seem to be fighting between fear and...awe? She's appraising me with a curiosity I don't understand. But I understand one thing. My anger. My eyes move to focus on her hand gripping Logan's arm and then back up to meet her eyes. Her hand slowly drops away from Logan and I know, if looks could kill, she would be a pile of ash on the floor.

Then I see Ana's face. She's stepped directly in front of me, cutting off my line of sight to Logan, and she's holding her hands out to stop anyone else's approach. Her lips are moving but all I can hear is the fire roaring in my veins. I stay staring at the spot behind Ana, as if I can see right through her, to where I know the other woman is standing. As if nothing or no one can interfere with me and my target. Then, Ana takes a few more cautious steps toward me until she's mere inches away. I blink and the world comes slamming back around me. There's a circle of bodies around me but no one besides

Ana has gotten close. There's something on their faces I never thought I would see because of me. Fear.

I look back at Ana and finally see her, really see her. Her yellow, sunlit hair is tied in a braid behind her, but some strands have come loose, framing her face. Her face. It's smudged with dirt. Or is that soot? From smoke? A fire? There are traces of blood on her cheek, neck, and some dried clumps in her hair, next to her forehead.

"You're hurt," I whisper, as I reach my hand out to touch her face.

She flinches and steps out of my reach, and that's when I notice my hand is on fire. White fire. My power. I didn't even realize I lost control. I didn't feel anything but my anger. If Ana hadn't stopped me, what would I have done? This just reiterates the fact that I'm dangerous. I'm not only a danger to my enemies but everyone around me. A familiar image flashes through my mind.

Blood.

Pain.

An unmoving chest.

Lifeless eyes staring at me.

A hand turning cold in mine.

Gone forever.

Because of me.

The memory helps sober my mind. I close my eyes and pull my power back in. When I look again, my hand is just my hand. "I'm sorry. I didn't mean...I wasn't going to...I wouldn't..."

"I know," Ana gives me a small smile and places her hand on top of mine, squeezing it reassuringly. "I know."

"You're hurt," I repeat.

"I'm fine, I promise. Everything has been healed. Now, let's have a seat and I can answer any questions you have."

She keeps a hold of my hand and leads me to the table.

Everyone gives me worried and curious glances, but thankfully, no one says anything. My eyes slide to Logan as I take my seat next to the Queen. He would typically sit next to the Queen as well, next to *me*, but now, he stays where he is. He has a pained look on his face, like he wants to come to me or at least say something, but he remains silent. The other unknown woman stays next to him, but keeps her distance now, as everyone else decides whether to take a seat or remain standing around the table.

"As you all know, there was an attack here earlier today, and as you can see, I'm fine. A large part of that is thanks to Prince Emrick who happened to be visiting, to discuss your training, Amarah, and heard the fighting."

I look around the room and find Emrick. He also shows signs of being in the fight but he also appears to be completely healed. He nods his head at the Queen's acknowledgment but doesn't say anything or look in my direction. I know I need to continue my training but it hasn't been something I've thought about in recent weeks.

Being so focused on Logan, I didn't even notice Prince Emrick. Hell, I didn't notice anyone, so I take some time to look at the crowd gathered around me. I recognize Prince Vadin and Princess Arabella, along with familiar faces I've seen when we gathered Leaders and fighters at the Air Fey home just one short month ago. Princess Hallana isn't here yet, but Ethan is here along with a handful of Werewolves. No one I recognize, but that brings my attention back to the unknown woman. Who is she? Why do I care? I decided to break things off with Logan. I shouldn't care. Why do I care? Not the time, Amarah, I remind myself. I refuse to look in their direction again, instead, I look at Ana and focus on what she's saying.

"From what I can gather, it was a direct attack on me, no one else was targeted or injured in any way, thank God," she says, with a heavy sigh. Her voice is calm and strong but I know she's tired.

Tired of betrayal.

Tired of losing people.

Tired of fighting.

Tired of always being on guard, and now, not even safe in her own home.

The room is quiet for a moment, waiting to see if The Queen will continue speaking. When she doesn't, Princess Arabella speaks up, "and the person who attacked you? Was it her? Was it my sister?"

Arabella stands with her arms crossed and her chin tipped up defiantly. Even now that she's the Princess of the Ōhk Family, she still seems to have a chip on her shoulder. Like she still has something to prove. Maybe she does? Maybe she just doesn't want to show an ounce of weakness? Maybe this is just who she is? I don't know her so I can't really say.

The Queen holds Arabella's gaze and her face shows no emotion as she verifies what we all already know. "Yes, it was Aralyn who attacked me."

The room erupts. Everyone starts talking at once, causing the tension in the room to rise again. It's now Prince Vadin who voices his concerns.

"How did she get in? Her face is known to everyone in the Church. She wouldn't be able to just walk in. She would have been noticed and stopped." His sapphire eyes betray him and show a hint of the anger he's trying to conceal with more relaxed body language. Vadin is always the quiet one, but those eyes…they're shrewd and intelligent and never miss a thing.

"You're right, Prince Vadin, and unfortunately, I don't have an answer to your question. The staff of the Church has already been questioned and no one saw Aralyn come in or out. The silent alarm was triggered as soon as I could get to it and everyone was on high alert. No one saw her exit through the Church."

"What about the tunnels?" He asks. Is it possible she could

have accessed one of the hundreds of tunnels that lead here from throughout the city? She could have left the same way or, she could still be hiding in one of them."

The Queen shakes her head, "only a handful of people know these tunnels completely and it's kept that way for exactly this reason. Is it possible? Yes, I suppose it is, but it's not likely."

Vadin continues, "I know the tunnels are a maze, and those who do not know them do not venture out in them, but... that's not to say someone *hasn't*. Specifically, Aralyn. She may have been mapping the tunnels this entire time. We need a new safeguard in place where the tunnels are concerned and they need to be scoured for any traces of her."

I finally speak up, "I agree with Vadin." Since I had a recent experience with a boundary spell, I knew something similar could be done to Headquarters. Of course, I didn't bring up the fact that I had my house warded against all magical beings. That information is need-to-know, and they don't. "I can contact Iseta and see if there's something she can do to protect the tunnels."

"Thank you, Amarah." The Queen gives me a warm smile before she looks back out at the group, "there's one more thing Prince Emrick and I have discussed and feel it's important to mention." The group stills again, all attention on the Queen's next words.

"Something was...*different,* about Aralyn today. Logan has been unable to scent her presence. How she's managing to mask her scent, I'm not sure. She's worked with Witches in the past. Perhaps she's working with one again, and, this is the strangest part, she didn't attack to kill me. It's like she was just here to prove that she could be. Like she was just toying with us. Toying with *me.* She didn't fight offensively. She only fought back to defend herself, almost like she was just playing with me. Taunting me. And she didn't say a word. We all know Aralyn loves to hear herself talk whenever possible, but she didn't speak. Not one word. It's the strangest thing and I don't know what it means."

"It's true," Emrick confirms. "She fought us back, she caused injuries, but she held back. She had the element of surprise and yet she...*waited*. I feel like it was more of a message than an attempt on the Queen's life."

"And what message exactly is she trying to send?" Arabella asks, in her cold voice.

"That she's still here. That she can get to us. That she's still one step ahead. After the last battle, I think she's trying to regain control and gain her confidence. I also think she wants to play on our fear and show us our weaknesses. It's all mind games," Emrick says, matter-of-factly.

"It doesn't make sense," I say, shaking my head. "Aralyn has never held back before. She's always gone in fighting and gone in for the kill. She wants to be Queen and the only way to do that is to kill you. Why would she not take the chance when she clearly had the advantage?"

"As I said, none of it makes sense," the Queen raises her hands and shrugs her shoulders. "I can only tell you what I know and what I saw. It was Aralyn who attacked me. I saw her clear as day, Hell, I physically fought her and it *was* Aralyn. As to why she held back? I don't know. Perhaps something has changed and she has a new motive."

"It doesn't matter. Whatever her motive is now, she's still our biggest threat and she needs to be stopped. We know she's in the City, at least for now, so what's the plan to go after her? I'm ready to go right now," I say, my anger and power still itching for a fight.

"Ethan has agreed to lead a team of his best tracking Werewolves. Logan is also going to be a part of the tracking team and you will join them, Amarah. The other Fey Leaders and I are going to get ready for another battle that is destined to happen sooner rather than later. Things seem to be escalating and we need to be prepared and not scurrying to react to an attack like we have in the past. It's time to get ahead of this once and for all. Does anyone else have any questions or suggestions?" The Queen asks.

I've been so out of touch recently, I need an update on the demons, and, remembering the gruesome things I had just been shown earlier, I want to know what the plan is for this new issue too. "I know I've been a little MIA recently, and I apologize for that, but what's the update on demon attacks?"

The Queen answers, "surprisingly, the demons have been quiet. We haven't seen much possession or sensed them anywhere."

"Why would the demons just suddenly stop and disappear?" I ask, even more confused at this situation.

Could it be because I'm in contact with Lucifer? Has he pulled the demons back because of me? But why? I'm the one seeking his help. He has no reason to control his demons. Granted, no one knows I'm having vivid dreams with the Devil and openly working with him. Hell, kissing him. Yeah, no one needs to know *that* piece of information.

I can't help glancing at Logan, his peridot eyes are already watching me. I can't help the heat that creeps up my neck and onto my cheeks under his scrutiny. It feels like he knows my every thought. It feels like he knows about the kiss with Lucifer. Then I remember he's already sleeping with someone else and I sit up straighter. The Queen is answering my question and I return my focus to her.

"I'm not sure why, but I'm going to take the small wins where I get them. As of right now, the demons are not presenting an issue so, we focus on Aralyn, but stay aware of potential demon activity."

"But don't you find it odd that the demon activity has slowed down? After all of these years of them gaining strength, what? They just stop?" I scoff, "that's not likely. Something has to be happening.

Aren't you worried about that at all?"

The Queen sighs, "I appreciate your concern, Amarah, really, I do, but I don't see the issue here? Fewer demon sightings and attacks is a *good* thing. I'm not going to question it."

"And what about the attacks they're talking about on the news? Do you think that could be Aralyn's doing as well? What if it is demons? What are we going to do if the attacks come here? Which, if the path continues as it has been, they will."

"That is another problem for another day. We can't focus on something that may or may not even happen. We don't know if those attacks will end up happening here, but we do know Aralyn is here, right now. She is our focus."

"But those attacks could very well be connected with Aralyn. We know she's worked with Witches in the past and has tried to work with Valmont. Hell, she's led an army of demons before! This could be another rogue group that she has gathered and is leading. Those attacks are not from a human serial killer and you all know that. This is a credible threat that we need to be ready for as well."

"Amarah, I've given the order and the direction we are all to take," her voice is hard and her stare is pleading, asking me not to make a scene. "This is the plan, and as our Võitleja, you are a part of it, like it or not."

"But that doesn't make sense to prepare for one and not the others. We need to..."

"Enough!" She jumps out of her seat and slams her hands down on the table, sending a wave of her power rippling through the room. "I am the Queen, not you! You are a Warrior, not a strategist. You will learn to use your sword and not your mouth! You will do as you're told and go with Logan and Ethan to hunt for Aralyn, and then resume your training with Prince Emrick and the Maa Family. End of discussion!"

I know Ana's outburst at me isn't personal. I know she's

shaken up from the recent attack, and I know she's needing to reclaim her ground and her authority. As much as the Fey are a family, she can't afford to look weak in front of the other Leaders. I know a part of her is scared of what Aralyn will do next, causing her to have tunnel vision. Her life is literally on the line, so I understand her decisions, but I don't agree with them. Once again, Lucifer's voice echoes in my mind.

Who do you want to be? What do you want to do?

I don't appreciate being ridiculed and talked down to in front of the other Leaders. In front of Logan and especially, in front of this new woman standing by Logan's side. Call it ego, call it pride, the fire inside of me doesn't like the water being thrown on its flames. It roars up inside of me in defiance. After all, why should I care what any of these strangers think? They don't know me, yet they're so desperate to mold me into their vision of what and who they think I should be.

I stand up with so much force my chair is sent flying and tumbling behind me. Everyone jumps back a step and watches as I clench my hands into fists, slowly placing them on the table, and lean in towards the Queen.

"Yeah, your plan doesn't work for me, so good luck with that. I'll find my own way to deal with *all* threats," I pull my power, my anger, out and into my fists. They glow red hot as I burn two holes into the table, "and don't try to stop me," I never lose eye contact with the Queen and I see her register the warning for what it is. A threat to *anyone* who gets in my way. They want a Warrior, they'll get one.

I pull my power back in, turn my back on the Queen and everyone in the room, and head for the exit. Nobody stops me. Everyone is left in shock at what just happened. Hell, I'm not even sure what I've just done, but I refuse to accept the role of just being told what to do and when to do it. I keep walking, my head held high as I put distance between me and the growing silence.

"Amarah!" Logan finally calls after me and I hear his heavy footsteps as he runs towards me.

He catches up to me quickly and I feel when he's about to reach out for me. I turn so abruptly that he takes a step back. "Don't," I say, through clenched teeth. "Don't even think about touching me." All I can think about is his hands on another woman's body and that sends another hot wave of anger through me.

"Amarah, what's happened to you? This isn't you. This isn't you at all." His voice is quiet, almost sad.

"Don't act like you care anymore, Logan. You know, I should've known," I scoff. "Guys are all the same. I don't know why I ever thought you would be different, but thank you for making this easy for me."

He looks like I physically slapped him in the face. He opens his mouth to say something and then closes it.

I put my hand up before he can get his thoughts together, "don't waste your breath. There's nothing that can pass those lying lips that I ever want to hear. So why don't you just run back to those comforting arms you were just in before you make a fool out of yourself and her."

I turn and start walking away again, feeling nothing but rage and fire. I know my heart will yell at me later, but right now, my heart is drowning in flames.

Logan finally snaps out of his shock and continues to follow me across the huge room to the back door, yelling after me. "You're in denial, Amarah! You only see what you want to see. Anything to make your decision easier on yourself. Because don't forget, this was *your* decision. You left me, remember? You refuse to see me, remember? You have no right to be angry with me. You have no right to say I'm no different."

I cannot get out of this room fast enough! I'm completely

ignoring everything he says but that doesn't stop him.

"All you have to do is open the connection, Amarah. Let the truth in. You refuse to listen to anything I have to say. You refuse to believe me but you can't deny the truth of the bond. You know I'm right but you're afraid. Come on, Amarah! What are you afraid of? Open the damn connection!" He yells, from right behind me.

I've finally reached the door and open it, eager to put this all behind me, but I hesitate. I turn to face Logan and his presence utterly consumes me. The added size and muscle, makes him even *more* imposing than normal. He's taking up my space, my air, my sanity, my resolve. There's nothing in this world except him, his smell, his fingers twitching at his side ready to reach for me, his arms ready to hold me, his lips ready to kiss me, and his eyes…his beautiful green eyes.

Eyes that I used to see the world in.

Eyes that I used to see my future in.

Eyes that still pull me in like gravity.

I can't deny that I want to go back to that, to those moments and those feelings. He will always have a pull on me like he's a magnet and I'm the helpless piece of metal being dragged against my will towards him. My heart starts to rise through the flames and it begs me to be in control. It aches to be whole again.

Logan must see the change in my eyes. No matter how small of a change it is, he sees it. He always sees me. Every damn inch and piece of me. It would be so easy to fall into him both physically and emotionally, open the connection, and let myself be free again. I'm suddenly having a hard time remembering why I pushed him away to begin with.

Logan is standing right in front of me now, he reaches out and caresses my cheek. I can't help but close my eyes and lean into his touch. I feel that cool, calming breeze dance across my skin and start to tame my fire. The yin to my yang. I want to walk into his strong arms and feel my body melt into his. I want to feel those soft, perfect lips on mine. I want *him*. I want him in a way that's selfish and all-consuming. This is why I've fought seeing him for so long. I'm strong in theory, but in reality, I'm weak when it comes to Logan. He will always be the one to reach me. To find me. To see me. The *real* me.

I open my eyes and all I can see is his handsome face smiling down at me. The hope in his eyes is cracking my defenses.

"There you are, Angel. I miss you so much," he rubs his thumb across my cheek lovingly before he leans in and rests his forehead on mine, closing his eyes. His lips are inches from mine.

Soft.

Full.

Delicious.

They're begging to be kissed and I have to close my eyes to focus on anything else. This only allows me to *feel* him. His body heat is pressing in on me and I want to snuggle into it. He smells like a rainy day in the woods. He smells like Logan. He smells like home and I desperately want to take everything he's offering. Just him. My whole world.

He cups my face in his hands and we stare at each other from inches away. "God, Amarah, you have no idea how good it is to see you, to touch you. I'm so lost without you. I miss you every second of every day."

I'm consumed by his touch, by his words, by him. It's like all of my fight is just gone, poof, never there. My eyes start to water as all of my emotions flood through me. Even without our link to each other, I still feel my emotions, I still love him with my entire heart and soul. The connection just allows us to feel what the other is feeling, it just intensifies what we already feel. I'm so in love with him that it physically hurts.

"I'm so lost without you, too" I admit. "I miss you so much,

Logan."

"Open the connection, Amarah," he whispers. "Let me in and let's get past this. I need to feel you, here," he places a hand on his chest, over his heart.

I know exactly what he means. The connection fills us up. Completes us. Gives us what we could never possibly have with anyone else and I desperately want to do what he says. I want to let him in. I want to go back to loving him and letting him love me. I want to go back to being a team and facing all of these new threats with him by my side. I want to be *whole*.

"Please, Amarah, let me in," he begs.

"I…"

"Logan? Is everything ok?"

My eyes snap to the voice that so rudely and inconveniently interrupts us. *Her*. She followed him across the room. My heart is quickly shoved back down inside the flames and now I'm more pissed than ever! I almost let him get to me. I almost let my guard down and let him back in. After he shows up here, with another woman on his arm, in front of everyone! I'm the one making a fool out of myself.

I step out of his grasp, "you will *never* feel that connection again." My eyes fall to the girl standing a few feet away from us, "stay out of my way. This is your one and only warning."

I walk through the door, slam it shut behind me, and race up the stairs. My anger and adrenaline propel me forward and I run. I run away from everyone and everything. I don't care about the quiet, reverence of the Church, as I come tearing down the aisle, causing people to jump out of my way. I run all the way to my car, quickly get in, and drive off as fast as I can. I don't want to risk anyone attempting to follow me.

I angrily wipe the tears that have somehow escaped off my cheeks. "This is seriously the last time you are going to cry over that man, Amarah." I scold myself. "It's time to move on for good and get him out of your mind and out of your heart. It's time to put yourself first and have some fun for fuck's sake!"

I made a few stops on my way home and lay out my new purchases on my bed. A little, black strapless dress that shimmers in the light, some thigh-high black leather boots with a heel that's almost too high, and two boxes of my old, fire-red hair dye.

"Alright, J.T, looks like you had it right. Time to bring sexy back."

12

Amarah: Daydream

Confident by Demi Lovato

A couple of hours later, I step back from the mirror and look at the woman staring back at me. She's familiar, and yet, her eyes belong to someone new. Someone...*dangerous*. My hair is pulled half up, in a high ponytail, and the rest flows like a fire-red flame down my back, all the way to my ass. My hazel eyes pop, a mix of honey brown, green, and yellow surrounded by black liner, and my lips, a devilish shade of crimson. My black, strapless dress puts my neck and shoulders on full display. Small diamond earrings sparkle brightly, matching the sparkle of the dress as I move, but I'm wearing no other jewelry. The dress hugs my chest, waist, and hips and leaves a few inches of skin bare before my legs are lost in the thigh-boots.

I strap one of my daggers to my right thigh. You can see the holster as it disappears under the dress and into the boot, ruining the look just a bit, but then again, the scars on my left arm from the last demon attack do that already, which is why I refuse to go anywhere unarmed anymore. I don't plan on seeing any demons where I'm going, but then again, a girl can never be too careful. The human world isn't without its own type of demons and there's just something comforting about the weight of a weapon against my skin. I spray on some Acqua Di Gioia and head to the one place I know will have a party.

I'm immediately greeted by, what seems to be, my very own personal valet. I wait patiently as he runs towards me and opens my car door.

"Good evening, Miss Andrews. Wow," I see him take a hard swallow as I step out of my car. He quickly takes control of his eyes and his composure. "You look stunning this evening," he says, as he bows his head, obviously not wanting to offer any offense.

I stand in front of him as he holds my door open, then I reach out, grab his chin, and lift his face so I can meet his eyes. His eyes are wide, and poor thing, is he shaking?

"I didn't mean any offense, or to come off as a pervert, or...or like I was checking you out or anything. Please..."

"Josh, calm down. Valmont wouldn't mind you paying me a compliment and *I* surely don't mind. A woman doesn't dress like this and expect *not* to be looked at. You *were* just complimenting me, right?"

He's still looking at me with wide eyes that are glued to my face. "Yes, Ma'am. With the utmost respect," he swallows hard again.

"Then I do believe a thank you is in order," I say. A devious smile appears as I take one slow step into Josh's personal space and lean my chest into his. Still holding his chin, I tilt his head slightly to the side as I bend my head towards his. I press my lips lightly against his, in a chaste kiss, then move my mouth to his ear and let my lips touch his earlobe as I whisper, "thank you for the compliment, Josh."

I let him go quickly and turn to head into the casino without another word or look in his direction. The devious smile is still playing on my lips as I feel a rush of satisfaction zing through me. We women have so much power at our fingertips when we want to use it. The power to manipulate. To control men with their basic needs and desires. Sex. Always, lust and sex. Yes, a confident and strong woman is a powerful thing and I'm looking forward to wielding it tonight.

I hold my head high as I strut through the casino, heading towards the nightclub, with an extra sway in my hips. I ignore all the hungry looks I receive from men and all the disgusted, *jealous* ones I receive from the women. I seriously wish women could support each other without trying to be competitive or jealous but I'm not going to think about that tonight.

As I approach the entrance to the club, I notice the familiar *private party* sign being displayed. "Perfect," I purr to myself, as I walk right past all the other women waiting in line. Luckily, I know one of the bouncers standing at the entrance.

Ignoring all the shouts of anger and confusion erupting behind me, I walk right to the front of the line. "Pierce, what a lucky night for me that you're here, right where I need you."

He gives me a once over and his eyebrows shoot up in surprise but he, unlike Josh, keeps his thoughts to himself. "Amarah, what are you doing here?" He asks in his deep, authoritative voice.

"Isn't it obvious? I'm here to party and have a good time. I'm afraid my name isn't on the list as this was a last-minute decision, but I'm sure Valmont won't mind me crashing his party."

He steps aside, and unhooks the red velvet rope admitting access to the club, "I'll radio Valmont and let him know you're here."

"You do that," I pat his arm as I walk into the club, leaving the scoffs and disgusting comments behind me.

As soon as I enter the tunnel leading into the club, I hear

the music and know it's going to be deafening once I step into the open room. The vibrations from the base and the energy hit me like a physical force. I feel the music thumping on my skin and feel the same sinful energy I felt last time I was here. Sex. Except this time, it isn't off-putting. This time, I'm not scared for the people I see being bitten. I know what those Vampire bites do now and I want to be a part of it. I want to feel that sensation and thrill again. My blood seems to sing inside of my body at the memory of it and the anticipation of feeling it again. This is what an addict must feel knowing they're going to get their next fix. Yea, this time, the vibe is intoxicating.

I head straight for the bar to my right and squeeze my way to the front. It takes a couple of minutes but the bartender finally makes her way over to me. She has powder blue hair pulled into a messy bun, hot-pink eyeshadow that accentuates her matching blue eyes and she's wearing a Care Bear t-shirt, cut and tied together to show a lot of skin, and ample cleavage.

Her face is soft and pretty but her eyes hold the mischief someone needs to work in a place like this. I can't tell if she's a Vampire or a human. I'm still learning the signs, but I don't care one way or another.

"Love the hair!" She says as she stops in front of me.

"Likewise!" I gesture to hers.

She leans across the bar, closer to me so we don't have to yell at each other. "I've never seen you here before. I *definitely* would have noticed you," she smiles sweetly, as she smacks her gum and lets her eyes roam over me freely.

"It's my first time," I lie. Technically, I had been here once before, but not in the same capacity as I am tonight. Tonight, I'm here for me. Tonight, I'm here to let loose.

She extends her hand out to me and I take it. "I'm Sky," she says sweetly, as she holds my gaze and hand for longer than is usually appropriate. Tonight, I don't care.

I hold her hand and her gaze, leaning forward even more. "I'm Amarah," I say, with a sexy smirk, fully aware that we're flirting.

"Well, Amarah, it's a pleasure. What can I get for you?" She asks, still holding my hand.

"Something strong to sip on. *Really* strong. And a shot of whatever alcohol you use to make this really strong drink with."

Sky's smile widens enough to show her fangs and my heart speeds up, and not in fear, as I stare at them. Knowing what they would feel like against my skin and the pleasure that would no doubt come crashing through me from her bite. The fact that she's a woman, and I've never been with a woman sexually, doesn't matter to me. She's attractive and I have no problem admitting that I think a woman's body is sexy. Besides, I don't have to sleep with her to let her bite me. And if it did lead to that? Well, shit, maybe I'd have better luck with a woman anyways.

"I'll make you my signature drink, Daydream. Be right back, babe," she winks, and then moves quickly behind the bar. Her Vampire speed is noticeable now that I'm watching her. She's curvy and has beautiful liquid grace as she dances to the music while making me a drink.

She comes back and places a tall glass filled with a powder-blue mixed drink that matches her eyes and hair perfectly, and a shot glass with clear alcohol in front of me. She jumps, to lean all the way over the counter, and whispers in my ear, "on the house if you promise not to go to any other bartender tonight."

She leans back just enough so I can see her eyes, then she pulls her bottom lip under her fangs, causing me to stare at her lips as my mouth waters. "God, you smell amazing, too. Come and see me all night and maybe we can hang when I get off later?"

We're still so close, I can feel her breath on my face and smell the minty gum she's chewing. Her pointy fangs are so close.

They had been centimeters away from my neck, and just the thought of them scraping along my skin, sends goosebumps across my body.

I reach up and trail my thumb across her bright pink lips, "now that sounds like a damn good deal to me."

Sky slowly slips off the bar. "Then find me later. Enjoy your Daydream, Amarah," she smiles, flashing her fangs again, and moves on to another customer waiting for a drink.

I slam the shot in front of me, realizing it's more like a double shot. I have no idea what kind of alcohol it is but it leaves a tingling, burning trail of devilment down my throat and settles comfortably in my belly. I grab my glass of Daydream and head out towards the dance floor.

Two Daydreams and two double shots later, I have no care in the world, as I dance my life away, grinding on strangers, men, women, it doesn't matter which. I'm here to have a good time and that's what I'm doing. I feel two strong hands grip my waist from behind right before I'm pulled into a hard chest. The body behind me moves with my body, matching my rhythm perfectly.

I reach up and put my hands around his neck, because there's no way this is a woman, and I lean hard into him. I move my body to the beat of the music and he mimics me, never missing a beat.

"Now, *you* are a great dancer," I say, with a smile on my face as his body moves fluidly with mine.

"And you are too sexy for your own good," he says, as he trails his hands up my arms and intertwines his fingers with mine.

I move our hands from around his neck and trail them down my body. I want his hands on me and he obliges, wrapping his hands across my waist, holding me tightly, as our bodies move as one to the beat of the music. He leans his head down, I feel his nose trail across my shoulder and up behind my ear.

He inhales deeply and moans, "fuck, you smell delicious." I feel his tongue slip across my neck and I move my head further to the side allowing him more access.

"And you feel fucking amazing," I whisper in a daze. In a Daydream.

"But do you taste as delicious as you smell?" I feel the sharp point of fangs gently scrape across my skin. I gasp in surprise and shiver as he keeps his fangs against my skin. I can feel his cock stirring against my ass as he pulls me even tighter into him.

I move my ass against him causing him to hiss against my neck. "Only one way to find out," I say, anxiously waiting for his fangs to penetrate me and deliver that instant, orgasmic pleasure I know will follow.

"Do you want to do this here or find somewhere more private?" He asks, still trailing fangs, tongue, and lips across my neck and shoulders. His hips gently thrusting his now hard cock against my ass.

I don't know who's behind me. I don't know his name. I don't know if he's attractive or not. And none of it matters. All that matters is he's here, right now, offering me what I came here for. And I'm done waiting.

"I want it now. Stop teasing me and give it to me," I say, breathlessly. Anticipation and adrenaline tighten in my chest.

"As you wish," the silky, smooth voice whispers against my skin, as he settles right in the middle of my neck. Right on the big vein, hammering like a beacon, guiding him.

I feel his fangs press against my skin, and the sharp pain as he punctures my flesh, but I don't even finish wincing before the pleasure takes over. My body is instantly languid, as a rush of pleasure sweeps through every inch of my body, from the inside out. Only his strong hold on my waist keeps me standing. I moan and let my head fall lazily against his chest as he drinks down my blood.

The pleasure coursing through my veins is heady, but not nearly as powerful as what I felt from Valmont's bite. It takes the edge off of my craving but it doesn't satisfy me completely. I want more. I *need* more. Just as I'm about to say something, I feel my body turn from languid with pleasure to a little light-headed and dizzy. This doesn't feel right. This feels like...*weakness,* not pleasure. I feel the strong pull of the man sucking my neck. It's too much. He's taking too much blood.

"Too much," I try to pull away but my body is limp in his arms. I focus on getting my feet under me and try again. "Stop," I try to say it loudly, but my voice is drowned out by the loud music blaring around us.

The pleasure slowly fades and fear is taking its place in my body. My fuzzy thoughts are clearing up and I realize what's happening. My blood. My *Angel* blood. He isn't going to stop. I feel the fear for a moment but then I push it away. Maybe this is meant to be. If I die, I won't have to feel loss and heartbreak anymore. I won't have to feel the pain anymore. I can just give in and let go.

I'm suddenly wrenched free from the arms that had been tightly wrapped around me. I stumble forward but more strong hands catch me before I fall. I look up to see my savior is Pierce, but his eyes are locked on whatever is happening behind me. I turn just in time to see Valmont rip out the heart of the guy, I'm assuming, was the one I was just with.

My hands slam across my mouth, stopping my scream. The man's eyes are still locked on me, my blood staining his mouth, dripping down his chin, and I watch as whatever lifeforce is in him, leaves his body. He crumples to the floor and Valmont drops his heart next to his unmoving body. All I can see is the bright red stain of blood coating Valmont's hand and it brings back the image of my bloody hands in my dream.

Valmont removes a handkerchief from the inside pocket of

his midnight black suit. Thankfully, the handkerchief is black as well and I can't see the blood as he wipes his hand with it. The music has stopped, everyone has stopped what they were doing, all eyes are trained on us.

Valmont's voice rings out cold and menacing across the club, "do you all see this woman?" He motions to me with his bloody hand. "This is Amarah Rey. Look at her!" He yells aggressively to the crowd. "Remember her name, remember her face, and let it be known that she is strictly *mine*! She is not to be touched by anyone or the consequences, as you can see, will be life-ending. This is your only warning." His voice changes to something less threatening and more jovial as he continues, "Now, let's all get back to enjoying the party!"

His voice may have been light and fun at the end of his little speech, but as the music blasts back to life, he turns his full attention on me and there's nothing nice in his stare. He grabs me by the arm, with his clean hand, and starts to drag me out of the club.

"Hey! What do you think you're doing, Valmont? Let me go!" I yell, as I try to plant my feet and pull against his hold.

He snarls, showing me his fangs as he stops, picks me up, and throws me over his shoulder. I continue to yell my protest as well as flail my arms and legs as wildly as I can. It doesn't even slow him down. We're up the stairs and in the privacy of his office before he finally throws me down, unceremoniously, onto the couch.

"What in the bloody Hell are you doing, Amarah Rey? Do you have any idea what you've done?" Valmont's disappointed voice rips into me as he stares at me with disdain.

For a moment, I'm struck by his words and his disapproving stare. He's been the only one here for me in this past month and I don't want to push him away. Then I remember Logan and the other woman. Her hands on him. Whispering intimately in his ear. If I can't trust Logan, or have him, I can't trust anyone. I don't want anyone or anything else. I'm done caring about what other people want. What other people expect. I twist the ring on my finger.

Who do you want to be? What do you want to do?

My anger rises through my inebriated state, helping to sober me even more than what I just witness.

Fuck Logan.

Fuck the woman he's with.

Fuck Valmont and his controlling issues.

Fuck this, that, and everything in between.

Valmont: Take It

Come And Get Me by Sleeping Wolf

I watch her closely, as she stands up from where I threw her, gathering herself and adjusting her dress. Gods, that damn dress. Her shoulders and neck are left bare, like a damn spotlight. Like a lighthouse leading the wayward ship home. I want my lips and tongue on her. I want to taste every inch of her creamy skin. And she's dyed her hair red again. It suits her. This whole outfit, her demeanor, and those boots that hug her legs tightly, have my cock stirring. I have to close my eyes, force myself to see *anything* else, and get my emotions in check. When I open them again, I give her nothing but disappointment in my eyes, as she lifts her chin stubbornly, and finally sets those wonderful hazel eyes on me.

"Yeah, I was having fun until you came and ruined it!"

"*That*... is not having fun and you know it. You let another Vampire taste your blood!" I yell, angry at what she's done, about the complications of it all, but more than that I'm...*jealous*. I feel possessive over her and I have no right to. These are such foreign feelings to me, I have absolutely no idea how to process them so, I focus on something she seems to understand.

Anger.

The sight of her pressed against another man's chest.

Another man's hands on her body. Another man's fangs in her skin, tasting her glorious blood. Anger doesn't even begin to cover how seeing that made me feel. I'm furious at her recklessness, yes, but just as furious at myself for feeling this way when I know, I shouldn't.

I rub my forehead, "do you have any idea what your blood would have done to him?"

"Kept him alive," she says, sarcastically.

"Do not be ignorant, Amarah Rey, it does not suit you. Have you forgotten that I've tasted you? Have you not realized what your blood can do? Or do you just not care?"

She shrugs. She fucking shrugs her beautiful, delicate shoulders at me. As much as I hate that disrespectful gesture, it brings my attention back to her bare shoulders. Her neck.

"Amarah Rey, your blood," I close my eyes to steady myself at just the mere memory of it, "your blood is a *drug*. The only reason I have not taken more from you is because I am Virtuoso, and even so…" I clench my teeth fighting for control, "…it takes every ounce of control I have *not* to take it. A lesser Vampire would not be able to control his craving for it. For *you*. As you clearly saw from what happened tonight."

She stands there with her arms crossed, listening to what I'm saying, but she doesn't seem to care. She seems almost void of any emotion or feeling. I look in her eyes and I don't see the strong-willed, ferocious Amarah Rey I've come to know. The one that speaks her mind regardless of the consequences. The one who fights when no one else will. I see nothing. Like she's finally just given up on…*everything.*

"There are worse ways to die than getting drained of blood and enjoying it," she keeps ignoring the seriousness of the situation and it's so frustrating to see her like this.

"Damn it, Amarah Rey! I'm trying to not only protect you but protect my Vampires *from you*! Tonight, I had to kill one of my own...for *you*! To keep *you* safe! To keep *your* secret safe!"

"Well, I don't exactly promise not to do it again so, what are you going to do about it then, huh? Punish me?" She laughs, harshly.

"I've claimed you as mine. No other Vampire will dare touch you now, and if they do, it's a direct disregard for my rule, and that's punishable by death. So, your plan on using and manipulating *my* Vampires is futile. I'm done playing games."

She snorts, "all you've ever done is play games with me. Toy with me. Claim you have...*feelings* or whatever for me, then in the same breath, threaten to kill me easily if you wanted to. Well, I'm tired of *your* games, Valmont."

She walks towards me and I see the anger rising. I see the fire lighting her eyes and I feel relief that she's coming alive again. I don't even care that it's anger she's directing at me. It's *something* and that's so much better than nothing.

"I'm tired of *your* idle threats," she uses both hands to push me as hard as she can, but I hold my ground, and her effort doesn't even budge me. That seems to piss her off even more.

"Claim me," she says, mockingly. "You haven't *claimed* me. You've been the goodie-two-shoes, Mr. Proper with your fucking British accent, too scared to make a move, Vampire." She scoffs again, "so why don't you stop making yourself look weak and either claim me as yours for real or kill me and get it over with."

Her fire is contagious and lights my own. I do want to claim her. I want to claim her in every way possible and I think she knows that. She's taunting me with my own truth. I want to reach out to her, to grab her, and pull her hard against me. I want to feel every inch of her bare skin on mine. I'm fighting for control as I clench my fists to keep them from reaching out for her.

"Do not threaten me, Amarah Rey, you will not like my response," I say, through clenched teeth.

"How many times do I have to tell you that I'm not scared of you? Maybe you're the scared one. A Master Vampire who's too scared to take what he wants. What would happen if others found out just how fucking weak and pathetic you actually are?"

In an instant, I'm in front of her, my blood-stained hand wrapped around her tiny throat, lifting her into the air. She's testing all of my control. I'm a Master Vampire, I *need* my people to fear me, and they do. She's right that I'm fucking weak and pathetic, but does she realize it's only when it comes to her? I know she affects me this way and yet, I can't fucking help it. The fact that Amarah Rey is always so bold and fearless in front of me makes me feel alive. It sends my blood racing in my veins and I want to sink my cock and fangs so deep inside her. Fuck!

"Finally," she chokes out the words. "Is this what you want? Kill me then. Take what you want, Valmont."

I'm looking up into her big, beautiful eyes, not an ounce of fear in them. I'm struggling with my own desires. What I want versus what I *should* do. I should put her in her place. I should make her utterly terrified of me.

"I can break your neck right now with the slightest twist of my wrist," I say, matter-of-factly.

She looks me directly in my eyes, Gods, another turn on. No one looks Vampires in the eye, no one. Yet here she is, challenging everything I thought I knew, and she still has absolutely no fear. Her eyes are only filled with hurt and loss. A part of me knows she wants me to end her suffering. Her eyes say it all even if she can't speak the words.

"Is that what you want, Valmont? Is that what you truly desire? To take my life? Or would you rather take my body? Which one is it? Come on Mr. Master Vampire, take what you want."

She's outright challenging me and calling me out. A Master Vampire that has survived as long as I have doesn't put up with challenges of *any* kind. I should kill her. I know it down to my very core. She is going to be my downfall. A flick of the wrist and I destroy any and all weakness. Because *she* is my weakness. I hold her stare as I struggle with what to do. Those eyes seem to see into my very soul. They see everything I try to keep hidden. Everything I thought I left behind with my humanity.

"Take it," she struggles to say.

One second, I'm considering breaking her neck, the next second, I'm slamming her back into a wall. She tries to cry out in pain but I silence her cries with my lips crashing into hers. There's a moment when she doesn't kiss me back and I hesitate. I'm about to pull away from her when her legs wrap around me and she pulls me into her. Gods, her lips are even softer than I imagined. I hungrily and greedily claim her mouth as if it's the only chance I'll get to taste her. And once she realizes what's happening, it might be.

So, I don't hesitate. My tongue is in her mouth, sweeping from side to side, exploring every inch of her. She's lighting my blood on fire, my very fucking soul is burning like a beacon to the Gods above. Just the feel of her hands desperately pulling me into her, wanting this, wanting...*me*, makes me feel like my entire body has been doused in gasoline and she's the match. But it's still not enough. I want more. I *need* more.

I reluctantly pull away from her lips to quickly discard my suit jacket. Her hands have already undone my vest and are deftly moving from button to button on my shirt. She's frantic, almost like she's as desperate for this to happen as I am. I don't fight her, and in a matter of seconds, I'm standing naked from the waist up before her.

"Wow! This is...ummmm, you are...wow."

I look down at my exposed body, "what is it?"

"Unexpected, this," she says, as she trails her hands down my chest and across my stomach. "This was not at all how I imagined you."

"So, you admit you've imagined what I look like naked?" I say, with a confident smirk.

"What? No!" She exclaims in mock denial.

"Amarah Rey, you really shouldn't lie to me, but I'll let this one slide because, I know you have, and I'm happy to see I've not disappointed you."

She's still fucking me with her eyes so, I take the time to return the favor. She's still pushed up against the wall, her legs wrapped tightly around me, causing her dress to bunch up at her waist, revealing the dagger she has strapped to her right thigh and red lace underwear. Fuck me. She's so fucking sexy.

I let my hands trail up her thighs, and grip her ass, lifting her higher. Gods, her skin is like silk. I want to dig my nails into her soft flesh and see her blood run down her thighs before I lick it off her. I want to devour her. To take her right here, right now, but I've dreamt about being with her for so long, I know I have to slow down. I need to make this moment last. I need to make sure she's satisfied in every way so that she wants to come back for more.

Now that I know she's not going to change her mind, I pull my eagerness back and move slower, taking it all in. Taking *her* in. I lean back in for another kiss. I love her lips, her mouth, her taste. I slide my tongue across her lips, coaxing her to open her mouth to me. She does, and the moment her tongue touches mine, I ignite again. This woman sets my very soul on fire and I can't help the frustrated groan that escapes my throat. I want her *now,* but instead, I make the kiss deeper. I take time exploring her mouth with mine as I move a hand between her legs. I rub my fingers lightly over her clit, her panties are already soaking wet, and she moans into my mouth. Fuck, it's the sexiest sound I've ever heard. I store it in my mind for later as I continue to tease her through her panties.

Her hips are moving against my hand and she moans again.

Her kiss has become desperate and reckless, just like I feel inside. I feel her tongue trail under my fangs and I immediately taste her blood. She lets out a small gasp in response and pulls back.

"Fuck," she gently touches her tongue and her fingers come away with blood.

"The wound will heal with my saliva as you kiss me," I say breathlessly, my eyes fixed on her blood-tipped fingers.

"I'm not used to kissing someone with fangs," she laughs, softly.

I grab her wrist and slowly move her fingers toward my lips. We lock eyes as I slip her fingers into my mouth, her breath hitches and she gives me another small moan, as I gently suck her fingers clean. Sweet Gods, she's the best thing I've ever tasted. Just this small amount of blood has me feeling invincible. My strength feels off the charts and my body feels alive in ways that aren't possible.

I want more.

More of her blood.

More of her mouth.

More of her desire.

More of her.

I hungrily claim her mouth again, letting the pooled blood coat my tongue until I swallow it down, fighting the urge to bite her again.

I move from her mouth and kiss across her jaw, underneath her ear, and down her neck, as my fingers start once again, gently moving back and forth across her clit, and she throws her head back and moans her pleasure to the ceiling.

"Amarah Rey, do you remember the last time we were in a similar position?" I ask, with my lips against her skin.

"Yes," she whispers.

"You were scared of me then and yet, you still wanted it. You still wanted me to fuck you, didn't you?"

"Yes."

"I can taste your desire now, Amarah Rey, and it's intoxicating. Only this time, there's no fear."

"No, there's not. There's no fear. I want this," she says, more forcefully, as she loosens her hold on my waist. I let her slip down my body to stand on her own.

Her hands land on my chest, my muscles constrict under her touch as she traces the ink embedded in my skin, covering almost every inch of me. "Your tattoos are unlike anything I've ever seen. I had no idea you had all of this hidden underneath your fancy suits," she says in awe, as her eyes follow her hands. "I wonder what else you're hiding?" She smiles up deviously at me as her hand continues south and brushes over my already hard cock.

"Jesus," she whispers.

I close my eyes at the feel of her hand squeezing my cock. She's teasing me and I love it and hate it all at the same time. My body feels like it's going to snap with all the tension and the need to be inside her. I'm so hard my cock aches with the pressure.

"Fuck," I manage to get out.

Her focus is on her fingers, as she works to unclasp my belt, and starts unzipping my pants. I watch her eagerly, anticipating what comes next, as I kick off my shoes. She pulls my pants down, I step out of them, and then I'm left standing completely naked in front of her.

I've been one with my body for longer than I care to remember, but I'm suddenly nervous, standing naked in front of Amarah Rey. I feel vulnerable and strangely, more alive. Just being in her presence causes me to second guess everything. I *care* about what she thinks and I haven't given two-shits about anyone's opinions in a very long time. It's unnerving and thrilling. I feel like a new man around her. Not a monster. Not a Vampire. Just a man. And I want to be the man she needs. The man she wants.

I watch as her eyes take in every inch of me for the first time. She's biting her bottom lip and I don't think she even knows she's doing it. I see the lust in her eyes as they finally make their way up my body and connect with mine again. The way she looks at me makes me feel like I've never truly been seen until now. The way it makes me feel is heady and also... terrifying.

"Jesus, Valmont, you're fucking beautiful," she says in awe, as her hands explore my body, sending bolts of desire through me with every touch. She grips my cock in her hands and starts to kneel.

"Wait," I grab her arms and stop her. "I want this off," I demand, as I grab her dress from the bottom and start to peel it off her body. She doesn't fight it and holds her hands up over her head for me.

I discard the dress somewhere on the floor and she's left standing in a red strapless, lace bra that matches her panties. The black boots are still hiding most of her legs. I let them stay, for now.

"The color of blood. How fitting, Amarah Rey," I smile devilishly, as my eyes explore her curves and everywhere I'm going to touch, lick, and kiss her.

"Do you like it?" She asks, as she watches me and starts to kneel again.

"For now," I say dismissively, but the truth is, I love it. I love the color of blood against her skin, but right now my attention is focused on every move she's about to make.

My cock twitches in anticipation, she smirks confidently as she takes me in both of her hands and strokes me before rubbing the tip and precum across her lips like she putting on fucking lipstick, and then she licks it off her lips with a moan of pleasure. Son of a bitch she's fucking sexy. Her eyes are still on my face, still watching me watch her, as she moves her head lower and licks me from base to tip, then back down again, excruciatingly slowly. Teasing me. I'm close to pushing my cock in her mouth where I want it. And *not* gently.

"Amarah Rey," I warn.

She smirks again and then finally takes me. I watch as my throbbing cock disappears inside her mouth and I focus on how warm and wet her mouth is. She moves her mouth back and forth, coating my dick with her spit, allowing her hands glide easily matching the rhythm of her mouth. She's working every fucking inch of me. Her hands pumping at the base and her mouth, lips, and tongue stroking the rest. Her eyes are closed now and I feel her moans vibrate across my cock and up my spine as she gives me the best fucking head I've ever had.

"Holy fucking Gods, Amarah Rey, that's so fucking good," I groan as I close my eyes, throw my head back, and relish in the feel of her devouring my cock.

I gasp in surprise when she takes my balls in her mouth but continues to stroke me the entire time. I'm so sensitive to the heat, to her touch. Nothing has felt this good in centuries and I don't understand it. It's almost too much, almost. She moves back to my cock and this time she's more aggressive, stroking me harder and I feel a graze of teeth. I rest one hand on the back of her head as she continues to moan her pleasure around my hard cock. My hips start pumping and she lets me take control, but I'm hesitant. I don't want to hurt her.

She pulls away and looks at me, "don't go easy on me. Make me gag and gasp for air. I've always been drawn to you because your dark energy calls to mine. I want the thrill of danger. I want it rough, Valmont. All of it. I like a little pain if it's mixed with a lot of pleasure. Am I wrong to think you can give me that? To give me what I've always desired but never had?"

I take a second to register what she's asking and to look into her eyes. No fear. No hesitation. I see only someone as desperate to feel alive as I am. We have a perfect understanding of each other in this moment and all my hesitation and resignation fades. We want the same thing. And I can give it to her.

"No. You're not wrong, Amarah Rey. Hold on," I say, as I flash my fangs.

I roughly take hold of her ponytail as I push my cock inside her mouth again. I don't hold back and I fuck her, hard. I feel her throat tightly wrap around my cock as I push my way down. Her reflexes fight against me but I force her to swallow me. I pull all the way out, allowing her to breathe before I do it again and again. She gags, her eyes are watering and her mascara starts to run down her cheeks, but her eyes are bright and alive sending reassurance flooding through me. The sight of her on her knees in front of me as my cock slides in and out of her mouth, has me seconds away from pouring my release down her throat. I've never felt so sensitive and out of control.

In a blink, I have her lying on the couch, my body on top of her as I take her mouth again in a desperate kiss. I thrust my hips, rubbing my cock against her clit over her panties and she claws at my back. It's my turn to tease her with what's to come.

I sit back, my hands move to one of the boots, and find the zipper. I unzip it and slowly peel it off of her, revealing her smooth, sexy leg one inch at a time. Then I take the other one off, trailing my fingertips down her thighs, behind her knees, and across her calves, before I lick my way back up, until I'm met with red lace in my face.

I unsheathe the dagger still strapped to her thigh and trail the blade slowly and gently across her skin, up her stomach, and bring it to make teasing circles around her nipple through the thin material. I see her nipple harden, begging to be touched and she arches her back, practically throwing her breasts at me.

"So eager for me to touch you," I say, as I continue to only use the dagger to touch her skin.

"Yes," she whispers, as she watches me. Her chest is rising

and falling with her heavy breaths.

I quickly cut the bra in the middle and it falls away, revealing her full, naked breasts. I hold her gaze as I press the dagger in harder against her sensitive skin.

I want her blood, but I don't want to give her my bite, not yet. "Are you sure this is what you want?" I ask, as I let the dagger sink into her skin right where her breast meets her chest.

She lets out a small whimper of pain but her eyes never waiver, "yes."

My eyes follow the trail of blood running down her breast. I move the tip of the dagger across her skin again, down her belly, and across her clit. I contemplate cutting the panties away too, but there's something about the act of slowly pulling them down her thighs that appeals to me, so I sheath the dagger again.

I hook my fingers into her underwear, "Amarah Rey..."

"Yes, Valmont?"

"Lift that beautiful ass for me."

She complies immediately, and it strokes my ego to have her at my beck and call. To have her body responding to my every touch. I take my time pulling her panties off inch by slow inch, until only the dagger remains, as she's left lying naked in front of me. Her body is even more beautiful than I've ever imagined. Her skin isn't flawless, she has scars from her battles with demons, and colorful tattoos adorning her skin, but every inch of her is perfect.

My eyes settle between her legs and my cock twitches again at the mere sight of her. I have to roughly squeeze my cock to keep from cuming at just the sight of her glistening, soaking wet, and ready for me.

I gently stroke her pussy right up the middle and her hips rock against my touch. "So wet. So beautiful, Amarah Rey," I whisper breathlessly, as I continue to tease her opening, rubbing her desire across her sensitive clit.

"Fuck, Valmont, I want you," she says, eagerly, as her hips continue to rock against my fingers, her eyes locked on what I'm doing.

Gods, my name on her lips. Her declaration of wanting me. I want to shove my aching cock inside her, right now, and get lost in her, but I somehow manage to control myself. Thousands of years of control almost come undone in minutes by her. Almost.

"All in good time, Amarah Rey," I say, as I lower my head and start licking up the trail of blood I left from the dagger wound. I push two fingers inside of her as I take her nipple into my mouth and bite down.

"Oh my God, Valmont," her body jerks underneath me, and her breathing gets even heavier.

I continue sliding my fingers in and out of her, as I position myself lower and slide my tongue across her pussy, finally tasting her desire. I can't help but groan as her sweetness coats my tongue. Her hands grab a hold of my hair and hold it back, her eyes watch me hungrily, until the pleasure builds and her head falls back. Her hands are tightly woven in my hair as she starts to move rhythmically against my tongue, fucking my mouth, instead of the other way around.

Her body starts to lose control, I feel her legs shaking as they fight to stay open, and I feel her pussy tighten against my fingers. My other hand possessively holds her hip and helps to keep her from losing all control. I moan into her core as I anticipate tasting her first orgasm.

"Holy shit, don't stop, please. It feels so good. Right there. Yeah, just like that," she commands me, as she moves her hips and rubs her clit against my tongue just the way she likes it, and I'm more than happy to comply.

I keep pumping my fingers into her as my tongue works her sensitive clit. I apply more pressure with my tongue and she let's me know how much she likes it.

"Oh my God, Valmont." Her whole body tightens, her rhythm falters, "you're going to make me cum," she strangles out, as her body spasms underneath me, her back arches, and she cums on my fingers and tongue, screaming my name. I remove my fingers and lick up every bit of her sweet juices before I give her my fingers to clean with her mouth.

"See how good you taste, Amarah Rey? Your blood, your pussy, everything is so sweet and addicting. *You're* fucking addicting," I admit my weakness and hope she's too far gone to notice.

She pulls me up her body so my eyes are directly in front of hers and my cock is brushing between her legs. She reaches down and grabs my cock angling it to her opening, desperately trying to get me inside of her, but I hold back.

"Valmont, please, give me what I want. I want you inside of me and I want your bite. I *need* your bite, please."

"I love to hear my name on your lips like this, Amarah Rey. I love to see your body begging for mine. And I promise, this is going to be worth the wait, but this isn't where I want to take you."

I pick her up easily, my Vampire strength and speed only intensified by her blood in my veins. We're suddenly standing, completely naked, in front of the floor-to-ceiling windows overlooking my club. All anyone has to do is look up and they'll see everything I'm about to do to her. The thought of people seeing me take her, claiming her, is almost enough to make me cum. Everything about her and this situation has me riding the edge, again and again.

"Valmont, what are you doing?" Her voice is shaky with hesitation but still husky and laced with pleasure.

"Despite what you might think, I'm far from weak and pathetic. I'm going to claim you, for any and all to see, Amarah Rey. You're mine now," I say, as I spread her legs apart and push her face to the glass. I reach down and caress her leg, slowly sliding up her thigh. As I do, I let my nails grow into sharp points as I dig into her soft skin. She cries out in pain but doesn't move.

"Stay here," I whisper against her ear, then take a step away from her. She's standing, pushed up against the windows, legs spread, her hair is like a living flame cascading down her back, all the way to her ass.

I pull my hand back and let it fall with enough force to leave a mark across her ass cheek. She cries out in pain again, but she still doesn't move. She has no fear and complete trust in me. She's so fucking sexy.

"Do you have any idea how sexy you are with blood running down your lovely skin and my hand-print on your ass?" I ask in admiration.

I take in every glorious inch of her body, committing it to memory before I step back into her, grabbing her chin and pulling her head back towards me.

"Is this what you want? A little pain," I smack her ass again, in the same spot, and she cries out, "before I give you the best pleasure you've ever fucking had in your life?"

"Yes," she struggles to say.

I let her go, and squat down so I can lick up the blood running down her leg, as my hand moves between her legs. I sink my fingers back inside her pussy and I swear she's even more wet than before. She moans deeply and pushes greedily into my fingers. I'll never get enough of her blood, her body, her scent, her sounds...*her.*

I can tell she's close to another orgasm so, I remove my fingers from her and stand behind her. I wrap her ponytail around my wrist and pull, until her neck is arched at an almost painful angle.

"Do you still think I'm weak and pathetic, Amarah Rey?" I whisper in her ear as I start to rub my dick across her clit.

"Valmont, please," she begs me for her release.

"I'm the one in control of your pleasure now. Tell me, Amarah Rey, who am I?"

"You're Virtuoso. You're a Master Vampire," she struggles to talk with her neck pulled back.

I move her head to the side, my lips and tongue caress her neck, right where my fangs are going to sink into her flesh. I scrape my fangs across her skin and I feel her heart rate spike, her vein pounding like a drum in my mouth.

"And who's Master am I, Amarah Rey?" I move my hand to squeeze her breast and hold her tightly to me for what's about to come.

"Amarah Rey, I asked you a question," I remind her, as my cock slides against her slit.

"You're mine."

"I'm your what?" I demand.

I want to hear her say it, but I'm barely hanging onto my control, as the tip of my cock sinks inside her tight, velvety soft pussy. She gasps and I don't wait for a response as I penetrate her with my hard cock and fangs at the same time. Her pussy hugs my dick tightly and I feel her second orgasm explode around me. I thrust in and out of her in long, hard strokes, drawing out her orgasm, my fangs still locked in her neck, pouring her heavenly blood down my throat.

I want it all. Every last drop and then some. It's like she's the elixir of life and I've never lived before her. Everything is more vivid and clear. All my senses are heightened. I feel like my blood is lava and I'm a volcano about to erupt. I have to pry my mouth off of her neck with a growl as I focus on fucking her.

I pull out of her just long enough to spin her around and lift her up. Her legs automatically clamp around my waist as I drive my dick inside her again. Gods, she feels so fucking good. My body is feeling every touch, every breath, as if I've never experienced physical touch before. Her mouth claims mine and it's a raw and savage kiss. Like she's clawing her way out of the darkness and I'm her lifeline. And she's mine.

I hold her easily with one hand as I wrap my still blood-stained hand around her throat and squeeze. She tries to moan but I'm cutting off her air. I pull back to watch her, as I continue to pound inside of her. Her hold on me starts to loosen, her eyes start to flutter and I know she's close to passing out. Still, no fear in her eyes.

I release her neck and immediately sink my fangs in her again. I hear a desperate gasp for air along with a scream of pleasure as an orgasm hits her again. I reluctantly break away from her neck and we watch each other as I feel my own orgasm building. I'm driving my dick in and out of her with so much force, the windows are shaking with every thrust I make. Her body is still clenched hard around me but she's so wet there's absolutely no resistance.

"Blood," she manages to breathe out as her eyes drop to my mouth.

I feel her wet tongue lick the corner of my mouth before she kisses me with the taste of her blood on her tongue. It's enough to send me over the edge as I finally erupt inside of her. The orgasm consumes every part of my body as I give her everything I have. All of me is now hers, and I am left with only her blood in my veins, sustaining me. Consuming me. She fills me up so completely, there's no room for anything or anyone else.

Only her.

Does she have any clue what's just happened? The line I just crossed? Does she realize how much control she truly has over me now? I wanted to hear her call me her Master, but the truth is, she's mine. Does she know that I'm addicted to her? Does she know that I'm hopelessly and deeply in love with her?

"Amarah Rey," her name falls like worship from my lips, as I twist us around so my back is to the windows and I slide us safely to the floor, before my legs give out from under me.

Amarah: Who The Fuck Is She?

Dangerous Woman by Ariana Grande

I'm still straddling Valmont, my head resting on his chest, listening to the steady thump of his heart echo in my ear. I still feel his large, hard cock inside of me, pulsing, as we sit tangled up in each other on the floor, catching our breath and coming back down to Earth. I've never felt so utterly and completely relaxed before. I feel weightless and there's not a single thought in my mind, which is a miracle, and a much-needed reprieve from the constant pain and nightmares that plagued me every minute of every damn day and night. I focus on my body. It's completely spent from the pain and, fucking Hell, the pleasure. I've never felt an orgasm, like the ones I just had, in my life. Can you die from too much pleasure?

I finally, lazily lift my head off his chest to look at him. There seems to be a blush to his normally pale skin, and his beautiful lips are pinker than I've ever seen them. I trace his defined cupid's bow gently with my thumb and then make my way up to meet his eyes. His turquoise eyes are a brilliant pop of color like I've never seen them before and his hair is sparkling silver in the light.

"You're breathtakingly beautiful," I whisper, as I caress his cheek. "I've never seen you look like this before. I mean, you've always been attractive, but…" I shake my head, "you look more…*alive*."

"I feel more alive." His brows furrow and he has a faraway look in his eyes. "I haven't felt like this in… a *very* long time."

"It's a good thing. Right?"

He looks at me and I see the raw honesty in his eyes, "I don't know."

"I haven't felt this…*free*, in what feels like a very long time either. I don't have a care in the world," I giggle, obviously still high on whatever Valmont's bite is. "How can this be anything but good?"

My eyes drop to his mouth and just thinking about Valmont's bite, has me wanting more. Even though I literally *just* had it, I want it again. I need it again. I want to feel that quick stabbing pain, the feel of his fangs breaking my skin before I explode with pleasure from places I've never felt before, as I ride him to orgasm, again, and again, and again. I close my eyes and ride the memory of that pleasure.

"Amarah Rey, if you keep rocking your hips like that, we're going to have round two," Valmont's voice comes out a little strangled.

"I'm sorry, I didn't even realize I was moving," I say impassively, as I look back up to his eyes and focus on moving my hips against him. My body is quickly responding to him, still hard and sheathed inside of me. I know I should be thinking about…something. *Someone*. But I can't grasp any real or solid thought so, I stop trying.

He lets out a groan, "Amarah Rey…"

"Shut up and kiss me," I say, with my lips against his.

He takes my head in his large hands and does as I say. His mouth claims mine but this time it's slow and deep. He's caressing my tongue with his, kissing me as if he has forever to do it. I lift my hips up and then slide back down the length of him, slow and steady, matching the way he's kissing me.

The dominating, pain-inducing Valmont, is hot and sexy, but there's something about this more reserved, tender Valmont that has my heart racing. His hands drop from my face as he caresses my breast, teasing my nipples gently, then gives a painful pinch, making me gasp, before he continues down to my ass. He grabs me and takes control of my movements, lifting me higher so I can get the full length of him, as he strokes me in and out. I can already feel the pleasure building between my legs but I know it won't be the same without his bite.

I pull away from the kiss, breathless, as I lean my head to the side giving him access to my neck. "Bite me."

He shakes his head, "you've already given up too much blood tonight."

"Just take a little. A little more won't hurt," I argue. My body is shaking with anticipation. My pussy is throbbing with excitement, my mind only thinking of his bite.

"Amarah Rey…"

"Please," I beg. I feel anxiety crawl up my throat at the thought of him denying me. I know he can take too much of my blood. I know this is dangerous, like an addict overdosing, and now I understand how it happens. I just want a little more. Just a taste.

I lean closer and I feel his breath on my neck. "Don't you want to?"

"That's the problem," he says, as his lips brush against my neck. I feel his arms tighten across my body as he pulls me in hard against his chest. "I don't want to stop."

I feel that sharp pinch of pain as his fangs dig in, and then, I'm flooded with feel-good endorphins. Although, that doesn't quite describe it either. It's like my entire body is filled up with every good feeling I've ever known. It fills me up so completely it threatens to break me apart. I only have one choice. Let it break me into a million, vibrating pieces of pleasure.

I scream his name as the force of the orgasm erupts from my body sending shockwaves of pleasure crashing through me. It's like a hurricane and I'm threatened to be drowned in it. To be destroyed by it until there's nothing left of me. I ride it out as Valmont thrusts inside of me, riding my orgasm like a surfer trying not to be thrown into the relentless waves.

We're holding on to each other so tightly, I don't know where I end and he begins. Our skin is on fire, sweating and sticking to each other. He pulls away from my neck as he growls his pleasure against my skin. His release fills me up, then I feel his warm pleasure slide down my thigh, and it turns me on even more. When we've both stopped cuming, I lean my forehead against his and try to catch my breath once again.

"Bloody Hell," Valmont says.

"You can say that again," I agree, as a smile starts to pull at my lips.

Valmont pulls his head back so he can see me. He takes my head gently in his hands again as he kisses me softly. Just a brush of his lips against mine but it sends goosebumps across my skin. He pulls back, and I feel like an idiot with this stupid smile plastered on my face, but I'm too high to care.

"You're devastating, Amarah Rey," he shakes his head and looks at me with too much emotion in his eyes for me to understand.

"What?" I laugh, nervously. "What does that mean?"

He continues shaking his head, "you really have no idea."

I'm trying to focus on the words coming out of his mouth but my head is in the clouds. My mind is fuzzy and slow. I feel like I'm swimming through molasses, trying to reach the shore where all my intelligent thoughts are just out of reach, when a knock on the door steals our attention.

"I'm busy!" Valmont shouts from our position still on the floor.

"No idea about what? What are you talking about?" I ask, as I desperately try to clear my mind from the haze.

"Isn't it obvious?" Valmont is searching my eyes for understanding, but I don't understand. I'm completely lost in this conversation. It's as if he is speaking a completely different language.

The knock comes again, more urgently this time, and Valmont's entire demeanor changes. His body is tense and his attention is now one hundred percent on the closed door. He stands with me still in his lap and gently sets me on my feet.

"Amarah Rey, get dressed. Quickly," he says, as he rushes to answer the door, still naked.

I turn to watch him walk across the office, more confused than ever, but can't help but admire his ass as he heads to the door. His body is covered in tattoos like I've never seen before. Everything about him, from his hair, to his eyes, to his body, is a work of art. I could stare at him for hours, trace every single line and drop of ink in his skin, with my tongue. I close my eyes and try to focus on what's going on.

"Why? What's going on?" I ask, as I take a step and stumble towards the couch. I still feel weightless and high, a little dizzy, and I can't help but giggle as I fumble with putting on my underwear correctly. It feels like the hardest and most unnecessary task I've ever had to do.

"Why do I need to get dressed? You've already seen me naked. Hell, everyone has seen me naked," I giggle again. The thought that Valmont fucked me against the window overlooking the club, for everyone to see, should mortify me but I can't bring myself to care. Later, I know I'll care later.

With a lot of effort, I finally have my panties back on, the bra is destroyed, and I throw myself down on the couch. The material from the lace underwear is rubbing against my sensitive clit. I trace my fingertips across my chest and down to my stomach. My skin feels sensitive, as if my nerve endings have been stripped bare. I've never been on ecstasy pills before, but I imagine this must be what it feels like.

I close my eyes and imagine it's Valmont's fingertips instead of my own. My fingers continue south until I'm gently rubbing my clit over the thin, wet material the same way Valmont did earlier.

I moan, "Valmont."

"Amarah Rey!" His voice is louder now and he's pulling me up by my shoulders so I'm sitting up on the couch. "Amarah Rey, you need to get a hold of yourself. I need you to get dressed, now." His voice is ice across my skin, quenching the fire, but still causing desire. Ice can be a whole other type of torturous pleasure.

Valmont pulls my bottom lip out of my teeth, "Amarah Rey, please, stop that." I can hear the strain in his voice. He grips my chin and applies pressure, pulling my head down so I'm forced to look at him.

His face is back to the blank slate I'm used to seeing him wear when he's around everyone else. His eyes are pleading with me to pay attention and I see a muscle in his jaw twitching every few seconds as he tries to maintain control. He's dressed in his three-piece suit, the same one that was discarded and thrown on the floor earlier. The Valmont I had in private is gone. He's now the business owner, Virtuoso, serious and threatening pain and death at the slightest offense, Vampire. This side of him is what I've always been attracted to. I imagine him tying me up, stalking around me in a fancy, expensive white suit, making me bleed, and tasting my blood before he heals me again and again, my blood leaving bright stains on his lips and suit. I imagine the immense pleasure that will come after the pain and I groan.

I feel a sudden sting on my cheek, my hand automatically reaches for my face and my lips are frozen in an *O* of surprise, as I register what just happened. He slapped me. Valmont just slapped me!

He lets out a frustrated growl, "I don't have time for this." He pulls my hair in front of me, giving a bit of coverage to my bare chest, and then leaves me sitting, with my shock, as he stands up and turns back to the door. "Just bring them in," he orders. I finally look up and notice Pierce standing just inside the doorway. He nods and disappears. I watch Valmont pour himself a drink as he speaks to me.

"I do not want you here for this, but I can use your current...*state*, as a distraction." He walks back over to the couch, drink in hand, and sits down on one end. He looks at me and his eyes are focused and determined, but there's something else sliding behind the bravado. Fear.

"This is a dangerous situation and I need you to act like a completely besotted lover. Even if you start coming to your senses, which you will as soon as the high passes, I do not want you to show your true identity. Do you understand?"

I'm trying extremely hard to listen to his words. I know this is a serious situation, whatever it is, and I know I need to do as he says, but I'm having a hard time understanding anything other than the need to have sex with him. The need to remove the suit and feel his sculpted body again.

"Ok," I whisper. "Whatever you want," I say, as I move closer to him, throwing my leg over his and leaning in to smell his neck.

"Bloody Hell," he pinches the bridge of his nose before he leans back and throws his arm around me, pulling me further onto him.

I'm busy exploring his neck, and jaw with my lips and tongue when I hear a voice that slithers across my skin and sends a feeling of dread straight to my chest.

"Well, well, well, Valmont Sinclair, aren't you a sight for sore eyes? And I do believe you've only gotten so much better with age.

My goodness, look at you." Her words are complimentary but her tone is seething with poison.

I move slightly away from Valmont so I can see who's speaking. My breath catches in my throat at the beautiful woman standing before us. She's taller than me and her frame is small and petite but with enough curves to be very sexy, and she apparently has no qualms about showing...*everything* off.

Her hair is black as night, with the tightest curls I've ever seen. It's styled up and away from her shoulders and back, parted to the side with curls framing her face. Her skin is the perfect mix of coffee and cream and shows no tan lines in the plunging v-neck, black and gold dress. The entire dress is sheer, leaving her nipples on full display underneath the thin material. Her body is covered from the waist down in a waterfall of cascading layers leaving *some things* to the imagination at least.

When I make my way back up her body, I'm met with a strong, yet delicate jaw, full lips painted with a shimmering gold that matches her dress, and cold, dead black eyes that threaten to drag me under the deepest, treacherous parts of the unknown ocean waters. I immediately look away and bury my face in Valmont's neck again. His smell is distracting, and I focus on the feel of his body underneath mine, and the pleasure I know it can bring. It's a nice distraction, but I feel the high slowly starting to dissipate as he said it would, and I'm desperately wishing I had paid more attention to his words.

"Viveka," Valmont inclines his head in a greeting. "This is an unexpected surprise. What brings you all this way? To *my* territory?" His words are calm and bland, but I feel how tense his body is. I know he's not happy about, whoever this *Viveka* chick is, being here.

"Come now, Valmont. Is that really how you're going to greet me after everything? Come here, give your mother a hug, and let me have a look at you properly." Her voice is demanding yet has a hint of amusement in it.

"Mother?" I mutter, confusion still clouding my brain, as I lift my head and look from her to him and back again.

Valmont is the most powerful person I know and I don't expect him to listen to her. He doesn't listen to anyone. No one pulls his strings, but the next thing I know, I'm suddenly being pushed aside like vegetables on a plate as he stands to do as she says.

"Hey! What the Hell, Valmont?" I say angrily, as I right myself, realizing that I'm still just in my red lace underwear.

Viveka lifts her eyebrows and looks at Valmont, "that one's a bit mouthy, isn't she?"

"I like the feisty ones, and I like for them to think they have some say in what I do or don't do. What can I say," he shrugs, "I like to play with my food. It adds to the fun, and you know as much as I do, after all this time, we need to get entertainment where we can," he says nonchalantly, talking about me as if I'm no one and I don't matter.

"What the fuck, Valmont? That's not true and you know it!" I'm getting angry now, and honestly, a bit jealous at this new woman running her hands all over Valmont as she walks around him with a lustful gleam in her eyes. Jealousy is definitely helping push through the last of the high.

"Oh, Valmont, how I've missed you and this beautiful body. You're even more beautiful than I remembered. You almost look...*alive* again. Like you did when I first met you. Mmmm, I can't wait to get reacquainted."

"Like Hell you will!" I stand up so quickly it sends a rush straight to my head and the room starts spinning. I have to sit back down and clutch my head in my hands, trying to suppress the rolling nausea in my stomach. The high is almost gone now but the blood loss has left me weak.

Viveka throws her head back and laughs. The sound is

wicked and reminds me of Revna. Evil. I shiver and feel cold sinking into my bones. "Oh, Valmont, you really do give your pets a lot of feigned freedom, don't you?"

I don't see her walk towards me, but I feel the material of her dress rub against my bare legs, and then I smell her perfume. She smells like roses, and the floral aroma is so strong, I can taste it on the back of my tongue. I have to swallow hard to keep from gagging. I've never been the typical girl who likes flowers or their pungent scent.

She kneels in front of me and roughly grabs my chin. "You are a pretty thing though," she says, as she stares at me. The scent of copper on her breath mingling with the scent of overpowering roses is dizzying.

I may not be able to stand up, but I'm not just going to let this bitch think she can have her way with me. I pull the dagger I still have strapped to my thigh, thank you Valmont for your wicked little turn-ons, and place it under her chin, letting the sharp tip press against her skin. I'll draw blood if she pushes me, but for now, the threat is there.

"Take your hand off me or lose it," I say, through clenched teeth.

Her black eyes sparkle and she laughs in my face, completely ignoring the dagger, and my threat. Instead, she stands up and gives me her back, as if I'm no threat at all, and walks back to Valmont with laughter in her words.

"Oh my, what a treat! I may have to give this a try sometime. Thank you for the idea. Oh, where are my manners? Valmont, this is Kordeuv, he's my darling companion," she gestures for him to step forward. I was so focused on Viveka that I hadn't even seen him. The high I'm finally fighting off is obviously a hindrance to my awareness. Hell, to *everything*. Not good.

This new guy, Kordeuv, steps forward to introduce himself to

Valmont. He has long black hair, past his shoulders, and he's wearing leather pants, combat boots, a leather jacket that he left open to show off slightly chiselled chest and abs, and heavy silver chains around his neck.

"Where's Kiefer?" I ask, with a chuckle.

He looks at me with a dead stare, there seems to be no life in his dark eyes. There's certainly no humor. "What? You mean to tell me you aren't one of The Lost Boys? Then you must be dressed for Halloween which, I'm sorry to inform you, you missed by a month."

He cocks his head slightly as he continues to stare at me. There's no anger or offense from my comments in his eyes or body language. In fact, he looks like he's...*curious*. Like I'm a riddle he's trying to decipher. My humor fades as I start to feel really uncomfortable and extremely exposed, sitting in my underwear with three pairs of eyes watching me.

"Pleasure, mate," Valmont says, bringing the attention back to him as they shake hands.

"Wonderful! Aren't we all going to get along marvellously," Viveka claps her hands together. "Now, I'm going to go back downstairs and have some dinner and fun for myself. I will need a place to stay, of course."

"Of course, you shall have our very best suite fitted for your needs but, you have not yet answered my question. What are you doing here, Viveka?"

She places her hand on her chest in mock offense, as if he's hurt her deeply, "I didn't know I needed a reason to visit one of my very first children. Once upon a time you would have been..." her gaze slides down his body and stops just below the waist, "*extremely happy* to see me."

Valmont doesn't let her comment get to him, "it's been almost a thousand years, if I remember correctly, since I've seen you. There must be a reason for you to show up here, now, after all this time," he persists.

"Maybe I just missed you," she whispers, as she steps in close and wraps her hands around his neck.

Valmont gives a half-smile before grabbing her wrists and stepping away from her. "I may have believed that once upon a time, Viveka, but I'm not the young boy you once knew."

"No, you sure aren't, and I can't wait to get to know the new you and all the new devilish things you've learned," she takes a step towards him again, placing her hands on his chest as she leans in and whispers something in his ear. I see his jaw tick as he clenches his teeth at whatever she's saying. She pulls away with a confident smile before she sashays out the door.

I look at Valmont more confused than ever and it has nothing to do with being affected by his bite but the scene that has just unfolded in front of me.

"What in the fuck was that all about and, more importantly, who the fuck is she?" I ask, as the confusion fights with jealousy for a spot in my mind.

Valmont turns to look at me and I see the fear flash in his eyes before he takes control of his emotions again, "that is Viveka Bolverk," he hesitates and then whispers, "she's my Valmistaja. My Maker."

Valmont: Memories Long Forgotten

Indestructible by Disturbed

I push all my rambling thoughts away and focus on the woman standing in front of me. Not much surprises me or rattles me. Hell, when you're over two thousand years old, what haven't you seen or done? There's also not much I fear, but ironically enough, both things I do fear come in seemingly harmless little packages with beautiful faces and sexy curves. And I don't fear them physically, well, Viveka may just be the exception. A Master Vampire is extremely hard to kill but we *can* be killed, and no one knows my weaknesses like my Maker.

Amarah Rey is standing in front of me, hands on her hips, determined to get answers. I see the fire in her eyes, her stance, and her energy is like she's getting ready to go into battle. She has no idea that a battle is exactly what she needs to prepare for.

"Hello! Earth to Valmont!" Amarah Rey snaps her fingers in my face, "did you hear anything I said?"

Not a better situation. She's still only wearing her little red lace underwear and my eyes hungrily roam over her body. The action is now accompanied by memories. Memories of her body shaking underneath mine, in my hands, at my mercy.

Lips on mine, on my body.

Hands and nails scraping.

Moans and screams.

Tight and wet.

Soft skin, slicing open.

Blood dripping.

I close my eyes against the overwhelming memories which does nothing to dispel them. I force my eyes to connect with hers and challenge myself to keep them there, "if you want to have this conversation, you're going to need to get dressed. Preferably in a bloody damn potato sack."

She looks down at her body as if she's forgotten she's practically naked. A beautiful blush climbs up her cheeks and she quickly picks her dress up off the floor and shimmies into it. She sits on the couch and starts slipping on the boots, "ok, so talk to me, Valmont. What's going on?"

"I'm going to need another drink," I head to the bar and pour myself one. After thinking about what I'm about to share with Amarah Rey, I pour her one too. I head over to the couch and hand her a glass as I sit down next to her.

She takes a sip and immediately coughs, "sweet baby Jesus! What the Hell is this?"

"Mead, from my hometown. I have it imported because it brings me comfort and reminds me of who I was. Who I am. Mead used to be the only alcohol available to drink if you can imagine it. I find that nothing else quite hits the spot for me but I do agree that it's an acquired taste," I chuckle, as I see the mead already flushing Amarah Rey's cheeks. "Perhaps, no mead for you at the moment," I suggest, as I take her glass and set it on the table. "You did lose a lot of blood tonight."

"Good idea," she agrees quickly. "Exactly how old are you, Valmont? I heard you tell, what's her name? Vivian?"

"Viveka. Viveka Bolverk. And if she's here, nothing good is coming. She causes chaos and destruction everywhere she goes."

"C'mon, Valmont, she can't be *that* bad, right? I mean, she's a tiny little thing and you're like… one of the strongest and scariest people I've ever met. You're not afraid of her. Are you?"

"Her first name means war and her last name literally translates to, evildoer," I say, as I take another drink. "To say she's evil from her namesake to her core is an understatement, Amarah Rey, and you would be wise to not only fear her but stay far away from her."

"You're joking, right?"

"I would never joke about Viveka or your safety."

"Well, that's tragic and…terrifying," I'm watching her wrestle with the information and I feel like I can almost hear the gears and cogs cranking away in her brain.

"Let's circle back to her in a minute. Back to my original question, how old are you? I heard you tell… *Viveka*, that it has been a thousand years since you've seen her. That can't be right. I didn't hear that right, did I?"

I can't help but chuckle at her sweet naivety, "oh, Amarah Rey, I forget that you've lived your life as a human and you're so far from understanding what it means to be Fey. Although, you're not *just* Fey. I imagine you will live longer than all of us, but yes, you heard correctly. I am just over two thousand years old."

She's staring at me, her mouth agape, "you're being serious?"

"Quite," I nod and take another drink.

"Wow. I can't even wrap my head around that. Two thousand years! I mean, what was going on two thousand years…" she stops and stares at me. I can see the light bulb illuminate behind her eyes as she figures it out. "Your characteristics, the hair, the tattoos, the mead…" she shakes her head, "holy shit! Were you a Viking? Like from Norway?"

"Gods, no!" I scoff at the thought.

She sighs in relief, "ok, yea that would be *crazy!*"

"The Norwegian Vikings were crazed brutes. Ruthless and dangerous. They only cared about fighting and conquering, even if it was against their own people, like us. I'm from Denmark, and we were far superior in our ways and thinking, compared to the other Scandinavian Vikings, although my opinion is biased." I can't help but smirk at the complete shock on Amarah Rey's face.

"Wow. I guess that would explain why you're so confident with your sword."

"Amongst other things," I wink.

That earns me another blush, "well, I must say you've adapted extremely well. Wait, so why do you have a British accent?"

"I think we're getting distracted. Didn't you want to discuss Viveka?"

"Yes, who is she? Why is she here? And who is she to *you*?" She asks as she crosses her arms in defense.

I lift my eyebrows in surprise, "is that jealousy I'm sensing, Amarah Rey?"

"No," she says sternly, but I know she's lying. I can't help but fight an arrogant smile at the thought of her being jealous, possessive even, but she has no reason to be jealous of Viveka. Maybe once upon a time, but not anymore.

I sigh, "you may as well get comfortable. I'm about to tell you more about my past than I've ever told anyone. It's been a long time since I've re-lived these memories."

"Valmont, you don't have to if you don't want to. I know how hard it can be to face your past." She places her hand on my thigh in a gesture of comfort and support. Her eyes are pools of understanding and sympathy. It evokes feelings in me that it shouldn't.

I reach my hand out and caress her cheek with the back of my fingers. The slightest touch of my skin on hers sends a thrill through my body and stirs my desire. Now that I've had her completely, and had more than just a taste of her blood, I'm ruined in the best, and worst, possible ways. I want to give her everything. All of me. I want her to know me. *Truly*, know me. Everything I've done and everything I am. Every second of every century I've been alive and every second yet to come. They all belong to her and she doesn't even know it.

"No, it's alright. I want you to know my past and understand the threat Viveka brings." I fight to return my arm to the back of the sofa and not lose myself in her for the third time tonight. If I was anything less than a two thousand year old Master Vampire, I wouldn't be able to control myself.

"I grew up in what is now known as Copenhagen, Denmark, but back then it was just known as, Havn, meaning harbor. We were mainly a fishing and farming community. We thrived living off the land, hunting, and growing what we needed. Living off of what the Gods gave us. We kept to ourselves and were content, until we were *forced* not to be."

I'm physically sitting on the couch next to Amarah Rey, but my mind is now back in Havn, reliving my past. "The village was preparing for a fast-approaching winter, and the unusually warm autumn day prompted a last-minute hunting trip to gather more meat. My father and older brother, along with a handful of other men from the village, set off at first light. There was no way of knowing that ships from Norway had descended on us in the night. They had pulled their boats onto the land, out of sight, then surrounded us. It was madness for them to be on the water so close to winter when the waters would freeze over. It was the last thing any of us would expect."

I take another long sip of my mead, "the hunting party walked right into their trap in the woods without ever knowing they were in danger. No one came back from that trip. The rest of us in the village were just as unprepared and caught off guard when they attacked."

The chaos and screams echo in my mind from that memory. The dead bodies, the glazed over, lifeless eyes staring at me. The smoke and smell of burning flesh. The blood. Always so much blood.

"They attacked without mercy. Raping and then killing women, they killed children too, it didn't matter to them if you were a threat or not. Crazed. Brutes. No better than wild animals, bloody Hell, they were worse than wild animals because they weren't killing just to survive. They killed because they could. Because they enjoyed it. I saw it in their eyes. The excitement. The thrill. They laughed and joked with each other while my entire village was being obliterated."

Amarah Rey is sitting quietly next to me, listening to my history, with sorrow and sympathy written across her features. I meet her eyes as I'm about to admit something I'm still ashamed of to this day. I want to see her reaction. I want to see the disappointment and disgust as I admit to her that I was a coward. I was weak.

"I hid," I say, quietly. "I was a coward and I hid. But...someone found me anyway. Curled up in a dark corner, scared and crying. He was a giant of a man. He looked like a monstrous bear towering above me, blood splattered on his face and clothes. His eyes were dancing with excitement and he laughed as he said, *I'm going to enjoy killing a little coward shit like you. You're no Viking,* and then he raised his axe above his head, ready to strike, and I didn't move a muscle. I was frozen in fear, just staring up at this monster, who was getting ready to send me to the afterlife."

Amarah Rey's eyes never leave mine and I'm confused when I see no signs of disgust or disappointment. I see nothing but deep concern and sorrow for my story, for me. No pity, just...*sadness.*

"Then, out of nowhere, two ravens flew across his face, wings flapping wildly, their squawking piercing my ears, but they provided a distraction. I know they were Huggin and Muninn, Odin's ravens, and they were there to help me. To save me. I managed to scramble to the warrior, took the knife from his boot, and stabbed him between the legs. As he fell to his knees, I slit his throat. The memory of his warm blood splattering across my hand and face feels like it was just yesterday." I take a deep breath, "the ravens were just suddenly gone, as if they'd never even been there, and I had just taken a life for the first time. I was only seven."

"Valmont, I am so sorry," she whispers, as she slides closer to me and places both hands on my thigh. It isn't in a sexual way, she's providing comfort, but I barely register it, as I'm lost in my memories of the past.

I stop long enough to take another drink as the memory washes over me and then I push it away so I can continue. "They took all of the food we had stored, any gold or piece of treasure they could find and carry, and then they set fire to our crops and homes. They raided and destroyed our village for no reason. They had no cause. Those Vikings were just selfish and savage. They killed more than half of the village and we were left with mostly women and children. A few men had survived, but not many, and the ones who did survive were near death."

"When the attack was finally over, we gathered everyone inside the meeting hall. I was the only one without a single wound. Luckily, our healer survived and was able to tend to all the injuries. Once that was all done and everyone seemed to be settled, more in a daze of loss and confusion, mourning their loved ones and trying to understand what happened, we were able to discuss what needed to be done. Winter was approaching, and now, we had *nothing* to survive on. The only Blessing, if there could be one, was that we didn't have many mouths to feed. We needed to gather what we could from the land around us. We needed to fish and hunt and gather any type of plant that could either be eaten or used for medicine. Unfortunately, all of this came down to women and children to do. The oldest boy to survive was thirteen and a lot of the pressure and responsibility fell on him."

I shake my head, "can you imagine a thirteen-year-old boy now, in this day and age, going to hunt and provide for his family?" I scoff, "this new generation, all this new technology at our fingertips and convenience of cars and fast food, supermarkets, all of it has made the world soft. I admit to enjoying the many luxuries of this new world, but I've earned it, and I have never forgotten where I come from and who I am. This is why I've risen to Virtuoso when so many others fail. I've been forced, since a young age, to either be strong or die, and dying is not an option. Well, I suppose technically I did die," I chuckle.

"I love that I'm getting to learn more about you, Valmont, and again, I'm so sorry for what you had to go through when you were just a child, but what does this have to do with Viveka?"

"Patience, Amarah Rey, I'm getting to that. See, in this new world, everyone wants everything immediately. Everyone is so used to instant gratification, instant and at the touch of their fingertips, but I digress. Where was I?"

I set my empty cup on a coaster, pick up Amarah Rey's full glass, and continue. "At the direction and guidance of the few men still alive, the women and children managed to gather enough meat and supplies to get us through winter. Barely. We rationed and stretched all the food out for as long as we could. We were barely eating enough to survive, but we *did* survive by the will of Odin alone."

"When Spring finally came, the real work began. We had to start our crops from scratch, rebuild houses, and restore our food and supplies. We also had to prepare for another attack, because if they came once, and defeated us so easily, we would be targets again. We all knew it to be true. So, we worked from sunup to sundown, all of us. The men that survived started to train us in battle. I took this very seriously, as I was now the man of the house, and needed to protect my mother and younger brother and sister. So, I started training to kill at the age of eight because it was necessary. It was for our own protection. Even the women picked up shields and swords and learned how to fight."

"The first year was the hardest, of course, but every year after that it got a bit easier. We were stronger and slowly rebuilding our lives and our village. The fighting and hunting seemed to come naturally to me. I had a way with a blade that was unmatched. As if it was just a part of me and always had been. I don't know why, but I knew I had been chosen by Odin the day His ravens saved me. I felt His spirit all around me. Inside me. Giving my strength. As I grew older and stronger, my people started to look to me for guidance and answers. I had ambitions of traveling across the waters to trade and open our port to others as well. We needed more people in our village, we needed numbers if we were going to continue to survive and thrive."

"We were the first Vikings to offer trade and became very successful with our Viking friends up North in Sweden and even Finland. We even traded some with the German port near us but I refused to trade with the Vikings of Norway. The anger in my blood for them was unrelenting and blood calls for blood. When our village was finally flourishing again, many, many years later, I knew in my heart, that I would never be able to move on until I made my way to Norway and made them pay for what they had done to us."

"And so, I did. I gathered warriors, men, and women, we were also the first Vikings to let our women fight in battle by the way, and together, we attacked the people who attacked us. We destroyed with a vengeance that was led by my sword. I was furious and bloodthirsty and I killed with no mercy and no guilt in my heart. I killed women and children in my first ever taste of battle. I was numb to the killing. It didn't excite me. The revenge didn't fulfill me. I was an empty vessel. A weapon of destruction and I was dangerous because of it."

"We continued raiding every village up and down the coast of Norway until there was nothing left. I was untouchable in battle, as if I was being protected by Odin himself. No one ever came close to killing me. I was unstoppable and I relished in the power. I enjoyed the way people spoke of me and looked at me in awe and fear alike. I became a legend in my own right. We settled in Norway and I somehow became the ruler of all of Denmark and Norway at the age of twenty-five."

"Wow, Valmont, I can't even imagine what you've been through and all that you've seen and done in your lifetime. It's actually really hard to wrap my head around."

"Yes," I nod, "I've done it all and seen it all. Nothing surprises me anymore, but then came you, Amarah Rey."

She laughs, nervously, "what do you mean?"

I ignore her question, "I was just getting to the good part, shall I continue?"

She nods and sits back on the couch getting more comfortable. "As you can imagine, I was very popular as the ruler of these lands. Other villages came to trade at our ports just to get the chance to meet me. Others brought gifts and offerings of all kinds, mainly daughters," I smirk, as what I say registers with Amarah Rey and I watch her eyes widen.

"Oh," she whispers.

"Potential brides were constantly being thrown at me. Every village wanted their chance at being connected to me. Don't get me wrong, I thoroughly enjoyed the offerings," I smile, wickedly.

Amarah Rey crosses her arms and looks upset, "I'm sure you did." The thought of her being jealous over me is exhilarating. I almost want to delve into some details, just to see exactly how jealous she is, but I don't.

"Oh, aye, but I never found any of them compelling enough to marry. Until *she* walked into my life." My humor dies as I relive the memory.

"Viveka."

"Yes, Viveka. She was stunning and unlike any other woman I had ever met. She wasn't a Viking woman, she was so much more. It's really hard to explain, but...she was just..." I'm grasping for words to try and describe her but nothing seems fitting. "She was just *extraordinary*. She had this otherworldly energy about her, this confidence that dazzled like a light through the darkness. And if you weren't careful, it would blind you."

"Let me guess, you were blinded."

I nod my head and sigh heavily taking another long sip of mead, "She claimed to be Freya, the Goddess of War, and that she had come to help me. She stroked my ego, told me how powerful and strong I was, but that she was here to help me be even more. More than just a man. She claimed that with her help I could become more than just a ruler of these two lands, I could be King of Norway, Denmark, and Sweden. She even talked about sailing across the sea further than anyone had ever gone and conquering lands no other Viking has ever even seen. These lands are what you now know as the United Kingdom."

I laugh, tiredly, "of course, I believed her. I believed that Odin had been with me since the day I killed that man when I was seven. I believed that he had sent his Goddess of War to guide me in becoming the most powerful Viking that ever lived. She told me that she had to drain my body of my weak, human blood, and replace it with her blood, the blood of the Gods. Only then could I become something more. Only then could I also lay with her and have her body. Gods, I was a fool. A horny, ignorant fool."

"She was just a Vampire and she wanted to turn you,"

Amarah Rey whispers.

"Yes. I had no idea what a Vampire even was. She was strong, stronger than any mortal man, and she could appear and disappear as if by magic. I was certain she was who she said she was. A Goddess. And so, as you can guess, I let her bite me. I let her drain me of all of my blood, and I was in ecstasy the entire time she killed me. My heart rate slowed, but before my heart gave its last beat in my chest, she poured her blood into my mouth and down my throat. I felt my heart take one final, desperate thump in my chest before her blood smothered it. Her blood took over my body, giving me life in a whole new way."

"It was excruciating, those first few months as a new Vampire. The hunger is unlike anything I've ever experienced before or since. I was no better than the savage Vikings who had attacked us, except now, I had the love for battle and spilling blood just as much as I had for drinking it. I became terrifying. I became an unstoppable monster. And Viveka was by my side the entire time, manipulating and controlling me. See, she was drawn to my power and strength as a mortal. She knew I would be a hundred times more powerful as a Vampire, even before I ascended to Virtuoso. That's what she wanted and I happily gave it to her. I was addicted to her. I would do anything for her and, I would learn much later, that I couldn't betray her, even if I wanted to."

"Amarah Rey, Viveka has only ever been drawn to one thing. Power. She wants it, and most importantly, she wants to control it. She doesn't care about anything else. She loves to create chaos and fear everywhere she goes. It's the only thing that thrills her after all the centuries she's been alive. She's extremely dangerous, not only because she's powerful, but because she has no rules. She has no moral code whatsoever. She does what she wants, when she wants, with no regard to anything or anyone in her way. And her being here now…" I trail off and slam the rest of the mead not wanting to finish the thought.

"You don't think it's a coincidence that she's here now, do you?" Amarah Rey asked.

"I'm afraid not."

"Is she here for your power? Now that you're a Master Vampire?"

I close my eyes and sigh, "no. When I became a Master, I broke any hold she had over me. That's the only way for any Vampire to break a hold from their Maker. Not many Vampires can become Masters, so most Vampires live their lives devoted to their Maker. No, she has no control over me now. At least not in the sense you're thinking."

"Then what control does she have over you?"

"You, Amarah Rey. I believe she is here for you."

Amarah: Always Another Threat

I heard what Valmont said but it takes a minute for his words to settle within me. It doesn't help that my brain is still a bit fuzzy around the edges from the alcohol, blood loss, and mind-blowing orgasms. A Vampire's bite might be a lot of deliciously devious things but it's also a hindrance. And in my life, that's not a good thing.

"Wait, what?" I ask, taken aback, as his words finally hit me. "Why on Earth would she be here for *me*?"

Valmont lifts an eyebrow and looks at me as if saying, *seriously*?

"I'm serious. Why would she be here for me? As far as anyone else knows, I'm just another member of the Müstik Family. I'm just Fey. Sure, I'm related to the Queen but that doesn't give me any power."

"Well, you and I both know that you are *so* much more than *just* Fey, and we must keep it that way. No doubt Viveka has heard about you and the astonishing things you've done. Like what you did at the Fire Fey's home when you killed all those demons. That was your *Angel* power, Amarah Rey, not Fey magic. And people gossip. People love to talk about things they cannot explain and you and I both know how gossip ends up. Every event ends up being more elaborate and exaggerated than the truth. However, in your case, all the exaggerated gossip is still not even close to the truth."

"Yeah, but...it still doesn't make sense. She didn't act like she knew who I was earlier. And you were just playing me off as some damn...*floozy*! Thank you very much for that by the way," I say, sarcastically.

"I did that for your safety, Amarah Rey!" His voice is angry and agitated.

"I get why you did what you did, but that doesn't mean I have to like it," I grumble.

He looks at me and his turquoise eyes burn into mine. I've never seen such emotion in his eyes but it isn't just fear. His voice is soft when he speaks again, "if she even thinks for a second that you mean *anything* to me...fuck!" He grabs the two glasses off the table and quickly walks back over to the bar. His body is tense and not like the relaxed, dangerous feline he usually exudes. He's scared.

"Under no circumstances can Viveka find out your true identity and what you're truly capable of. Bloody Hell, do *you* even know what you're capable of?" He looks back at me but he doesn't wait for me to respond. "I don't want you alone. Not until Viveka leaves and is no longer a threat. You can move into the Penthouse and a bodyguard will be with you at all times. Only those that I trust with my life."

Now it's my turn to be angry, "what?! You can't be serious?!" I stand up and cross my arms over my stomach, "I think you're forgetting that I *am* powerful and I *am* capable of protecting myself, Valmont. I don't need to be locked up and I sure as Hell don't need a babysitter."

"For all the Gods' sakes, Amarah Rey, I love your fighting spirit, truly, but do not fight me on this! You do not know Viveka as I do. You do not know how twisted and demented she is. You don't want her anywhere near you and you sure as bloody Hell don't want her gaining any type of control over you."

"The only way she could control me is if she turned me into a Vampire and, trust me, that's never going to happen," I scoff.

I gasp as he's suddenly standing in front of me. I never even saw him move. "And what about earlier tonight? You couldn't even protect yourself against the Vampire you let bite you! *I* had to save you! What makes you think you could handle yourself against the most powerful Vampire I've ever known?"

"I didn't need saving, Valmont! You were just jealous! I would have..."

"Was I?" He interrupts me and takes the last step towards me, putting our bodies touching and I have to crane my neck back to keep eye contact. "Is that what you think?" He grabs my chin and holds my head still as he leans closer to me. "That I was jealous of a lowly, weak Vampire?"

"Yes," I whisper.

It's hard to speak with my throat stretched out at such a hard angle and his body against mine brings my breaths faster. My eyes drop to his lips, I can smell the sweet honey mead on his breath and I desperately want to taste it off his tongue. I want to feel his hands on my body again. My blood seems to be screaming in my veins, begging to be freed.

"Don't fool yourself, Aamrah Rey." He keeps leaning closer until his words are whispered against my lips, "it is you who is addicted to me. I am Virtuoso. I'm always in control, I do everything for a reason, and I am jealous of no one."

He lets me go so quickly I stumble into the empty air where he had just been standing. "You are not only in my Territory but you are my ally. I keep my people safe and you are no different. I would never ask you not to fight or defend yourself but I refuse to allow you to do it recklessly. You will do this and allow me to *help* protect you until the threat passes. It is my duty and something I take very seriously. Nothing else. Are we clear?"

He speaks with his back to me as he pours himself another drink. I'm still reeling from his body being pressed to mine and his words that cut into my pride.

It is you who is addicted to me.

His words settle in my stomach and the hurt and rejection help fuel my fire. I won't be that weak, pathetic woman. I won't be the *floozy* I had just accused him of treating me as. I claim to be powerful and strong and I need to act like it. Walk the walk.

I head to the door, "fine. I'll stay here. I'll accept your protection, but I'm not going to be locked up day and night. If that means you assign me a bodyguard, so be it, but I plan on continuing my training with Prince Emrick. I need an outlet and I desperately need to hit something," I say, as I open the door and shut it loudly behind me.

I storm through the casino shaking my head and muttering to myself how ridiculous this all is, but if he wants to put me up in a luxury Penthouse, where I'll have everything I want at my fingertips, so be it. I can live with being spoiled for a couple of days. It'll be like a stay-cation.

"At least I'll get to use that bathtub," I mutter to myself, as I head outside and towards my car.

As soon as I step through the doors, the cool night air finds every inch of exposed skin and makes me shiver. I feel the weather starting to turn the corner from Fall into Winter and I'm not ready for it. I'm never ready for the coldness of Winter and even more so now. Now that I'll be alone, again, with nothing to keep me warm except my darkness. Maybe that will be enough this time around since I'm choosing to embrace it. I can only hope.

As soon as Josh sees me, he runs over to my Camaro and holds the door open for me, dangling the key fob in front of him, head bowed, not making eye contact. Guess I rattled him pretty hard earlier. I smirk at the memory of it, but I'm in no mood to flirt now.

"Thanks, Josh," I say, as I take the key fob from him and slide into the driver's seat without another word or look.

"Drive safely, Miss Andrews," he says, eyes still on the ground, as he shuts the door and practically runs away from me.

I sigh as I start the car thinking about everything that's just happened. Now that I'm out of Valmont's vicinity, I feel a pang of emptiness and betrayal in my chest.

Logan.

Always Logan.

I thought that perhaps by getting under Valmont it would help me get over Logan, but everywhere I go, there he is. The Texas-size hole in my heart is a constant reminder of what I had but can no longer have. Not to mention he moved on quite quickly. I grit my teeth at the memory of her hands on him.

"Am I ever going to escape him?" I say, to the empty air of the car.

My only reprieve from the constant pain in my chest and hurtful memories has been in the afterglow of sex with Valmont. The high from his bite obliterates every thought in my mind. That feeling of complete emptiness and weightlessness is a gift in itself. Sitting here, alone in my car with nothing but my own destructive thoughts and feelings, I desperately want the reprieve again. My body craves the bite and my mind craves the freedom only Valmont can give.

It is you who is addicted to me.

"Fucking arrogant prick, piece of..."

The passenger door opens and a stranger slides into the

seat next to me. I have my dagger out and pressed against his chest, right above his heart, before his ass completely feels the seat beneath him.

"Who the fuck are you?"

He holds his hands up in surrender, "well, this is awkward. I don't normally get this kind of reaction until after the first date." His words are light, but his brows are furrowed, and his grey eyes are focused on the dagger drawing a small pool of blood onto his light-blue t-shirt.

"Who the fuck are you?" I repeat. "And what the fuck are you doing in my car?"

"Apologies," he reluctantly pulls his eyes from the dagger and extends his hand out in greeting. "Alistair Carmichael, at your service."

I ignore his outstretched hand, keeping my eyes locked on his body for any movement, and keeping pressure on the dagger.

His grey eyes lock on mine and they start to shine ever so slightly, "please remove the dagger, you've quite ruined my shirt already, harm done."

I push the blade in just a bit harder but he doesn't even wince. "I don't know you, Alistair. I will only ask one more time, why are you in my car?"

"Isn't it obvious?" He takes his offered hand back and rubs his beard covered jaw, "Valmont sent me to protect you. Although you seem quite capable of handling yourself," his eyes move to the dagger again.

"I told him I don't need a babysitter," I growl out in frustration.

"Are you so sure about that?" His face is menacing as he raises his hand, places it on top of mine, and starts to push the dagger further into his chest. It's my turn to be caught off guard, as I struggle against his strength, trying not to hurt him now.

"You see, your little dagger can't hurt me. It might be a great defense against a human, but a human I'm not, and neither are Valmont's guests." The dagger is now over an inch deep in his chest. "You may have some abilities against us, which I wasn't sure I believed until now, but those abilities are mere child's play compared to what you would be up against. Valmont is insistent on your protection, so you're stuck with me until he says otherwise. Capeesh?"

I pull my gaze away from the dagger in his chest, meet his cold, grey eyes, and nod. Alistair slowly pulls the dagger out of his chest and I watch as the wound heals almost instantly, the only sign of a wound is the bloody, torn shirt.

"Now, shall we try this again?" Alistair runs his hands through his light-brown hair, brushing it back. It's just long enough to curl under his ears and stay there. Then he moves his hand to straighten his, now ruined t-shirt, before he looks up at me. He offers his hand again, "I'm Alistair Carmichael, at your service."

Still, in a slight shock, I manage to take his hand in mine and give it a shake, "Amarah Rey Andrews."

A dazzling smile emerged from underneath the fearsome look the Vampire had just been giving me, not enough to flash his fangs, and it changes his entire look and demeanor. His scruffy and manly appearance somehow softens and makes him look almost...*harmless*. His smile is unarming and the drastic change is unnerving.

Dangerous. Everyone around me is just plain scary and dangerous.

"Amarah! I've heard such great things about you and it's my absolute honor to meet you and protect you. Let's be off, shall we? We need to be back here before sunrise if you don't mind."

I pull my still reeling mind back to my present reality and my body goes into autopilot as I buckle myself in, put the car in drive, and pull out of the casino. I desperately wish that Logan was with me or at least waiting for me at home. Although I know Alistair can and will protect me at Valmont's order, I don't know him, and I sure as Hell don't trust him. I find myself wondering for the millionth time.

How did this become my life?

Logan: Losing Control

Impossible by Manafest

"This is such a fucking waste of time," I frustratingly run my hand through my hair, as I pace the never-ending, winding, labyrinth of tunnels. "There's no sign that Aralyn was ever here. No scent. No tracks. I mean, look at the cobwebs strewn across here," I wave my arms in the air. "It's clear no one has passed this way in a very long time."

"Well, maybe she used another tunnel? It's not like she doesn't have several to choose from. This place is insane. Not to mention a bit creepy," Atreya admits, as she points her flashlight into the surrounding darkness, rubbing her hands up and down her arms.

I shake my head, trying to clear my mind and stay on task. Amarah's scene at the meeting is replaying over and over in my mind. This isn't her. She's still hurting and I don't know how to help her. How to get to her. If she refuses to open our connection ever again...I don't want to think about that possibility. Her words echo in my mind on repeat.

You will never *feel that connection again. You will* never *feel that connection again. You will* never *feel that connection again.*

I don't know how she's managing to be so strong and keep the block in place. Just thinking about never feeling our connection again, our bond, is enough to drive me insane. Fuck! And now this useless manhunt for Aralyn. How do you track someone who was never here? I mean, ok, the Queen saw her but other than that, there's no sign of her, and she didn't use these tunnels. Between seeing Amarah, barely able to touch her when I want her so greedily, and this stupid hunt, I can feel my anger boiling under the surface.

"Ahhhh!" I let my anger out of my chest and send my fist flying into the hard-packed dirt wall with all I have. All of the pent-up rage of my past flooding back like a hurricane slamming into me.

There's a burst of blue light as my fist lands, a boom reverberates off the walls and echoes eerily through the tunnels, for what seems like miles. I hear a scream, a harsh thud, and a grunt of pain. I look over my shoulder to find Atreya laying in a heap on the floor.

Forty feet away.

I rush over to her and kneel beside her. I reach out to help her sit up. Her skin is ice cold.

"Jesus," I whisper, "are you alright? I didn't mean to...I don't know what happened," I swallow my anger and uncertainty in a painful gulp.

She groans and slowly lifts her head, "son of a bitch that hurt. It felt like blades of ice slamming into my body. What was that?"

"I'm sorry. I've never done anything like that before," my voice is steady but my mind is panicking. I remember what happened at Amarah's, not long ago, when I left frozen fist imprints in her door. I have no idea what's happening to me and I don't like not being in control. And right now, I'm not in control of one fucking thing! "Well, I mean, I don't know what's happening with my power. It's never been like this before."

"I've always sensed something different about you. Something I've never sensed on any other Werewolf. Did I just experience what I was sensing?" Atreya asks, as she sits up straighter and rubs the back of her head.

"Are you sure that you're ok?" I ask, still kneeling beside her and looking for any visible injuries.

"I've been thrown around in fights before, I'll be ok as far as that's concerned. Nothing's broken. I just feel...*cold*. Like my blood is going to freeze solid in my veins at any second and my heart is going to stop beating as it's being encased in an ice tomb," her body shivers violently. It's...*terrifying*." She looks up at me and I see something in her eyes I've never seen in all the time we've trained on the mats together. Fear.

"You're scared of me," I whisper, as I pull back and sit on my heel, giving her space.

She scoffs, "uhhhh, yeah, but I'm not scared of *you,* I am a little bit scared of what you just did though. What was that?"

I run my hand through my hair, frustrated and just as confused as Atreya. I sigh, "I was given a Fey life-force a long time ago." I let myself get lost in the memory of Analise. Reliving that awful moment that terrorized me for centuries.

Until Amarah.

"As far as I know, it only gives me some power over the elements, like all the Fey from the Müstik Family have. I'm the only non-Fey to ever have a Fey life-force given to me, so I'm kind of like a science experiment. No one knows what I am or what will happen. The life force seems to give me a small portion of their power, but it also makes me stronger, faster, harder to hurt." I shrug, "I've honestly never felt it physically until I met Amarah. It sort of...came to life when I met her, but still, it's never reacted like this before. I don't know what's happening."

The sound of chattering teeth brings me back to reality.

"Atreya!"

She's shaking uncontrollably, eyes closed and unresponsive. I gently tap her cheek, "Atreya, open your eyes. Come on, stay with me." Nothing.

"Fuck," I quickly pulled my shirt off and struggle to get hers off, too. Once I have it off, I scoop her up in my arms, hold her as close to my chest as I can, and then cover her with the discarded shirts. I call on my Wolf, using my Wolf eyes so I can run as fast as I can through the dark tunnels, back to Headquarters, and pray that my body heat will start to warm her up. Werewolves are hot-blooded creatures. We don't do well when our internal temperature falls, which very rarely happens.

I'm yelling as I run and approach an opening into the inner, used tunnels of Headquarters. "Healer! I need a Healer!"

Ana comes running to me as I storm into the throne room. "Logan! I'm here. What's wrong?"

"I...I..." I struggle to explain and to believe that *I* did this. I don't know how to explain it or what to think. I stare at Atreya's face pressed against my chest. Her entire body is convulsing and her face is pinched in pain.

"Logan," Ana grabs my face and makes me look at her. "Focus. Tell me what happened so I can help her."

"I honestly don't know. My power," I shake my head. "It was my power but I don't know how...please, we need to get her warmed up. She is freezing from the inside out."

"Get her to Amarah's room. Quickly!"

We dash across the throne room and into the archway on the other side that leads to the rooms. Ana is leading the way and opens the door for me as we rush through.

"Lay her on the bed and help me get her shoes and jeans off. We need to get her into the hot spring."

I do as I'm told and we quickly get her shoes off. Even

unconscious, Atreya's body wants to curl in on itself and gather as much heat into her center as she can. It takes a lot of careful strength, holding her down, before we wrangle the jeans off her spasming body.

"You too now, quickly!" Ana remains calm but her voice is urgent and I know she's just as worried as I am.

"Wait, what? You want me to..."

"You want to put her in a deep pool of water by herself, while she's unconscious?" Ana puts her hands on her hips and glares at me as if I'm stupid. At this moment, I feel stupid. I can't think past what I've done.

Without any further arguing or hesitation, I strip down to my briefs, pick her up again, and rush into the bathroom. I quickly step into the natural spring that also acts as a bathtub for this bathroom. The water is hot, almost too hot, but I ignore the shock and sting of it against my skin and quickly lower myself and Atreya into its healing depths. She lets out a whimper as we settle into the hot water.

I keep her in my lap, cradled against my chest, her body is still shivering violently as I whisper comforting words to her to try and ease her mind. "I know you can hear my Atreya, don't worry, you're going to be just fine. We just need to get you warmed up again, that's all. Don't worry, just relax and let your body heal. Don't fight it. I'm here with you. You're safe."

My whispers slowly fade as I lose myself in my racing thoughts and try to understand what's happened. My power has been more alive since meeting Amarah but it's never been so...*physical.* I've never seen it leave my body before, much less, lash out and attack. It feels alive. Powerful. *Dangerous.* This is the second time I've seen my power solidify instead of just being inside of me. Why now? What's different? Is it my anger or something else affecting it? I close my eyes and lean my head back, willing it all to make sense.

"Logan."

I feel a hand on my shoulder, gently shaking me. I open my eyes and see that Atreya is still unconscious in my arms, but she's no longer shaking, and her face is no longer pinched with pain. It looks like she's just sleeping.

I sigh and look up at Ana, "I must have fallen asleep. How long have we been in here?"

"Just about fifteen minutes or so. The spring has soothing and healing properties in addition to its warmth. Her outside body temperature is almost back to normal, you can bring her out now but she should remain bundled up in blankets just to be safe. Come, let's get her dry and into bed."

After some struggling, we're both as dry as we were going to get. Ana has removed the rest of her wet clothing and tucked her into a pile of cozy covers, as I remain sitting next to her on the bed.

"She's doing much better, but..." she shakes her head and I see the worry etched in her eyes and face. "Her skin is warm but I don't know what's going on inside of her body. Her still being unconscious worries me. Logan, what happened?"

I stand on the opposite side of the bed, in nothing but a towel wrapped around my waist. Now that most of the danger around Atreya's condition has passed, I suddenly feel uncomfortable being so exposed to the Queen.

I clear my throat and meet her questioning gaze. I shake my head as I try to put into words what happened, "honestly, I'm not sure. We were searching the tunnels and I got frustrated when we kept coming up empty, tunnel after tunnel, and then what happened in the meeting with Amarah..." I run a hand through my hair and let out a heavy sigh, "I just...*burst*. My anger came out physically and this is what happened. Ana, I don't know what's going on. I've never seen my power do anything like this before. Do you have any experience with this?"

Ana shakes her head, "no, I'm sorry. I've never seen Fey

power do anything like this before. I've never seen anything outside of element manipulation, control, and healing. I suppose our power for healing could be used to hurt instead but I've never seen it done. Then again, no other non-Fey has ever had Fey power so…" she shrugs.

I scrub my face in frustration, "so I'm an anomaly. I'm just stuck trying to figure it out as I go and hope I don't do something I can't take back." I look down at Atreya, she looks peaceful now and I'm grateful for that, but I need her to wake up and tell me she's ok. I need to know there's no internal or permanent damage. "Ana, if she had been human…"

"She's not. And she's going to be fine. Don't go there, Logan, it won't do you or anyone a bit of good. We'll figure this out together but right now, those thoughts won't help you or Atreya."

I nod but don't meet her eyes. I just keep staring at Atreya, willing her to open her eyes.

"I need to go take care of some things but you should stay with her. I know you've been a Lone Wolf for a long time, so you're used to being alone, but Atreya isn't. She's used to Pack life and she needs that comfort right now. Comfort you can provide her. Stay with her, hold her, as much skin on skin as you can manage."

"I…"

She quickly holds up her hand to stop any of my protests, "it's not about anything sexual, just physical. Keep her body heat up and help remind her of home, family. Wolves are Pack animals and need the comfort of other Wolves in times of healing. You know this," she lectures.

I just nod my head again in understanding. I know she's right. Even though I've been on my own for centuries, I've never stopped longing for the feeling of being back with my Pack. My family. It's a hole in my soul and an ache in my body that only ever abates when I'm with Amarah. My chosen family. My chosen mate. I feel the emptiness and loneliness now more than ever.

"When she wakes up, have her drink that," she points to a thermos sitting on the bedside table.

I nod again and Ana seems satisfied that I'll do what needs to be done. When the door quietly clicks closed behind her, I let the towel drop to the floor and I climb under the covers, pulling Atreya's naked body against mine. A part of me protests because this isn't the body I'm familiar with. This isn't the body that fits perfectly into mine. This isn't the body that I *want* to hold. But another part of me welcomes her Werewolf energy. I can't help that it stirs memories and feelings of home in a way that I haven't felt in a long time.

But the piece of me that accepts Amarah as home, doesn't like this one bit, and a chill of guilt runs down my spine. There has to be something I can do, some way that I can reach her. But what? How? I reach for my phone that's sitting on the nightstand where I left it. I can't let Amarah think I've stopped fighting for us. I send her a song that will tell her exactly what I need to say.

Spotify Link: Gotta Be A Way by Chase Matthew

I need to get through to her because I can't live without her. Look at what it's already doing to me? I can feel my frustration and anger rising at just the thought of losing Amarah for good. What if...no, I quickly shut out the worst-case scenarios and focus on the warmth emanating from Atreya. She needs me right now. She needs me to help her heal, and my Fey power isn't what she needs. No, it's the reason we're even here in the first place. She needs me to be the Werewolf I am and that's the least I can do for her now. I swallow my rising anger, slowly relax around Atreya's body, listening to her steady breathing, and let sleep gradually pull me under.

Amarah: Will The Pain Ever End?

Bruises by Lewis Capaldi

The ride to my house with Alistair takes little participation on my part. He can make conversation out of thin air, literally. No really, he's jumped from the air quality in the city, to a billboard he saw an advertisement for, to vehicles and license plates and places. He loves to hear himself talk and it seems impossible for him to sit in silence for even a second.

"You're lucky to live this close to the mountains. Do you go hiking often?"

"No."

"Why not? You should take advantage of your backyard! Do you not like hiking or the outdoors? Or is it physical activity you don't like?"

I sigh, "I like the outdoors and physical activity just fine. I've just been a little preoccupied with more pressing matters besides *hiking*."

He rakes his eyes over me, "uh-huh. Pressing matters like driving my Master to kill another Vampire or banging his brains out maybe or...?"

"Ok!" I yell more forcefully than I intend. I can't stop the heat that creeps up from the pit of my stomach, up my neck, and into my cheeks with a force that feels like my head is about to pop off my body. My palm then ignites for another furious second, adding to my discomfort, as I pull into my driveway with a Vampire in my car. At least I know the wards really do work. I put the car in park, rest my head against the headrest and close my eyes, getting control over myself before I turn and look at Alistair.

He's completely relaxed in the seat, as if he's been in it a hundred times before. His face betrays nothing, no emotion, as he waits patiently for me to speak. These damn ancient-ass men and their infuriating self-control! It not only pisses me off, but makes me feel so young and inexperienced compared to them, which makes me feel insecure and that just leads back to pissing me off!

I take a deep breath before I ask the question I've been dreading, "does everyone know?"

"Darling, you've been the talk of the night!"

"But why? I'm sure I'm not the first girl Valmont has given his," I clear my throat, suddenly struggling to get the words out to have this conversation, "…*attention* to."

"God, no! Valmont can have any girl he wants, when he wants her, and she'll be forever happy with the slightest scrap of attention he chooses to give her."

"Great. That's just…great, thanks. That made me feel a whole lot better about myself."

"Hey, you asked, and I run on a brutally honest policy. So, if you don't truly want to hear the truth, darling, don't bring your questions to me."

I nod, "good to know." I reach for the door handle so I can run away from this conversation, and the entire night for that matter, as fast as I can when his next words stop me.

"But… I've never seen Valmont kill for *any* woman before. None of the women he takes to his bed mean a damn thing to him.

He would just as quickly snap their neck than kill one of his Vampires." He holds up his hand as if he knows I'm about to spew my outrage at the thought of Valmont killing innocent women. "I'm not saying he goes around just killing women, or any humans for that matter, I'm just using it for context. He doesn't act on anything more than a purely physical need with women. I've never seen him do what he did tonight. Not to mention the way he claimed you as his, loud and clear, and made sure everyone," it's his turn to clear his throat, "saw it."

I can't help the damn blush that erupts again at the thought of what I let Valmont do. The fact that people *did* see. Away from Valmont's intoxicating presence, and left completely sober, I *am* mortified! I can't believe that my hurt about Logan's betrayal let me go that far. The alcohol didn't help, but at the end of the day, I have to take responsibility for my reckless and completely idiotic choices.

"Oh my God," I mutter through my hands as I hide my embarrassment. "What the Hell did I do?"

"Oh please," Alistair laughs, trying to lighten the mood. "No one at those parties is innocent. Those parties are exactly about what you and Valmont did together. No one is going to be thinking twice about that. What I don't understand is why he killed one of our own for barely touching you. And when he called me into his office to give me this position of guarding you, he was overly passionate and adamant about your safety. I'm sure you figured out that if I'm here with you, Valmont trusts me beyond a shadow of a doubt. He trusts me with his business, with his life, and apparently with what's most precious to him."

I just stare blankly at him as he keeps delivering insight into the mysterious Valmont.

"You," he says seriously.

My head is reeling at everything Alistair is saying but then Valmont's harsh words come back to sober me up yet again.

It is you who is addicted to me.

I laugh, nervously, "I'm pretty sure you're deeply mistaken with that truth. I'm just his ally, that's why he wants to keep me safe."

He points to himself, "brutal honesty, remember? You can lie to yourself and Valmont can try and lie or try and hide it, but it's obvious to those that are paying attention, at *that* is a truth that scares me. Who else has figured out what I have? Who else has deciphered this little bit of information, and more importantly, why? Why are you so important to him?"

He's staring at me now with those intelligent grey eyes, that see and know too much, waiting for an explanation. I try to clear my face of any thoughts or emotions the best I can. And with what I hope is a nonchalant attitude, I say, "I have no idea what you mean."

"You know, you can't lie to any Vampire that's older than a few months, and I'm far beyond a few *centuries.* I can hear your heart speed up because you're nervous, I can smell the sweat that's threatening to break out of your pores, and I can just generally sense when your energy changes from one emotion to another. So, shall we try again?"

I look up to the roof of the car, "seriously, how am I always so out of my league with everyone around me?" I look back at Alistair, "you want an honest answer?"

"Always."

"Ask Valmont." I reach for the door handle again, and again, his words stop me.

"Amarah."

I go still but I don't take my hand off the handle and I don't turn towards him.

"Be careful. I know Valmont puts your safety as a high priority but he is my Valmistaja, and I put his safety as a high priority. The two of you together is a dangerous thing and he's not entirely safe when he's with you."

Now he has my attention and I turn to face him, offended, and more confused than ever. "I would *never* hurt Valmont."

"Not intentionally or even knowingly, I'm sure. But he's distracted beyond all senses when he's with you for reasons I can't understand."

"And I don't understand what you're saying."

He sighs, heavily, "Valmont should never have been taken by surprise by Viveka's arrival. He should have sensed someone as powerful as her the *second* she crossed into his territory. He should have sensed the potential threat in an instant and sent someone to look into it immediately. One of the deadliest and most powerful Vampires, Viveka Bolverk, walked right up to his doorstep, didn't even bother to knock, and waltzed right in as if she owned the place, with no opposition. No doubt this is something she noticed and is now wondering how weak Valmont is. No doubt she's wondering what that weakness is, how to use it against him to gain an advantage, and how to utterly destroy everything he's built because that is what she does."

I'm frozen in shock at his admission. I know I'm a danger to those around me because of the demons, and Aralyn, trying to get to me, it only makes sense that I'm now a danger to the one person I thought could handle me and the threats that come along with me. But apparently, I'm a danger to every single person in my life. No one is safe around me and the only thing I can do is remove myself from as many people and situations as I can. The thought of now having to give up Valmont, his companionship that's kept me going through losing Andre and Logan. His bite that's given me my only true escape from my mind and pain. My only sense of peace, no matter how fleeting, is now being taken away from me too. Why am I cursed? Why am I forced to constantly lose people?

My mother was taken from me before I ever got the chance

to know her.

Andre, whose death is on my hands.

Logan, who is the love of my life.

And now, Valmont.

It's too much. It's too unfair and I'm not strong enough to let them all go. I'm not strong enough to live this long life, alone. This new revelation sits like a weight on my chest. My heart can't possibly break any more than it already has, and yet, I feel it splintering inside my chest.

"I didn't know," is all I can whisper, as a tear falls down my cheek.

"Well, at least now you do and you can make your decisions accordingly."

I nod as I sniff to keep my nose from running and wipe at my face. "I'm just going to grab a few things, I won't be long," I say, as I finally push the door open, and escape Alistair's brutal revelations and astute gaze.

Alistair has been blabbing his head off for the last ten minutes as if nothing has changed. As if he hasn't just dropped a bomb, several bombs actually, on me tonight. I hear him making noises in the passenger seat, but I can't decipher a word he's saying, much less put together his sentences or actively participate in the conversation.

My mind is still stuck on the fact that Valmont put himself in danger because of me. I don't know if he did it knowing the consequences and doing it anyway, or if he was just as clueless as I was. Either way, I can't let him compromise himself like that again, which means, we can't be alone together. According to Valmont, I'm the one who is addicted to him, not the other way around. Maybe he did know exactly what he was doing and maybe he only acted surprised to see Viveka? Maybe this is all a ploy on his part somehow? A way to give Viveka false confidence to lower her own defenses?

But the look in his eyes when we were together. I can't get the emotion I saw in them out of my head. I thought I saw something…*more*, in his eyes tonight. Hell, maybe I saw what I wanted to see, to make myself feel better about my fucked up decision. Maybe I'm lying to myself to ignore the truth of what actually went down.

A revenge fuck for Logan moving on so quickly. I used Valmont for selfish reasons and now I'm trying to make something out of nothing. I used him to try and make myself feel better. But the truth of it all? With his mind-numbing bite out of my system, I feel worse than I've ever felt. I feel like I've fallen so far and so low that there's no way I'll ever climb out of this hole I've dug.

I pull into a parking spot at Headquarters. It's eerie how quiet a city of almost six hundred thousand people can become in the sleeping hours of the morning. It's just past 4:30 a.m., which is so far past my usual bedtime, I'm shocked I'm still functioning. The exhaustion is only adding to the effects of this crazy, long, impossible night. I'm drained physically and mentally, emotionally I'm a wreck, even with bottling it all up the best I can, and my body aches from the literal pounding it took against the glass.

I put the car in park but leave it running, "I'll be right back."

"I'm going with you," Alistair counters.

"I need you to stay here and watch Griffin," at the sound of his name, my little dog lifts his head off my lap to look at me.

"Valmont put me in charge of your safety tonight, Amarah, I'm not going to fail him. It's not an option."

"And you won't. This is Headquarters, and after the attack, trust me, it's safer than it's ever been. Plus, I've got both daggers with me and I'm not exactly helpless. I do have power to protect myself which everyone seems to forget. I'll be fine."

I open the car door and slide out from under Griffin, leaving him staring up at me, waiting for me to say something he understands. If I'm going to be living at the casino for a while, there is no way I'm leaving Griffin. He's the only thing with a beating heart that I have left to love and that loves me back. I need him with me now more than ever.

"Amarah…"

"Please, just…stay here. The sooner we stop arguing the sooner I'll be back and get you back to the casino. I just need to find Prince Emrick. I won't be long."

Alistair peers out the window into the night sky. It's still pitch-black and the stars that we can see through the pollution of the city are bright and strong.

"Sunrise is still at least three hours away," he says, almost to himself. "But please hurry, Amarah, I need to be back to the casino quickly. My body starts to weaken once I feel dawn approaching and I don't want to take any chances."

"So, the sun really is a weakness for you guys then? Not just direct sunlight but just the act of daylight itself?" I'm intrigued.

I don't know much about the Vampires, their different strengths and weaknesses. There are moments, like these, that are so eye-opening and sobering. Moments that show just how ignorant and selfish I am. I should be immersing myself in The Unseen, learning everything I can about it and the preternatural and magical beings I'm living alongside. Instead, I focus on myself, my problems, and live in the little three-foot world that revolves around me. I swear, sometimes I get so disgusted with myself and I can only imagine what others around me see and think.

And then I think back on the lessons Lucifer has given me. Why is being selfish and putting my needs and wants first wrong? This is my life to live and I only get one shot at it. Shouldn't I be selfish? Shouldn't I be doing or focusing on the things I want to? Why should I care what anyone else thinks or believes? This is my life! No one gets to live it but *me*.

And that is yet another war waging inside of me. As much as I want to follow Lucifer's advice and live my life for me and no one else, it's just not that simple. I'm constantly fighting with myself on what to do, how to act, who to be. Why is life so damned complicated and exhausting?

"Amarah, what is it? Are you ok?" Alistair finally breaks the silence. I'm not sure how long I've been standing here, staring off into space, getting lost in my thoughts.

"Yeah. Yeah," I shake my head to clear the fuzz. "No, I was just thinking that there's a lot about you that I don't know or understand. I mean, not you-you but just Vampires in general. I think I've been relying on the fact that Valmont is my ally and it's become a crutch. Just because he's my ally now, doesn't mean he always will be. And even if he is, that doesn't mean all the Vampires in this world are. I just realized I've been very trusting and I need to start opening my own eyes. I need to do better." Even if it is only to benefit my knowledge base and therefore, better protect myself. Back to being selfish.

"A wise revelation," he dips his chin in agreement. "Perhaps you can have more of these revelations once we're back at the casino though?"

I nod my head, "right. I'll be right back." I close the door and jog off towards the one place around here that keeps its doors open 24-7, the San Felipe de Neri Church, the entrance to Headquarters.

Once inside, my body shivers at the change in temperatures. Winter is right around the corner and I'm grateful for the long-sleeve tee, sweatpants, and sneakers I changed into earlier. As sexy as the little black dress is, it's just not running-around-at-all-hours-of-the-morning attire. As I'm descending the stairs that will lead me into the throne room, I'm suddenly very aware of what time it is. What in the Hell am I doing coming to have a conversation about training with Emrick at almost five in the damn morning? Just because I'm awake doesn't mean anyone else will be.

"Way to use your head, Amarah," I say, sarcastically to myself, as I push through the door. I'm already here, so I may as well have a look around and see if anyone else is as unstable as I am and awake.

This place is usually fairly quiet, but in these early hours of the morning, it's eerily quiet. I feel the immense, cavernous size of this room, my soft footsteps are the only sound, as I make my way towards one of the many tunnels that lead off from this room.

My hunch pays off when I approach the library and hear muffled voices coming from inside. As I walk through the doorway, I spot exactly who I came to see. Emrick is lounging in a chair across from Ana, who is talking to someone else. Their back is facing me so I'm unable to tell who it is. Ana notices me, as I make my way closer, and her eyes meet mine. There's a flash of hesitation I see in her entire body, from her appraising eyes, to the frown of her lips, and her tense body language. Queen that she is, she schools her features into relaxed and indifferent quickly, but I saw the hesitation first. Our last encounter plays through my mind and a part of me wants to run to her and tell her how sorry I am for the way I acted. Another part of me, the part that is fuelled by my fire and rage, refuses to back down.

Torn between the two, my right hand seems to move without my permission to twirl the ring that sits tightly on my left middle finger. My reminder that this is *my* life to live and no one else's. My reminder that it's ok to put myself and my needs first. My reminder that I don't need to be anything for anyone other than myself. I hold my head up high as I approach the seating area. Ana's eyes on mine alert the others to my presence. When the other woman on the couch turns to face me, I can't help but return the infection smile being thrown my way.

"Amarah!" She's off the couch quickly and embraces me with the warmest hug.

I can't help the laugh that escapes me, despite the otherwise dismal reception. "Hey, Mariah," I chuckle, as she squeezes me and I squeeze her back. "It's good to see you."

I pull back from the hug and look down at her. I'm not the tallest girl, but at barely over five feet tall, Mariah is tiny. Her face is scrubbed clean of her typical expertly applied makeup and she looks so fresh and so much younger. She has a smattering of freckles across her nose and cheeks that I've never been able to see before.

"What are you doing here so early?" She asks, bringing my thoughts back to my reason for being here.

"Oh, I ummmm, was hoping to speak with Emrick about my training," I say, as my eyes finally travel to the Prince sitting to my left.

His emerald eyes meet mine and scrunch at the corners as he bestows one of his brilliant smiles on me. "I'd be delighted to discuss our training."

His reaction seems genuine and it thaws me a little bit more. I think back to the very first time I met him. Out of the four Leaders of the Fey Families, I liked Emrick instantly. His aura is warm and comforting and with everything going on in my crazy, unpredictable, and anguished life right now, I desperately want to be around his energy.

Ana stands from the couch, still giving me cold, vacant eyes before she turns her attention to Mariah. "Come, Mariah, let's check on our patient and leave them to it." She walks past me without another look or thought. I'm left feeling like a scolded child, dismissed and thrown aside, as I mumble a goodbye to Mariah and watch them leave.

I can't help but feel a bit of pain in my chest. Ana is the only blood relative I have. This distance between us isn't what I want. I know I'm at fault for our current situation but the blame isn't wholly mine. Ana lashed out at me in a way I've only ever seen once before. And it was in front of everyone else which makes it that much worse. Is it my pride that's hurt? Maybe. But it's my heart also. I don't want this for us but I'm also not going to apologize for my actions. At the moment, they were right for *me*, and I won't apologize for putting myself first. I can't. But I also can't lose my aunt. Once again, I'm impossibly torn.

Turning back to Emrick, I let out a frustrated sigh as I take a seat on the now vacant couch across from him, "well, she officially hates me."

He shakes his head, "she doesn't."

"Did you not just witness that lethal winter stare that froze me where I stand?"

"You've both reacted poorly to incredibly terrible situations. Actions always have consequences whether good or bad. Of course, there's going to be some discomfort but she doesn't *hate* you."

"I'm not so confident. She's never been like this with me before."

"You both just need to figure your shit out," he waves his hand in the air nonchalantly. "Have some wine and girl talk, bond, and everything will be fine."

I laugh, "yeah, because there's so much time for hanging out, having wine, and girl talk."

"Girl, there's *always* time for wine and girl talk," he winks and gives me a playful grin.

This is the first time I've actually spoken to Emrick one-on-

one and not in a public setting. I'm seeing a whole new side to him and I'm wondering if he's gay? Bi maybe? Then I'm wondering if it would be rude to ask? Not that it matters to me either way.

He interrupts my thoughts, "so you wanted to discuss training?"

"Of course, yes. I need to start training again but I don't really want to leave right now. I'm hoping that you'll be able to stay here for a while and we can start training at Valmont's casino? I'm sure they have a gym and training area somewhere and we can figure out a place to do the Fey training. I just need to stay here for now. There's some stuff going on that I want to be around for. I hope this isn't too much to ask, but if you need to go back home, we can postpone training for a while."

"It's no problem at all. I can stay here, and home isn't very far away, actually. Though, I am curious about what's keeping you from coming back to my home since you've visited both the Fire Fey and the Air Fey homes?" He arches a brow in question.

"Unfortunately, a threat," I sigh. "I don't have time to get into it all right now but I'll tell you more about it when we start training. Tomorrow? Or rather, today?"

"Today would be great," he smiles genuinely at me. "I've heard a lot about what you can do. I'm excited to witness it for myself."

I scoff, "don't believe everything you hear, and don't get your hopes up. Not with me."

"We'll see," he smirks, as if he knows a secret I don't.

I shake my head and get to my feet. "So, are you staying here at Headquarters or do you have someplace else you stay when you're visiting?"

"You can always find me here, but perhaps we can exchange numbers as well, in case we need to reach each other."

"Great idea. Do you have your phone on you? Mine is back

in my car."

"He shakes his head and stands, "it's in my room. Let's save some time and walk there together and then you can go about your day."

"After you."

I follow Emrick through some tunnels and turns leading towards the living quarters. We get to the tunnel where my room is located but we turn in the opposite direction. A few doors down, Emrick stops in front of the one I assume is his, opens the door, and walks inside.

I'm hovering near the doorway, not sure what to do when he calls out, "you can come in."

I slowly walk into his room, not wanting to intrude, but also curious to see if his room is as nice as the one dedicated to me. I'm stunned to see that this room is little more than a hole in the wall, literally. The full-size bed and dresser take up most of the room leaving very little space to walk around. There's a door on the other side of the room and I can vaguely make out that it's the bathroom. It looks tiny as well. Considering my room is at least five times this size, I'm shocked. I guess I didn't know what to expect but it sure wasn't this.

"This is where you've been staying?" I ask, as my eyes sweep the bleak bedroom.

Emrick follows my gaze and looks around, "I know, it's not the Ritz Hotel by any means but it's a place to rest my head and that's all I need. Here," he hands his phone to me. "Enter in your number."

I take his phone, punch in my number, and hit the call button so I can also have his number too, before I end the call and hand the phone back to him. "I've only ever seen the room Ana gave to me and this is definitely not what I was expecting. I mean sure, it's good for a day or two but not for an extended stay," I shake my head.

"Especially if we're going to start our training. No, you need a more comfortable room. You should use mine."

"Nonsense. This is fine. I only..."

"I insist," I interrupt. "It's just down the hall in the other direction and it's not being used. It's just sitting there empty. I've never used it. Not once. Please, say you'll use it?"

"Amarah, it really isn't necessary."

"I know it's not, but I would feel better knowing you're there. Plus," I give him the I-know-a-secret-you-don't smirk, "it has a natural hot spring as the tub!" My smile widens. "It will be perfect for recovery from training."

"Okay, okayyyy, now I'm listening!"

"Come on, I'll show you!" I grab his hand before he can argue and pull him out of his room and down the hall.

"You're seriously going to die when you see this room. It's beautiful, and there's a fireplace, which will be nice for the colder nights that are coming." We reach the end of the hall quickly and I don't stop when we reach the door and burst in with my excitement. "And there's a walk-in clos..."

I stop in my tracks at the sight in front of me. My brain seems to have malfunctioned. It doesn't want to process the image my eyes are sending to it. It can't be happening. I mean, I assumed it was happening, but to think about it is entirely different than actually seeing it.

"Well, this is awkward," she's sitting up against the headboard clutching the blankets to her chest. Glancing between me and Logan.

Logan.

Logan.

Logan.

In bed with another woman.

My eyes take in Logan's exposed chest. It's so much bigger

than I remember, and his arms are bulging with muscles, and he's not even flexing. I can't help but drink in every new and every old detail, remembering what his body feels like under my hands and pressed on top of me, and the new desire I have to explore every new muscle with my mouth. My eyes travel down his newly acquired washboard abs. I've never cared much for abs before but now they're suddenly my favorite things. The blanket is low across his hips, barely covering him, and he's naked.

Naked.

Naked.

Naked.

In bed with another woman.

My mind is glitching. Working in pieces of information. Time seems to have stopped, as I process all this information, but I know it's only been seconds. Seconds is all it takes to feel like Logan has just used his Wolf claws to pull my chest wide open, cracking my ribs to expose my barely beating heart. He then grabs it and crushes what's left of it in his massive, muscular hand. It's over. And I can't bring myself to feel the rage or fire inside of me. It's like every defense I have has disappeared. The anger has disappeared. All I feel is anguish. Unforgettable and unforgivable pain. I've tried to cope. I've tried to be strong. I've tried to move on. I've tried to push my emotions down, to smother them in fire. But the truth is I *feel* too much. I told myself I was done crying over this man but I can't stop the waterfalls cascading down my cheeks.

I'm drowning…

Drowning…

Drowning in pain.

"Amarah," Logan throws back the covers, reaches down then stands, pulling on his briefs.

He walks towards me with purpose and I can't help but notice he's hard. My mouth waters at the sight and desire pools low in my belly. The truth of him hard, naked and in bed with another woman seems to have slipped my mind, as I stare at him. Craving him. His briefs leave absolutely nothing to the imagination and he doesn't seem to care who sees it. He suddenly stops several feet in front of me as if he hit an invisible wall. His nostrils flare, his jaw clenches tightly, as do his fists, right before his Wolf claws emerge. His eyes rage into amber as every emotion seems to flit over his features.

Confusion.

Hurt.

Betrayal.

Disbelief.

Disgust.

Anger.

"I swear to God I am going to fucking kill him," he snarls.

"What?" I ask, confused and glance back at Emrick. "I was just going to show him the room and..."

"Valmont. I can smell him on you. His scent is covering every inch of you," he lets out a growl that's far from human. He's a glass house right now and he's throwing stones. Considering the scene around us he has no right to be angry with *me*!

"And if I could smell it, I'd smell *her* scent all of *you*! You have no right to be pissed at me when you moved on first! You men and your double standard hypocrisy! I'm done! You want her? You can keep her!"

"Oh my God! I swear you are so fucking frustrating lately! You have no idea what you're talking about!" He yells back at me. "I don't fucking want *her*. It's not like that. I want *you*, Amarah. Nothing has changed for me. I know this looks bad but I can explain."

"I don't want to hear your lies and excuses, Logan. We're done. Officially done. We can't come back from this even if we wanted to."

"And I'm sure you have lies and excuses as to why Valmont's

scent is all over you?" His voice is deep and angry.

"We're not together anymore, Logan, I don't need excuses and neither do you." My words are true but they contradict everything I'm feeling and showing. I desperately want to hear his excuses. I want to pretend none of this happened. I want to run into his arms and go back in time. I want so many things to be different. But…this is our brutal reality.

The anger drains away from both of us, and we're left standing a few feet apart physically, but it might as well be oceans between us. I see the ache in his eyes and it matches the ache in my heart. My tears are streaming freely, I can't contain them. This is the downside of all-consuming love.

All-consuming pain.

"Amarah, please, just open the connection. Let me show you the truth." He moves to close the space between us, his arms outstretched towards my face. The need to wipe my hurt away is evident in his eyes.

I'm finally unfrozen and take a step back. "Don't you dare fucking touch me with the hands that just touched *her*."

I'm screaming.

I'm crying.

I'm breaking.

I'm dying.

His hands fall back to his sides. I see the agony on his face, the agony that so perfectly reflects how I feel, before his face is blurred out by tears. I open my mouth but I no longer know what to say. I shake my head and catch watery glimpses of Logan before I turn on my heel and run like Hell.

I run as fast and as hard as I can. I run from the truth of that room. I run from the sight of Logan in bed with another woman. I run from the truth that Logan and I will never be together again. I run from the guilt of sleeping with Valmont. I run from everything. But no matter how fast or how hard I run, I can't outrun the pain.

When I reach my car, I'm inside and shoving the car into reverse before the door even closes. I burn rubber as I exit the parking lot, a choked sob escapes my throat as I grip the wheel tightly with one hand and try to clear my blurred vision with the other.

Alistair is holding Griffin in his lap and doing nothing to give me a pretense of privacy. He is openly staring at me, no doubt judging my weakness, but all he says when he finally speaks is, "perhaps I should drive?"

"I'm fine!" I yell too loudly in the small space of the car, as I speed across I-25 heading back to the casino. Back to Valmont. Back to the only salvation I have. His numbing bite. I need it now more than ever.

Amarah: Alone Again

My Immortal by Evanescence

Alistair has taken Griffin and my bags up to the Penthouse and I've managed to compose myself as I make my way to Valmont's office. My feet moving urgently towards the only cure for my pain. A bite so powerful it leaves me truly empty of all other thoughts and feelings. The lightest, happiest moment of peace I've ever had.

I quickly climb the stairs to his office and knock urgently, "Valmont, it's me. I'm coming in."

Locked.

I wiggle the handle back and forth for good measure. "Valmont, come on, open the door."

I wait a few seconds but the door doesn't open. I knock again, "it's been a really rough night," my emotions are threatening to break the surface again. I can't seem to push them down far enough. "Please. I really need you."

Silence.

I stand still and press myself against the door. I close my eyes and focus on the other side. I listen intently for any sound, any sign that Valmont is there. The door is locked so, I know he must be in there. The door is *never* locked. Why now?

"Valmont, I know you're in there and I know you can hear

me. Please just let me in so we can talk."

Silence.

Locked out.

I turn around and slide down the door to sit on the floor. I close my eyes but all I see is Logan, naked, in bed with another woman. A beautiful, stunning woman. The tears seep through my closed lashes as I bring my knees up, hugging them to me, and bury my face in them.

"I just don't want to be alone," I admit the truth in a whisper to myself.

I don't know how long I've been here but I'm pulled out of my shell by a familiar voice.

"Amarah, come on. Let's get you into the Penthouse. Some food and some sleep will do you good."

I lift my head to see Emerson crouched down to my level. His glacial blue eyes show no feelings about me or my current situation. They're just the cold, calculating eyes they've always been, and for once, I'm grateful for them. The last thing I want from anyone is pity. The, *oh bless her heart*, look.

"But I need to see Valmont for just a quick minute. I just..."

He shakes his head, "he doesn't want to see you right now, Amarah."

"What do you mean he doesn't *want* to see me. You mean, he *can't* see me? He's *too busy* to see me?"

He holds those cold eyes on me and I fill the chill slip down my spine as he repeats his words, "he doesn't *want* to see you."

You are the one who is addicted to me.

I try to swallow the lump in my throat that's making it hard to breathe and talk. The only other person I have in my life right now, the one who refused to let me slip away in the weeks I was suffering at home, the one who fought for me, and now he doesn't want to see me. The truth of that statement cuts me to the core and adds to the destruction of my heart and soul. Did he finally get what he wanted from me? Sex? Is that all I've ever been to him? Another one of his Viking conquests? Or does he know I used him as revenge for Logan? Maybe he doesn't want to be used and this is my punishment. Either way, I feel the cut of his sword deep in my chest.

I finally take in a deep, shaky breath, refusing to let the emotion slip out my throat in front of Emerson. All I can do is nod as he extends his hand to help me stand. I take it, and follow silently behind him towards the private elevator. What else can I do?

I'm sitting on the edge of the bed after I pulled all the blackout curtains closed to keep out the inevitable daylight that is slowly pushing against the darkness. Whether I want it to or not, the day will come and shed light on my life and the tragic consequences of all of my decisions. The sad truth about life? Life continues on with or without you. And because I'm a glutton for punishment and torture, I grab my phone and open up Spotify. I hit play on a sad breakup songs playlist. I need to hear words bleed out the emotions pent up inside me.

The tray of food that was brought to me sits untouched on the nightstand. I finally reach for the bottle sitting next to the glass of water. Sleeping pills that I requested. If I can't have Valmont's bite to help numb my mind, the next best thing is a state of over-the-counter- comatose.

I read the directions; two pills are what the professionals

recommend. Well, the professionals don't know my life and my pain. I shake out four pills. I'm fairly confident that four sleeping pills aren't enough to overdose, but if I'm being honest, I don't think too much about it either way. Popping them into my mouth with no hesitation, I down them with water, click off the lamp, and slip into the silk covers, next to Griffin, who seems to have no problem with the new scenery or with finding sleep.

Curled into a protective ball on my side, I'm desperately trying to climb into myself and hide. If I had a hole to burrow into and never leave again, I would. The best I can do is cuddle into a luxurious bed as my mind refuses to move past the image of Logan with another woman. *You Were Good To Me* by Jeremy Zucker and Chelsea Cutler comes through the speakers and I break a little more. Will the breaking ever stop? How much and how long can I break? How can I possibly survive?

Tears are drying on my face when I finally feel my muscles relaxing. The sleeping pills are kicking in and I can feel them physically pulling me under. I'm close to oblivion when I feel a gentle touch at my temple. A faint brush of lips and a tickle of silky hair on my cheek.

I swear I hear his words, "Everything I do is to protect you, Amarah Rey, but Gods, you make it so hard."

"Valmont," my voice is groggy with forced sleep and I can barely open my eyes to slits. The room is dark, I can't see him or feel him but I swear I can smell a hint of honey and bergamot as I'm finally pulled into the darkness.

The noise is deafening. Resounding in my mind. Flooding my body with its power. I can feel it vibrating through me as if a hand has penetrated my skin and is shaking me from the inside out. Splashes of ice-cold water pelt every inch of my exposed skin with so much force it feels like I'm being stabbed over and over again with sharp icicles. The cold is seeping onto my bones threatening to shatter them. My hair is plastered to my face and chest doing little to protect my nakedness.

The sensation is too much and I cry out as my knees slam against the unforgiving rock beneath me. I curl in on myself, trying to make myself a smaller target, as I pull my head to my chest and cover my ears with my arms. My body is shaking in forceful fits, my teeth chattering so hard it feels like they're going to break. Pain. Pain is all I can feel and I can't think against the roar of the Falls next to me.

The Falls? Niagara Falls? The thought pushes through for a brief second against the pain. This has to be a dream but it feels so real.

The pain.

The cold.

The noise.

It's all so real. I just want it to stop! I want the pain to stop! I want the ear-splitting noise to stop! If I can just get my body to move. If I can just get myself over the side of the cliff, the force of the Falls will crush me instantly. No more pain. No more noise. Just blissful quiet. Blissful peace. Inside and out.

I slowly inch my aching body towards the cliff with one purpose in mind. Ending it all. My brain knows this is a dream but a part of me is hoping it's real. Real like Lucifer's ring that followed me from my dream into reality. Maybe this will manifest too. My frozen body feels like it's going to break and shatter with every move I make. My lungs are seizing as I pull in more of the cold air into my chest.

"Amarah Rey," his voice steals my attention.

I look down and Valmont is in my arms. Blood coats his skin, as deep gashing rip open every inch of his skin, his body trying to heal them, again and again, and failing.

"No, no, no! Not again!" I squeeze my eyes shut, willing all of this to end, "this isn't real. It's just a dream. This isn't real!" Open my eyes again and Valmont is still in my arms, blood spilling out of his mouth as he looks up at me with fear in his eyes. I know he fears dying but I refuse to let him leave me.

There's suddenly a dagger in my hand and I don't hesitate, cutting across my forearm. "Here, drink my blood," I push my bleeding arm towards his lips.

His eyes widen in fear. Fear of *me*. He shakes his head and pushes my arm away, "no, no anything but that. Please! Anything but that!"

"What are doing? I can heal you! Let me heal you, please! I can't lose you." This isn't right. This isn't what happened in real life. My brain is confused as it tries to grasp my memory of this moment and stay present for this new one.

"Valmont, take my damn blood! It will save your life!" I struggle against his strength, as I fight to move my arm to his mouth.

He shakes his head, holding my bleeding arm away from him. "No," he whispers. "You won't save me, you'll destroy me."

"What are you talking about? Valmont, my blood is the only thing that can save you! Please!" I beg.

The sound of blood gurgling in his throat makes me close my eyes again. I smell smoke and hear the battle raging on around me. When I open my eyes again, Valmont is no longer in my arms and a choked sob escapes me.

"Andre," I cradle his head in my lap and caress his cheek. His hand reaches up and touches my face, his eyes look up at me, full of love, and I feel my heart breaking all over again.

"Amarah," his voice is strangled and he coughs on the blood filling up his lungs. His eyes turn from adoring to fearing. Fear of *me*. No! This isn't right. It didn't happen like this. His hand falls away as he chokes out, "you did this to me."

"No! I didn't mean to! I didn't know! I would never hurt you, Andre, I would never hurt you! Please, you have to believe me!" I hang my head, closing my eyes so I don't have to see the fear in his eyes, as tears stream down my face, "I didn't know."

Another voice has me jerking my eyes open. My greatest fear is laying before me. "No, no, no, no, this isn't real! Wake up, Amarah, damn it! Wake up!" I yell to the sky but the Falls swallow my pleas as soon as they leave my mouth.

"Angel," Logan's voice brings me back to his broken body beneath me. Blood is gushing out of a wound in the middle of his chest.

"This isn't real, Logan, you're not really here," I blink back the tears trying to keep his face in focus. It feels real. He feels real in my arms. The warm blood leaving his body feels real as I try to stop it.

"Oh, Angel, you were right," his voice is laced with pain.

"Right a-about w-w-hat?" I choke through my tears.

"I should have let you go... so I could live."

"No, Logan, you *are* alive! This isn't real. Please. Lucifer!" I scream. "Lucifer, stop this! Please, don't let me lose him too!"

I look up and Logan is suddenly standing at the edge of the cliff, the raging waterfall framing his beautiful body. The fear in his peridot eyes pierces right through me, sinking into my chest. Into my soul.

"You're going to destroy us all," he closes his eyes, spreads his arms wide, and falls back over the cliff.

"Logan!!!" I scramble to the edge of the cliff, determined to follow Logan over the side, but an arm catches me around the waist before I can jump.

"Amarah," that's all he says, as he brings my head to his chest and holds me safely to his body.

I wrap my hands around him and cry into his chest. The ragged sobs jerk my body violently. He soothes my hair as he whispers, "it's alright. It's not real. It's not real, Amarah. Calm down. Just breathe. You're safe. Shhhhh, you're safe. It's not real."

I finally manage to catch my breath, "make it stop, please, Lucifer. Make it stop."

His hands cradle my head as he pulls me away from his chest so he can look at me. "This isn't my doing. You're in control of this one. I can't control this dream, Amarah, you have to."

I shake my head in disbelief as the tears keep falling, "no, that can't be right. I wouldn't…"

"Shhhh," he says softly, as he rests his forehead against mine, whipping my tears away. "Just breathe. You're safe. Focus on something else and change the dream. You can do it."

My breath shudders in my chest, I close my eyes and desperately hold on to Lucifer, feeling his solid body under my hands. I focus on the rhythm of his steady breaths and match mine to his. I breathe in the scent of him, smoky, burnt wood and ashes, yet fresh, wild, and free. The thundering of the falls slowly dissipates and the freezing drops of water retreat.

"Aye, good girl," he presses a kiss to my forehead and steps out of my hold, taking a hold of my hands.

I open my eyes to see that we're in a small clearing, surrounded by trees on all sides and a huge bonfire next to us. He leads me to a thick patch of grass and pulls me down to sit next to him. The heat from the fire feels real against my skin, but the coldness is still deep in my bones, making me shiver. I'm relieved to see I'm wearing jeans and a tank top and no longer completely naked and vulnerable.

"This is much better, Amarah," his sexy Scottish voice

caresses my skin. "Are you ok?" He asks, as he rubs his hand up and down my arm closest to him.

"I…I don't know. I don't know how I got there." I finally lift my eyes to meet his. "I thought you controlled these dreams?"

He shakes his head, "I only controlled the first two. The others have been all you. You have been calling out to me," he smirks, arrogantly.

I roll my eyes, ignoring his teasing, the image of the men in my life, dying in my arms is still too real. I'm not in a playful mood when my heart is raw and bleeding inside my chest.

"I don't understand. Why would I dream that?"

"Dreams are a part of your subconscious. A mix of reality, and emotions, your hopes, and fears. Your *guilt*. You can face things in a dream that you can't, or won't, face in real life. Sometimes we choose not to face things in our waking hours because they're too painful. But dreams, for the most part, you have no control over. They come when and how they want and they come with a vengeance. Especially if you're blocking the feelings and thoughts in real life. Your mind devises dreams as a way to *make* you face the truth whether you want to or not."

"But this dream wasn't real. Things didn't happen that way. And Logan is safe. Everything I've done is to make sure he's safe and far away from me," the tears are back as I relive all the hurt of pushing him away. Pushing him into the arms of another woman. I did that.

"Dreams aren't the past or the future. They simply are. And it's clear that your dream tonight was a clear representation of your pain, Amarah. You're drowning in your pain. You're drowning in your guilt about Andre and you're drowning in your fear that you'll lose the rest of the people you care about."

"If dreams aren't real, then how can I have this on my finger," I lift my hand up to show him his ring, "in real life. It's real, Lucifer, not just here."

"That ring is not a normal ring. It's celestial, like you and me, and isn't bound to the same rules. This is also why we can communicate in your dreams. Well, you gave me that power when you brought my calling card into your home a few months ago," he chuckles, "but still, you're not human, Amarah. You need to remember that. The normal rules don't apply to you."

"I wish I was," I whisper.

"You wish you were human? Why on Earth would you ever want that?" He looks confused.

"Because then I wouldn't be important and I wouldn't be a target. *Your* demon target by the way."

"Aye, that's true. You were a threat in the beginning, but have any demons come near you since we made our little truce?"

"Well, no. But still," I sigh. "I'm different. I'm powerful. And people will always fear what's different and people will always chase power. People will always expect more of me, try to control me. I'll never just be… *me*. I'll never *not* be in danger and a danger to those around me. I'll never have a normal life."

"And is that what you want? A *normal* life?"

I think about the month I had with Logan when we were hiding away from the world and our responsibilities. It was simple. It was all I needed. All I wanted. It was perfect. But I never would have met Logan if I hadn't come into my power. If my power hadn't *called* to him. And I wouldn't have found my aunt or all of the amazing magic and beauty of The Unseen. Would I really choose to go back to the life I had before everything changed?

At least this way, I still have Logan in my life. He's no longer mine, but I at least *have* him in my life. Would I give this all up just to avoid the pain and guilt that consumes me? *Yes!* Yes, I think I would, because the thought of never feeling Logan's body again, or his love, is worse than anything! Is it truly better to have loved and lost than never to have loved at all? I can't say I agree with that right now.

I stare off into the flames of the bonfire not wanting Lucifer to see the truth in my eyes. "I don't know," I finally answer his question. "I don't know."

We're quiet for a long time before I speak again. "I wanted this dream to be real. I wanted to follow Logan off that cliff and end it all. End everything. All of this pain that consumes me every second of every damn day. I wanted to die and I wanted it to be real. There has to be peace in death because being alive is too damn painful."

Logan: A New Ally

Hope In Front Of Me by Danny Gokey

"Let it out! Come on, I can take it."

"You can't! You can't take it. No one can! I almost *killed* you," I run a hand through my hair, as I pace the mat, my anger and frustration clawing at my skin with no way of escape.

We've been sparring for two hours, we're both drenched in sweat, a little bloody and bruised. I should be tired but my body is pulled tight as a bowstring and I need a release. A release beyond what the mat can provide. I need to unleash my power and I desperately need to unleash my pent-up desire. It's been a month since I've had sex and my body is about to fucking snap. But I don't want to have sex with anyone else but Amarah.

I refuse to believe that she slept with the Vampire. Even though I know she did. I smelt him all over her. I smelt their sex. It has a very distinguished scent and there's no mistaking it. Still, I can't believe she would do that to me. To us. She thinks I'm with Atreya, and I know without the connection open, there's nothing I can say that will convince her otherwise.

Is that why she did what she did? To get even? Or did she do it because that's what she's wanted to do? No. I don't believe it. I've felt her love for me. It's more than skin-deep. Our love is carved into our fucking souls. That love doesn't just go away, ever.

I'm so fucking lost!

I'm so fucking confused!

I'm so fucking angry!

I'm so fucking horny! Fuck.

God, when I saw her this morning, that red hair I fell in love with, and even in sweats, she's the sexiest thing I've ever seen. Being naked in bed with a beautiful woman did nothing for me. I wasn't the least bit turned on. But the second I saw Amarah, I was instantly hard. My cock ached to push inside of her and feel her tight body around mine. Accepting me, loving me, healing me. My body wants only hers, my Wolf wants only his mate, my soul wants only our connection.

I want to fuck her, punish her for what she's done, but I also want to make love to her, and tell her that everything is ok. I want to completely consume her until there's no other touch, kiss, or dick, she remembers but *mine*. I want to erase everyone before me and ruin her for anyone after me. Not that I plan on letting her go, ever again, once I get her back. Fuck!

Just thinking about taking her, again and again, making her mine again, my cock starts to stir. I turn my back on Atreya and take a moment to settle my thoughts. I breathe in through my nose and slowly let it out between my lips. Then do it again, and again, until I'm as controlled as I'm going to be. I turn back around to the woman standing in front of me. She's stood beside me since the day I met her and I can't fathom why she's still here. Putting up with the drama that is my life. The unstable bomb that is me, threatening to detonate at any given moment.

"Jesus, Atreya, I almost *killed* you and you're still here, trying to help me. Why?"

"You know why."

"I don't," I shake my head. "You told me you were a Lone Wolf before you came here. I know the Los Lobos Pack took you in, but I don't know anything besides that, and I don't know why you've chosen to befriend me. I *am* still a Lone Wolf. I will never be a part of this Pack or any others. Is that it? Do you pity me?" I growl out, angrily. Just the thought of anyone pitying me pisses me off.

She crosses her arms and looks insulted, "you really think I pity you?"

"I don't know," I yell. "I don't know anything!" The anger is starting to get the best of me, I close my eyes, clench and unclench my fists, and try to steady my breathing…again. When I can finally speak calmly, I look at Atreya and try to have a civil conversation, no yelling. "I don't know what you want or what your motive is so, why don't you tell me."

"Pity is the last thing I think of when it comes to you, Logan."

"Then what is it? If you're hanging around in hopes of me giving up on Amarah then you're wasting your time."

Atreya looks at me with a blank stare before she erupts with laughter. She throws her head back and laughs at me as if I just delivered the punchline of a joke. She's doubling over, clutching her stomach, and gasping for breath. All I can do is stand here and stare at her, confused as all Hell.

"What? What did I say that's so funny?"

"I'm sorry," she wipes at the corner of her eyes. "No offense. You're very attractive, Logan, in the intimidating, brooding, look-at-me-wrong-and-you'll-regret-it type of way, but I'm more likely to try and steal Amarah away from you, than I am of trying to steal you away from Amarah," the laughter lingers in her tone, as I digest what she's telling me.

"Oh. *OH!*" I say, as it all comes together. "Really?" I cock my head, feeling like I'm seeing her for the first time.

She chuckles again, "really. It's not like I've given you those types of signals."

"Well…"

"What?" She asks, indignantly. "No way! How?"

"Well, you are very…*touchy-feely*."

She laughs again, this time more in disbelief, "ok, two things." She holds up two fingers and starts ticking them off, "one, this is why it's so difficult for women. We're either stuck-up bitches or sluts. There's no in-between," she shakes her head. "It's impossible for women to show any type of *niceness* to a male without his mind automatically going to sex. Honestly, it's sad, ridiculous, and sick. Second, you really have been away from Pack life too long. I'm a *Werewolf*, Logan, a Võltsimatu, Pure Blood, like you. Physical connection means more than sex to us. It's about comfort, healing, love, friendship, support, sympathy. Physical touch is *everything* to us. It's how we communicate without needing words. You've truly been alone for too long if you've forgotten what being a Werewolf is."

I feel like an absolute asshole, as she's explaining the simple truth about life to me as if I'm no more than a fuckboy, seeing her as *something* to play with instead of *someone* with their own intentions. Plus, she has to remind me of our nature, who we fucking are at our core, as if I'm no more than a newly turned Werewolf, unfamiliar with the customs, instead of a Pure Blood, born into it.

I run my hands down my face, "I'm sorry. I'm an idiot and an asshole. You're right, I've been alone for too long. I haven't had that type of family in…" I pause, thinking back to my youth and the feelings of love and wholeness that I had with my Pack. The feelings I've gotten again from being around Atreya. Family. "…a very, very long time. Amarah is the only family I've had in so long and our physical relationship is *very* much about sex," I laugh, embarrassed at my admission. "But you're right, it's so much more than that too."

She nods in agreement, "I know what it's like to live without it. Without family and connection but I was only a Lone Wolf for a few years. I can't imagine what it's been like for you but I can relate on a small scale. And I know what it's like to be filled up with nothing but anger. I sensed that in you the first time we met. I know how hard you fight it and I know that nothing helps the anger except one thing. Love."

"I don't know about that. This love that I have with Amarah, right now, it just fucking hurts," I admit.

"Everyone always says that, *love hurts*, but that's not true. You wanna know what hurts, Logan?"

"What?"

"Loneliness hurts. Rejection hurts. Losing someone you love and care for hurts. Everyone gets these things confused with love, they blame it on love, but the cold hard truth of it all is, love is the only thing in this world that covers up all of the pain and makes you feel wonderful again. Love is the only thing that can truly heal you."

My throat is tightening, as emotions rise at the truth of her words. The memories of Amarah and how incredibly peaceful I feel around her. It's profound and rare. It's something you're lucky if you even find once in a lifetime and I can't fathom why she's turning her back on it. On me. I don't trust my voice so I just nod in agreement to what Atreya said.

"I feel like we're kindred spirits, Logan. That's why I've befriended you. I know that you're friends with Ethan but it's clear it's a professional friendship. And I understand his hesitance when it comes to you, and letting you close to his Pack, but I'm not like the rest of them. I don't share their fear about who you are or what you're capable of. I saw it plain as day the first night we met. No one wanted to step on the mat with you. Too many people are controlled and lead by their fears and insecurities. I'm not one of them. I want to be your friend, Logan. A true friend and hopefully someone you can consider family one day." She shrugs, "if you'll let me?"

I'm floored at her offer. No other Werewolf has offered me

what she's offering me. A connection to another Werewolf. A two-Wolf Pack so to speak. The trust and generosity of her offer is heart-warming and it helps temper the anger stirring inside of me a bit.

I clear my throat of its emotion, "under one condition."

"What's that?"

"You keep your damn hands off of Amarah."

She laughs heartily and makes an X sign over her heart, "cross my heart and hope to die. My hands will remain off of your woman. Besides, she definitely has the wrong impression of me and I don't think I'd have my hands for long if I tried to even get *close* to her."

"Can you blame her? She did walk in on us in bed together. *Naked*," I shake my head. "She's been living as a human her whole life. What she sees is what she believes. She doesn't know or understand all the different customs of The Unseen. Hell, you had to remind *me* of my own Heritage. I can't blame her for assuming the worst. And I don't know how to reach her. To tell her the truth."

"We'll figure something out. Come on," she places her hand on my arm, "let's go get some breakfast. My treat. You can tell me more about this power of yours." She removes her hand from my arm and grimaces as she cleans the sweat off on her leggings, "but perhaps showers first." She sniffs at the air around me, "you stink."

We're sitting at a corner table in the back of The Range Cafe's dining room. I'm not usually one to eat out, as I prefer to eat home-cooked, healthy meals, but recent situations have led me to break that rule and I have to admit, I see the appeal. Greasy, salty food is addicting.

Luckily the recent hardcore training has prevented me from getting a dad bod. In fact, I'm in better shape now than I have been in a long time, both my physical appearance and strength, as well as my . cardio and endurance. Not to mention, Werewolves just have a higher metabolism in general, which is causing our waitress to give us, and the table overflowing with a variety of foods, very curious glances when she thinks we aren't looking.

"Mmmmm," Atreya closes her eyes as she takes another bite of the Carne Asada Huevos Rancheros I recommended. "I swear, you guys have the *best* food here. I can't believe the rest of the world doesn't seem to know about red and green chile. They are *so* missing out. I think, no I *know*, I'm addicted."

I cock an amused eyebrow, watching her savor every bite as I make quick work of my own plate filled with my favorite breakfast.

"So, tell me about this terrifying power that almost killed me. What is it exactly?" She asks me in-between bites.

The thought of her body literally freezing, makes my stomach turn and I'm suddenly not as hungry as I was before. I put my fork down and sigh, not really wanting to relive any of these memories but knowing that she deserves an answer.

"Back when I was not much younger than you, I had...someone special." I clear my throat as images of Analise flood my mind. "We were very much in love but things were different back then." I shake my head, "Human men were ignorant and fearful of what they didn't understand. Now that I say that out loud, I guess not much has changed when it comes to that aspect, but it was a much different time. Anyone that showed any signs of being different were persecuted as Witches or accused of being possessed by something evil. Werewolves were in hiding, never to show their true selves, as were the Fey," I explain, in disgust.

I take a drink of coffee as I prepare myself for the next reveal of my past. "Analise worked as a Midwife. As a Healer from the

Müstik Family, she helped many women overcome complications that could have taken their life, or the lives of their unborn babies. She was discovered using natural herbs, as medicine, but ignorance and fear caused them to accuse her of Witchcraft. She was taken, tied to a stake in the middle of town, and set to burn alive as an example to others."

"Oh my God," Atreya stops eating and is intently listening to my story.

"I tried to save her," my voice breaks. "I tried and I couldn't. I was young and hadn't Mastered my Wolf yet. I was still controlled by the moon, and even with my supernatural strength, I wasn't strong enough to save her."

"You had to watch her...burn alive?"

"Almost. I was beaten down, badly, but I never took my eyes off her. We were locked on each other, watching each other die slowly. But my Analise was a fighter." I smile sadly, as I remember her fire. Her spirit. "She unleashed Hell on everyone. She gathered all of her Fey power and released it with such force, she cut down everyone right where they stood. In doing so, she also caused the rip between our world and the demon realm. So, there's that," I laugh, sarcastically.

"Her power also cut through her bonds, and with the last of her strength, she crawled to me. She was dying and nothing and no one was going to be able to save her. She knew it. I knew it." I blow out a heavy breath. "She kissed me with her last breath, and as she left this world, she gave me her Fey life-force. Essentially her essence, her aura." I shrug, "that's honestly all I know about it."

"Oh, Logan," Atreya reaches for my hand, "I am so sorry. I can't even imagine what that must have been like or how that still affects you."

"I lost everything that day. The woman I loved and my Pack. We didn't find out the life-force gave me additional power until months later, but the Pack determined I was too dangerous and a threat to the Alpha, so they disowned me. But it was that day, the day it all happened, is the day I lost everything."

"Your Pack was just like those ignorant fearful men! They shouldn't have turned their backs on you. You don't turn your back on family! Especially when they need you most," her voice comes out in an angry whisper.

"You sound just like Amarah," I say, with a sad smile. "It is what it is," I shrug. "And it was a long time ago, but that's when the anger started. It's been with me ever since and the only time it has been quenched is when I'm with Amarah. She's the only one I've truly *seen* in centuries. And she's the only one who makes *me* feel seen. My power feels right when I'm with her. It feels safe and comfortable but also incredibly powerful. Power like I've never felt before. And I love her more than I've ever imagined loving anyone. More than I ever thought was possible."

I run my hand through my hair suddenly feeling embarrassed, "I know it sounds cliche but she makes me a better man. She's my soulmate. She's my home. She's my *everything*, Atreya, and I can't live without her. I *can't*."

"So...what happened then? It doesn't sound like you would do anything to hurt her or betray her. And I've seen the way she looks at you, Logan. She's head over heels for you. So, what happened?"

A frustrated growl escapes me and I'm thankful we're a few tables away from anyone else. "She's struggling with who she is. With her power. Someone she cared for died at our last battle with Aralyn and it was her power, essentially, that killed him. But it wasn't her fault. It's a long story but she blames herself for his death. She only sees herself as a danger to anyone around her. She left me because she thinks she's protecting me. I know it's ridiculous, but I also understand where she's coming from."

I look at Atreya and I'm overcome with gratitude that she's sitting next to me. Alive. "Yesterday, when I hurt you unintentionally with my power, I understood. I almost killed you because of my lack of control. I'm potentially dangerous in the same way Amarah is, but the difference between us, is that I've lived a long life. I've seen and done *terrible* things. I also know that this world is dangerous, every single day, with or without preternatural beings. People are in danger just sitting in their homes, stray bullets or random burglaries, mass shootings, Hell, simply driving to work, every second that passes is a second something bad can happen. Yes, The Unseen has a few more monsters, but at the end of the day, we're all in danger. She doesn't understand that tomorrow is never promised and I'd rather spend one more day with her than a hundred more without her. She thinks she's protecting me by pushing me away when she's actually destroying me."

"Have you tried to tell her all of this? How you feel?"

I look at her incredulously.

She laughs softly, "ok, ok, calm down there, killer. Just keep reaching out. Keep trying. She loves you, Logan, just as much as you love her. The fact that she's sacrificing her own happiness to keep you safe speaks volumes. She'll come around, just give her time."

I nod because there's nothing more I can say. I don't want to give her time. I don't want to spend another second without her. But what I want doesn't seem to matter. She's made up her mind and... damn her! She's so incredibly bull-headed and stubborn!

I take a drink of my now cold coffee. It seems the waitress has disappeared. Probably because she saw the intensity of our discussion so, I don't blame her for steering clear.

"Now that you've heard my life story, it's your turn to tell me yours."

She sits back in her chair, crossing her arms defensively, "yeah, I suppose I owe you some of my history after everything you've shared." She lets out a heavy sigh, "I don't even know where to begin."

"I would say the beginning but I have no clue to any piece of you, so start wherever you see fit," I shrug.

"I guess the beginning is as good a place as any. I'm the eldest of five siblings, all girls. My father is the Alpha of my Pack," she clears her throat, "of my *old* Pack, and my mother is Beta."

"Wow, that's impressive. You don't usually see such a strong Alpha unit in Packs."

She snorts sarcastically, "no, you don't, and let me tell you, it's not all it's cracked up to be. My parents are assholes, both of them. They were always extremely tough on us but that's putting it lightly. We had to be, and do things, better than anyone else. We trained hard from an early age, both in hand-to-hand combat and Wolf combat, but as the eldest, I got the majority of my father's attention. He was always disappointed that I wasn't a son and he never let me forget it. Not that women aren't capable of doing what men can, because we *are* capable, but my father didn't see it. His so-called *training* was more abuse than anything else."

I want to speak up and tell her I'm sorry that she was treated that way by her father, but I know she doesn't want the pity any more than I do. She's used to being treated like a man, and emotions are a weakness so, I stay quiet and just listen. She's staring blankly at the table as she continues and I know she's reliving memories best left forgotten.

"I had to be better than everyone else in the Pack. Faster. Stronger. Smarter. He insisted on perfection and refused to accept anything less. When I failed, and I *did* fail, because no one is perfect, I was...*punished*. I was repeatedly abandoned in dangerous woods, forced to survive on my own, with nothing but my Wolf's instinct to protect me, and itself. Well, these fun little adventures caused me to make my first change *years* before I was ready and without the help of a full moon."

At this revelation, I can't hide my shock. "That's..." I shake my head. "I can't even wrap my mind around what you just said. I've never heard of that happening to *anyone*. The initial transformation is significant in a Wolf's development and life. Packs revere the change, it's sacred, and they train everyone fiercely on the connection to our Wolf and the acceptance of the process."

"Well, not in my family."

"What happened to you is, is...*beyond* barbaric." I shake my head again, "they're lucky you survived."

She scoffs, "yeah, lucky me. The only thing my father acknowledged was that I showed extreme strength in being able to survive the unnatural change without *significant damage*. The pain was excruciating but he had no idea what it did to me mentally and emotionally. No one did, and no one seemed to care either," she shakes her head. "Going through the change alone, scared and without knowledge of what to expect or what to do, was terrifying. I wasn't trained for it, I hadn't bonded with my Wolf, and I wasn't strong enough to control the her once I changed."

"Your Wolf was in complete control." It's not a question but she answers it like one.

"Yes," she whispers. "They tried to monitor me, contain me, and keep me safe, but my Wolf was always in control. She could force the change at any time and her power and control only intensified during a full moon."

"I know how powerful and dangerous our Wolves can be, especially on a full moon. I have excellent control over my Wolf now, but it's still not easy. Even seasoned Werewolves struggle with controlling their Wolf on a full moon," I shake my head at the thought of Atreya as a little girl going through everything utterly alone. "I can only imagine the horrors you survived."

"Horror. Yeah, that word is accurate. My Wolf fought me for a long time. She was used to being in control, being dominant over me. It took me a long time to finally be able to control her. To hold her inside. We fought for dominance constantly, and when I was finally strong enough to contain her, she settled. She finally respected me as her Alpha, so to speak, but by then..." she shakes her head and I can see the pain reflected in her glassy eyes... "it was too late. I have so much innocent blood on my hands, Logan."

She finally meets my eyes, as a single tear escapes down her cheek. She quickly swipes it away and sits up a little straighter in her chair.

"We all have innocent blood on our hands, Atreya. You're not alone," I try to comfort her, but I know from experience, comfort can only come from forgiving yourself. "Is that why you left your Pack and became a Lone Wolf?"

"Part of it."

"Something else happened."

She nods and I see her swallow down the thick ball of emotion threatening to clog her throat. I know the feeling all too well. "You don't have to tell me if you..."

"No," she interrupts me. "No, I want to tell you. I know the worst days of your life. If you're going to understand why I feel the connection I do to you, if you will ever accept me as family, you need to know mine."

"Ok," I nod, voice steady and patient. I don't want to seem too eager or uninterested. I just need to be here for her. I just need to listen without judgment.

"I was seventeen when my father decided I was in control enough that I could leave our Base and go into the city. Granted, I still had to go with a chaperone," she rolls her eyes. "I was with my mother, and we were in a grocery store getting supplies for the Pack, when I first saw her. I swear she was the most beautiful thing I've ever seen. Onyx hair, straight and shiny like silk, cascading down her back, light-brown, flawless skin, and the biggest, deepest mahogany eyes. When we locked eyes, I swear my feet stopped walking, my lungs stopped working, my heart stopped beating, and the whole damn world stopped spinning." The ghost of a smile pulls at the corners of her lips.

"It took me a few seconds to realize she was speaking to me. When the world finally snapped back into place, all I could do was take a huge gasp of air into my lungs and stare at her like an idiot. She had a soft smile on her lips and her eyes were sparkling with amusement. She was asking me if I could help her reach something from the top shelf," she laughs softly, "man, she was the tiniest thing, under five feet, but her energy filled up the whole damn isle. I finally came to my sense enough to speak. I told her that I would help her under one condition, that she had to let me take her out on a date. I couldn't believe it when she said yes."

"Her name was Minwaadizi," she laughs again, "I could never pronounce it right, no matter how hard I tried so, I just called her Izi. She was from the Ojibwe Tribe and her name means, *is kind*, and it suited her. She was the kindest, most gentle soul I'd ever met. Granted, I had never met anyone outside of my Pack before. And I know, you're probably just thinking I grasped onto the first person I saw, but it wasn't like that. To this day, I've still never met anyone else that comes close to her."

"I know exactly what you mean," I agree.

"Well, we exchanged numbers and we spoke every day. We went on date after date and I swear she was my soulmate. It was love at first sight for both of us. She had the softest voice I'd ever heard, but when she spoke, her voice drowned out everything else. She commanded my attention without ever raising her voice. She had me wholly and completely. She still does."

"Where is she now?"

She let out a heavy sigh, "we were together for eight months. It was just shy of my eighteenth birthday when there was a rare super blue blood moon. I thought by this point I could handle it. I was wrong. The moon's power and pull was intense, and my Wolf came through with a vengeance. The members of my Pack that were with me tried to stop me. I almost killed them, but luckily, Werewolves can take one Hell of a beating and still heal, as long as it's not silver. The same thing can't be said about humans."

Sitting across from Atreya, I watch as she recedes into her memory. She's still here sitting at the table with me physically, but her mind is back in the memory, and all I can do is sit here and listen to her confession, as I watch her relive her most painful memory.

"Izi knew what I was and knew all of my history, my struggle for control, and the progress I had made. She never once recoiled from my truth and she never showed an ounce of fear toward me. Until that night. She had never seen me in my Wolf form before but she knew it was me. I saw the recognition in her eyes, and even worse, I saw her fear," she closes her eyes against the memory as the tears flood down her cheeks. "Her fear was so intense, I could taste it on the back of my tongue, and my Wolf *relished* in it. I was trapped inside, forced to watch and feel everything as my Wolf's claws, *my* claws, tore through her skin like a knife to butter. I was forced to feel her bones cracking between *my* teeth, and the sour taste of fear-laced blood, as it slid down *my* throat," she chokes on her words, as if she's choking on the blood all over again.

"I wasn't strong enough to control my Wolf and stop myself from killing her. It's like my Wolf wanted one last shot at control. My Wolf never acknowledged her as a mate and she'll never approve of anyone I choose. We were never given the chance to learn about each other and connect to each other in that crucial bonding stage. She's possessive over me in a way that most Wolves are possessive over their mate. I will *never* let what happened to Izi happen to anyone else."

She takes a few minutes to compose herself. She wipes her face clean, blows her nose on a napkin, and fusses with her hair. Her breathing settles and she looks at me with sheer determination in her eyes.

"I keep saying my *Wolf* did this, my *Wolf* did that, but it was *me*. I was in there, lucid and conscious the whole time, too weak to stop what happened. *I* killed hundreds of innocents in my uncontrollable years. *I* killed the woman I love before I got to share a life with her. *I. Am. A. Monster.*"

"I fled that night, with no possessions, and told no one. I became a Lone Wolf and lived as remote as I could for a couple of years. At first the anger and guilt consumed me. That's why I went as remote as possible. Less chance of hurting or killing anyone in my rage. I still struggle with the anger and guilt every single day, but I can confidently say, that I am a thousand percent in control of my Wolf now and that is *never* going to change." She looks at me as if daring me to challenge her about her control. I don't.

"Once I resurfaced, and started to get back into society, I kept my ear to the streets and eventually heard about Ethan and his Pack. I knew he was the kind of Leader that would take me in and one that I could respect. He knows some of my history but he doesn't know about Izi. No one knows the truth about that night except her, me, and now you," she blows out a relieved breath.

"I'm honored that you trust me enough to share all of this with me. You're right, I do feel like I know you on a deeper level now. I understand anger and guilt better than I understand anything else. You're stronger than you realize. You gained control of your Wolf and your anger in the blink of an eye compared to me. Not that this is anything to compare, but just to give you an idea, your hundreds are my *thousands*. I won't get into my details, just know that I understand you. I do." I let out a sad chuckle, "we are definitely broken and fucked up kindred spirits but kindred nonetheless. Did you ever go back to see your Pack? Your family?"

She shakes her head, "no. I *abandoned* my Pack, Logan. That's just not something Werewolves, especially Pure Bloods, do. And if I know anything about my father, he'll either kill to get me back, or kill me if I ever go back. I ruined his attempt at a Legacy. I was supposed to be the next Alpha of the Roone Pack. I was supposed to carry on the infamous Stone name," she shrugs. "As if I want anything to do with the man who calls himself my father or the bitch that sat by and watched him treat me the way he did."

"Roone? That name is familiar. Michigan?"

Atreya nods in confirmation.

"Ahhhh, I see it now. The Roone Pack is known for not only their brutality and ruthlessness but their red hair and fur. I should have put it together earlier," I shake my head at my own oversight.

She laughs, sarcastically, "yup. That would be my family. Roone is an Irish word that literally means red-haired. They refuse to take in anyone that is not Pure Roone blood. If a human is *accidentally* turned, they die. There's no acceptance outside of the Pack. Another reason I would have left eventually anyways. I could have a fling with anyone I wanted, but in the end, I was always destined to marry within the Pack and provide pure-blooded heirs."

"But if you had stayed, and become Alpha, you could have changed those rules. You could have made the Pack into your vision. A better vision."

"And at what cost to myself and my happiness? Why would I sacrifice any more of my time, my body, and my soul, for a potential dream? A what-if chance?" She shakes her head, resigned in her decision, "no, that Pack stole the most important thing from me. The bond to my Wolf. I'll never do anything to help them, and if I ever get caught or taken back, I'll kill myself before anyone else has the chance."

It's a harsh reality. Most people would probably think she's overreacting, or has ideas of being a martyr, but I understand her. The most sacred thing in a Werewolves life was stolen from her. A relationship, a bond, with her Wolf. I couldn't imagine fighting my Wolf at every turn. I can barely contain him at times *with* the bond.

"I have the chance to have a decent life here, with the Los Lobos Pack, with you. I may not ever get the life I wanted or the happily ever after, but I do still choose to live, Logan. I'm living on my terms, to the best of my ability, and no one is going to take that away from me. You still have a chance to have what I lost. Amarah is still alive! And I'll be damned if I'm going to let you end up like me. No, we are going to fix this and we are going to get her back! You will have your happily ever after if I have anything to say about it."

Her truthful words hit me like a brick in the face. She's absolutely right. Amarah is still alive. And as long as we are both alive and breathing, there's a chance for us.

Atreya suddenly stands up, bringing my attention back to her, as she drops cash down on the table to pay for our half-eaten buffet. "Now, if we're done sharing sob stories for the next century, let's go figure out how to get your girl back, yeah?"

"Hell yea!" A spark flares up deep in my chest. One that I had let slowly suffocate underneath my anger.

Hope.

Amarah: Time To Start Again

Phoenix by Olivia Holt

Intense sunlight suddenly streams across my closed eyelids. How is it possible that we can detect light so well behind closed lids? Why can't my own eyelids work as blackout curtains for my eyes? I groan and pull the covers over my head. I'm not ready to get up and face the day. Face the hurt and truth of my disaster of a life. I'm not done sleeping my life away. But then I start to remember last night's dream. No, nightmare.

Andre dying in my arms.

Valmont dying in my arms.

Logan dying in my arms.

Logan telling me it's all my fault. Everyone I love is in danger. Because of me. I don't want to sleep my life away if I'm going to have nightmares. I'm plagued by demons and losses literally day and night. I have no reprieve. I guess I don't deserve one.

The warmth of the covers is suddenly stripped from my body. My instinct is to curl my body in on itself, preserving as much heat as I can, as a shiver runs through my body from head to toe. But is it from the sudden lack of warmth or from the memory of my nightmare? I can't tell. I can feel the heat radiating off a little curled up body at my back, Griffin. My brain starts to wake up and put two and two together. The curtains didn't just suddenly open by themselves. Covers don't just get up and walk off the bed on their own. *Someone* did this. My first thought is that it must be Emerson but why does he care if I'm up here in the Penthouse asleep?

"What in the actual fuck, Emerson!" I try to sound as annoyed as I am, but my voice is still heavy with sleep, and it comes out as more of a mumble than a yell.

"Rise and shine, Sleeping Beauty."

My brain is still a bit foggy from sleep, and the help of the sleeping pills I swallowed last night, but this voice *doesn't* belong to Emerson. This realization causes adrenaline to pump through my body faster than the speed of light. I wrap my hand around the handle of the dagger I stashed under my pillow at some point last night. I sit up, fully alert, and face the direction of the voice, dagger positioned in front of me, ready for an attack.

I'm met with an amused smirk and sparkling emerald eyes. His eyes stand out even more in his face with his normally unruly hair pulled back into cornrows. The five o'clock shadow he's sporting accentuates his jawline and the overall new look makes him look a lot meaner. Tougher somehow.

Prince Emrick crosses his arms in front of his chest, "well, I'm pleased to see you stay armed and prepared for danger, but I'm afraid it would have been too late if I *actually* wanted to hurt you."

I shrug, "this Penthouse is one of the most secure places I can be. If an enemy can get to me here, I don't think I stand a chance either way. How'd you get in?" I ask, as I set the dagger down at my side.

His smirk turns into a grin, "the handsome blonde one let me in."

I nod in understanding, "Emerson."

"I could get swim and get lost in those deep cerulean eyes all day," he sighs.

I can't help but feel like I'm seeing him for the first time. The thought crossed my mind last night that he may be gay or bi but his comments about Emerson confirm it. I think I'm in a bit of shock because I didn't expect it. Not that I know Emrick on any level, so why should I be surprised? The only times I've been around him he's always been very professional and on task. There's never really been a time or place for me to truly *know* him. The shock must show on my face.

"Is there a problem?" He asks, defensively.

I shake my head, "you'll freeze."

His defensiveness turns into confusion, "excuse me?"

"Those deep cerulean eyes. You'll freeze in those frigid depths," I tease, my lips twitching, as I try and remain serious and fail.

His body visibly relaxes. I think my initial shock had him concerned that I would judge him. That I wouldn't accept him for who he is and that our working together would be an issue. I get the feeling that he hides his truth more often than not, and for some reason, he's decided to be open with me. I've always liked Emrick's calm energy and I can't help but like him even more now for taking a chance on trusting me with his honesty. His vulnerability.

We stare at each other another moment longer before we both bust out laughing.

"He is pretty cold and rigid, that one," he agrees.

"Well, if anyone could thaw out that glacier, my money is on you and that easy, disarming, and brilliant smile you wield as a weapon."

"I'm not one to brag but it is one of my best features," he flashes said smile my way to prove his point.

I can't help but smile back. "Do you remember the first time we met?"

"Of course. In the throne room when Hallana burst in like a blood-thirsty bat out of Hell and you and Logan put on *quite* the show." He wiggles his eyebrows.

I chuckle and can't help but blush a bit at his teasing. "Yeah, well..." I clear my throat, "that part was fun but honestly, I was so damn terrified. I felt so lost and out of place, and then Hallana's blatant hate towards me threw me for a loop. I had no idea why she hated me without even knowing me."

"That's just who she is, it's not personal."

"I know that now but I didn't back then. I swear I just wanted to run back to my old insignificant but *safe* life, and then you were introduced. You smiled at me and it was so genuine and heart-warming. You made me feel like maybe I would have some people in my corner after all. Maybe all this wouldn't be that bad. Your warmth towards me in that moment was everything I needed. I never did thank you for that. Thank you."

"Hey now, just because you're throwing all these amazing compliments my way doesn't mean that I'm going to go easy on you in training." He puts his hands on his hips in defiance but he's smiling brightly.

"I wouldn't dream of it, Coach."

"Good," he gives me a curt nod. "Now get your ass up and dressed for training. Wear layers because where we're going will be cold outside."

I groan at the thought of leaving the comfort and warmth of this bed and heading out into the chill and bite of fast-approaching winter weather. Not to mention my head is still groggy, I need to eat and hydrate before I can function much less start training, but I get out of bed without protest. After all, I'm the one who asked for this.

It takes another hour for me to get dressed, eat breakfast and find someone to take care of Griffin for me while I'm out training. Lucky for me, Valmont has a slew of employees for the casino, hotel, restaurants, bar, and dance club. Some employees even live on-site and have children. Children love dogs and they have endless energy to play fetch for days. Griffin will be a happy pup. After ensuring Griffin will be in good hands and threatening Emerson's life if anything happened to him while I'm gone, Emrick and I are finally headed out of the casino.

Emrick hands his valet ticket to an attendant and we take a seat on a nearby bench, waiting for his vehicle to be brought around. I scan the area and don't see my trusted valet, Josh, anywhere. He must only work the night shift and has gotten off work already. I've definitely gotten used to the celebrity status treatment here. Ok, maybe not *celebrity* status but never having to wait for my car is a simple convenience but a convenience nonetheless.

"This is us," Emrick rises as a dark blue, 4-door Toyota Tacoma pulls up. The attendant jumps out of the driver's side and rushes around the front to open my door for me.

"Thank you," I say, as I climb inside. I already know better than to try and offer a tip. No one here accepts money from me. Valmont's orders I assume.

We're quiet as Emrick pulls out of the casino and takes us South on 1-25 and then East on I-40. The sun is shining, there's not a cloud in the sky, but I can still feel the bite of winter in the air. This is going to be one of the last nice, sunny days we have before the snowstorms start sweeping in. I can feel it. I lean forward in my seat and lift my face up to the sun shining through the windshield and focus on the heat that caresses my skin. My head feels clear from the sleeping pills but still muddled from the nightmare. From my demons that haunt me even in a drug-induced sleep. I need to get my mind off of it all and focus on today's training.

"Where are we headed?" I ask, as I sit back and give Emrick my attention.

"I'm taking you to my home. You'll finally get to see where the Maa Family live and meet everyone. Well, maybe not literally everyone but you'll get to meet most of my people."

"What? No, you can't take me there! I need to stay close to the casino! I can't leave, not right now! It's not safe!" I start to panic.

"Amarah, calm down. We don't live that far and no one else knows I'm taking you there. *You* didn't even know. I promise you'll be safe. We are safeguarded and protected and we can handle threats. Plus, we're close enough that you don't need to stay with us for training. We can come back to the city but it's important that you know where we are and only fair that you visit my family too."

"You live close by?" I ask. in confusion.

"Compared to the other Families, yes. We live up in the Sandia Mountains. It's still quite the drive, it will probably take us an hour to get there."

"Oh. I just always assumed you would be further away."

The Fire Fey and Air Fey both live a decent distance away from Albuquerque, it's about a two to two-and-a-half hour drive to each. You then have to hike another eight or so hours to even reach the Fire Fey, which is the first place I went for training when I was brought into this world.

"I like that you're close, but still, we shouldn't take this risk. There's a new Vampire in town and Valmont insists she's not only dangerous but he thinks she wants something to do with me. Once again, I'm a target and therefore, anyone around me is in danger."

"You can't hide your whole life, Amarah. The more training you do, the better equipped you are to handle these threats. If you stop running away from the idea that you're a target and therefore a threat, and instead start running towards it on offense instead of defense, you'll have a better chance of winning and protecting those around you. Hiding and running never does anyone any good."

I let out a defeated sigh and cross my arms, knowing he's right, but not having to like it. I also know I'm not winning this particular argument, so instead, I focus on the here and now.

"If you're the closest, then why didn't I start my training with you? Why did I start with the Fire Fey?"

He cocks his eyebrow and glances at me as if I should already know the answer to my question. "Hallana insisted you train with her Family first. She obviously wanted to get in the middle of you and Logan and squash anything before it started. It had nothing to do with training and everything to do with Logan."

"God," I let out a sigh, "that sure was a Hell of a way to get inducted into The Unseen. The hike alone nearly destroyed me, then a demon tried to kill me, and I'm not talking about Hallana," he chuckles, "dealing with Hallana's fiery hatred and jealousy, finding out about Logan's past and then a full-blown demon invasion that nearly destroyed the Tulekahju Family." I scrub my hands down my face, "I would have much rather started training with you."

"You've definitely been through a lot in your short time as our Võitleja but I firmly believe that everything happens for a reason."

I scoff in disagreement.

"I'm serious. You might not see it or understand it when you're going through it, but things all make sense and come into focus eventually. You can't see the forest through the trees. That saying is true. Think about it. When you're inside the forest you can't see it. You can only see the beauty of it, as a whole, once you're standing a good distance away. But when you're inside, you notice things you can't see from afar. The beauty in the details, the sounds, the smells, the life thriving inside. The cycle of life and death and how they go hand in hand and compliment each other. Life is the same way. You need to literally stop and smell the roses along the way and have faith that you'll see the bigger picture eventually. Things always work out just the way they're meant to."

"Yeah? Tell that to Andre. Oh wait, you can't. Because he's dead. I killed him."

He shakes his head, "you didn't kill him, Amarah. He died in battle and he lived more in his final days than he had in a long time. Andre is resting now and he's at peace. You need to accept that death comes to us all and it will never seem like the right time. It will never get easier. You need to find your peace with both life and death or you'll only suffer and cause those who love you to suffer right along with you."

We sit in silence as I contemplate everything he said. He's right, I know he is, but it's easier said than done. We finally pull off the winding Sandia Crest road that leads to the peak of the mountain and onto a dirt road I would have missed on my own. The dirt road starts off fairly smooth but it quickly turns into a narrow, bumpy, off-road trail. I can see why he drives this truck now.

"This is definitely off the beaten path."

"It is. You know the Fey like their privacy. We need places that allow us the freedom to be who we are without always having to hide and use glamour."

The road doesn't even resemble a road at this point and I'm gripping the oh-shit handlebar for dear life. There's a straight wall of rock and dirt to our left and a cliff to our right. I glance out the window and down, big mistake. My heart is in my throat and I squeeze my eyes shut only to see Logan throw himself off a cliff. I take in a gasping breath and try to calm myself and focus on the piece of land I can see in front of us.

"It's ok, Amarah, it's not as bad as you think. This road is very secure. I promise you're safe."

"Road," I try to laugh but a huff of air is all I get. "What road? This is just a barely wide enough path with sure death at the slightest mistake."

"Well, training 101, we obviously need to work on your glamour detection."

"Glamour?" I ask through my rising fear. How did I forget about glamour?

Emrick grins and then bites his bottom lip as he tries not to laugh in my face. "The cliff you're seeing isn't really there. I promise this road is wide and safe. Yes, it's very off-road for obvious reasons, but it's safe. You're safe."

"Shit," I let out a relieved sigh. "I'm sorry. I'm distracted and I haven't trained in a while. Guess I've forgotten more than I'd like to admit."

"We'll get you back on track," he says with a wink.

I return my focus to the road in front of us. It looks like a dead end with a huge mountain looming in front of us. Emrick continues at the same pace, not once tapping the breaks to slow down. I immediately know it must be more glamour and it's confirmed once our truck plows right through the mountain. I roll down my window and stick my arm out, immediately feeling the tingle of glamour against my skin. Once I feel it on my skin, I remember what it's like to see it, and see *through* it. Details of past training sessions are coming back to me, I cling to them as we round a bend in the road, and I'm suddenly looking upon a village built into the mountainside.

It's similar to the Fire Fey's home in the sense that there is green everywhere. Plants and trees and flowers as far as I can see. There are roads and trails cut out of the mountain leading up to cabin homes, all various sizes and shapes, but they're all built out of logs and stones. Everything is natural. There's a field off in the distance and I can just make out the shimmer of water snaking through the greenery.

"Oh my gosh, Emrick, this is beautiful," I whisper, as I try and look at everything around me and take it all in.

"It is," he smiles and the pride in his eyes is undeniable. "Welcome to the Maa Family's home."

He parks in front of a building built like the cabins above, but I can tell it's not a home. It's got more of a big building vibe than a cozy home vibe.

"This is our community building. This is where we meet to discuss important events but it's also a place to hang out. There's a movie theater and a huge game room for the kids. Well, we say it's for the kids but honestly, the adults use it just as much," he laughs happily. "Come on, the Vanemad are waiting for us."
"Vaneman? I'm not familiar with that term." I admit.

"Our Elders"

"Elders?" I ask, in confusion. The other Fey Families don't have Elders. At least not that I know of."

"Yep. We are a bit more old-fashioned than the others."

That's all the explanation he provides, as I follow him into the building. We walk into an enormous entry way with floor to ceiling windows, as well as sky lights, letting in all the natural light. There are also huge chandeliers hanging from the ceiling. It's just past midday, but as the sun sets, it's going to fall behind the mountain and leave this settlement in the shade until the darkness envelopes them completely.

I hear the sounds of voices and laughter filling up the huge space and the pure happiness radiates throughout the building. I can feel the joy hanging in the air around me. I feel suddenly more at ease with the energy I feel. I follow Emrick, as he leads me down a short hallway to our left, and we enter what I assume is the game room.

There are a mix of kids and adults, lounging on couches and cushions, that seem to be on every available floor surface. There are people scattered around at tables with puzzles and board games, pool, air hockey, foosball, pinball machines, darts, ping pong, you name it, they have it. I stand here, no doubt with my jaw on the floor, as I take it all in.

"This doesn't look very traditional to me."

"We're traditional in our beliefs and understanding of the world but we do adapt and evolve. We love modern technology as you can tell. The movie theater is through there," he points to the back wall. There is a door on the bottom floor and also a staircase, balcony, and another door on the second level.

"The movie theater is two levels?" I ask in awe.

"Is there any other way to watch movies besides on the big screen?" His smile is enormous and the love he clearly has for his home is so beautiful to see.

"You're welcome here any time but we have introductions to attend first. Come on."

We leave the game room and head in the opposite direction, down the same type of hallway, but this time we enter what must be their version of a throne room. Only, it gives me more of a church vibe with benches lined up in rows on either side of a wide walkway that leads to the dais. Instead of a single throne sitting on the dais, there is a long table with five chairs. The chairs are currently occupied, by who I assume are the Elders, and I'm immediately in awe of their beautiful, vibrant colorful clothing. It's all modern but obviously custom. It reminds me of what I've seen represents indigenous tribes, exuberant colors and shapes, adorned with beads and accented with bold jewelry.

As we approach the dais, I notice that the Elders, two females and three males, are not using any glamour, instead, they remain in their true Fey forms. Their varying shades of dark skin are textured like the bark of a tree. But the texture is just that, texture. It doesn't hide the youthfulness their faces still have. The Elders aren't what I expected. I was thinking I would see men and women in their eighties and nineties, skin delicate and wrinkled, bodies hunched and fragile, but that's not at all what I see. They all have similar dark hair. Some wear it short, some long, some more unruly than others and some have grey in their hair while others don't. They all have the same short horns sticking out of their hair. I remember seeing them on Emrick when I first met him and forced him, and the other Fey Leaders, out of their glamour.

Once we're standing right beneath the dais, I'm met with five pairs of intense green eyes. Shades from emerald, like Emrick's, to jade, moss, lime, and apple. All intense shades of green but none with any hint of yellow, like Logan's, or any other color. I know I'm staring but I can't help it. I feel like I'm in a whole new world. I feel like Dorothy and we're definitely not in Kansas anymore.

"You're all so beautiful," I whisper, more to myself than to them.

"Vanemad," Emrick bows his head in respect. "This is Amarah Rey Andrews, the Võitleja, Warrior of the Fey, and she has come to learn and train with us."

I suddenly feel extremely self-conscious standing before these powerful Elders in my black hoodie over bulky layers, sweat pants over leggings, and a pair of old sneakers. My daggers strapped to my thighs are the only thing that resembles any type of Warrior, but they look ridiculous with the outfit I'm wearing, and I suddenly wish I had the suitcase full of leather again. There's something to be said about looking fierce and feeling fierce.

Following Emrick's lead, I bow my head, "thank you for allowing me this time in your home. I will respect it as my own and treat all people here as my own family. I'm looking forward to the training and knowledge I will learn here."

The woman in the center of the table speaks for them, "Amarah, we're so happy to have you here. This is Kyanna Hale," she gestures towards the woman on her far-right and proceeds to introduce the Elders. "Theodore Robinson, Kian Smith, Carson Williams, and I am Emmaline Marshall. We welcome you to the Maa Family and look forward to getting to know you and assisting you in learning about Earth magic. Please, consider our home your home while you're here."

"Thank you," I bow my head again, because I feel so awkward in my hoodlum attire, looking like a hobo compared to the majestic vision of the Elders.

I feel a slight tug on my hand and hear Emrick whispering in my ear, "Amarah, come on."

I glance back up at the dais and I see the humor in Emmaline's eyes and curiosity in the others. I dip my chin again, and turn on my heel, as Emrick tugs my hand and leads me out of the throne room.

Once we're safely in the hallway and out of earshot, I let Emrick have it, "you should have warned me! Or prepared me better!" I whisper yell. "They're your *Elders* and they're sitting up there like kings and queens and I look like you took pity on me and picked me up off the street!"

He grimaces but shrugs, "I had no idea they were going to go full-on traditional and meet you like that. I thought we would all shake hands, maybe a hug or two and some small talk. I had no idea they were going formal. They're not that bad, I promise. You're going to love them."

I just glare at him with my hands dangerously close to my daggers.

He puts his hands up in defense, "Amarah, I swear! I didn't know!"

"Oh, you are going to pay for this, *Prince*," I seethe. "Where's the training mat because you're about to bleed all over it." If there's one thing I really don't like, it's to be embarrassed and feel insecure. I feel *both* and Emrick is going to be the one to pay for it.

He grins at me but this time it's more sinister and I see the excitement in his eyes, "we'll see whose blood decorates the mat. Follow me, *Sleeping Beauty*."

He leads me back outside and down the road to another large building, but this one is only one story. As soon as I walk in, I smell the rubber, sweat, and blood in the air. I stop at the end of the mat and take off my hoodie and sweats. I leave the dagger harnesses on the floor and take the daggers in my hands and step on the mat.

"You haven't trained in a while, are you sure you want to go with those and not some practice ones first?"

"Is the little Prince scared?" I tease.

"You wish," he pulls his own set of daggers from the wall rack and joins me on the mat. "Show me what you've got, Sleeping Beauty."

I let out a battle cry and attack without hesitation. The adrenaline rushes through my veins, and the sound of metal against metal in my ears is a song I didn't know I was missing until I heard it and felt it again. This is just what I need. A balm to my wounded soul. An outlet for all of my anger and frustrations. The steps and movements all come back to me as if I've never stopped. It's just like riding a bike, but more ferocious, and potentially deadly. I imagine it's someone else I'm attacking. A beautiful female, with natural red hair, and roaming hands that I want to remove from her curvy body.

I feel the maniacal grin on my face as my dagger connects, the first slice of skin, red droplets flying through the air, painting the mat.

Amarah: Moving Forward

Fight Song by Rachel Platten

We're both spread out like a couple of starfish on the mat, chests heaving, muscles that feel like jelly, and skin peppered in knicks and cuts.

"I have to say..." Emrick manages short bursts of sentences through his gasping breaths, "I wasn't expecting that."

"If I'm being honest, I wasn't either."

"You've had great training when it comes to fighting."

I think back to my time on the mat with Andre. He was the first person to train me and he was so incredibly patient. He taught me so much in my weeks at the Fire Fey's home. Then I trained with Jon at the Air Fey's home and he really helped refine my skills. Not to mention training I've done with Logan, too. Although, that typically ended up being more of a...*cardio endurance* workout most of the time. They're all incredible fighters and trainers. Andre is no longer here to train me and Jon nearly died in the attack at their home when I was there. Again, an attack meant to target *me*. Well, me and the Queen, but still. I'm always going to be a target of some kind.

My heart feels heavy in my chest with all my memories, "yeah, I have. Some of the best. Though I'm not good enough yet to avoid *your* blades." I hold up my arms and inspect all of my wounds. "Nothing too deep though, thank goodness. I should be able to heal them," I say, as I sit up.

He sits up, too, and faces me, "that's right, you're from the Müstik Family, your Bloodline excels at healing."

I scoff, "my Bloodline, sure, but I wasn't raised as Fey. I'm like a child learning for the first time. Hell, a Fey child can probably heal better than I can at this point."

"Words have power, Amarah. You need to have more confidence and grace with yourself. Start building the habit to think and speak positive thoughts. Being self-deprecating doesn't make you humble it just makes you a negative Nancy and no one likes to be around a negative Nancy."

"Ouch," I physically wince at his harsh words, "that was another blade nick to my already battered soul there, Dr. Phil."

He shrugs, "you can't start to make conscious changes until you're aware of your habits and behaviors. So, let's start with some confidence, and let me see some of those healing powers."

"I don't know if it's enlightening or infuriating being around you."

Emrick delivers one of his confident grins, "girl, I'm the best friend you wish you always had. Now, come on, stop stalling," he gestures to my arms.

"Definitely infuriating," I sigh, as I drop my head to hide my smile.

I have two wonderful friends but they're human. It would be really nice to have someone to confide in who actually knows about and understands my unique situations. Like the fact that I'm really half Fey and half Angel, my sister, who's not really my sister, is a Witch, Vampires are real, and my boyfriend is a Werewolf. Ex. My *ex*-boyfriend.

I let out a heavy sigh that has nothing to do with recovering from our training as I try to focus on my left arm. There are cuts and bruises alongside four nasty-looking scars. Two scars on top of my forearm and two underneath. They're scars left from when a demon nearly bit my arm right off. Luckily, I had been healed by an amazing healer almost immediately. Still, the scars remain due to dark blood magic. Magic fuelled with *my* Angel blood. I shake my head and try to focus again.

"Amarah, it's ok if you can't do it. You've been out of practice for a bit." He shrugs nonchalantly again, "nothing to be ashamed of."

"It's not that," I shake my head. "My past just keeps distracting me."

"Perhaps it's a sign that you need to stop ignoring it and instead *address it* so that you can move past it and finally allow yourself to heal. On the inside."

I glare at him and try to convey how much I don't like all this wisdom spewing. He's saying all the thoughts I've buried deep inside of me out loud. He's illuminating truths I'd rather not face because I'm a coward and running away from problems is easier than trying to grow through them. He makes it sound easy when it's anything but. And my insecurities and confusion about who I am, who I *really* am, and what I want, make me feel like a child again. An immature, spoiled little brat who never has to face her responsibilities and consequences of her actions.

I know I'm just being stubborn when I say, "my past is just that, in the past. I'm moving forward how I want to move forward and I'm doing just fine, thank you very much. Now, if you'll stop talking for two seconds, I have some healing to do."

I ignore his condescending smirk and focus back on my arm, only seeing the cuts. I think back to Iseta's words the first time she explained to me how the healing process works. I focus on the deepest cut and then I access the power that's inside of me, the power that *is* me. I've become very comfortable with my power although, still unsure of exactly what it can do. What *I'm* capable of. But the warm, tingling feeling as my power comes alive on my skin comforts me. I imagine the wound stitching back together. I picture my skin closing, and with no more than a quick, vague burning sensation, the cut is gone and my skin is whole and smooth again.

"That's wonderful, Amarah!" Emrick smiles brightly, as I meet his eyes with my own smile.

"Thanks!"

"Now, don't take this the wrong way," he immediately holds his hands up in defense. My smile falls and I give him another death glare.

"What now?" I ask, in irritation.

"If you have to literally heal one cut at a time we'll be here forever. Have you tried to heal on a bigger scale? A bigger area of focus?"

I shake my head, "no. I told you, I'm not experienced when it comes to this and I haven't had any training."

"Well, you're never going to know what you're capable of if you don't try and push the boundaries of what you think you know. Why don't you give it a shot and try to heal all your cuts at once?"

Again, it's like he can read my damn mind. So much so in fact, that I narrow my eyes in suspicion, as I look at him and ask, "can you read my mind?"

"Is that a legit question or are you being cheeky?"

"Dead serious."

He studies me for a few seconds, to gauge if I really am being serious or just joking about his ability to read my thoughts, before he answers just as seriously.

"Amarah, The Unseen is a magical world, yes, but no one has the power to actually read minds. Witches may be able to use spells to try and get inside your head but that's not full-proof, and Vampires can hypnotize and simply ask the truth out of you, but no one can read minds."

I let out a sigh of relief and nod my head. I think about how Logan and I can talk to each other's minds but I've never wondered if the opposite is possible. Could I read his thoughts? I can already feel his emotions through our link which is...*intense* but still somewhat of a guessing game. Being able to know his actual thoughts, or him being able to know mine...now that's a terrifying thought.

I pull my focus back to the task at hand but this time I close my eyes. I pull on my power as if I'm tugging on a string that's connected inside of my chest. My power rushes through me and I can feel it in my hands. I caress the power and focus on my body. I can feel every inch of my bruised and beaten skin. The cuts are like little heartbeats that I can feel pulsing, so I focus on healing them, healing my body as a whole. I picture my skin whole and smooth and will my power to make it so. I feel the tingling sensation of my power intensify for a few seconds before it returns to its normal warmth around me.

I'm about to pull my power back inside of me when I have another thought. I extend my power to envelop Emrick. I hear his gasp as my power connects with his skin. It's been a while since I've shared my power with anyone else, in a peaceful way. I will my power not to hurt Emrick but instead, heal him. I imagine his skin whole and smooth as well. I hear him hiss in pain before I pull my power back and finally open my eyes.

Emrick is looking back and forth between his outstretched arms, moving them this was and that way, trying to see every inch of his skin. I look at his outstretched arms as well, and notice that there are no more open wounds. The only evidence there is, that he was ever hurt, is the dried traces of blood.

"Holy Mother of the Earth!" Emrick exclaims. "That was amazing! A little uncomfortable...and maybe a lot a bit scary," he laughs, nervously, "but amazing nonetheless! I've never experienced anything like what you just did. Your power is like a *physical* thing. I could feel it all around me. It...it wasn't exactly painful, but..." he shakes his head. "I don't know how to explain it."

"But you've been healed before." It's not a question but he answers like it's one.

"Yeah, but never like that! Our healers have to use natural herbs and remedies to heal. The Müstik Family can heal with their hands, yes, but it's concentrated. They have to literally place their hands on or near wounds and use their own auras to heal. Even the most skilled and powerful of the First Fey can drain their energy in the healing process. They can give too much of themselves in order to save someone else. What you did was different. I don't exactly know how. But it was way different."

He's looking at me with a mix of awe, curiosity, and fear in his eyes. I quickly look away so he doesn't see the lie in mine as I shrug it off. "I don't know about all of that, I just did what felt natural to me. Maybe others just don't know they can do it any other way? They've been taught the same way for generations and I'm just winging it. I'm sure it's nothing."

The lie tastes bitter on my tongue because he's been so open and honest with me, the last thing I want to do is lie to him. What kind of friendship can I hope to have with him if I start it off with lies? But what choice do I have? He can't find out what I *actually* am.

"So, now that we're all healed, are you going to show me your skills with Earth magic?" I quickly change the subject.

He appraises me again but seems to give in for the time being. "Girl, I've got *mad* skills! You ain't even ready."

I can't help but smile at his confidence and easy swagger, "alright, well, I'm done giving you compliments for the foreseeable future. I don't know how you manage to fit through any door with that big head of yours."

"Confidence and cocky are two different things. Yes, I'm very confident in who I am and what I can do, but by no means am I arrogant. My momma taught me better than that."

"I know you're not, Emrick, I was just teasing you," I say, as I follow him outside.

The sun is still out, it can't be much past mid-afternoon, but the mountain sits entirely in shadow. The temperature has dropped at least ten degrees already and I shiver as I put my hoodie back on.

"Now I understand why you told me to wear layers."

"Oh, this is nothing compared to the winter months. Those days can be pretty brutal."

"Consider me a summertime patron then because I do not do well with the cold."

"What? Amarah, the cold months are the perfect excuse to find a hottie to snuggle up to. Trust me, everyone has the same thought, that's why they call it cuffing season."

Emrick's words pierce an already gaping wound and rip it open wider. The image of Logan in bed with that woman cuts me so deeply no magic power will ever be able to reach it and heal me.

Emrick must see the pain in my eyes because he stops short and turns me towards him. "Amarah, I'm so sorry. I didn't even think about what we walked in on last night. I'm an idiot. I didn't mean to stir all of that up. I'm so sorry."

I shrug, not knowing what to say and not trusting my voice as the emotion claws its way up my throat. What is there to say?

It's ok? Because it's not.

It doesn't matter? Because it does.

I'll be ok? Because I won't.

I've moved on? Because I haven't.

"Do you wanna talk about it?" He asks, softly.

"What's there to even say? Just like everything else, it's my fault, and he made his choice." I cross my arms in a defensive position and shrug again as I try and maintain my willpower not to break down and cry in front of the Prince.

"Follow me," he commands, as he turns around and heads towards the mountain.

There's a well-worn trail snaking up the side of the mountain leading to the homes nestled snuggly in the mountainside. Some homes have lights on inside while others remain dark. The further we climb, the homes get fewer, and farther apart. By the time we come to our destination, I'm sweating, gasping for air, and my legs are on fire.

I collapse on the top stair that leads up to a small porch, "man, I'm so out of shape it's not even funny. I didn't think a month off would hit me this hard."

He leans against a porch beam, arms and ankles crossed, as he looks down at me where I'm trying not to die, "It's not like you took care of yourself in that month. I don't know exactly what's going on, but I notice you've lost weight and muscle tone, then I saw the trainwreck of last night and it doesn't take a genius to put two and two together."

"That obvious, huh?"

He arches his eyebrows at me with a look that says, *really?* He shakes his head and walks towards the door. He opens it without knocking or unlocking the door. A light comes on and Emrick calls from somewhere inside, "get your butt in here, Amarah. We're going to have girl time!"

Even in my hurting and wounded state, both emotionally and now physically thanks to training and this steep climb, I can't help but smile. I don't know if I want to talk about all that's happened but it's nice to have someone I *can* talk to. I pick myself up off the porch and follow Emrick inside. I shut the door behind me and take in my new surroundings. It's not at all what I expected from the outside. I was expecting dark wood, old rusty metal decor, and deer heads hanging from the walls, but what I actually see is sleek, modern decor, clean precise lines and bright colors.

I follow the noise and enter the kitchen. New stainless-steel appliances stand out against the warm shade of blue cabinets and light golden wood countertops. The lighting is bright to fight against the shadow of the mountain, but there are a couple of skylights in the ceiling too. I imagine the natural light in the mornings and mid-day is phenomenal in here. It's a fairly small space, but it's open and inviting. I take a seat on one of the island stools and watch Emrick as he bustles about. He places two oversized mugs on the island just as the tea kettle whistles on the stove.

"Honey? Cream?" He asks.

"Both, please," I answer, with an amused smile on my face. I'm getting a sense of who Emrick is outside of being the Prince of the Maa Family, and I'm completely shocked because he's not anything like I thought he would be. I knew he had good energy but he's downright wholesome and it eases something in my chest to know that he's in my life.

"Thank you," I say, as he places a mug in front of me. I wrap my hands around it and that familiar, comforting heat seeps through my palms and straight into my soul. I take a sip of the tea, "mmmm, is that coconut?" It's not coffee but it's a damn good second choice.

"Toasted coconut black tea, one of my favorites," he explains, as he takes a sip and then leans his arms onto the island, giving me his full attention. "Now, tell me what happened."

I sigh as I stare at the cup in my hands, not sure if this is even something I want to rehash but words start spilling out of my mouth instantly. "You know what happened at the Air Fey's home. You were there."

"Yes, I was there. It was a nasty, bloody battle."

I nod in agreement, "it was. We lost too many people and it's my fault."

He scoffs, "ok, talk about being arrogant. Do tell how you've managed to come to the conclusion that Aralyn's traitorous play for the crown is *your* fault?"

"I'm Võitleja, Emrick. I'm supposed to be the one helping defeat the demons and end the war. Everyone is counting on me to be this...*miracle*, and I'm not. I'm not what, or who, the Queen and everyone else thinks I am. I'm not *good* and I can't protect anyone. My power is dangerous to those around me either because I can't control it or because I'm a target for threats."

"Alright, you said a lot there. First, no one, myself included, puts winning this war all on your shoulders. I've actually never understood why the Queen thinks you're different. Maybe because you're the last of her blood, I don't know. Care to elaborate on that?"

I shake my head.

"I didn't think so," he sighs. "No one can end a war on their own, Amarah, and no one expects you to. Second, I can't speak to if you're good or not. Not even sure what that means. Everyone's definition of good is different. If you're upset because you're not perfect, well, honey not everyone can be me," he smirks and pretends to flip hair over his shoulder.

I can't help but laugh, and I know that was his intent, to lighten the mood. "Not cocky, huh?"

"We're not here to talk about me," he waves off my statement. "Lastly, your power is no more dangerous than mine, the Queen's, Logan's, or Valmont's for that matter. We're all dangerous, Amarah, and your power has never hurt anyone."

I scoff and I'm about to argue when he holds up a hand, "I know you blame yourself for Andre's death. That's not exactly a secret, and I know it's been explained to you that it wasn't your fault. It was evil blood magic at play that took Andre's life. Not you. Since you're obviously not getting over this detail any time soon, let's fast forward to the present and bring out the big guns."

He takes another sip of his tea and I do the same, preparing for hard truths about to knock the shit out of me.

"I've seen the way Logan looks at you. From day one, it was *impossible* not to see. And I've seen the way you look at him. There is something undeniably special between the two of you. So...why on Earth was he in bed with another woman? What happened?"

I swallow down the ball of emotion threatening to suffocate me. I take another sip of my tea trying to force it down. The tea does nothing to comfort me now.

I sigh and finally look up at Emrick, "yes, I blame myself for Andre's death. He died in my arms, Emrick. And Valmont barely survived. I held two dying men in my arms and it terrified me. I loved Andre, in my own way, and I've come to deeply care about the frustratingly arrogant Vampire."

"But...?"

"But it's child's play compared to what I feel for Logan."

"I'm struggling to understand how that's a bad thing?"

"I won't survive if Logan dies in my arms," my chin starts to tremble, the tears are suddenly building up, threatening to spill, and I can't stop them. I can't stop the flood of emotions and words spilling out of me.

"I've dreamt about it happening again and again. I see them all, dying in my arms, and when I wake up, the only thing that brings me peace is knowing that it wasn't Logan that died. That's he's still alive and breathing. Someone died! Someone lost their life, in my arms, and all I can think about is Logan. What kind of monster does that make me?"

"Amarah..."

"So, I made the decision to keep him alive. I left him, to give him a chance at life, because his days are numbered if he's with me. I'm *dangerous*, Emrick. And I won't survive knowing I'm responsible for killing the only man I've ever truly loved. I know that sounds cliche but it's true. Whatever else I've felt for anyone before him was surface level. Logan is etched in my mind, in my body, and in my damn soul! I can't lose him. I *refuse* to lose him."

He sighs heavily, "let me see if I got this right. You let him go...in order to...to *keep* him?"

The tears are flowing and I'm sobbing like a baby so I just nod.

"Amarah, that is so...*fucking twisted.*"

"I know, but he's obviously moved on. So, I'm glad it happened sooner rather than later. I don't know that he ever loved me the way I love him," I sniffle, trying to keep my runny nose in check. The last thing I want is boogers running down my face. I've already sunk low enough.

"I know you don't believe that."

"I don't want to! But what else is there to believe? He says one thing but his actions prove something else entirely! I've been blinded by all the right words before, choosing to ignore the actions, and I'm not doing that again."

He's quiet for a long time before I see a devilish smirk pull on his lips, "so you're saying I have a chance with that sexy Werewolf then?"

I'm leaning over the island in an instant, batting at him half-heartedly, "not if you value your life!"

He laughs and steps out of my reach, "kidding! Kidding! I would never cross that line. Chicks before dicks, right?" He winks, "but damn, that man is sexy."

"Ugh, don't remind me," I slump on my stool.

"Well, from what I gathered last night, you seem to have rebounded quite well," he doesn't ask it as a question, but he's looking at me eagerly, awaiting a confirmation.

I think back to my night with Valmont and the things I let him do to me. Heat creeps up my neck and face as I duck my head.

"It's true then! Valmont, really? I've never been with a Vampire. What's it like?" He asks, enthusiastically.

"First of all, it's not what you think. It happened after I saw Logan with that woman at the meeting. They were clearly together and had been for a while. I just...*acted*. I didn't have intentions of sleeping with Valmont. I went to his club to get shitfaced and find a Vampire to bite me. One thing led to another and Valmont had to make the choice to either kill me or fuck me," I shrug. "I was hoping for the former, but he chose to think with his dick instead, and here we are," I gesture with my hands. "It's true what they say about their bites being pleasurable but what I didn't realize is how *addicting* they are. If you value your sanity and sobriety, don't *ever* let a Vampire bite you because it won't be a one-time thing."

"What's it like?"

I shake my head and shrug, "how can I even explain it? It's like...intense pleasure from the roots of your hair down to the end of your toenails," I laugh. "It's all-consuming and the best fucking thing I've ever felt physically. It leaves you so high you might as well be floating in outer space. It's actually the only time I've been at peace since everything that's happened. It wipes my mind completely and for a little while I can just...*breathe*. I think that's another reason why it's so addicting to me. I crave the numbness."

"That makes sense and definitely sounds dangerous. Men are addicting enough as it is, I think I'll steer clear of any added possibility."

"Smart," I chuckle.

"So, what are you going to do then? About it all?"

I look at him and shake my head, "I have no fucking clue. I need this, I need training. I can't let myself fall victim to my emotions any longer. There's a lot of weird shit going on. We need to find Aralyn, we need to try and find out what the demons are doing and why they've been quiet, and I'm worried about the stuff that's been on the news. All those bodies can't be good for The Unseen *remaining* unseen."

"I agree with you about that. The Elders have also been tracking the killings and are concerned as to what it might mean for us."

"Well, that's good to know. Maybe they can include me in their discussions about it? I want to help but not sure how."

"Yeah, of course, I'll talk to them about it right away."

"Thanks. Ana is just too distracted. She has a single purpose, to find Aralyn, and I get it. I do. But we can't turn our backs on anything right now. Plus, Valmont has visitors that are supposedly crazy dangerous. The last thing I should be worrying about right now is my pathetic love life."

"You mentioned these visitors, tell me more about them," Emrick's teasing has subsided, and I see the brain of a Prince, working hard to understand and analyze all threats and situations. This is the Emrick I'm used to seeing in the meetings.

"I really don't know much. Viveka is like, one of the very first Vampires *ever*. I mean, Valmont is over two thousand years old…"

Emrick chokes on his tea and stares at me with wide eyes.

"I know! It's crazy! Well, Viveka is the one who turned Valmont into a Vampire so, I don't even want to know how old she is. She's traveling with some guy, Kordeuv, but I don't know anything about him at all. Valmont is concerned that Viveka is here for me."

"For you? Why would she be here for you?"

"My thoughts exactly! Valmont said she's drawn to power. That it's the only thing she wants, and apparently, what I did with my power at the Fire Fey's home is enough to spark her interest in me," I run my hands down my face. "Hell, I don't know Emrick. I don't know what's up from down anymore or where to focus my energy. It's like everything changed in the past month and I got left behind and now I'm running, trying to catch up."

"We'll figure this out," he reaches across the island to squeeze my hand in reassurance. "I'll talk with the Elders and get a meeting for us to discuss the attacks. I'm honestly not sure what connection we have to find out why the demons have suddenly stopped attacking and possessing bodies. We just need to keep our eyes and ears open. And as far as this Viveka chick, can you find out more about her?"

I nod, "yeah, of course. I can meet with Valmont and I can watch her as closely as I can. That's going to require me to become more of a night owl than an early bird though."

"Do what you can and we'll stay in touch." He reaches for his jacket that he placed on the island when we came in and pulls his cell phone out of the pocket. "It's getting late, I should get you back to the Casino. We don't want Valmont to go defcon one trying to find you when he wakes up and you're nowhere to be found."

"You have a point, but we didn't even get to practice with Earth magic."

"There will be plenty of time for that. I'll come to you tomorrow and we can start with the basics, somewhere close to the casino, and then we'll come back here when the Elders are ready to meet with you."

"Sounds good, Coach." I smile, as he grabs our mugs and places them in the sink.

"Let's go, Sleeping Beauty."

Valmont: At All Costs

Heavy Is The Weight by Memphis May Fire, Andy Mineo

My office is usually my sanctuary but it's currently being used as a war room. At least that's what it feels like in my mind. Viveka and Kordeuv are intruding on my personal space and I need to be on high alert, prepared for anything. I can't let the smallest thing distract me. So, why in the bloody Hell am I thinking about Amarah Rey? I know she's safe. Pierce confirmed that Alistair is shadowing her and last I knew, she was up in the Penthouse. Alone. So, why am I worried? And why do I want to be up in the Penthouse with her? Why do I want to take her onto the balcony, slowly undress her, so I can admire her naked skin under the moonlight, before I sink my fangs and cock deep inside of her?

The drink glass I'm holding shatters in my hand, bringing me back to reality, "bloody fucking Hell."

"Eveyrthing ok, Valmont?" Viveka's deceptively sweet voice asks from across the room.

"Fine," I say, through clenched teeth. I need to get myself under control. This is not the time for fantasies.

I pour mead over ice into three glasses and walk over to where Viveka and Kordeuv are looking out the windows, down into my club.

Viveka takes an offered glass, "I'll take that, but I'm afraid Kordeuv will have to pass. He doesn't drink."

I glance at him but his stoic expression gives nothing away. He seems fine letting Viveka speak for him, and clearly, make decisions for him. Then again, I do remember how controlling and influencing she can be. I don't envy the position he's in and can't help but wonder what stage he's in? Infatuated and eager to please or trapped and desperately trying to find a way out? With Viveka, there's no in-between.

"Very well," I toss back the extra drink and set the empty glass on the table. The Gods know I'm sure gonna need the extra alcohol to survive whatever this night has in store.

"So, this is all yours," she gestures with her hand to the office and the club.

"It is."

"It's a bit...*insignificant*, for you, don't you think?" She continues before I can answer. "I mean, don't get me wrong, it's great and all, but I know what you're capable of, Valmont. You could be worshipped as a king somewhere else. Why are you settling for owning a casino and a meager territory?"

"I have been worshiped as a king," I remind her.

She takes a sip of the mead and groans in ecstasy, "oh, Valmont, this is glorious. It's like traveling back in time." She approaches me and lays her dainty hand on my chest. "We were quite the pair, you and I. I have so many fond memories of our time together, but I must admit, they're starting to get a little fuzzy around the edges. Perhaps we can make some new ones," she holds my gaze, as her hand travels down my body, and she runs her hand over my cock. "Seeing you again reminds me how much I loved your body and your dick." She continues rubbing me over my pants, trying to get me hard, but it does nothing but disgust me.

I grab her wrist tightly, and she gasps, surprised at the pain, but her eyes sparkle with mischievous desire, clearly enjoying it. I pull her hand away from my body and take a step away from her.

"You may not think of me as your equal, but I am Virtuoso, and you *will* show me the respect my title demands. You've already crossed my territory without permission and touched me, *twice,* now. This body is no longer yours to touch, Viveka, and if you touch me again without my permission, or break any more of the Konsiilium's rules, I won't hesitate to report you and let the Täitjad deal with you. Are we clear?" I ask, as I grip her wrist even tighter, feeling her delicate bones close to snapping.

She scoffs and I let her pull her wrist out of my grasp, "You wouldn't dare report me to The Council."

"I'm no longer the scared little boy you can control, Viveka. I'm not afraid of you anymore. I don't want to report you, and I'm willing to let these few transgressions slide, but *do not* push me."

"You're right, I'll never consider you my equal, and I won't be threatened by you either," she tips her chin up in defiance. "I'm still more powerful than you and I *always* will be. So, be careful who you choose to throw your threats at. You do not want to push *me.*"

Her words are strong and confident, but I see the doubt flash in her eyes before she conceals it. I just spread my arms out and shrug. We both know there's only one way to find out who's more powerful and that only ends one way.

With one of us dead.

And Viveka is not one to fight her own battles and get her hands bloody. Not when it counts. No, she's manipulative and cunning. If she's going to prove her power over me, it's not going to be in any way I see coming. I know it, can do my best to prepare for it, but it still terrifies me. She has no lines she won't cross and I don't understand how The Council hasn't sent their Enforcers after her yet.

"Why are you here, Viveka? What do you want? No games."

She takes another sip of her drink, making a show of humming her pleasure, licking her lips, and trailing her fingertips seductively down her chest, between her breasts. A simple, yet effective method, of causing your eyes to follow her hand and watch her nipples harden under the thin, silk material of her top. If I hadn't just had Amarah Rey's beautiful body underneath me a few nights ago, I might have been tempted, but to her frustration, I'm not.

She's never been one to quit easily, I'll giver that. I understand why she often gets what she wants. If someone doesn't know any better, if they're not aware that she's the literal, walking, talking, Vampire of Death, giving the Goddess of Death, Hel, a run for her money, then that's they're mistake. A mistake they quickly realize, but often not quickly enough, before they're trapped in her web, being drained of their blood and life-force.

Viveka has turned her attention toward her companion, who stands ever stoically at her side. He's wearing a similar outfit to the one he wore the first night we met. Leather, leather, and more leather, silver chains around his neck, and an exposed chest and stomach, where Viveka's hands are now exploring.

"You must have forgotten how much you used to love my touch too, Valmont. I remember you used to be *insatiable* for me." She speaks to me as she's exploring another man's body. She moves to stand beside him, her left hand, holding her drink, goes around his back, while her right hand moves south. She makes eye contact with me as she starts to rub his cock. He responds quickly to her touch, growing harder with every stroke of her hand. "Perhaps a little demonstration will remind you of what you're turning down. Surely, I must be better than the insignificant women you play with."

I sigh, and rub my forehead, unable to hide my exasperation, "Viveka, truly, I appreciate the gesture, but I asked for no games. This," I gesture to what she's doing, "is not going to make me jealous.

If you do not wish to discuss why you're here, then might I suggest you go and enjoy the fruits of my labor? The casino, the club, or perhaps the suite should be your next stop, so you may stop teasing this poor bloke, give him his release, and put him out of his misery."

"You used to be jealous if another man even looked at me with desire in his eyes. You were down right possessive. I remember when…"

Viveka's voice fades out as my attention is pulled towards the office door. I sense her seconds before I hear her raised voice, arguing with Pierce.

"I don't give one single fuck, Pierce! You're going to have to lay your hands on me to stop me and how do you think Valmont will react to that? Yeah, that's what I thought! Ugh, I fucking swear, I'm so sick of this shit." The office door slams open, "Valmont, you're going to fucking talk to…oh, ummmm," she clears her throat, "I didn't realize you had company."

Amarah Rey stands a few steps inside of my office, where she stormed in, guns and cuss words blazing, before she stopped short at the sight of Viveka and Kordeuv. Her hands are still balled into fists at her sides, no doubt she furious with me since I've been avoiding her. Not that it's been easy. After our night of pleasure, all I've wanted to do since, is take her in every position and on every surface possible. I want to hole-up in the Penthouse and get lost in her for days, but the untimely visit of my new guests, keeps me away from her.

Seeing her now, in a pair of leggings that are clinging to her legs like a second layer of skin, a large, off-the-shoulder sweater that, once again, spotlights her shoulder and neck, her hair styled in a messy bun, leaving her neck achingly bare. My eyes rake over her exposed skin, I see the vein in her neck start to throb harder, faster, just the way I want to take her. My cock twitches and I have to pull on every ounce of my control to not react to her. Every second I'm in the same room as her, is a second Viveka can pick up on my secret. And if she suspects I feel even the smallest sliver of *anything* for Amarah Rey, she will use it against me.

Viveka is once again ruining my life.

Amarah Rey's sweet voice pulls me back to reality, it's low and a bit shaky, and I can't help but wonder if it's because she's reacting to me as well. "I see that I clearly interrupt…*something*," her eyes dart to where Viveka's hand is still stroking Kordeuv over his pants.

"I really can see why you like this one, Valmont. She's always so feisty, and clearly, impatient and desperate to be with you. Not that I blame her," Viveka comments and she takes a step away from Kordeuv and closer to Amarah Rey.

"Yes, you have, indeed, rudely interrupted my meeting. If I want you, I will call for you. Do you understand?"

She scoffs, "since when do I need to wait for a damn invitation to talk to you? You've been ignoring me for days and…"

I slam her back against the wall, my hand tight around her throat, and déjà vu hits me like slug to my chest. The memory of our night together comes rushing back, her sweet scent consumes me, and I have to clench my jaw tightly, grinding my teeth, to stop the urge I have to taste her beautiful mouth.

Her hands are gripping my forearm, her toes barely touching the floor, and her sad, hazel eyes are locked on mine. I see how lonely she's been. How lost. And I hate myself for making her feel this way when all I want to do is be with her every second of the day. I want to do whatever it takes to bring back the fire and happiness in her eyes. Her eyes drop to my mouth, her lips part in invitation, as her chest starts to rise and fall more quickly. She's arching herself away from the wall, fighting against the hold I have on her neck, fighting to get closer to me. Her desire sets my damn heart on fire.

Before I can stop myself, I lean in and brush my lips against hers. She eagerly reciprocates the gesture, pressing her lips against mine, then her tongue darts out, licking across my lips. I can't help the groan that escapes my throat. The sound is loud in the suddenly quiet room and it helps sober my mind. I remember that Viveka is no doubt watching every move I make. I can't even whisper a warning to Amarah Rey because Viveka will hear every word I say. All I can do is continue to act like Amarah Rey is just a girl I *play* with, as Viveka put it.

"How quickly your anger disappears at the thought of me fucking you again," I whisper, with my lips against hers. I slide my lips across her jaw and whisper my next words in her ear. "I told you, sweetheart, you're positively *addicted* to me."

At those words, she starts to struggle against my hold. I pull back to see the anger and hurt in her eyes. I try to reveal my truth, my apologies, to her with mine, but I don't know what she sees. I clench my jaw, desperately pushing down all of my emotions, as I step back and let her go.

She gasps for air, but quickly regains her voice, and uses it as her only weapon against me. "you're such a fucking arrogant piece of shit! I'm *not* addicted to you. You refuse to let me choose anyone else over you because you're a fucking control freak! You were a revenge fuck and nothing more to me than a means to an end."

She tips her chin up defiantly but her eyes betray her. Her eyes always show the truth of her heart and soul. Instead of the anger she's trying so hard to portray, her eyes are fighting to keep her tears at bay. I see the conflict of her words and emotions, but there's always a bit of truth in everything people say, and I can't help but feel the stab of her words like a stake in my heart. Yes, I am a Vampire, long since losing my human feelings and emotions, but when it comes to Amarah Rey, they're as real as they've ever been. I can't help but be affected by her words.

Revenge fuck.

Means to an end.

Is that her truth? Did I force her hand to be with me? Did I give her no alternative? Was I not her choice? I'm frozen in place, frozen by doubts. Doubts that are so foreign to me. I've forgotten what it feels like to feel...*insecure*. It's utterly miserable. To second guess yourself. Now is not the time for me to have *any* doubts. I need to turn this around and I need to get Amarah Rey out of here.

I shrug, and take a sip of my mead, that I'm still somehow holding. When I'm sure I've composed myself and my voice will be calm and normal, I respond.

"That may have been your goal initially, but what about the second time? When you fucked me slow and sweet, and begged me to bite you? You can't tell me you get the same pleasure from any other Vampire's bite. Hell, the way you were begging for it, I know you don't get that kind of pleasure *anywhere*. You can lie to yourself all you want, sweetheart, but you can't lie to me. I know you and I know your truth. And your truth came all over me, multiple times."

She scoffs, "you're unbelievable, Valmont. I *almost* believed you were different. I don't even know why I'm surprised. You're all the same."

"Yes, well, why don't you run along. As we've already established, you're not wanted right now. Perhaps I'll call on you soon, and as much as you want to deny it, I know you'll come running, eager and wet, when I call."

"I hate you," she seethed.

"Hate can only stem from some sort of love or caring," I turn my back on her, before I can see her reaction, or allow her to make another comment. "Pierce," I raise my voice for the bodyguard standing outside my office door.

He steps inside the office, hands clasped in front of his body, "boss."

"Please escort our uninvited guest out and make sure she stays out. See that Alistair keeps her in line going forward. You have my permission to handle her in any way you see fit to make that happen."

He dips his chin in confirmation as he takes a step towards Amarah Rey and grabs her arm, ready to haul her out.

"Hey! Get your hand off of me, I know how to walk, and I'll *happily* leave!" Amarah Rey growls out angrily.

"Not so fast, Valmont. You may not want to play with this one tonight, but she piques my curiosity." I don't like how she's appraising Amarah Rey with her predator eyes. "I may just take your earlier advice and take my leave to enjoy this feisty snack. What do you think, Kordeuv? Should we have some fun with this one?"

"Whatever pleases you," he responds, calmly.

"We haven't finished our discussion, Viveka," I argue, trying to keep her attention on me.

She waves my words away, "nonsense, you were just dismissing me if I remember correctly."

"I'd much rather finish our conversation, if you don't mind," I try to keep the pleading tone out of my words.

"Oh, Valmont, when did you stop being fun? All this business, business, business, doesn't suit you, and honestly, it's so boring. We used to have so much fun together, don't you remember? Perhaps that's what you need. Would you like to play with her together? You and I? Like old times?"

Viveka walks towards Amarah Rey with a vicious gleam in her eyes. I know the way she plays, and Amarah Rey would only make it worse by fighting back. Not to mention, Viveka can't find out the truth about her. About her blood.

I step between them, blocking Viveka's path to her. "She is not yours to play with. She's mine and I'm not in the mood for sharing."

"Why not? What makes you keep this one to yourself while you open up all others to me? Why is she so special?"

"She has a fierce fighting spirit, as you've clearly seen, and she's mine until *I* break her. I won't let anyone else have her until she's nothing more than a servant, bending to my every whim, grovelling at my feet."

"Oh, Valmont, how delightfully wicked of you!" She laughs deeply and claps her hands together. "Perhaps you haven't forgotten how to have a little fun after all. And perhaps, once you're finished with your little pet project, you'll turn that wicked attention my way," she slowly rakes her gaze down my body again, causing me to shudder in disgust. Of course, she doesn't take it that way. "Oh yes, I'll be waiting. Until then, all of this talk of play has me feeling left out. Come, Kordeuv," she holds her hand out and her companion moves to take her offered hand without hesitation, "let's see where the night takes us."

I watch as Viveka and Kordeuv walk out of my office without another word or glance back. My body sags and I sigh in relief.

"I don't know what's gotten into you, if you're just acting this way because *she's* here, but I know this isn't you," Amarah Rey says softly, then jerks her arm out of Pierce's hand, giving him a death glare, before she storms out of the office, not waiting for me to explain.

It kills me to watch her leave, knowing how angry and upset I've made her, that I've caused her even more pain than she's already in. I've made her feel insignificant, when she's anything but. All I want to do is run after her and beg her to hear me out. Beg her to forgive me. Beg her to let me take her to bed and show her how truly remorseful I am. To worship her body and give her pleasure again and again, until she's delirious with it and can't cum anymore, and begs me to stop.

That's what I want to do, but I just nod at Pierce and he nods back before he heads out of the office, shutting the door behind him.

It has to be this way.

I have to keep her safe.

And once Viveka is gone, I'll do whatever it takes to prove myself to Amarah Rey. Because I know she didn't mean what she said earlier. There are feelings in her heart that are for me and only me. What they are, exactly, I haven't had a chance to explore. *We* haven't had a chance to explore what could be. I know what could be on my end. I know how I feel, even if I have to keep my feelings hidden, for now. I've lived long enough to know that days, weeks, months, even years, is no time at all. I'll wait until the time is right, but will it be too late?

Amarah Rey isn't used to life as I know it. Simple *days* may be too long for her. If she believes my act, I may just lose her before I've even had the chance to have her. To love her. No, I'll do whatever it takes for her to forgive me.

But she needs to be alive in order to forgive me. I *will* keep her alive.

At all costs.

Even if those costs are my own happiness.

Amarah: Trickery Is A'Foot

Unshatter Me by Saliva

I storm out of Valmont's office feeling all sorts of conflicting emotions. Valmont has been a friend from the very beginning. Ever since the very first night we met, he's been on my side. Ok sure, he more often than not has his own agenda, but that agenda has never been to hurt me. He was there for me after I lost Andre and Logan. He's the sole being on this planet that I let see me at my worst. He's the only one I let in. He's the only one I bared my vulnerable and ugly truth to. And during his many visits, he gave me exactly what I needed.

Comfortable silence when I couldn't find the words to speak.

A safe embrace when the nightmares consumed me.

Comforting words when I cried in his lap.

Unwavering belief in me when I wanted to give up.

A body to abuse when I needed an out let for my anger.

Valmont had become a lifeline for me. A rope pulling me out of the pit. A light leading me out of the darkness. And nowhere in any of his visits did he try to take advantage of me. In no way did he try to use me or manipulate me. In no way did he ever attempt to cross a line. To say that he earned my trust, my friendship, and my feelings, whatever they may be, is an understatement. He gave me everything and never once asked for anything in return.

The night we slept together I could have sworn I saw something more in his eyes. Emotion I couldn't quite decipher, but raw and deep nonetheless. I felt like he was showing me something real and true. And the way he kissed me...

You don't kiss someone like that without reason. Right?

Now, I can't help but wonder if it's all been a lie? If it's nothing more than a game? A ploy? Another agenda on his long list of things to keep him entertained? An opportunity to exploit me for what he wanted most.

To claim me.

But why? To make Logan jealous? To say he won? Was his goal this entire time just to fuck me? Add me to his list of conquests and then treat me like I'm nothing to him? Am I really nothing to him now because he's had me? I feel like I'm a pawn in a sick, twisted game I've never played before. I don't know the rules, I don't know the end goal, and I'm completely lost and out of my depth. Who he is in private, with me, is so different than who he is in public. So, which Valmont is the real one? Do I want to find out the truth to that question?

I have a literal link to Logan and his feelings, and I never would have expected his betrayal. For him to claim he loved me more than anything else in the world, only to replace me within mere weeks. If you would have asked me a month ago, if he was capable of hurting me like that, I would have bet my life on the fact that he wasn't. If I misjudged Logan so badly, with insight into his heart, how can I ever imagine to understand and know Valmont? The answer is a cold hard truth.

I can't.

Feeling frustrated, angry, hurt, and completely confused, I decide to head outside for some fresh air. Maybe just go for a drive to be alone and clear my mind. Maybe stop for a hot fudge sundae to smother my emotions in. Extra fudge.

I look up just in time to see Viveka and Kordeuv heading out the front doors as well. The gut decision to follow them, and see what they're up to, flares up inside of me. I hesitate for a second, remembering what happened the last time I attempted to follow someone. I was knocked unconscious and held captive by the evil Witch, Revna, for almost a week.

But I'll be on alert this time. I won't t be caught off guard, and besides, I'm still on casino property, under Valmont's protection. What's the worst that can happen? I tell myself not to answer that, as I weave through the crowd, rushing towards the front doors.

The icy wind immediately wraps around me as I step outside. I'm trying not to rush or bring attention to myself but also trying not to lose my potential lead into learning more about this unsettling duo. Just act cool, Amarah. I shiver and hug myself against the chill, this is not exactly the best outfit to be outside in. Although, yes, I am wearing a sweater, it's more of a fashionable choice than a practical one.

I glance around me, looking left and then right. I see no sign of them and have no idea which way they could have gone. I see my ever-reliant valet, Josh, standing near by so, I hurry over to him.

"Josh," I speak up so he can hear me approaching and I don't just suddenly show up in his face.

He turns around and gives me one of his warm smiles, "Amarah, what can I do for you? Will you be needing your vehicle?"

I slow my steps as I approach him, inspecting him a bit more carefully. Something is different about him, but I can't quite put my finger on it. He looks the same as he always does. His valet uniform is the same, his name tag is in the same place as it always is, his hair, although freshly cut, is still the same as it usually is. Maybe I'm just being ridiculous and overly suspicious considering my current status of stalking.

"No, no, actually I'm looking for a couple that walked out right before me. A woman, tall but petite, with short, curly black hair, and a guy wearing leather," I laugh. "You literally could not miss him! He looks like he just stepped out of the 80s. Did you see which way they went by chance?"

"Your description is spot on actually," he laughs along with me. "I did see them pass this way just a minute ago. Come on, I'll show you which way they went," he says, eagerly, and flashes me another brilliant smile.

Something is definitely different about him tonight. Maybe he got laid and that's why he seems different? Maybe he got a really good tip? I search for anything amiss but I can't find anything wrong other than a feeling. Again, I shake it off as I follow him and huddle into myself a bit more, trying to maintain whatever warmth is left in my body.

I follow Josh around the side of the building, away from the parking garage and open-space parking. There's nothing on this side of the building except for some storage sheds and a few employee vehicles. The security light high above us makes a loud popping noise, before it burns out, throwing us into darkness. The next light isn't for another thirty feet or so, illuminating everything around it but falling short to where we've stopped.

"Josh, are you sure they went this way? I don't see them, or anyone, for that matter."

"Yeah, I saw them come this way. People come back here all the time to be *alone*, if you know what I mean," he chuckles. "Don't worry, I won't let anything happen to you, Amarah."

"Ok, stop. I don't know what's going on and I don't know what you're up to, but this isn't you, Josh."

He turns around to face me, I can barely make out his features in the dim light, but it's hard to miss the devious sparkle in his eyes, and the slight upturned corner of his lips in a mischievous smirk.

I take a step back, "what's going on?"

"I wanted a chance to speak with you. Alone."

Again, something isn't quite right and I don't know what it is. All I know, is that it's making my spidey senses tingle. And considering I'm deathly terrified of spiders, any tingles related to anything spidery, is not ok!

I squint my eyes, hoping if I zero in on him, maybe I'll spot the difference. "Why?" I ask, suspiciously.

"Because I'm in need of assistance and I think you may be the only one capable of helping me."

"You're a valet, Josh, what on Earth could I possible assist you with? Do you need me to ask Valmont for a favor or something for you?"

"You mean you haven't figured it out yet? Not even an inkling in that big brain of yours that Valmont tries to downplay?" He tsks, "perhaps I'm mistaken and you can't help me at all."

"What are you blabbering on about? Stop speaking in riddles and just tell me what you want."

"I must admit, I'm a bit disappointed in you, Amarah. You're not at all what I expected from what I've heard about you." He walks over to the wall and leans his shoulder against it, crossing his arms and ankles in a very, *I'm bored*, manner.

He isn't acting, or even speaking, like the valet I've come to know. Josh is sweet and shy. He speaks to me with the utmost respect. I've never heard him speak so much in all of my time coming here. Granted, I've never tried to have a conversation with him, but this isn't right. He's never once called me, Amarah. He always calls me, Miss Andrews, and now that I'm thinking about it, his voice doesn't sound quite right either. I'm suddenly regretting not carrying one of my daggers with me, but still, I'm not helpless, and I call to my power, bringing pure white flames to life in my hands.

"Ok, this ends now. Who, or what are you? Because whoever you are, you're not Josh."

A wicked grin erupts across his face, "now this is more like it. I've heard about this power you have. If the rumors are, in fact, true, then why don't you give me a little demonstration? Wow me with *something*, Amarah. Can't you figure out who I really am?"

"Have it your way," I sneer at the imposter, as I push my power towards him, forcefully.

Had his body not rested against the wall, I'm sure he would have staggered with the force of it. My power is very intuitive, but I mentally focus on what I want my power to do, reveal the truth. Push aside whatever magic, or glamour, is being used to trick me.

In seconds, the illusion of Josh is stripped away, and I'm left standing with the enemy. His wicked grin is even more unsettling in his true face. I shiver, and this time, it's not because of the cold.

"I take back my earlier disappointment," his voice is deeper, rougher, but not unpleasant. He has a slight accent but I can't place it. "That is indeed, quite the trick, if I do say so myself, and I am quite versed in trickery." He makes a show of adjusting his jacket and wiping off the sleeves, as if he's wiping away any traces of Josh.

"It's not a trick to reveal the truth of something, quite the opposite actually."

He shrugs.

"What do you want? Why did you…" I think about what I just witnessed. What *did* he do?

He *was* Josh. In almost every single way. Except, unlike a demon, he didn't actually possess Josh's body. I'm still alert and watching his movements, not trusting him in the slightest, my power is thrumming right below the surface, ready to be called in an instance, should I need it. I know I need to be asking more important questions but my curiosity gets the better of me. "What exactly *did* you do?" I ask, utterly confused. "How were able to look exactly like

Josh?"

"It's who I am. It's what I do."

I wait for him to say more. To explain everything to me, so that I can understand what's going on, but he seems satisfied in his response. Well, that makes one of us.

"Listen, Kordeuv, is it?"

"It is."

"Well, Kordeuv, I'm going to need a bit more than that. What exactly are you? Because you're definitely not a Vampire."

"How do you know I'm not a Vampire?"

I sigh, "one, I've never seen a Vampire take on the appearance of someone else before. I think if Valmont could have done it, he would have already flaunted that power in front of me, and two, you don't have fangs." I motion to my mouth and he grins again, revealing his pearly whites for my inspection. "Case in point. Now, can you please cut the bullshit and tests and just answer my questions?"

"I will answer your questions, in time, but I can't right now. I must go before Viveka suspects I'm up to something. She doesn't ever let me out of her sight for too long," he huffs out a frustrated breath, all earlier teasing and nonchalance evaporated in the cold night air. "If you want to know more, you're going to have to help me."

I cross my arms, no longer worried he's going to attack me. If he wanted to hurt me, he's had plenty of time to do it, but he hasn't. The urgent and desperate look in his eyes is shining through now that he's no longer *testing* me. I do want to learn more. I want to know how he was able to imitate Josh. I want to know what him and Viveka are doing here. I want to know their motivations and I want to know Viveka's weakness. Not that he'll probably share that with me but it's worth a shot. I must hesitate for too long because he takes a slow step towards me, his arms out in front of him, treating me like I'm a wild animal about to bolt.

"Amarah, please. I need your help. At least give me the opportunity to share my story and what I know. If you still don't want to help me after you know everything, then so be it, but please just hear me out," he begs with more than just his words.

His eyes are pleading more than any eyes I've ever seen plead. And I've been up close and personal with Andre and Logan's sad, pleading eyes, but these eyes, Kordeuv's eyes, are absolutely devastating. I can't help but feel a little bad for him. I don't know why, I don't know his story, but his eyes are downright forlorn.

"Fine," I give in. "What do I have to do?"

I see the relief flood through him like a physical force, "we need time to talk, just you and I. I need Viveka distracted long enough for that to happen."

"Ok, and how do we make that happen?"

He quirks a brow at me, "how do you think?"

I sigh in defeat, "Valmont."

"Yes. Do you think you can get Valmont to agree to meet with her...*privately*? To keep her distracted long enough for us to meet?"

The thought of Valmont meeting with Viveka, alone, grates on my nerves. The thought of her pressed up against his chest, her hands touching his body, exploring him in places *I* want to explore, tasting him, and reminding him of all their time together, has me clenching my jaw tightly and white flames dancing through my fingers. But this isn't anger I'm feeling.

It's jealousy.

Scorching, blistering, I want to drive a flaming stake through her heart, jealousy.

"Amarah, can you do it?"

His voice brings me back to the task at hand. Can I convince Valmont to do this? Maybe. Do I want to convince him to do this? Hell no!

"I don't know. He hasn't been the same with me since you guys got here. I'm not exactly sure where I stand with him or if he'll even talk to me long enough for me to discuss this with him."

"Make it happen. Trust me when I say that it's for his benefit too. He'll want to hear what I have to say." He looks around nervously, "I have to go."

"Ok, I'll try," I agree.

"Don't try, Amarah." He holds my gaze, and again, I see the desperation clutching him like a vice, but behind the desperation, is a small glimmer of hope. "Make. It. Happen," he orders, then turns and walks into the darkness.

"How will I find you?" I yell after him.

"I'll come to you," his voice carries back to me on the cold breeze, sending another shiver through me, as I stand in the darkness staring after him.

Now that the immediate danger and distraction has passed, my body starts to shake from the cold. "Fuck me, I really do hate winter," I mumble to myself, as I jog back towards the front of the casino.

Once I'm back inside, walking along the loud, bustling playing floor, I relax. Nothing is going to happen to me when I'm surround by innocent humans and Valmont's guards on watch. But even though I relax at the thought of being safe, my mind and body are still tense from the strange encounter with Kordeuv.

Why did he seek me out? Why did he try and trick me by pretending to be Josh? What can he possibly need help with and how can I possible be the one to help him? And why is he sneaking around behind Viveka's back? Or is he? What if that's not the case at all? What if he's only pretending to be doing something she wouldn't approve of? What if it's another attempt to trick me? To get me to let my guard down? Ugh! I hate this feeling!

I'm almost to the private elevator to the Penthouse when

Alistair casually strolls up beside me.

"Need to head up?" He asks.

Valmont has refused to give me a key and the access code to the private elevator, which frustratingly, leaves me at the mercy of my babysitters. He insists that I be escorted and that the Penthouse be thoroughly inspected for *any* potential threats before I enter it. Every, single, fucking time! Honestly, it's beyond ridiculous but I've stopped arguing. There's simply no getting him to change his mind where my safety is concerned.

"I was planning on it but, Alistair," I gently grab his arm, halting his steps to the elevator, "is there a gym around here somewhere? I mean, there's gotta be like a special place you all go to workout and train, right?"

He hesitates before answering me and I'm not sure why. It's not like I asked him to share his secret family recipe with me.

"There is," he admits, hesitantly.

"Great! Can you show me where it is so I can continue on with my training? I'm sure there will be plenty of..."

Alistair is shaking his head at me.

"What's wrong?"

"I can't take you there. Not without Valmont's permission."

I cross my arms, irritation at this entire situation really starting to rub me the wrong way. "I swear, he's so infuriating! He has so many rules and is so damn controlling and secretive! I'm tired of it! I'm tired of him dictating everything. You tell him, that if he wants me to continue to stay here, he needs to give me more free-reign! He's the one who insisted I stay here so, he better agree to letting me train, or I'll go somewhere else. I'll move back home and ask Ethan for a place to train if Valmont doesn't stop with this dictator shit."

"I'll talk to him."

"Ugh, fine. Well, then I guess in the meantime take me up." I can't even storm off by myself. I have to wait for Alistair to operate the damn elevator.

Once inside the Penthouse, I try to relax further, but it's no use. My mind might as well be locked onto a treadmill running a million miles a minute. I pick up my cell phone, only to see Logan's name flash up on the screen, making matters worse. No doubt he's texting me about missing me, sending me songs to tell me how he feels. I've attempted to block his number sooo many times, but like everything else in my life, I fail to do that too. The truth is, I need to see his name on my phone. I need to read his words, no matter how much they hurt. I torture myself, listening to the songs he sends me, and have even saved them into their own playlist.

It's sad.

It's pathetic.

It's all I have left.

I know that when I stop seeing Logan's name pop up on my phone, I'm going to be truly alone. Truly lost. But some stupid, ignorant, and hopeless romantic part of me, still feels the tiniest bit of hope. Like one glorious and golden grain of sand struggling to be seen in a black sand desert.

It's with this hope, that I unlock my phone, and open his message.

Logan: I know you're still reading my messages, Amarah. Which means you haven't blocked me. Which means there's hope inside of you. And I know you don't want to hear from me, I know it makes this harder on you. On both of us. But this is the only time I will ever not care about what you want. Some things have happened recently, and I desperately want to talk about it with you, because honestly…I'm scared. I'm barely holding onto the man I am when I'm with you. The man I want to be for you. I understand why you feel like you're dangerous now, I did something to...someone. I get it now. But pushing me away is not the answer. I know there's still a future for us because our type of love can't be broken by anything in this world or even the next. It's eternal. There is absolutely nothing that you can do to make me stop loving you, Amarah. I'm fighting or you, for us, until there's no life left in me to fight. I love you, Angel.

Spotify Link: Unshatter Me by Saliva

I swear, even without a connection, he knows all of my deepest, loneliest secrets. He knows I read and cherish every single word he writes. He knows I'll memorize every lyric to every song he sends. He knows that I have the smallest spark of hope inside of me. He knows *me*.

I take a few minutes to listen to the song he sent me. It's actually the first song he's sent where I feel like he does understand what I'm feeling.

Alone.

Afraid.

A ghost.

Voices in my head.

But one lyric stands out to me above all the rest. I know it's not meant to be literal, but that's where my mind goes.

Demons in my bed.

Demons in my bed.

Demons in my bed.

How can he be sending me these types of messages when he's sleeping with someone else? How can he literally stick his dick into another woman then turn around and tell me he's fighting for us?

I'm not judging him for sleeping with someone else, Hell I kissed the Devil and slept with Valmont, I have no room to point fingers, but I'm not the one lying or pretending. I'm not the one doing one thing and then saying another. How can he continue to do this to me when he knows that I know? There's no better proof than what I witnessed with my own damn eyes! Him in bed with another woman! And even knowing all of this, and how utterly betrayed and heartbroken I am, when I read his messages, I still have hope. I still want to believe there's an explanation for it all. That there is a future for us.

I'm so fucking *weak*.

I dash away the tears running down my cheeks and send a message of my own.

Me: I know it's late, so I hope that I'm not waking you up, but I really need a distraction. And I hope I'm not crossing a line, or making things awkward, but if you're up for it, can you come to the Penthouse? I could really use a friend. If not, I totally understand.

Literally, ten seconds later, my phone vibrates with an incoming message.

Emrick: On my way, Sleeping Beauty.

Amarah: All The Things I Don't Know

Head Above Water by Avril Lavigne

"That's good, Amarah, really good!" Emrick praises me. "You're very in tune with the Earth, if I didn't know any better, I'd think you were Maa. Now, let's take our training a step further, what can you do to use the Earth as a weapon? Or to protect yourself?"

We're sitting at the base of the Sandia Mountains, basically the casino's backyard, as I practice my Earth Magic. We're bundled up against the frigid twilight hours, my eyes are closed and my hands are resting palms down against the cold, hard ground. I'm so focused on the magic all around me that I don't feel the chill at all. If anything, the wintry air is adding to my alertness and focus.

I think about Emrick's words, how can I use the magic at my fingertips as a weapon or to protect myself? The only thing that comes to mind, no doubt from watching too many movies, are vines or roots. I search the Earth around me until I locate roots from the plants, cacti, and trees around us, and use my power to reach out to them, to call to them. I imagine them growing longer, stronger, pushing through the ground to come to my aid. I wrap them around Emrick's legs first and then coil them up and around his body, until his arms are pinned, and the roots are wrapped around his neck, threatening to restrict the life-saving air from reaching his lungs. Of course, I'm not actually applying any pressure.

Emrick chuckles, "how very human and unoriginal, Amarah."

I open my eyes and see Emrick's amusement at my feeble effort. "Hey, it *would* work," I pout. "I'm really not sure what else I can do to use Earth as a weapon," I admit.

"You're absolutely right, this would work, and at the end of the day, as long as you survive, it doesn't really matter *how*." He uses his own Earth magic to unwind the roots from his body and return them to the Earth, where they belong. "But, you also need to dig deeper, pun intended, and think bigger."

Without any warning, I'm suddenly falling through the Earth, it's cold, hard walls rising up all around me. I gasp at the sensation of falling *through* the Earth. It's unnatural and very unnerving.

Emrick leans over the edge from above, smiling down at me, "We can literally have the Earth consume our enemies. Bury them alive, deep down, where no one will ever find their bodies, in this life or the next."

Emrick's face is now swiftly rushing towards me again, as I'm being propelled back up to the surface. Once I'm sitting, solidly, back in front of Emrick, and I'm sure the Earth has stopped moving beneath me, I let out a nervous laugh.

"That was the *strangest* sensation, and honestly, a bit dizzying. Kind of like being on some crazy theme park ride, not to mention, fucking terrifying! I would never have thought to open up the literal Earth and bury someone in it," I shiver in unease.

"Yes, well, when it comes to your life or theirs, it's important that you know all of your options." Emrick is suddenly hidden from view, behind a wall...of dirt. "You can use the Earth to blind your enemy in many ways, to hide yourself from them, or allowing you to escape completely." The dirt falls back onto the ground, revealing Emrick is no where to be seen. I look around, but wherever he is, he's completely hidden. "Amarah," his voice pulls my attention to a nearby tree. It's far too thin of a tree for Emrick to hide behind, yet, I can't see where else his voice could have come from. I'm staring directly at the tree when Emrick steps away from it. It's almost as if he *was* the tree. He's now in his true Fey form, and walks back towards me, wearing a successful grin.

"Holy shit!" I exclaim. "I would never have seen you standing there! You blended in perfectly with that tree."

"Yes, our original form allows us to blend in, almost like a chameleon, with the Earth. Once we've Mastered Earth magic, we can slightly alter our appearance to blend in with whatever natural Earth element surrounds us, but the texture of our skin works best for blending in with trees, though we can change it enough to get by with blending into other things."

He sits back down, cross-legged in front of me, his glamour back in place, leaving him looking like the *human* Emrick I'm used to seeing.

I'm struggling to find words, after being utterly shocked by Emrick's display of power. "Wow, that's amazing! I had no idea you could change your skin to blend in. I can defintiely see how that can come in handy. And of course, you know, burying someone alive is always a fun time," I scoff.

"I told you, I have mad skills," he smirks and pretends to dust dirt off his shoulder.

I laugh out loud, "you're unbelievably arrogant is what you are."

"Confient, Amarah, confident. There's a difference.

"Yeah, yeah, so you've said. Ok…so, you're a Master of Earth, and you're the Leader of the Maa Family, you're the one at all the meetings and well, *leading*, but yet, you have the Vanemad."

He nods, "yes, that's right."

"I guess I'm just confused at how it all works, and how the

Elders come into play. Are you really the Leader or are they?"

"I'm the Leader but I lead with their guidance and Blessing. It's not really something that's black and white. Can I make decisions against their council? Yes. But their advice and insight is not something to ignore. The Vanemad are special and have a unique ability, superior to even becoming a Master, but having this gift doesn't automatically make someone qualified to be a good leader either. So, Elders are Elders and the Leader is the Leader."

"Okayyy, I mean, I get that, that makes sense. What exactly is this special gift the Elders have? Or is that something you're not able to share with me?"

"No, it's not a secret in the Fey community, or The Unseen, for that matter. Upon becoming a Master of Earth, a select few also awaken their Rändaja, their Traveller."

I rest my elbows on my knees, as I lean in, eagerly soaking up all of the information Emrick is sharing with me. I still find all the details of the The Unseen absolutely fascinating. I want to learn about every little thing that makes this world so special, and yet, I'm afraid I'll never know everything. I'm afraid I'll always be behind the curve and out of my depth. Emrick continues his lesson, and I push my self-doubts out of the way for now, making room for this new information.

"Basically, what the Traveller is, is the ability to separate your spirit, your essence, from your body and send it out into the world on its own. A Traveller can only travel through the Earth though, not through the air or on the wind, but down underneath the surface. By being able to do this, the Rändaja can uncover and provide insight and knowledge about what may be happening in other places very quickly. But, it's not always foolproof or easy to translate."

"What do you mean?"

"The Rändaja has to listen to the Earth and gather clues as to what's happening. It's a lot of interpreting what the Earth has to say, because the Earth *does* talk, Amarah. During times of war, the ground, the trees, the plants, are all witnesses to its brutality and death. When blood seeps into the soil, the Earth *feels* it. The agony, the death, the loss of life. It radiates its sadness, its frustration, its helplessness, and it's up to the experience and strength of the Rändaja to take these nonverbal feelings, and understand the actions behind them. Does this make any sense?"

"Oddly, yes. I have this link, this connection to Logan, which allows me to feel what he feels, but I have to interpret his feelings. I may feel his sadness but I may have no idea what caused the sadness."

"Yes, exactly! You have to then know more about the situation. You have to do more research to find out the truth and not just assume you know what the feelings mean. It's dangerous making assumptions based on feelings and not truth. So, yes, the Elders insight is crucial, like I mentioned, but not always one hundred percent accurate. It's then up to me, as their Leader, to make decisions based on the information they provide."

"Wow," I repeat, seemingly out of better ways to express my awe. "That's incredible! To be able to travel the Earth, wait, how far can they Travel?"

"That depends on the strength of the person and how much they practice and hone their skill. The Head Elder, Emmaline Marshall, has Travelled the furthest. She's the only one who has been able to send her Rändaja across oceans, Travelling deep down, underneath the waters. It's different for all, but to be seated at the Elder's table, means you've fully accepted your Rändaja and accepted the risks of using the gift every day, to Travel the Earth, and gain invaluable knowledge."

"Marshall," I hadn't made the connection when I was being introduced to the Elders, because of my utter state of shock, but now the name rings familiarly in my mind. "Your name is Marshall, are you related to Emmaline?"

He smiles and his whole face lights up with pride, or maybe it's the light finally creeping over the horizon brightening his features, but whatever it is, he's glowing when he says, "Emmaline is my mother."

"She's absolutely lovely, Emrick! Instead of a power couple, you guys are like a power family! What about your dad?" I ask, excited to learn more about my new friend. I regret my question instantly, as I watch the light fade from Emrick's eyes.

"My father passed when I was just a kid. I have a few memories of him, but not much."

"Oh, I'm so sorry, Emrick. I didn't mean to bring that painful topic up." I hesitate, not always great with tackling these types of conversations. "I don't want to downplay or disrespect your loss in any way, but you're very lucky to have memories of him, even if they are only a few vague ones. I never knew my real mother and I would give anything to know her. Even for a little while. But losing someone you love is never easy, regardless of when or how. I understand if you don't want to talk about him."

"No, it's alright. I don't mind talking about him. It was a long time ago, and although it never gets easier, I don't mind it. He was a hero and I know I'm very lucky to have known him, even if our time together was cut too short. I'm sorry you never got to know your mother, Amarah."

"Me too," I shrug, remembering her beautiful face hovering above me, her warm touch on my cheek. A vision, a dream or a straight up hallucination, whatever it had been, I cherish the memory. She came to me when I was held captive by Revna and she saved me. "My mom was a hero, too. She gave up her life for mine," I smile sadly, "what about your dad?" I ask, again.

He shares my sad smile, "my dad is the one who discovered the rip between our world and the demon world. My dad was also a

Rändaja, the most powerful our Family had ever known, until my mother, of course." He smiles and laughs softly, "She never could let anyone do something better than her, not even the love of her life."

"I'm sure your father adored her for her determination and ambition."

Emrick nods, "he did. They loved pushing each other, making each other better. It was always done with respect. Never once did their competitive spirits ever come between their love and partnership. They did everything together and trusted each other completely. Their love was clear to see, even as a child."

"That's beautiful, and honestly, sounds like a fairy tale love we all dream of having."

"It was," he agrees, his voice thick with emotion. I can only imagine what kind of beautiful memory he's reliving. I stay quiet, giving him time to live in his memories and live with his father once more.

He clears his throat and looks up at me, "yes, well, my father was Travelling and came across a section of Earth that was ripped open, literally. As if some giant, alien claws reached down and tore it in two. The Earth was in agony and terrified. Later, we came to the conclusion that it was terrified at what was crawling up from depths of an unknown realm."

"Damn, the odds of your dad finding the rip, in the vastness of the world, even just the States, is nothing short of a miracle. Maybe he didn't just randomly discover it. Maybe he was guided somehow? Even unknowingly."

"It's very possible," Emrick agrees. "How he found it is a mystery, but he did, and it ended up causing him his life. With great power, comes great responsibility, and great sacrifice. That's what we teach and that's what we believe. Power is not something to take lightly."

"No, it's not," I shake my head, thinking about my own power and how it had backfired, killing Andre. Regardless if it was my fault or not, my power took a life. "How did your father's power and his discovery of the rip...kill him?" I ask, hesitantly.

"Once he discovered the turmoil in the Earth, he told my mother, and they Travelled together. She confirmed it was something that needed further investigation. At this time, all they knew was the Earth was ripped but they didn't know how or what was happening. My father offered to go, physically, to the spot of the rip, to look for more answers. My mother wanted to go with him, but they agreed I was too young for such a long journey so, my mother stayed to take care of me. My father set out and promised to keep in touch every day. You see, a spirit that's left the body in order to Travel, cannot communicate with a spirit that's still in the body, but it can communicate with another spirit that's Travelling, just like we can talk to each other in physical form."

"This is all a bit mind-blowing, Emrick. Everything you're saying that's possible, is...I mean it's just...hard to wrap my brain around, ya know?"

He chuckles, "I can imagine. This is how I've been raised. This is my normal, my reality, and I don't know any different, but I can see how crazy it all must seem to you. Do you need me to explain anything in more detail?"

"No, I'm following along, just..." I mimic explosions with my hands, "mind-blowing."

He laughs, genuinely, and continues, "well, my father made it to the rip. Luckily, it was located out in the middle of nowhere. Not much of this land was occupied back then, and even if it was, it was small villages few and far between. So, it appeared that my father was the first to discover the rip. He monitored it for a few days, constantly reporting back to my mother. That's when he saw the first demon emerge and walk the Earth. When he Travelled to alert my mother of what he had seen...he was attacked. Do you remember I told you that to become an Elder, means you have accepted your gift and the risks?"

"Yes," I whisper quietly, not wanting to hear where the rest of Emrick's story is going but understanding that I need to. If he can re-live this pain, the least I can do, is listen and appreciate his history.

"When you Travel, and your spirit leaves your body, you're left in a trance like state, unaware of this plane and the physical body you leave behind. My father's body was attacked, and destroyed, while his spirit was Travelling. When the spirit tried to return, there was nothing left to return too. For this reason, no one is allowed to Travel alone anymore, there must always be someone standing guard over the body."

"Oh, my goodness, Emrick, I don't…I can't even imagine…" I'm lost for words. "I'm so sorry," I finally say.

"Thank you, Amarah," he smiles, sadly. "We honestly don't know what happens to the spirit when the body is destroyed while they're separated. My mother left immediately, she found my father's body and laid him to rest, but sometimes, I wonder if my mother spends so much time Travelling because she still believes she'll find my father's spirit out there somewhere."

This story is one of the saddest stories I think I've ever heard. I haven't even lost Logan, not like that, and I'm barely functioning through the pain of not being with him. I can only imagine what depth of pain his mother must deal with on a daily basis. To lose the love of her life so drastically, and even worse, not even knowing if his spirit is at rest. At peace.

"It took several years, but we eventually relocated here, to Albuquerque. It was only a handful of Fey from each Family, but others have joined us throughout the centuries, and of course, we've grown our own population. Years later, when the Fey started growing, Anaxo was elected Queen, and we truly began to fight the demons and control the rip. We found out the hard way, that if you spend too much time being too close to the rip, you start to lose your…" he waves his hand in the air, grasping for a word, "essence, I guess, is the best way to describe it. Our Fey energy, our auras. It's almost like the rip feeds on it or sucks it in."

"No one has mentioned that to me before."

He shakes his head, "they should have. The land around the rip is dangerous, almost toxic, and it just seems to be getting stronger and stronger." He sighs and rubs his hands down his face, "We did what we could to hide the rip by building the Earth around it. It's located deep in a cave and there's now a lake on top of it. Bottomless Lakes, is what it's called, out in Roswell, New Mexico. That's where the Vesi Family live and are the first line of defense against the demons. Still, they can't handle it all on their own, especially not being able to stand guard at the rip's entrance. We have to let the demons through and fight them on safe land. It's not easy, especially now that the demons seem to be coming through faster and stronger, but we do what we can."

"Ok, hold on, I'm seriously blown away by all of this information right now. I feel like I just got a crash course in my heritage, and not to mention, I used to swim in Bottomless Lakes as a kid! There were always rumors of the lake being *actually bottomless*. There were stories of a cavern underneath and creatures that were half man, half mer-*something* or half fish, living in the lake. Which, I guess," I laugh, sarcastically, "is all somewhat true!"

"Every piece of lore or fiction has come from some grain of truth, no matter how small."

I rub my forehead, making sure my head is still intact and my brain isn't being blown out of my skull. "*None* of this has been explained to me. I was told my grandmother caused the rip, but other than that, I haven't really received much information. I feel like everything is just being given to me in bits and pieces and it's so frustrating!"

"To be fair, and honest, you've only known about The Unseen, for what, four months give or take? And you've wasted half of that time. One, by being locked up with Logan for a month," he holds his hand up to stop my embarrassing protest, "not that I blame you, because girl, if I had a chance to have that man all to myself, I'd take it in a heartbeat. Oooo weee," he fans himself. "Speaking of, you've got to tell me all about the sex, is his junk as big as..."

"Emrick!" I lean over and punch him in the shoulder, my cheeks now burning from embarrassment despite the cold air.

"Ouch!" He holds his hands up in surrender, laughing, "ok ok, a topic for another time. Sheesh, you can't keep all of that goodness all to yourself is all I'm saying. Some of us have imaginations that need fuelling." I lift my fist and threaten to punch him again.

"Alright, alright, back to you and other ways you wasted time that aren't nearly as fun. You wasted a month grieving. Again, not that I can blame you, or tell you how you need to grieve, but that only leaves you with two months of training and learning about your Fey history. Two months is not a long time considering there are centuries worth of history. Again, give yourself grace, and if you're not happy with your progress, then you need to be the one to change tactics. Lose the training wheels and ride that shit, you know what I mean?"

I laugh, "ouch. Yet again, you cut me right where it hurts. Right in the middle of my own damn guilt and shame. You're right. I've been handling everything so badly."

"I didn't say *badly*," he lectures.

"No, but it's the truth. I don't think I've actually made *one* good decision since I've become Võitleja, not one," I shake my head, complete disappointment in myself. "I'm going to do better, Emrick, and I know I'll need your help along the way. To keep me in line and focused on what's important. Are you up for that immense challenge, Coach?"

"It would be my absolute pleasure, Sleeping Beauty."

"Be careful what you…" a huge yawn interrupts my retort. "Man, this switching to night owl status is kicking my ass. It's harder than I thought it would be."

"Give it a few more days, you'll get used to it, but let's head back to the casino and get inside where it's warm," he stands and offers his hand.

"Speaking of your new night owl activities, have you discovered anything useful about our unwelcomed visitors?"

"Not yet, but I'm close. Kordeuv actually sought me out earlier tonight. He said he needs my help but didn't have time to explain how or why. Apparently, he's going behind Viveka's back and needs her distracted long enough for him to talk to me. So, I'm working on making that happen."

"Ok, that's good."

"Maybe. I can't get a read on him and I don't trust him as far as I can throw him."

"No, you're right, be careful. Don't do anything that isn't safe, Amarah, and keep me in the loop. If you need me for anything, all you have to do is ask."

"Thanks, Emrick," I smile and I mean it. Another vicious yawn forces its way out before I can continue. "What about you? Did you have any luck securing a meeting with the Elders?"

"I did, actually. I can't believe I forgot to text you. We have a meeting with them tomorrow."

"Ok, good. I'll try and get everything figured out on my end in the next day or so too. Hopefully after both of these meetings, we'll have a better idea of what the Hell is going on and a plan to move forward with everything. I feel like I have a million pots cooking on the stove and I'm close to burning everything."

"We'll get this all figured out. You're not alone you know. You do have people that can, and want, to help you, but no one is a mind reader, Amarah. You have to ask for help."

I sigh, "I know. It's definitely not something I'm good at. I've never been one to seek help." I shrug "I never really had that type of support system growing up and I just sort of figured everything out on my own. I don't mean to be so independent or stubborn. It's just kind of…ingrained in me, I guess."

"At least you're aware of it, that's a big step in the right direction. You can't make any changes or adjustments if you're ignorant to the problem."

"Yes, but like so many realities of life, easier said than done."

"Well, my next piece of advice to assist you is this, go and talk to that deviously hypnotic and deliciously tempting Vampire, and ask him for his help. We need to find out what Kordeuv has to say."

I laugh at his words and the dreamy look on his face, "you're so boy crazy."

"Hey, not all of us are having the fun you're having. You'd be the same way if you were in my shoes, surrounded by all these scorching hot bodies that are basically demanding my attention, but not actually getting any action. Eye candy is nowhere near as satisfying as chocolate melting in your mouth. You get me?"

"Wow, you are unbelievable," I shake my head but can't help the smile spilling across my face.

"You know I'm right," he playful nudges me with his arm as we walk through the casino, heading towards the private elevator.

Emerson is coming down the steps from Valmont's office, I forgot, it's now daytime and Valmont and his Vampires are unavailable for the next twelve hours or so. Just as well, I need the sleep too. I'm exhausted from the change in my sleep cycle and the power training with Emrick.

"Amarah, good timing. You headed up?"

"I am actually." I turn to Emrick, "hey, thank you, for…tonight. For coming when I asked, even though, it was not at all a decent hour. I really do appreciate you and this was exactly what I needed."

"I'm always one call or text away. Remember what I said, ask for help. Keep me posted and let me know if you want to train later this evening again."

"Will do, Coach."

"And you," Emrick turns to Emerson, who is now standing next to us, "you make sure she stays safe, and my God, would a smile once in a while kill you?"

Emerson sets his cold, blue gaze on Emrick, his jaw tightening is his only response to Emrick's comment. He's obviously not amused at the suggestion.

"Apparently it will kill you, or perhaps me," Emrick mumbles, as he turns to leave. "Goodnight, Sleeping Beauty," he waves to me as he walks away.

I shake my head again, "goodnight. Oh," I yell louder so he can hear me, "and sweet dreams!" I tease.

"Melting chocolate, honey! Melting chocolate," he yells back.

Emerson raises an eyebrow but refrains from asking any questions about what we're talking about. "Ready?"

I nod my head and follow him to the elevator. I can't help but inspect him as I wait. Behind the total serious bodyguard vibe, Emerson is good looking. I can see what Emrick sees in him. He's tall and muscular, has smooth, fair skin, his blonde hair, although shaved on both sides, is full and think on top, his face is strong, always clean-shaven. The cold, artic eyes don't really help to give him an approachable look, but I bet a smile *would* change everything about him. I can't help but probe just a bit.

"Are you really not curious about anything at all or is your job just *that* important to you?"

His eyes quickly slide to mine, before he returns his attention to the keypad on the inside of the elevator, punching in the code that will get us moving.

"What do you mean?" He asks, gruffly.

I scoff, "what do you mean, what do I mean? You," I gesture to him, "you're always so…well, for lack of a better word, cold."

He stands at attention, one hand gripping the other wrist in front of him, even though it's just him and I alone in the elevator.

"This," I gesture to him again, "are you ever not in bodyguard mode? What do you do when you're not working?"

"No," he says. I wait for him to say more but he doesn't.

"Noooo….what?"

"No, I'm never out of bodyguard mode. When I'm not working, I'm sleeping, eating or training."

"Well, that sucks. I mean, I understand your commitment to the job but what about the commitment to yourself? Emerson is a person too, not just a bodyguard. Don't you ever have the desire to do something else? I dunno, spend time with someone? Have fun?"

His eyes slide to mine again, for a second, I swear I see something stirring under their cold depths. The elevator door opens to the Penthouse, and before I can get a read on Emerson, he's back into bodyguard mode in the blink of an eyes.

"Stay here while I sweep the premises," he orders.

I sigh, "yes, dad."

It takes him a few minutes to examine every room, nook, and cranny. When he's satisfied no one is lurking about, threatening to kill me, he unlocks the elevator and lets me out. I'm immediately greeted by a little black, wriggling, whining body. I squat down and pick Griffin up, letting him attack my face with his little kisses of affection. These days, it's the only affection I'm getting so, I'll take what I can get. As much as I hate to admit it, Emrick is right. Surrounded by men like Logan and Valmont, Hell, even Emerson, it's easy to be boy crazy and get a little tense and sexually frustrated with no release.

"Well, thanks, Emerson." He's about to get back in the elevator and continue his night of bodyguarding when I stop him.

"Oh, Emerson! Can you do me a huge favor? Can you please let Valmont know that I need to speak with him as soon as he wakes up tonight? Please don't let him blow me off. It's extremely important. Tell him it's about Viveka and Kordeuv. Tell him I have information he wants to hear."

He dips his chin in acknowledgment. "I'll deliver your message. Also, I was told I can show you to our training facility. Would you like me to show you this when you wake up?"

My hope rises, if Valmont agreed to let me into their training area, maybe he'll listen to me again after all. Maybe he's coming back around to being the Valmont I know. Or, the Valmont I think I know. Either way, this is definitely good news.

"Yes," I say, excitedly. "That would be fantastic! I'll text you when I'm up and ready to go. Thank you."

He dips his chin, and then the elevator doors close, leaving me alone once again.

26

Amarah: Top Secret Secrets

Fighter by Royal Deluxe

I wake up drenched in sweat. Tormented by another nightmare where I witness Andre, Valmont, Logan, and now Emrick, all dying in my arms. Lucifer didn't come to me this time, perhaps I didn't allow him to. I'm not sure how much of the dreams I control anymore. Either way, I had been left to face my subconscious torture alone.

I reach for my cell phone and see that it's a little past five in the evening. I slept for about eight hours, but because of the nightmare, I still feel exhausted. I feel like I can use an additional eight hours, minimum, of sleep, but there are too many important things to get done. As Emrick so graciously reminded me last night, I've already wasted too much time hiding.

I push the covers off me and sit up, throwing my legs over the side of the bed and stretch with an obnoxious yawn erupting out of my throat and ending in more of a loud, protesting groan. I pick up the Penthouse phone and order breakfast. Yes, it's technically almost dinner time, but considering I've just woken up, and evening is now my morning, I want breakfast. Coffee, eggs with red chile, crispy bacon, a tortilla, and pancakes with lots of syrup on the side. Mmmm, yes please! I also ask for someone to come up to take little Griffin out for his potty break. The kids that live here with their parents have fallen in love with him, not that I can blame them, and he gets more than enough attention, and treats I'm sure, when I'm too busy to take care of him.

Breakfast is delivered fifteen minutes later, by a young girl, who's being escorted by my cold, daytime bodyguard. She quietly and efficiently lays out my breakfast on the huge dining room table. It's enough food to feed two, maybe even three, people. In addition to what I ordered, there's a variety of fresh cut fruit and whipped cream, different flavors of syrup to choose from, along with fresh orange juice and water.

"Thank you," I say gratefully, as I take my seat at the table and reach for the coffee.

"Is there anything else I can get for you?" She asks, sweetly.

"No, this is beyond perfect, as always."

The first time I was brought a feast, after I only ordered a simple meal, I tried to protest, but nothing I say makes a bit of difference. It's been ordered that I'm to be treated like freaking royalty while I'm here, and so, I am. I sigh at the waste of it all but Valmont refuses to have it any other way. As if I'll think less of him if I simply get the eggs and bacon I requested. Boujee Vampire in every aspect of his life. And now, mine.

The young girl takes Griffin and promises to bring him back soon. Emerson escorts her back to the ground floor, since she does't have access to the elevator either, and then returns a few minutes later.

"Hungry?" I ask, as I motion to the pile of food on the table. "There's no way I can eat even half of this."

"Breakfast for dinner isn't really my go-to."

"What?" I exclaim. "What normal human doesn't like breakfast for dinner once in a while? Technically, this is my morning though, but still, there really is no wrong time for bacon."

"Bacon, maybe, but eggs and pancakes?" He shakes his head.

"Wow," I say, between bites. "Maybe that's why you're so damn cold all the time. You haven't experienced breakfast for dinner. Makes me wonder what else you haven't experienced," I eye him curiously.

He doesn't flinch under my scrutiny or even look interested in the slightest about continuing this topic of conversation.

All business.

All professional.

All the time.

"Would you like me to escort you to the training facility after you've eaten?"

I consider the time and realize that I'll have a few hours to kill before I have the chance to talk to Valmont about my plan. What better way to pass the time than by wielding my sword and daggers, learning and perfecting my fighting technique.

"That would be great."

He nods, "Let me make another round and make sure everyone is where they need to be. I'll come back for you in thirty minutes. Be ready."

"Yes, sir," I salute with all seriousness. He shakes his head, walks out of the dining room, and leaves me to enjoy my bacon alone.

Thirty minutes later, on the dot, the elevator doors quietly swish open. I finish tying my laces, pick up my weapons from the couch, and head over to the elevator.

Emerson holds the doors open for me and then enters his code once I'm inside. I feel the gentle fall of the elevator as we begin to descend but the decent lasts longer than usual. It usually takes us a handful of seconds to go from the Penthouse to the casino floor. I glance at the panel Emerson always uses, to see if there's any indication on how many floors this thing operates on, but other than the key insert, and the keypad, the panel is empty.

"We're headed underground." I conclude. It's not a question, but Emerson answers.

"Yes."

We're quiet for a few more seconds and then I feel the gentle bump as the elevator comes to a stop. I eagerly wait for the doors to open so I can see Valmont's secret underground lair. I mean, that's what it feels like to me. But Emerson doesn't open the doors right away. Instead, he faces me, his cold, serious eyes meet mine and I know I'm about to get a lecture.

"What I'm about to show you is top secret."

I can't help the laugh that escapes. Top secret. I feel like I'm in a James Bond or Mission Impossible movie, about to see the inner sanctum. The heart of the entire operation. Hell, maybe I'm about to walk into Batman's secret cave!

I stifle my amusement, "sorry, it's just, you're so serious and then you said, *top secret*, and I just can't help but feel like this is all ridiculous."

He crosses his muscular arms, his face clearly displaying that he's not at all amused by my amusement. "Amarah, when are you going to start taking The Unseen seriously? When are you going to realize that this is an entirely different world, with a whole new set of rules that you know nothing about? When are you going to realize that you're not playing by human standards anymore? Your ignorance can not only get *you* killed but those around you killed."

His words pierce right through my humor. My ignorance *has* gotten people killed. Not knowing or understanding magic, blood magic, not knowing or understanding anything about my power or the power of the Fey, the Werewolves, or the Vampires. I'm surviving on sheer luck and by the knowledge and protection of those around me. Others haven't been so lucky.

Seeing my reaction, Emerson's features soften, slightly, "shit, I'm sorry, Amarah. I didn't mean to suggest...I didn't mean..."

"No, you're right, Emerson. I need to take all of this more seriously. If Valmont is trusting me with this piece of information, I need to respect his trust and also understand what's at stake by this extension of trust. Tell me."

Not one to linger on silly details or silly emotions, Emerson nods, "the Penthouse is usually Valmont's resting place. As you know, it only has one way in and one way out. Unless, someone was to access it by scaling the walls and climbing over the balcony. That's why, someone is stationed to watch the perimeter, 24-7. There's also someone stationed on the roof, as well as motion censors, that are strategically place throughout the casino and premises."

"I had no idea security was that intense."

"This is the home of a Virtuoso and his Sigitis, Amarah, of course security is going to..."

"I'm sorry, his what?" I ask, confused.

"His Sigitis, his brood, his family."

I swallow, "wait, so, all of the Vampires live down here?"

"Yes."

Why am I suddenly not excited to be here anymore? I know I waltzed right into their clutches when I went to the club but I was also surrounded by other humans. The club is public and I still felt safe. Not to mention, Valmont was there, and he always makes me feel safe. Well, at least safe from everyone around me. Now, I'm about to walk into their home! Their resting place. Their turf. Chills erupted on my skin and I suddenly have no desire to continue training if it means I have to do it here.

"Valmont wouldn't have agreed to have you down here if you weren't safe, Amarah, but you also need to understand the magnitude of this knowledge. You're getting to see the inside of Valmont and the Vampire's most secret and sacred place. This is information people would kill and torture for. Do you understand?"

I nod my head, still trying to wrap my head around all this new information I keep getting thrown at me.

"I need to hear you say it."

"Yes, I understand what this is and what it means. I would never give this information away. I would never do anything to hurt Valmont." My words sound confident, because they're the truth, but a small sliver of doubt creeps up my spine and settles inside of me. I said these same words in a conversation with Alistair and his words still haunt me.

Not intentionally or even knowingly, I'm sure.

Is it truly safe for me to have this knowledge? I'm not sure, and yet, my indecision and my fear, is nothing compared to my curiosity. My need to know more, to know everything I can. As Võitleja it's my job to know as much as I can to help protect this world.

Emerson is still studying me, my reactions. So, I lift up my chin and square my shoulders, "I can handle it."

"Consider this Vegas," he says. "What happens here, stays here. Whatever you see or hear, doesn't ever leave this place. Understood?"

"Understood."

Emmerson looks me over again and finally seems satisfied. Not that he can honestly tell me no at this point. If Valmont gave him the green light to bring me down here, and I want to go, well, he has to obey the order. He keys in a code, the elevator doors glide open, and I tentatively step out.

I'm standing in an underground tunnel that looks strikingly similar to the tunnels at Headquarters. If I didn't know where we were, I wouldn't have been able to tell them apart. There are lights strewn across the hard-packed roof above us, and I still can't quite believe these underground hideouts are wired for electricity and plumbing. I can understand now, how the Fey have done what they've done with their underground Headquarters, they have the Maa Fey to literally move and work with the Earth, but how did the Vampires manage this?

I follow Emerson down the wide tunnel, until we reach the first split. We've come to a stop and we can either go left, right or straight.

"Although you've been given clearance to be down here, I highly recommend you do not ever roam around down here alone. Not only can you get lost, but young Vampires are not something you want to come across alone."

"Why is that?" I ask, curiously.

"Young Vampires are not yet in control of themselves and their hunger. The blood thirst controls them and they're dangerous. All young Vampires, or lapseealine, as they're called in The Unseen, are mentored by an ammune, an experience and older Vampire. Their mentor is charged with teaching them how to control their hunger so they can return to the life they knew. Well, kind of."

"How long does it take for a young Vampire to gain full control?"

Emerson shrugs, "it varies Vampire to Vampire. Some are stronger than others and gain control within a few weeks. Others, it can take months, and some never gain control at all."

"What happens to the ones who never gain control?"

"I think you already know the answer to that, Amarah."

"They're killed," I say, plainly.

"Yes, they have to be. They're a risk to humans and to the entire world of The Unseen. We survive because we stay hidden. Vampires, or any preternatural being for that matter, that jeopardizes our secrecy, safety, and our autonomy, is a risk that we can't afford.

The world is just not ready for The Unseen. They may never be ready."

"I never realized there was so much to consider. So, Valmont is in charge, and responsible, for every Vampire in this city. That's a big responsibility. What happens if he ever loses control?"

"That would be very, very bad news for us all. It would trigger the Konsiilium, the Vampire Council, to send in their Täitjad, their enforcers of the Vampire law, to handle the situation. I've never personally seen this happen, but I've heard stories of it happening in other Territories. Trust me when I say, we do not want the Konsiilium's eyes on us for any reason."

"Damn, I had no idea there was so much structure and politics to it all, although, I see how it's needed. Do the Werewolves also have something similar?"

"They do, although the details of their hierarchy are kept secret, as the Vampires are. It must remain this way for everyone's safety." He looks at me to make sure I understand the threat in his words. I'm being given information that only Vampires and their protectors have.

Without needing to be prompted, "I understand."

"Good. Again, I don't want you to think you're not safe here. You are. There are strict rules in place and Valmont is serious about your safety. They won't forget he killed one of his own over you any time soon."

I feel the heat creeping up my cheeks at the reminder of that night. I wonder if Emerson had seen what happened? It was late into the night before Valmont and I had our little…*display*. Emerson, hopefully, was asleep since Pierce is the head of night security, but no doubt he had at least *heard* about all of the events of the night.

"Yeah, there's that," I admit, embarrassed.

"Left is where all the young Vampires and their mentors rest, right is where everyone else rests, and straight ahead is the middle of the compound where the training center is. Don't ever venture down either of these other tunnels. Just stick to the center and what you came here for."

"I think I can manage that," I agree.

He nods and leads me down the tunnel straight ahead of us. We come to a large steel gate that takes up the entirety of the tunnel, barring our way. Again, there is a panel located on the wall next to the gate that Emerson has to insert a key into and enter a code.

"Wouldn't it be easier if you just used a fingerprint or something?" I ask.

"Easier? Maybe. But not safer if I'm killed and someone chops off my finger to use and gain access."

"Well, I ummmm, guess you have a point."

The gate groans and I hear the chains of a pully system working to pull the massive gate up.

"Hurry through. The gate will automatically lower again in fifteen seconds," he ushers me through the gate.

Once on the other side, I vaguely hear the gate lowering behind me again, but don't pay much attention to it locking me inside. I'm too focused on what's in front of me. I'm standing at the front of a massive room, at least the same size of the throne room at Headquarters if not bigger.

There are no mats here, just hard-packed Earth, worn down over centuries of use. There are sectioned marked off by ropes, designating fighting areas. There are weapons of all kinds, orderly stored throughout the room, next to each marked off section. There's a wide, clear path that looks like it completely surrounds the entire room, which I'm assuming is supposed to be a running track. I look up and there are planks of various shapes and sizes zig zagging across the room, at least fifty feet high. I can't imagine anyone who would be willing to train up on those ledges. There are ropes and chains hanging from the ceiling, and off to one side, more of the things I'm familiar with, like weights and benches, barbells and dumbbells, and punching bags. Things that a human would need in order to train. Although, Logan does hit up the weights too. I wonder if the Vampires also use them?

"This is where you will train, obviously. Through there," he points to a door on my right, "is a locker room, so to speak. Bathroom, shower, sauna, etcetera. Through there," he points to a door on my left, "is a kitchen. It doesn't come very stocked with human essentials but it gets the job done most of the time. And through there," he gestures to the door at the other end of the training room, "is a common room. Television, couches, games and such."

"Who knew Vampires needed all this human stuff."

"Eh, they don't really. It's more of a courtesy and security blanket to those who have recently turned. Although, being a Vampire doesn't mean they lose interest in human things. It just means they drink blood to survive now, that's the main difference."

"And they're dead. Their hearts no longer beat with life. I think that's a big enough difference."

"Perhaps, but not big enough not to sleep with them," his point hits its intended mark.

My cheeks flame but I don't deny it, "touché, Emerson. Touché." Tired of having the conversation directed at me, I decide to turn the table. "How did you get mixed up in all of this? Working with Vampires? And not just working with them, but being one of Valmont's most trusted men?"

"That's not something I talk about."

"Oh, come on! You basically know everything about me. Your story can't be anything I haven't seen or heard before."

He levels his hard, glacial eyes on me, with a look that sends a piece of ice sliding down my spine. "I won't discuss it. Don't ask again." He sweeps his arm out towards the room, "this is what you wanted so, train. Valmont should be up soon and, if he wishes to speak to you, he will find you here."

"Wait!" I plead, as he turns to walk off. "Who am I suppose to train with? I need a sparring partner."

He glances around the room and points to a solid wooden beam, "use that."

"What? No, that's not the same. I don't just need to practice my moves, I'm still learning. I need a live sparring partner to train me. Looks like you're it, buddy."

"I'm not sparring with you," he says, with finality.

"Why not? Are you too scared?" I taunt him.

He gives me an incredulous look and crosses his big arms over his chest, "I'll hurt you."

"I'm harder to hurt than I look."

"No."

I roll my eyes, "ugh, you're so infuriating! Emerson, come on, I need the help and you're the only one here."

He looks resolute in his decision so I try another tactic.

"I need to be able to protect myself in this world, Emerson, and you can help me with that. Please."

I see the muscle in his jaw twitching, he's obviously not happy about being put in this situation. Happy or not, he's obviously a badass and knows how to hold his own against monsters, I can learn from him. I'm not sure what he sees on my face or what thoughts are going through his mind, but he eventually uncrosses his arms and walks towards me.

"Fine," he says, through clenched teeth. "I'll train with you, but we aren't using these," he grabs the weapons I've been holding and places them off to the side.

"What? Why not? I need to practice my blade work," I protest.

"Not all of your enemies are going to come at you on the battlefield when you're armed. Do you know how to defend yourself with your own hands? Do you know how to take down an opponent? To disable them, and not just kill them?"

I wobble my hands back and forth, "kind of. I did a little bit of hand-to-hand training when I first started, but I tend to fight demons, and hand-to-hand doesn't quite fit the bill for that opponent."

"True, but they won't always be your only enemy. You have plenty of people to teach you how to fight with weapons, use my expertise and skill to learn some basics of hand-to-hand." He takes off his black suit jacket and loosens his tie, preparing to maneuver a bit more freely. "You can never be too prepared when it comes to protecting yourself, Amarah."

"Alright," I follow him and step over the low hanging rope, marking off one of the square fighting sections.

We're both standing in the middle of the fighting square, a few feet away from each other. Emerson motions for me to start, "ok, show me what you got."

I shake out my arms and shoulders, bounce on my feet a couple times, trying to loosen up my lips and get my body warm. I call on my power and pull it out around me, like a shield. If I'm going to be getting punched and kicked by a former Navy SEAL, I'm not going to do it unprotected. I'm stubborn, not stupid.

I steady my breathing, widen my stance, and put my arms up to protect my face. I move in quickly with a kick mid-body, he blocks me easily and returns a fast kick that I manage to block as well. He immediately leads in with a swing, which I duck under and land a punch to his stomach with my right and a quick left to his cheek as his momentum throws him forward. I immediately throw a high kick, trying to land it on his other cheek, but he grabs my ankle, spins me in the air and I come crashing down to the hard ground. My power protecting me from the force of it.

"Well, you landed a couple of hits, which I didn't expect," he says, as he rubs his jaw. "But you need to be quicker in your delivery.

Get in and get out and don't do something your opponent can predict. Again." He instructs.

I get up from the floor and try again. We throw a few punches and kicks that we both block. I see an opening for a solid front kick to his stomach. I make impact, but he recovers quicker than I thought he would. Once again, I'm not fast enough with my kick and he grabs a hold of my leg, swinging me off my feet, tossing me like a bag of trash, off to the side. This time, he doesn't stop the fight, he charges at me and I manage to land a kick to his knee, giving me time to scramble to my feet.

He's on me before I can gain my stance, I manage to block the first couple of punches, but he lands two to my stomach and hard third across my cheek. My power is protecting me, but I still feel the impact of the blows. They may not be breaking bones or breaking skin, but they would be if I wasn't protected.

I let out a battle cry and I charge him. I grab him around his waist, hooking his leg with mine, and bringing him to the ground with me. I know I only manage to get him down because he wasn't expecting a wild charge. I don't hesitate and give him two knees to the gut, before I climb on his back and try to grab onto him with a chokehold. He's on his feet now and doubles over as he pulls me off him. I go flying, feet over head, and land hard on my back. Even with my power protecting me, I feel the air leave my lungs from the force of the fall.

"Damn," he says, with a chuckle. "You're a little scrapper. Your basics were taught well. There may just be hope for you yet."

I groan as I roll onto my side and push myself back up to my feet. "Doesn't feel like it."

"Who taught you what you know?"

Andre had taught me a little bit of hand-to-hand combat, but Logan is the one who really spent the time teaching me what little I know. I would probably know more if our training sessions hadn't often turned into sex. Not that I'm complaining but also kind of wishing I had paid more attention.

"Andre a little but Logan mostly," I say, breathlessly.

"Well, then, I stand corrected. You have the perfect person to teach you how to fight without weapons. I'm not sure there's anyone alive, or undead, that can beat Logan in a hand-to hand fight."

"Yeah, well, I don't exactly have his help anymore so, you're stuck with me for now. Let's go again."

I completely lose track of time as we practice. Emerson is a surprisingly patient teacher. He slows me down, shows me how to position and maneuver my body for more fluid attacks and withdrawals. He shows me how to use my opponent's momentum against them, especially if they're bigger than I am, which is the case ninety-nine percent of the time. He corrects me when I pull back on an attack before it's landed. He says I need to commit and follow through, giving the attack more power. There's a skill to following through and still being able to withdrawal quickly. An art that is obviously going to take me time to perfect.

We practice, back and forth, defense and offense, until the hold on my power starts to fade and I'm too tired to give him one hundred percent effort. He leaves me sitting on the dirt in the fighting square as he walks through the door that he mentioned is the kitchen. He comes back with a couple of bottles of water and tosses one to me.

"Drink. Your body needs to rehydrate."

"Yes, dad," I say, sarcastically, but eagerly take the water and almost drink the entire thing in one go.

"Someone is enjoying my private training facility I see."

Valmont's smooth British voice floats through the air and caresses my skin, with promises of wicked deeds, sending goosebumps down my arms. I look up and see he's leaning up against one of the thick wooden beams Emerson had pointed out earlier. He's already dressed in an immaculate navy-blue suit, crisp white shirt, and dazzling silver tie that brings out the silver in his hair. His hands are in his pockets, legs crossed at the ankles, looking completely relaxed.

I drink him in, from his Brandy colored Oxfords, to his fancy watch that matches the blue of his suit and the brandy of his shoes, to his silver pocket square and up to his beautifully handsome face. Except now, I can imagine the Viking tattoos that remain hidden, like a dark, sexy secret covering his entire body. A hidden treasure just waiting to be discovered. And the fangs, hidden behind luscious lips, promising unfathomable pleasure. My blood starts to hum in my veins at just the thought of them piercing my skin.

The arrogant smirk on his lips tells me I've been a bit too obvious in my appreciation of him.

It is you who is addicted to me.

I immediately drop my gaze to the bottle of water in my hands but I know it's too late. He saw every second of me gawking over him, and even if he didn't, the blush on my cheeks would give my thoughts away anyway.

"I've been told that you wish to speak to me," he says, plainly, as if I'm no more than an inconvenient business meeting.

I force myself to look at him. I hold his turquoise gaze and lift my chin in defiance. If he can act like I'm nothing to him, then I can do the same.

I stand up to face him. "Yes," I answer just as plainly.

"Leave us," he orders Emerson.

Emerson bows his head, "yes, boss."

I watch as he steps out of the training square without a second thought or look in my direction. His steps echo quietly through the now deadly silent and cavernous room.

I feel Valmont's attention on me so I return my gaze to him. His turquoise eyes are heated with desire and I suddenly feel vulnerable in my leggings and sports bra. My breaths are coming faster now, and it has nothing to do with the training I was just doing. Valmont's eyes drop to my cleavage as my chest rises and falls heavily. My heart starts to race. The pounding in my veins drowns out Emerson's footsteps and I know Valmont must be able to hear it from where he's standing.

He pushes off the post, hands still remain in his pockets, and he walks towards me, slowly. Like a panther, quiet and deadly, creeping up on its prey. Only I see him coming and I don't want to run. He stops right in front of me. He can easily reach out and touch me but his hands remain in his pockets. My hands are clutching the bottle of water as if they're glued to it. I refuse to be the one to break. To reach for him. He smiles, a lazy smile, but makes sure to show me his fangs.

My blood is on fire.

My skin is on fire.

The pulse between my legs is on fire.

The memory of his bite, his pleasure coursing through my veins, has me close to panting. He's so close but still too far. I want him to take me in his arms. To push his body against mine. I want to taste him. I want to taste my blood on his tongue. I want to feel him pushing inside of me. Pumping his hard cock into my tight, wet pussy. I want his bite to take me and shove me over the edge. I want to fall into the bliss of sweet oblivion that only he can give me. I want him to claim me. I want him to want me. I want him addicted to me.

The way that I'm addicted to him.

"Amarah Rey," his voice brings me out of my racing thoughts.

I swallow hard, "yes?"

"You needed to speak with me? I suggest you say what you need to say before the other Vampires wake up and I have to go to work."

He's still so cold. Even though we're alone. So, this is it. This is the truth after all. I'm the one addicted to him and I'm nothing to him. The truth splashes like cold water in my face, helping me clear my head. I won't be his fool.

I clear my throat and take a step away from him. "It's about Viveka. I need a favor."

Valmont: Truth Shall Set You Free

My Heart I Surrender by I Prevail

I'm standing next to Amarah Rey and we're finally alone. I've wanted to be alone with her for days. I've wanted to say so much, to do so much. Her body is glistening in sweat and I want to taste it right off her skin. I want to learn and savor every flavor she offers up. I want to draw out every whimper, moan, and breath her body keeps secret.

I see the way she looks at me. I hear the song her body plays for me. The beat of her blood pounding in her veins. I can taste her desire for me as if it was rain falling on my tongue. The air is thick with it. With desire and electricity. Ready to shock me back to life the second I touch her. But I can't. I can't lose focus. I can't lose control. Not now, while Viveka is here. I clench my hands tightly, still hidden in my pockets, to keep from reaching for her.

I see her sheer determination take hold, but I don't miss the hurt that passes through her eyes first. She can't deny her addiction to me, but is that all she feels? Or is there something more? I desperately want to ask, and to tell her, to show her how I feel, but I can't! For her safety, I can't. So, I remain cold and continue pushing her away.

"Yes, well? What it is? I don't have all night to stand around here with you, waiting on you to ask your favor. Speak up before I change my mind."

"What has gotten into you, Valmont? I don't understand. You've never been this way with me. Maybe with others, but never with me."

"Oh, what, so now you suddenly believe what everyone's been saying? That you're special? Tell me, Amarah Rey, how should I be treating you? Shall I grovel at your feet, perhaps?"

"What? No! All I want is the old Valmont back! Where is the Valmont who came to visit me? Who made sure that I was ok? Where is the Valmont who believes in me? Where is my friend?"

Did she really just throw me into the forbidden friend zone? Is that what she thinks we are? Friends with benefits? When a man loves a woman, the last thing he ever wants to hear her say is, *friend*. It makes the cold act a little easier to deliver.

"Ah, I see. Your friend," I spit the word out. Even just saying it leaves a bad taste in my mouth. "Is that what we are, Amarah Rey? *Friends*?"

"Yes! At least, I thought we were. I thought that maybe...after the other night, I thought...Hell, I don't know what I thought but I didn't think this would happen," she motions between us. "I didn't think all you wanted was sex and then you'd just..." she throws her arms up in the air, "treat me like I'm nothing more than another one of your many conquests."

It crushes me that she believes that's all I wanted from her. I fucking hate Viveka for showing up when she did. I waited patiently for my chance to be with Amarah Rey and now it's all going to shit! And I don't know how to fix it without putting Amarah Rey in danger. She needs to believe my act, because if she doesn't react genuinely, Viveka will know. Viveka will smell the lie in an instant and use her to hurt me.

I do my best to give her a blank expression, even though my

emotions are raging, just below the surface. "If the shoe fits," I shrug.

She jerks back, as if I physically hit her. She's clearly shocked at my words, bloody Hell, I'm shocked at my words. They couldn't be further from the truth.

She scoffs and it turns into a sob. She's frozen, staring at me as if she's never seen me before, and tears stream down her face.

I swear, I feel my heart constrict in my chest. "Amarah Rey," my hands are now reaching for her and I'm taking a step towards her before I can reign myself and my emotions in.

"No," she steps back quickly and angrily wipes the tears off her cheeks. She's shaking her head, "no. You don't get to change your mind because you feel sorry for me."

Her pain has always been my undoing. I can't bear to see her hurt. I can't bear to see the truth of her pain glistening in her eyes, leaving trails down her beautiful face. It's even harder to face when it's because of me.

"Amarah Rey, please, let me…"

"Enough, Valmont! I thought if I had the chance to speak with you alone that I could figure this out," she shakes her head again, "but there's nothing to figure out. I see that now. I hear you, loud and clear. What I really wanted to talk to you about is Viveka. Kordeuv came to me last night and…"

Her words hit me like a punch in the gut. "He what? What do you mean he *came* to you, Amarah Rey? Did he hurt you?"

"What? No, why would he hurt me? I have power he wants but they don't know *what* I am, remember. If you would let me finish and not interrupt me, I'll tell you."

I manage to contain my control but the thought of Amarah Rey being approached by Kordeuv fills me with too many emotions to sift through.

Unease.

Suspicion.

Anger.

Jealousy.

Protectiveness.

And I'm not used to feeling *anything*, for anyone. Still, I manage to somehow keep my cool. No doubt the fact that she's standing here, in front of me, unharmed, is the only reason why.

"Apologies. That was indeed rude of me to interrupt. Please, continue."

She rolls her eyes at me, "he claims that he needs my help. He said he wants a chance to speak with me, privately..."

"Absolutely not. Out of the question."

"Ughhhh! You are so insufferable! We're allies, Valmont, and apparently that's *all* we are. You have no control over me or what I chose to do. You're not my keeper."

"That's beside the point, Amarah Rey, he's dangerous and..."

"I'm dangerous too, Valmont! Or have you forgotten the fact that I *killed* someone with my power? My *Angel* power! Despite what you, and everyone, might think, I'm not helpless."

"I have not forgotten anything about you, Amarah Rey, but you don't know him, *I* don't know him, and you sure as bloody Hell don't know Viveka. This is a trap for her to get to you, nothing more, and I will not allow that to happen."

"It's not a trap, Valmont. I believe him. He wants to help us so that we can help him with...whatever it is he needs help with. I can guarantee you, with my life, that this is not a trap for Viveka to attack me, or whatever."

"How can you make that guaratee?"

"Beause she's going to be with you."

"Come again?" I ask, taken aback.

"That's my favor. I need you to agree to spend time with her, to distract her long enough for Kordeuv and I to meet."

"No," I say, flatly and difinitively.

"This could be our only chance to find out why they're here, Valmont. We need to know what Kordeuv has to say. We don't really have any other options on the table."

"I don't trust him."

"Then trust *me*, Valmont. I believe him. I think he truly needs help getting away from Viveka. I don't think he's loyal to her. But it's all speculation unless we give him the chance to speak."

I start pacing, the emotions and sudden adrenaline rushing through me need an outlet. I know she's right. What other options do we have that will allow us to find out why they're here? Viveka isn't just going to *tell* me, and we've been unsuccessful finding anything out by following them and keeping tabs on them. This may truly be the only way we get information. But I don't like this plan.

"I don't like the thought of you and him alone together. I'm not going to put you in danger and I'm not enough to keep Viveka distracted. We'll find another plan."

"There is no other plan, Valmont! We need to do this."

"You don't know what you're asking of me," I growl angrily, as I loosen my tie, suddenly feeling suffocated.

"All you have to do is agree to meet with her prvately and keep her distracted for an hour or so and give us time to…"

I stop pacing so I can look at Amarah Rey. "You think it will be that simple? You think I can trick her with some fancy words and a drink? You don't think she'll see right through me and our plan to keep her distracted?"

"I don't know, I…"

"That's right, you don't know! You have no idea what you're asking of me, Amarah Rey."

Just the thought of what I'll have to do to convince Viveka that I'm sincere in wanting to spend time with her, alone, makes me want to kill someone. Hundreds of years I spent under her cruel, greedy little hands. Hundreds of years craving nothing but her and hundreds of years tortured by the same touch. When I became Virtuoso, I swore that I would never allow her to use me again, and now, here Amarah Rey is asking me to do just that.

And the sad part is, I probably would have jumped at the opportunity to trick Viveka, to turn the tables and use *her* for once, but everything has changed.

I've tasted Amarah Rey.

I've been inside of Amarah Rey.

I'm addicted to Amarah Rey.

I'm in love with Amarah Rey.

And the thought of tainting my body with Viveka, to bed the devil after I've tasted an Angel, is blasphemous.

Amarah Rey crosses her arms, "I don't understand what the issue is, Valmont? You may have to sleep with her. So what? You've never had a problem with fucking women and getting what you want before."

"That was before," I say, through clenched teeth and start pacing again, this time losing the tie and suit jacket completely. The enormous training room feels like it's caving in on me.

"Before what?" Amarah Rey asks, throwing her arms in the air in frustration.

"Before *you*," I yell back.

"Before me? I don't...I don't understand. What do I have to do with it?"

"Everything!" It's my turn to throw my arms in the air. I turn to face Amarah Rey. All of her frustration, anger and hurt are gone, replaced by a look of confusion.

"How can you ask me to let you go off alone, with another man, a *dangerous* man? How can you ask me to voluntarily sleep with another woman, someone I spent hundreds of years trying to break free from? How can you ask me to sleep with her when I..."

I can't say it. I can't tell Amarah Rey how I feel. This truth, once voiced out loud, cannot be taken back. This truth will only endanger her. And if I say these words out loud, they become true. And this is one truth that terrifies me. As long as it remains inside of my head, I can act like it doesn't really matter. Once she knows…it changes everything.

"When what, Valmont?" She asks, quietly.

"Never mind. It doesn't matter. You just can't ask me to do this. I can't do this."

"It *does* matter, Valmont," she takes a step towards me.

I inhale a big breath and stand up straighter, fortifying myself. Only the inhale brings her scent crashing into me. Covering every inch of my mind, body and fucking soul. She consumes me in every way.

I close my eyes, I don't want to see her pleading eyes, desperate for the truth. "I said forget it, Amarah Rey."

"No, I'm not ging to let this go. Why me? Why did I change everything? I don't understand what I have to do with this. You clearly don't want anthing to do with me anymore, since you've already had me, so why am I the issue?"

"Amarah Rey, we are done talkinig about this. This plan doesn't work, period."

She takes another step towards me, this time her anger decides to join her, "stop being a fucking coward, Valmont! Why is it always this way with you? Why do we have to get to this point? Why can't you ever just trust me? Why can't you talk to me and tell me how you feel? Why won't this plan work? For fucks sake, Valmont, be honest with me for once!"

I grab a hold of her wrists, as they're flying wrecklessly in the air, near my face. I raise my voice above hers to get her attention, "because I fucking love you!"

She freezes, once again, completely still in my hold and

under my gaze. The water bottle she's holding goes crashing to the ground, a loud thud in the suddenly quiet room. We stare at each other as my deepest secret comes crashing down around us. We're both breathing hard, as if we've been physically battling instead of just yelling at each other. Her mouth opens and then closes, several times, as she struggles to find words to the truth bomb I just set off between us.

"What?" Her voice is so soft I almost don't hear the question.

I lower her hands to her side and trail my hands up her bare arms, savoring the feel of her soft skin under my fingertips. Gods, I've been desperate to touch her again. She shivers and closes her eyes. I caress her cheek and she leans into my touch, ever so slightly, but I feel it, and it makes my heart leap in my chest. She's responding to me. To *my* touch. Maybe there's hope after all.

I gently pull on her chin, tipping her head up towards me, "Amarah Rey, look at me."

She slowly opens her eyes and I see all her questions written openly in her big hazel eyes. These last few days have been a rollercoaser of emotions for me, I can't imagine what it's been like for her.

"I want to make sure you're listening to me. Are you paying attention?"

She nods her head.

"You don't know what you're asking me to do. The thought of you alone with *any* other man, sets my blood on fire. I want to punch my fist into their chest and pull out their still beating hearts just because they *looked* at you. And Viveka," I shake my head, "the only way I can distract her long enough to give you the time you need is if I sleep with her. The thought alone makes me want to pull out my own cold, dead heart, because I can't imagine being with anyone else but you."

She lets out a shaky breath as I continue to split open my

chest and offer her up whatever is left of my heart.

"I only want *your* body pressed to mine. I only want to hear my name on *your* lips. I only want *your* blood in my veins. You see, the truth is, I lied to you, Amarah Rey."

Her eyebrows scrunch together in confusion, "when?"

"When I told you that it is you who is addicted to me. That may be true, but only because I'm far beyond addiction. I'm in love with you, Amarah Rey. I may not have a beating heart to love you with, but for what it's worth, you make me feel like I do."

She tries to shake her head, but I'm still holding her chin, holding her gaze on mine, "I don't understand. These last few days, you've been so cold and mean to me, and now you tell me...*this*. I don't understand."

"Amarah Rey, everything I've done has been to protect you. If Viveka finds out how I feel about you, you would already be tortured or worse. I have to push you away while she's here. You don't understand the danger you're in, not even because of what you are, but because of what you mean to me."

"Why couldn't you just be honest with me? All this time I've been thinking you used me." Her eyes start to water and her bottom lip trembles. "That all you wanted was sex and that I was nothing more than that."

I trail my thumb gently across her bottom lip, I want nothing more then to take her mouth with mine. To show her the truth of my words, to reassure her that she's so much more to me than sex, but I won't assume she wants what I want. Her previous words still haunt me.

Revenge fuck. Means to an end.

No, I won't force this on her.

"I tried to show you how I felt. I thought you would see right through me, and see how enamored I am with you. I tried to tell you, that night, Hell, many nights, but I never got the chance. And then everything that's happened since," I hang my head in defeat. I hate that I've made her feel like nothing.

I feel her hands gently rest on my chest. I move my hands to hold hers harder to me, her warmth seeps in through my skin, as my body greedily takes everything she has to offer. It's not enough. I want *more*. I want her body, yes. I want her blood, yes. But I also want her heart.

I want it all.

And I know her heart belongs to someone else, and as much as that truth destroys me, it doesn't change how *I* feel. I've said it before, and I'll say it again, if I was a better man, I'd walk away. But the hope that one day her heart could be *mine* is too tempting to resist.

"I understand," she says, softly. "I don't like it, but I understand why you did it. I've basically done the same thing with..." she shakes her head, "I don't blame you for trying to keep me safe. Thank you."

"There's nothing in this world that I wouldn't do to keep you safe, even if it kills me to do it. I will always keep you safe. Do you understand?"

She nods and looks up at me.

"Gods, you're beautiful, Amarah Rey." I caress her cheek and trail my knuckles lightly down her exposed neck. "You took my breath away the very first time you looked into my eyes and *saw me* and every single time since."

Her hazel eyes are locked on mine, she doesn't say anything for a few heartbeats, but I feel the vein in her neck pulse harder against my fingers. I delicately run my fingers along the throbbing vein. Her eyes drop to my mouth and in this moment, I know exactly what she's thinking. I may not know exactly how she feels about me, I may not have her heart, but in this moment, I know she's thinking the exact same thing I am.

"Valmnont?" She asks, hestinantly.

"Yes, Amarah Rey?"

"Come with me to the Penthouse."

"If you're sure that's what you want. That *this* is what you want."

She practically climbs up my body, tiptoeing, and reaching up to me with every inch of her body, and claims my mouth with hers. Just her soft, warm lips on mine, ignite my body like she's the match and I'm drenched in gasoline. Considering fire is one of the few things that can kill me, I should be terrified of this feeling, but I only want to burn hotter and brighter.

Before I can think clearly, to grab a hold of her and never let her go, she lowers her body back down, feet planted solidly on the ground once more. It was a gentle, soft, chaste kiss but it's completely knocked me off my feet.

"I'm sure," she says, as she holds my gaze.

I can see the heat in her eyes, and I'm not sure if it's from what she's feeling within, or the reflection of my own body on fire.

She walks to the end of the training square, picks up her weapons, and heads to the exit. I stand alone in my inferno as I watch her walk away. I haven't felt this exposed and vulnerable since I was seven years old facing death for the first time. I'm at a loss of what to do, what to say, how to act. All this time, I've imagined what it would be like to tell Amarah Rey how I feel. I imagined all of the beautifully intimate things that would take place afterwards. I imagined how I would devour her body and make her *feel* my love. And now, as I watch her walk away with expectations of what's to come, I'm nervous.

What if my love isn't enough? What if *I'm* not enough?

"Valmont? Are you coming?" Her voice pulls me from my thoughts.

I clear my throat, "yes, of course."

I pick up my suit jacket and tie from where I hung them across a weapon's rack and join Amarah at the large metal gate. I pull out the single key from my inner suit jacket pocket and enter the access code into the panel. The sound of the gate being lifted open is defeaning in the silence that hangs between us. We continue walking down the tunnel in silence, the only sound is coming from our shoes softly hitting the ground. I repeat the process of key and code to gain access to the elevator and we ride up to the Penthouse in our electrically charged silence.

I'm aware of her body inches away from mine. I feel the warmth radiating off of her, adding to the intensity of the flames licking my skin. I glance over, she's facing forward, seemingly unaffected by me, but I know better. I feel her desire and I can see her vein pulsing rapidly in her neck. But if I didn't have my heightened senses, I wouldn't be able to tell she was even slightly interested in me. Meanwhile, I'm practically chomping at the bit, barely containing myself. I want to take her, right here, right now, against the elevator doors. I want to engulf her in my fire until we're both nothing more than ashes blowing on the wind of our spent pleasure.

I open the elevator doors to the Penthouse and follow her inside. She deposits her weapons on the couch and kicks off her shoes, walking barefoot to the wetbar.

"I found your mead in here," she says, as she pulls out a bottle and two glasses.

Seeing her here, in my personal space, walking around like it's hers, stirs my heart. The scent of her, everywhere, and on everything, stirs my cock. Gods, this is everything I've wanted for the last few months, but it feels like I've been waiting for this, for her, all of my life.

Amarah Rey.

Here.

With me.

It's all I've wanted, and yet, in this moment, all I want is to know how she feels about me. I know she isn't in love me, not yet and maybe not ever, but is it a possibility? Will she eventually join me in this inferno? Or am I destined to burn alive, alone? I've given her everything that I have, made myself vulnerable in way I never have with anyone else before. Not even Viveka. That was always about manipulation and power. I never loved her. Back then, I may have thought that's what it was, but it wasn't. Not for either of us.

And now, here I am, confessing something so foreign to me, but it feels so right. It feels like it's a part of me, rooted so deeply, there's no way to cut it out. There's no way to cut Amarah Rey away from me. I'm falling rapidly towards heartbreak, towards a death I actually fear, and I can't stop myself.

These thoughts and all of the unknowns, all of the doubts, are spiraling through my mind. I feel dizzy, hot, and it's suddenly hard to breathe, because all I smell is her. I leave her rambling at the wetbar, pouring our drinks, and walk out onto the balcony. The cold, winter air hits me and helps to ease the burning of my skin. A half moon is just rising above the Sandias, lighting up the balcony in a soft white glow. There are storm clouds moving in, blocking out the stars, but the moon remains free of their touch.

"Valmont?" Amarah Rey's voice sounds nervous as she searches for me.

I hear the soft pad of her bare feet as she approaches. She finds me, standing in the middle of the balcony, staring up at the moon.

"Valmont, is everything ok?" Her voice is cautious, worried.

"Yes," I immediately respond, not wanting to voice any more vulnerabilities, but she deserves my honesty. We both do. "Actually, I don't know," I admit, as I take one of the drinks from her hand, still staring at the moon. I don't want to look at her, not yet, because if I do, I won't be able to say what I need to say.

"Are you going to tell me what's wrong? Or are you going to continue to keep your feelings hidden?" She asks, softly. There's no condescence in her tone, just a simple question of fact. She's used to me hiding behind my walls.

I take a large sip and the honey mead flows through my veins in a comforting embrace.

"I've told you everything that I feel for you, Amarah Rey, there's nothing left to say, and that's part of the problem."

"I don't understand?"

"Neither do I," I sigh. "I don't know how you feel about what I revealed to you. I don't know what happens next. I don't know what to do now, or what to say, if I need to say anything at all. I'm a two-thousand-year-old Master Vampire who doesn't know anything at all. This is all new territory for me and I'm feeling rather unsettled."

"What do you mean, this is all new territory for you?"

I finally look away from the moon and give my attention to Amarah Rey. One of my many fantasies, has been to see her body, naked and shaking with pleasure, in the moonlight. But her face looking up to mine, open and genuine, one hundred percent here, focused on me and my words in this moment, is one of the most beautiful things I've ever seen.

"I've been on this Earth for a long time. I've had many women, men, I've had them alone, I've had them together, there's not much I haven't experienced in this unnaturally long life."

I know my words aren't what she wants to hear. She looks away from me and takes a large drink of her mead and winces. It's strong and potent, it's an acquired taste and Amarah Rey isn't accustomed to it yet.

I take her glass from her hands and place both of our drinks on the table next to us. I don't want her distracted by anything. I want her attention on me and what I have to say next.

"I've done and felt a lot of things over the many, many,

never-ending years, but...I have never felt *this*. I've never been in love, Amarah Rey. And now that I've told you how I feel, it's real, and for the first time in my life, I don't have control. I don't know what comes next."

I see her throat bob in a hard swallow as she digests yet another unfathomable truth. I watch her try and collect her thoughts, her feelings, for what feels like an eternity. When she finally opens her mouth to say something, I move in.

"I..."

I cover her mouth with mine, swallowing down whatever she was going to say. I slip my tongue in her mouth, pushing back any new words she might try to speak. I'm suddenly terrified of them. My truth might be blissfully painful, but her truth will destroy me. I already know she doesn't feel the same way about me and I don't need, or want, to hear it. So, instead, I'll focus on my truth. I'll show her all the ways that I'm in love with her.

Her tongue is sweet, tasting like honey from the mead and just...*her*. I move my hands to pull her hair free from her pointail and let it cascade over them. I hold her head gently but firmly as I tip her head further back and to the side, allowing me to deepen our kiss. I kiss her slowly, dragging out every caress of my toungue on hers, every open and close of our lips, in a passionate dance of give and take. And she lets me kiss her this way, for as long as I desire too.

And I never want to stop.

Kissing someone has never felt so good.

I gently pull her bottom lip into my mouth and graze my fangs along the soft, tender skin. Her moan reverberates through me and I nick her lip, then quickly pull away.

Her eyes are heavy lidded as she looks into mine. No hesitaton, no doubt, no regret, no fear, anywhere to be seen. I drop my gaze to her swollen lips and the blood that's pooling on her bottom lip where my fangs broke the skin. A groan rumbles through my chest and out of my mouth from a need so deep it scares me. Need for her. Her blood.

"Take it," she says, breathlessly.

I never move my gaze away from her blood, vivid and bright, even in the moonlight, beconing me. I hold her head steady as I move in. I slowly draw my tongue across her lip, licking up the blood with the care and attention it deserves. It is Angel blood after all. It deserves to be savored and appreciated. Just this tiny bit of blood, explodes throughout my entire body. It's like her blood wakes me up from the inside out. I suddenly feel everything ten times deeper. It's as if I've been walking through this life hypnotized, and only vaguely aware of my surroundings, and her blood pulls me out of the daze.

Her fingers are blindly fumbling with the buttons on my shirt as she keeps her lips locked on mine. The fact that she's the first one to take the next step helps bring back my confidence.

I smile against her lips, "someone's in a hurry to get me naked."

"Is that a complaint?"

"Only if I'm not allowed to return the gesture."

"By all means," she raises her arms above her head.

An invitation and request for me to remove her sports bra. I finish discarding my shirt, tossing it somewhere behind me, and then I give Amarah Rey my attention. I start at the tips of her fingers, slowly making my way down her arms, as they're held up to the sky. She's standing so steadfast and trusting before me. I never want to see her standing before me with saddness ever again.

My fingertips carress her sides and she shivers as goosebumps temprarily mare her silky skin. I push my fingers underneath the bottom of the sports bra and begin to peel it off her body. It's tight, but I manage to get it off, and discard it somewhere along with my shirt.

Her hands come down but she doesn't try to hide herself

from me. She comfortable and confident in her skin and I love that about her.

"You're absolutely perfect, Amarah Rey," I say, as I soak up ever inch and curve of her body.

I reach for her breasts, so full and soft in my hands. Her nipples harden under my touch and I lean in taking one into my mouth. The sweat has long since dried but I still taste it on her skin. She's clean and salty and sweet and everything I can live off of for the rest of my life. I suck her nipple into my mouth, she moans and runs her hands through my hair, pushing it away from my face. I roll my eyes up to see her face and she's already watching me. A look of hunger in her eyes.

I bite down and she hisses as my fangs penetrate her skin, but it quickly turns into a moan, as the pleasure of my bite rushes through her body. Her head falls back in gratification, her hands tangle in my hair, as the rest of her body sags agaisnt me.

I take a drink of her blood but quickly release her. Just a taste of her blood and a taste of my bite. Not nearly enough for either of us. We're two addicts feening for each other. Her addiction is surface level, where mine is at the core, but in this moment, it's impossible to distinguish the difference. We're both desperate for the next hit and thoughtless about the consequences and the danger.

"Valmont, please," she begs.

"In time," I assure her.

I hook my fingers into her workout leggings and pull them down her legs, along with her underwear. Once she's stepped out of them, I pick her up and she wraps her legs around me, as I walk us to the balcony's railing. I sit her down on the ledge, it's about a foot and half wide, and she clings to me as she looks over her shoulder.

"Valmont, what are you doing? I can fall!" She exclaims. I can see her fear pushing its way through her pleasure.

"Do you trust me?" I ask, as I stand between her legs,

holding her tightly against me.

Here eyes dart back and forth between mine before she nods, "yes."

"Good girl," I smile, as I unhook her arms from around my neck and step back from her. "Turn around," I instruct her.

"What?" She looks at me with wide eyes.

"You said you trust me, now be a good girl, and turn around," I say, slowly. Demanding.

She swallows down her fear and hangs onto my hand as she throws one leg over the ledge and then the other. Her legs are now dangling over the edge of the balcony, thirteen stories up, her back is pressed solidly against my chest as she leans back into me. There's nothing to interfere with the view of the mountains and the glowing moon. The storm clouds are over us now, but somehow, the moon still manages to avoid their cover.

I'm holding her with one hand across her stomach as my other hand moves between her legs. My fingers slide through her folds easily, her body is already soaking with desire. She leans her head back against my shoulder as she moans.

I whisper in her ear, "I love how your body eagerly responds to my every touch."

I use the slickness of her own desire to coat her clit so I can glide my fingers across it effortlessly. I move in a slow, steady circle, feeling her clit swell under my touch.

"Do you like that?" I ask, as I pull her earlobe into my mouth.

"Yes," she breathes out.

She starts to rock her hips to my touch, her breaths become heavier and I listen to every moan and whimper she makes. I dip my finger inside of her, causing her to buck against my hand. All fear and thoughts of falling off the ledge are forgotten under the simple touch of my fingers.

I move my arm from around her waist, just long enough to

turn her head towards me, "I want you to cum while you kiss me, Amarah Rey. I want to feel your desire, your breaths, and your moans, as they leave that beautful mouth, and then I'm going to to make you cum again, so I can taste your desire as it rushes out of your body and onto my tongue. I want to taste and experience all of you, in every way."

I take her mouth, as I continue to hold her body against mine, and I move my slick fingers back to her clit. I move my finger up and down and gently use my fingernail to add some friction. Her moans are non-stop as she continues to recklessly kiss me and rock her hips frantically against my fingers. I increase my speed, her moans turn into whimpers, and I know she's close. A scream errupts from her throat and her body starts to shake as she cums. I swallow down her scream, as I start to tap her clit, drawing out her orgasm.

Tap.

Tap.

Tap.

She pulls her head away from me, gasping for air and grabbing my wrist, pulling my hand away, "stop, please, it's so sensitive."

I turn her head back to me and kiss her again, this time slow and deliberate, savoring every shared breath between us, as her body comes down from her high. I slip my finger into her mouth and she eagerly takes it and sucks it clean. I remmeber what it felt like to have her greedy little mouth on my hard cock. It twitches as it pushes against my pants, begging to be released, to join the fun, but not yet. This night is for her. When she's finally regained herself, and is breathing normally again, I pull back from our kiss.

"Lie down."

"What?"

"Lie. Down."

"Are you crazy? There's not enough room on here. I could

fall off!"

"I thought you liked the idea of a little danger?" I tease.

I see the sparke of excitement in her eyes and the smile tugging her the corners of her lips.

"You already said you trust me so, lie down. Don't make me ask again."

She doesn't hesitate, but she moves slowly, bringing her legs onto the ledge, gripping the sides, and then cautiously lying back. It's barely wide enough for her to lie on, any sudden movement will have her either falling to the floor of the balcony, or her death.

I take a few seonds to remove my shoes and pants before I climb up on the ledge, my Vampire abilities making it effortless. I could balance myself on something half this size if I wanted to.

I lower myself down, between Amarah Rey's legs. "Wrap your legs around my shoulders," I order.

She does, and I lie flat on my stomach, moving my arms under her legs and wrapping them around her thighs to help hold her in place. I don't give her any more time to prepare before I dive in. The first taste of her sweet pussy makes me groan as it coats my tongue. It's my second favorite flavor next to her blood. In fact, if I was given a choice to drink another person's blood to keep me alive, or have my tongue between Amarah Rey's legs, I would slowly die making her cum again and again.

I caress her clit with the top of my tongue, moving in small circles, as I listen to her body speak. She tells me what she likes and what she loves without ever having to say a word. I sink in one finger inside of her and then another. Gods, she's so wet and so tight. Her hips start to move in time to my strokes and I know she's getting close again. I suck her clit into my mouth as I continue to flick it with the tip of my tongue. Her hands are in my hair, gripping, and pulling my closer.

"Oh God, don't stop," she pants.

Who's she kidding? I could literally do this all day and never get tired. I feel cold, soft drops against my skin before I see the big, fluffy snowflakes, as they land on Amarah Rey's skin and immediately melt away. Her legs tighten around me as her body loses all control, only my grip on her thighs keeps her planted on the ledge. I feel her pussy throb and pulse around my fingers as she cums, screaming freely into the stormy night sky. A loud rumble of thunder shakes the world around us, followed quickly by a shockingly close flash of lightning, as if the world is experiencing her pleasure with her.

I unwrap myself from her and sit up with one leg on each side of the ledge. I look down at Amarah Rey, still lying on her back, her legs bent, both feet planted on the ledge. Her eyes are closed, snowflakes sticking in her lashes and hair, her hands are resting against her stomach, and her cheeks are flushed with the color of pleasure. She looks exactly like what she is.

An Angel.

I part her knees and grab her hands, lacing her fingers through mine, as I gently pull her up to a sitting position in front of me.

"Have I told you how absolutley stunning you are?" I ask, as I pull her closer to me.

"I think your Vampire eyes are finally getting old and betraying you," she teases, with a smile.

I slide my hands underneath her and lift her up, her legs wrap around my waist as I hold her above me. My cock is rock hard, ready to finally push inside of her.

"I would know you're beautiful even if I was blind," I say, as I lower her onto me. The head of my cock pushes into her and she gasps. "Your every breath, your every word," I say, as I continue to lower her onto me, slowly. I trail my nose along her neck, "the way you smell," I push the rest of the way into her, her mouth opens on another gasp for air and I take it with mine for a quick kiss before I continue. "The way you taste, and most importantly, the way you make me feel alive like no one else can. The way you make my heart beat again. That's how I know you're beautiful, Amarah Rey."

She holds my face in her hands, looking into my eyes, into my heart, into my fucking soul, like only she can. "You're beautiful too, Valmont, and so worthy of love."

She kisses me before I can ask her if that means she loves me, but the way she's kissing me, speaks for her, even if she can't say the words yet. She may not be in love with me, like I am with her, but she *does* have love for me. And where the bud of one love starts, allows for another love to bloom. I stop thinking about it and lose myself in her. She breaks the kiss and tilts her head to the side. She doesn't have to ask me this time.

I place my mouth over her vein, it's pounding thick and strong, leading me home. I let my fangs sink into her lifeblood and I hold on as she rides me through her orgasm. Her hips rising and falling, coating my cock with her pleasure, her pussy squeezing me so tightly I have to focus hard on not following her over the edge. I make love to her, out here on the balcony, under the moonlight as snowflakes land on our hair and skin. Cooling off our hot, sweating bodies, and I never want this to end.

But of course, it does. Another bite has her screaming my name into the stormy skies, and I finally let myself go. I cum long and hard, my body jerks with the force of it, and goosebumps travel across my skin. It feels like the first time I've ever experienced an orgasm. Maybe even better than the first time.

"Bloody Hell," I pant, as I lean my forehead against her shoulder.

We sit here for several minutes, wrapped up in each other, too much at peace to move. Finally, she leans back and holds her palms up towards the sky, catching snowflakes as they fall. She laughs, loud and deep, turning her face towards the thundering sky.

I've seen her in a million different settings but non of them compare to this. Her joy shines brighter than the moon, brighter than a million stars, and I can't help the smile that spreads across my face.

She's here.

With me.

And she's *happy*.

In this moment, she's truly happy.

She looks at me, still smiling brightly, her eyes shine with her joy. We just stare at each other for a few seconds, ridiculous smiles plastered on our faces. She laughs again, and this time I join her. A laugh that comes from deep inside of me, a place that I never knew existed until now. Where those roots are planted deep. Where my love for Amarah Rey grows faster and stronger every second.

"I don't think I've ever heard you laugh, truly laugh," she says, as she smiles at me.

"I don't remember the last time I had a reason to," I admit.

"That's really sad, Valmont," she says, but there's no pity in her eyes as she looks at me. "I think it's one of my favorite things about you now," she smiles, brightly. "And I'll make it my mission to make you laugh again, and again, just so I can hear it."

"If you want my laughter, all you have to do is ask. Whatever I have is yours," I say, seriously, as I brush her hair behind her ear.

She bites her bottom lip and drops her gaze. I know that she didn't expect any of this from me. I know she must be overwhelmed and still trying to process everything that I've thrown at her. I don't expect her to say anything. Not yet.

I pull her lip out from under her teeth, "that lip is mine to bite, Amarah Rey," I say, as I gently pull it into my mouth.

She shivers and I suddenly register the cold air and the cold snowflakes falling on us. Now that my body is returning to a normal, resting state, I feel it. It's cold. *I'm* cold. How am I cold? The weather hasn't affected me physically since I turned, but as sure as I see the snow, I *feel* it.

I pull back, away from Amarah Rey, in shock. I clear my throat and try to hide my reaction. "Come, let's get you inside and warmed up."

She nods and I finally notice the world around us. The snow has already started sticking and coats the balcony in a pristine white blanket. I move off the ledge, my feet quietly crunching in the fluffy snow, and I can't remember the last time I felt the texture so clearly. I shake my head and turn around reaching for Amarah Rey. She doesn't protest as she wraps her arms around my neck and I carry her across the balcony.

"What about your suit?" She asks.

"Probably ruined. The shoes absolutley are."

"Shit, I'm sorry."

"Why on Earth would you be sorry about that? It's just clothing."

"But they're so expensive!"

I chuckle, "oh, Amarah Rey, remind me to spoil you more."

Her brows crease, I see her trying to think clearly through her high, "you know I don't like fancy shmancy stuff."

I laugh again, hearty and deep, "well, then, I shall spoil you with cheap unshmancy stuff." I softly deposit her on my bed and kiss her nose, then lean back to admire her. It's like every new second I'm seeing her for the first time and she's more and more beautiful than she was the second before.

"I don't need anything. *Things*," she waves the word away. "I don't need things. I just need this," she throws herself back on the bed, arms splayed out, "this weighless feeling. I'm free," she says, more to herself.

I can stand here all night, just watching her, listening to her talk about anything and nothing at all. I want nothing more than to stay here with her but I've already done more than I should. I've already been distracted for too long. I have work to do. I have visitors to monitor. I have a role to play. So, I leave her laying on the bed, lost in her oblivion, as I head into the walk-in closet to get another suit for the night.

"What are you doing?" Her soft voice shocks me. I didn't hear her get off the bed or approach. Bloody fucking Hell, I shake my head. I'm distracted. Beyond distracted.

"Getting dressed."

She cocks her head to the side, "why?"

I smile tugs at my lips as I watch her trying to piece together this simple information as if she can't comprehend it. "Although I am rather skilled at giving you mind-blowing orgasms, I do have a rather large business to attend to, Amarah Rey."

She slowly walks towards me and my eyes travel down her still naked body. I take my time to admire every curve, muscle and scar. Everything that makes Amarah Rey, Amarah Rey. I bring my eyes back up to hers, and the way she's looking at me, stirs up my heart and my stomach like they've been placed into a blender. I feel like I need to throw up, and also like I deperately need to drink more of her blood, all at the same time.

She doesn't stop until her body is pressed against mine, her hands travel up my chest and end with her hands clasped behind my neck as she looks up at me.

"Stay." She whispers it so softly I barely hear the word

"You don't really want me to stay, Amarah Rey, it's the high talking. You'll come down soon enough."

She shakes her head adamantly, "I'm not as high as I was the first time. Yes, it still feels fucking amazing," she chuckles, "but I'm not delerious like I was the other night. I know what I'm asking."

I look at her, really look at her. Her eyes are clear and

focused, just slightly dialated from the high of my bite. They're not clouded or extremely contricted like they would be if she was beyond comprehension.

"Please, stay with me," her eyes beg.

Her words are hesitant, as if she's scared of rejection. She's been through so much in the past few weeks, part of her pain has come from me over the last few days, and I don't want to cause her any more. I can't bear to see the hurt of my rejection pass through her hopeful eyes. It will kill me to see her tears run down her cheeks as I walk away.

I lean down and lift her into my arms, her legs wrap around my waist, as I start walking us back towards the bed. We never take our eyes off of each other as I climb on to the bed, still holding her in my arms. I crawl to the middle of the bed and then gently lay her down.

Only this time, I follow.

I know this is a terrible idea. I know just minutes ago I was chastising myself for being distracted. I know I have other responsibilities. I know I have to keep her safe. But there's no safer place for her than here, with me, right now.

I keep my eyes locked on hers, "I told you that whatever I have is yours. If it's my time you want tonight, it's yours. All you have to do is ask and you never have to ask twice." I position my already aching cock against her opening, "is that all you want tonight, Amarah Rey?"

"No," she whispers, as her eyes drop to my mouth.

"What else do you want?"

"You, inside of me," she tightens her legs around my waist, pulling me into her as she lifts her hips up to meet me, "and your bite."

I realize she didn't say she just wants *me*. Only me. She wants what I have to offer. She wants my bite. Because she doesn't love me the way that I love her. The pang in my chest almost makes me change my mind but the feeling of sliding inside of her is too damn good to deny.

Then her mouth is on mine, stealing all of my senses. Everything else fades away, except for the woman underneath me, demanding my attention. And I told her she never has to ask twice.

I won't become a liar tonight.

Amarah: Hopeful Heart

It Feels Like Today by Rascal Flatts

I wake up the same way I've woken up for the past month and a half.

Alone.

It doesn't seem to matter how much time I spend with people when I'm awake, how much love and attention I receive in my waking hours, this...this waking up alone shit sucks. In these quiet moments before the world comes alive, and it's just me, a bed, and my thoughts, I'm lonelier than I am at any other time.

I spent the entire night with Valmont. I spent hours getting to know him in a way I didn't even know was possible for the arrogant Vampire. He's so much more than he appears. He's warm and affectionate. He's actually hilarious, and we spent a good time of our night laughing at nonsense. Underneath the cold, blocked off demeanor, Valmont is just a man who wants to be *seen*. Who wants to be treated as a man and not as a boss, a business owner, or a fix to satiate a craving.

And that last part is why I feel so guilty. I see him, I do. He's beautiful and surprising and funny and damn, the sex is *really* good. But even considering all of that, I can't make my heart feel something it doesn't. I can't make it change directions, even if I wanted to. And honestly, I don't want to. I'm not done loving Logan and I don't think I ever will be. I don't know, maybe one day. Maybe if I live another hundred years. Who knows what the future holds?

But that's why I feel so guilty. Valmont is just as lonely as I am although, I know being with me eases his pain, it's not fair to him. I know what it's like to have unrequited love. He's choosing to ignore it for now, choosing instead to hang on to what he can.

Hope.

And I can't even return that much for him. My hope lies in another direction. With another person. And the truth of that doesn't hit harder than it does now, waking up alone, wishing I was waking up in Logan's arms, even though I was just in the arms of another man mere hours ago.

Valmont has my body. He has my addiction. My body craves him like I've never craved another human being, not even Logan, but that's all it is for me. I do care about him, and similar to Andre, I have love for him, in some way. It would kill another part of me if something were to happen to him, but my heart doesn't crave him. My heart doesn't beat for him. My mind doesn't race for him. My soul doesn't cry for him. No, every part of me that matters still belongs to Logan.

I sigh at the complication of it all. Logan claims to still love me and wants to be with me, but how can he claim that as he beds another woman? Yes, I'm sleeping with Valmont too, but only because Logan betrayed me first. How is that love? And now Valmont is also confessing love. If what I've experienced is truly love, then I don't want it.

It's confusing.

It's manipulating.

It's fucking impossible.

And I seem to be drowning in it from all directions. I still can't wrap my head around everything that Valmont said last night.

Everything that he showed me. His walls came crashing down around us and I'm still recovering from the blast. I'm struggling to believe that he's in love with me. How did this happen?

I sigh as I reluctantly reach for my cell. I already know I'm going to have messages from Logan, I always do, and they always cut deep. I don't know what to do or what to believe anymore. My heart just wants to put the past month and half behind us and act like nothing happened, meanwhile, my mind can't unsee Logan in bed, naked, with that woman.

I unlock my phone, and sure enough, Logan's name is glaring at me. I open his messages.

Spotify link: If I Die Tomorrow by Florida Georgia Line

Logan: I've been thinking about us. Hell, that's all I do. I let you go. I've given you space and time. I've told you how I feel every day since you've left and it's obviously not working. I'm done, Amarah. I'm done letting you hide from me. From us. I'm done letting you cause us both unnecessary pain. I'm done letting you think you know what you DON'T. I'm coming for you and I'm not going to stop.

My heart starts to race at his words. He's coming for me? What does that mean? Like, he's physically coming for me? Here? I mean, he can't get to me while I'm in the Penthouse, but I don't stay locked up here all day, or night, rather. If he comes here, to the casino, it's not going to be pretty. Especially now that Valmont has opened up about how he feels. Things have changed and lines have been crossed for Valmont. Two alpha males, with intentions to keep each other far away from me, is not going to be pretty.

I grab a pillow and smother my face. "Fuck my life," I scream into it.

My phone vibrates on my stomach where I left it after reading Logan's message. I open the new notification.

Emrick: you better be ready, Sleeping Beauty. I'm leaving in 5 to go get you for our meeting. Meet me outside and I'll scoop you up so we can be on our way.

"Shit," I scramble out of bed and run to the bathroom to start getting ready.

It will only take him about ten minutes to get here. I start brushing my teeth first, one look in the mirror and I curse around the toothbrush. Not only did I get sweaty and gross when I was training with Emerson, I also had a night of non-stop, sweaty sex with Valmont. I don't just want a shower, I *need* one. Desperately.

I turn on the shower and type out a quick message as I wait for the water to warm up.

Me: gonna need at least 25 mins. I know, I know, I'm sorry! Don't yell at me! Just wait for me in the front, tell them you're waiting for me and they'll let you stay up front. Be down soon!

Thirty minutes later I'm running through the casino and burst out of the doors like a mad woman. There's still snow on the ground and the winter chill has definitely set in. I hug my jacket tighter around me as I run to Emrick's truck and jump into the passenger seat, steeling myself for the lecture I know is coming.

Emrick eye's me from head to toe. I don't know why, but I feel like he can tell I just had traces of sex dried on my skin minutes ago. I blush under his scrutiny and he shakes his head.

"Wow, Sleeping Beauty, just wow," he says, indignantly.

"What?" I ask, nervously. I look down at my black jeans, knee-high boots and waist-length, black leather jacket over a bright red sweater. "Am I dressed wrong for the meeting?"

"You're dressed fine," he waves away my question. "It's the, *I've just been fucked within an inch of my life*, look that I have a problem with.

"What?" I pull down the visor so I can look in the mirror. My face looks the same as it always does. Ok, I might be a bit flushed, but that's probably from the blush I'm experiencing. "I do not look like that!"

"Ugh, yeah you do, bitch. It's written all over your face, and you already know how jealous I am in that department. You don't just have one, but *two*, gorgeous men making all of your dreams come true. It's so not fair."

"Pretty sure all I have are nightmares nowadays, and no amount of sex seems to change that."

"Ok fine, you have two gorgeous men making all of *my* dreams come true then."

I don't know what to say so, I just shrug and look out of the window. Yes, I am getting mind-blowing sex but it doesn't mean anything to me. It's not at all what I dream about, or what I would dream about if I had normal dreams.

"So...you won't tell me about Logan, but will you spill the beans about Valmont?" He asks, hopefully.

I shake my head and look over at his excited expression, "you're unbelievable. And unbelievable horny," I laugh. "We seriously need to get you laid."

"Don't deflect, come on, dish! Is it good? It's really good, huh?"

"Three times, and lost count of how many orgasms I had, good," I say, with a big smile on my face as heat continues to warm my cheeks.

"Dayum, girl," he snaps his fingers, "you are getting it!"

"Did you know he was a Viking? Like an actual fucking Viking from like two thousand years ago?"

"Shut up!"

"You should see his tattoos," I moan. "Oh my God, they are so fucking sexy."

"What? Girl, stop playing. Tattoos? No way. Not on that clean-cut, well-dressed Vampire. I don't believe it."

"I'm dead serious! I was shocked as Hell too when I first saw them. He's nothing at all like he portrays himself to be."

"I've said it before and I'll say it again, you are one lucky bitch!"

I scoff, "I don't feel lucky."

"Still hurting over the sexy beast, huh?"

"Almost every second of every day. He sent me a pretty definitive message this morning."

"Uh oh, definitive how? Good or bad?"

I shrug, "I guess that depends on which side you're on. He said he's done letting me ignore him, ignore us. He said he's, and I quote, coming for me."

"Damn, sounds like he's done playing games and is pulling out the claws and teeth. What's fang face going to say about that?"

I run my hands down my face, "I don't even want to find out. He told me he was in love with me last night."

"Wow! Way to just kinda sneak that one into conversation! What did you say?"

"Nothing! What do I say to that? Thank you? I appreciate it? Ugh! What am I going to do, Emrick? No matter what I do, someone gets hurt. If I choose Valmont, not only am I lying to myself, Logan will get hurt. If I choose Logan, Valmont is going to get hurt. Not to mention the reason why I left Logan in the first place. He's not safe around me, I'm always *someone's* target. Oh, and...he's sleeping with someone else and I'm sleeping with Valmont. How do we even try and get past all of this?"

"Ok, maybe you're *not* lucky," he frowns.

"Gee, thanks for the assist there, Coach."

He sighs, "look, Amarah, I know you think you're doing what's right, but I have to be honest with you, your choice and reasons regarding Logan are wrong. He's not some fragile human you need to worry about. He can handle himself, Hell, probably better than you can handle yourself at this point. It's not fair that you've made this decision for him. How would you feel if someone made the same decision for you?"

"Actually, Valmont did the same thing to me. He pushed me away in an attempt to keep me safe. It hurt. It didn't feel good and I'm pissed, actually. I mean, I understand why he did it, Hell, I did the same thing! Of course I understand his reasons but he basically just showed that he doesn't trust me or believe in me enough to be honest with me. He took my choice away when I think we'd be better off handling this threat as a team."

"And I rest my case."

I sigh and throw my head back against the headrest, "fuck. As you would say, I'm such a stupid bitch."

"I mean, technically you said it though, not me."

"Damn, you should have your own TV show and be making loads of money like Dr. Phil or something."

"Naw, I like watching drama from afar and not getting into the nitty gritty. Yours is the exception, of course."

"Of course," I shake my head. "Well, enough of my Debbie downer love issues, what do you know about the meeting?"

"Nothing more than you at this point. The Elders agreed to sit with us and discuss the threats against The Unseen. As far as what they know, if anything," he shrugs. "We'll find out soon."

I nod my head, "I just want to have a solid plan on how to move forward. I hate feeling useless and constantly having to rally after an attack instead of getting ahead of it and stopping it all, once and for all."

"As noble as that sounds, I don't think it's quite realistic, Sleeping Beauty. There will *always* be threats to contend with."

"I know, but Aralyn is a threat we should be able to stop, as well as Viveka and Kordeuv. When it comes to the demons, there has to be a way to close that rip. There has to be."

"If there is, I don't know about it. Hopefully the Elders will have some insight."

I nod as we approach the dirt road that leads to the Maa Family's home. We'll either know more shortly, or we won't.

Ten minutes later I'm following Emrick into the community building again. Just like the first time, the game room is bustling with activity. I can hear the excited talk and laughter as we pass by the door and continue on down the short hallway to the door that leads into their official meeting room. I'm surprised to find the table and chairs on the dais empty.

Instead, the Elders are gathered on couches and comfy chairs that have been brought in, along with a coffee table and what looks like a rolling drink cart. They're also wearing casual clothing and all seem comfortable and relaxed. I thought for sure we would be entering into a formal setting but I'm relieved to see that it isn't.

"Ah, Emrick, my darling boy," Emmaline reaches her hand out, ushering him to her, "come, sit with me."

"Gladly, Mother," he says, as he grasps her hand and leans in to kiss her on the cheek.

She beams up at him and I can't help the smile that spreads

across my face at their loving relationship. A small twinge pulls at my heart, a reminder that I never got to experience my mother's love like this, but I don't begrudge them for their relationship. It makes me happy to see Emrick loved and cherished.

"Amarah, would you like a drink?" A smooth, rich voice draws my attention to one of the men, as he stands up and walks to the drink cart. He's dressed in a pair of dark blue jeans, black boots, and solid black sweater.

"Water would be great, thank you," I say, still a bit nervous.

"Psh, nonsense, we're all drinking spirits today. No need to be nervous or proper. White or red wine, perhaps?"

I smile and nod my head, "alright, red then, please."

"Come and sit," one of the other men taps the couch cushion next to him. "We don't bite," he says with a small, warm smile. He's lounging on the couch, his ankle propped up on his knee and one arm thrown cross the back of the couch. He's also in a pair of blue jeans, brown boots, and a blue and yellow striped long-sleeve t-shirt.

"Thank you," I walk over to the couch and sit. "I apologize, I don't recall all of your names," I say, slightly embarrassed.

The gentleman sitting next to me chuckles, his eyes are so dark green, they're almost black, but the green shines through against his darker skin tone.

"We didn't expect you to, after such a brief meeting the other day." He balances his drink on his leg and extends a hand to me, "I'm Kian." His voice is strong but common, not unique or recognizable. His hair is shaved short on the sides with thin dreadlocks on top. It's styled so that the top dreadlocks sit forward and hang over his forehead. He also wears a full beard and mustache but they're kept well-trimmed. It's impossible to tell his age but I'm assuming all of the Elders are, well...*elder*, but he doesn't look older than late forties.

"Nice to meet you, Kian. Again," I laugh, nervously.

"I'm Kyanna," a small and sweet voice comes from the other

woman sitting in the chair to my right, on the other side of Kian.

She has her legs pulled up into the chair with her and she's so petite, the chair seems to swallow her. She's wearing black leggings and an oversized red sweater with the word, *joy*, on the front, very festive. Her long black hair is styled in a braid that hangs over her shoulder and falls down into her lap. Her eyes are a warm and bright green, slightly lighter than Emrick's emerald beauties.

"Nice to meet you," I nod in her direction and smile.

"And I'm Theodore, but you can call me Theo," the man who addressed me earlier says, as he walks towards me and hands me my glass of red wine.

His sleeves have been pushed up revealing strong forearms. His skin tone is lighter than the others but still a beautiful light brown, darker than mine. I take my drink and finally look up into his face. His eyes catch me off guard. I saw the Elders the other day, but from further away, it was hard to make out all the details of their faces. Theo's eyes are a green like I've never seen before. Almost like a mix of green and blue and white. Not quite turquoise, no, they're definitely green, but so unique. If I had to put a name to the color, my best attempt to describe them would be, seafoam green.

His hair is kept short, but not buzzed, you can see the tight curl that is styled and managed neatly around a clean-shaven face, leaving his eyes to steal the show. Well, at least until he smiles at me. It's a dazzling white smile, paired with those eyes, I'm sure I would have been knocked off of my feet had I been standing. The actor, Michael Ealy, comes to mind.

"Use your words, Amarah," Emrick's voice teases from his seat next to his mom.

Chuckles erupt around the room and my cheeks flame. I clear my throat and manage a strained, "nice to meet you, Theo."

He takes a seat in the chair next to me, to my left. I pull my arms into my body, trying to make myself as small and unseen as possible.

"I'm Carson," the last man says, from his seat on the couch across from me. He's wearing black jeans, black boots, and a red and black flannel shirt. His hair is buzzed very close to his head and I can see some grey peeking through at his temples. He and Emmaline are the only ones who have grey in their hair and seem to be a little older than the others. His eyes are very lime green and they seem tired.

"Nice to meet you, Carson," I say, and then take a sip of my wine, hoping to calm my nerves and also drown my earlier embarrassment.

"And that just leaves me." Emmaline sits in the middle of Emrick and Carson with her legs crossed and her drink held in her lap. She's wearing light blue jeans tucked into knee high boots, similar to mine, and a beautiful green, flowing, button-up blouse. Her hair is tied up in a loose bun, loose strands frame her face with a mixture of black and grey.

"I'm Emmaline, no doubt Emrick has told you that I'm his mother," she smiles at him and pats his knee. Her eyes are the same emerald green as her sons, and even though they sparkle with the love she has for him, I can't help but notice the sadness in them too. I wonder if I would have noticed if Emrick hadn't told me about his father?

"Yes, he has. It's so nice to meet you, all of you. Thank you for agreeing to see me and allowing me this meeting."

"Emrick said that you wanted to discuss several threats, or potential threats, is that right?" Emmaline asks.

"Yes, that's right."

"And why not meet and strategize with the Queen?" Carson chimes in.

"Well, ummmm..." I clear my throat and sit up straighter in my seat. "We haven't quite been seeing eye-to-eye recently. I believe she's a little too focused on Aralyn, which is understandable, considering it's her life that's constantly being threatened," I add quickly. "It's just that there are other things that also need our attention, in addition to Aralyn, and the Queen doesn't seem to share my concern. And honestly, I'm at a loss at how to even move forward. I'm hoping to gather some intel and advice from you, at least with a direction I can start in."

"Emrick mentioned Valmont has some pretty powerful guests in town," Emmaline continues.

"Yes. Valmont claims Viveka is *beyond* dangerous and we don't know anything about her companion, Kordeuv, although, I'm supposed to be meeting with him tonight as well. Hopefully he can shed some light on why they're here and if they're a threat to anyone."

"Like everyone else, we've been following the news," Kian adds. "Do you think these new visitors could be the ones responsible for the trail of bodies?"

Honestly, the bodies mentioned on the news has been the last thing on my mind, until now. I guess because we haven't had any incidents here, I've let that threat fall to the back burner, not a good thing for the Võitleja to do. I need to handle *all* threats with equal focus.

"I saw the pictures of the bodies, before they were taken down, and I did notice there wasn't nearly enough blood at any of the scenes. The lack of blood suggests Vampire so, yes, absolutely I believe Viveka could very well be responsible. A trail of bodies that basically led right to our door, and the next thing we know, they show up? I don't think it's a coincidence but I don't have any proof either."

"Well, you have the potential meeting with this guy..."

"Kordeuv," I repeat.

"Yes, Kordeuv, so I don't think we need to spend any time speculating or discussing that further until you find out what he has to say," Kian responds, matter-of-factly.

"No, you're right. What can you tell me about Aralyn?" I turn back to Emmaline.

"Emrick told you how our Rändaja works?"

"He did."

"Then you know it's not perfect. It's not a precise or certain answer that we can give you. All we have are feelings and thoughts that the Earth provides, nothing more than that."

"I understand. Really, any clue that I can look into is more helpful than you know," I plead.

Theo sits forward in his chair, resting his elbows on his knees. "When Emrick mentioned you wanted to meet and what you wanted to discuss, we started Travelling, searching every inch of the city. Unfortunately, we didn't feel anything unsettling in the city. Well, nothing out of the norm."

I sigh.

"But," Theo continues, "we extended our search. That's why we took longer to meet with you. We wanted to be able to give you a confident response, whatever it may be."

"And?" I question. "Did you find anything…unsettling?"

He nods, "we did."

"There's still a lot of unnatural vibes coming from Revna's house," Kyanna joins in the conversation.

"Revna? But Revna died in the Air Fey attack. My sister killed her. I saw the body myself."

"I didn't say Revna was the one responsible for what's currently happening at her old house," Kyanna clarifies.

"Wait, so, you think Aralyn is hiding out there?"

Kyanna nods.

I sit back in my seat, resting my weary and shocked body against the back of the couch. "But why would she stay there? So close to the Air Fey?"

"Think about it," Theo says, "what better place to hide than the place people least expect you to be? Has Revna's house been monitored after her death?"

"I…I'm not sure. I know her house was searched and stripped of a lot of her supplies initially, but I don't know if it's been monitored. I mean, why would it be? We all know Revna is dead."

Theo spreads his hands in a, *that's exactly what I'm saying*, manner, and then sits back in his chair with a confident, half-smile gracing his lips.

"All we know for sure, Amarah," Emmaline interjects, "is that there's still activity happening out there. The Earth around that house is not at peace. Those are our truths, not facts, but what we know to be true. Is it Aralyn?" She shrugs, "the only way to know for sure is to go there and find out."

I take another drink of my wine, feeling it slide down my throat and settle in a warm pool in my stomach, filling the empty pit the thought of Aralyn being so close has opened. If it's true, the thought of her being right where we could take her, this whole time, starts to stir my anger. And my frustration. How did we not think to monitor Revna's house?

"I'll gladly go with you, Sleeping Beauty, to follow up on their lead and do some recon, but if she is there, we need to have a plan ready to move in."

I nod, "ok, you and I can plan a trip out there, but first, I need to see what's going to happen with Viveka. I should know more tonight and we can discuss that too."

"Ok, then, I can bring back whatever news you find out to the Elders and we can all go from there," Emrick agrees.

"That's perfect. Alright, that's two out of my three concerns."

"What's the third?" Carson asks.

"The demons. Or, lack thereof, rather. Where are they? Why aren't they attacked and possessing humans? Why aren't they causing any trouble?"

The Elders all look around at each other as if waiting for someone else to speak. I look around as well, eagerly waiting for one of them to jump in with some wise words or intel any second.

"What? What is it?" I finally break the silence.

Emmaline sighs, "we don't have any information regarding the demons. We're just as stumped as you are."

"But can't you sense the rip in the Earth?"

Kian draws my attention, "we can feel the rip, yes, but the Earth isn't telling us anything new. There hasn't been any change to the rip or the feelings there. The Earth is still in pain, ripped apart unnaturally, with no way to heal," he shakes his head. "But that's all the Earth feels right now. There's no sense of anything else happening."

"What about the Vesi Family? Can they provide any insight since they're the ones guarding the rip so closely?"

"I've been in contact with Prince Vadin," Kyanna says. "There isn't anything new to report surface level either. For some reason, the demons have stopped coming through the rip."

"But why? Why would they suddenly just stop? It doesn't make any sense," I look around the room again, desperate for answers.

"You're right. It doesn't make sense," Carson agrees. "And you're smart for noticing this and addressing it as a concern, especially when others drop their guard and slip into a false sense of safety. All we can do is stay vigilant. We can't take our eyes away from the rip just because it's suddenly gone quiet. What's that saying? It's always calm before the storm. I don't know what's going on with the demons and their underworld Leader, but what I do know, is that it can't be good. I just don't know how, why or when."

I finish my wine, "well, at least now I have a lead to follow when it comes to Aralyn. That's more than I had before so, thank you, very much."

"And keep Emrick in the loop on what happens with your meeting tonight. We need to all be educated and on the same page. We're a family and we're no good to each other if we aren't willing to work together," Emmaline says, in a very motherly tone.

It hits like an arrow, dead center on my guilt, thinking about how I've pushed Logan away and how I walked out on the Queen.

Emrick stands up so I move to join him. Emmaline stands as well and gives her son a big hug, "you be safe out there."

"Always, Mother."

"And you," she says, coming around the coffee table. "You be safe, too," she says, as she comes in for a hug. I'm momentarily taken aback. Shocked that Emrick's mom is giving me such a warm, tight embrace. She whispers into my ear, "thank you, for being a friend to Emrick. He's been happier since training with you. Please, promise me you'll keep him safe."

"He's been a good friend to me too, and I'll put my own life in danger long before I'll let him do anything stupid or crazy." It's not a promise, but it's the best that I can say. I will protect him, with my life, but I can't promise he won't get hurt...or worse.

She doesn't press the issue. She leans back, gripping my arms, smiles and nods. She understands I'll do all I can but won't make promises I can't keep.

We say goodbye to the other Elders, I thank them again and again for their time, their assistance, and their welcoming arms. As we're walking towards the exit, I hear Theo's smooth voice call out.

"Wait up!"

We turn around and he's walking towards us with that dazzling smile on display and those sparkling, unique green eyes. He stops and stand sort of between Emrick and I.

He offers me his hand once again, "it was a pleasure and an honor to meet, Amarah. Please, don't hesitate to reach out if you need anything."

"Thank you, Theo, that's very kind."

He offers his hand to Emrick next, only with Emrick, he places his other hand on top of Emrick's hand. Basically, holding it with both of his hands, and he holds onto Emrick's hand a little longer than is polite. I glance from their hands up to Emrick's face and then to Theo's.

"If you need anything at all," Theo reiterates. He finally releases Emrick's hand, slowly, and backs away. "You have my number," he winks at Emrick and gives him the full mega-watt smile. "Use it." Then, he turns around and walks back towards the other Elders, leaving us standing here dumbfounded.

It takes Emrick a few seconds to find his words, "did he just..."

"Yes."

"And the hand..."

"Mhhmmmm."

"And the wink..."

"Yup," I say, excitedly, as I lace my arm through his and turn him around, walking quickly through the door.

Once we're safely outside, alone and out of earshot, we stop walking and face each other. I'm smiling like an idiot and Emrick is biting his lower lip.

Then he reaches for my and we both start jumping up and down screeching like some kind of dying birds. I feel like I'm back in high school, with my best friend, and we just found out his crush likes him too.

"Alright,ok," he calms himself down, running his hands down his chest, straightening out his shirt. "I'm not dreaming, am I?" He asks.

I quickly reach out and pinch his arm.

"Owwww! Damn, Sleeping Beauty."

"Emrick! He basically just asked you out! I mean, not in so many words, but he told you to use his number. He clearly has a thing for you! And here I was feeling sorry for you! Poor, lonely and ignored, Emrick." I punch him in the shoulder, "you liar!"

"For the love of Pete, stop hurting me, woman! I didn't know!"

"Oh, come on! He basically undressed you with his eyes in there! How could you not know he's into you?"

"I've never noticed! He's never done anything like…like, *that*, before!" He waves his hand towards the building and then grabs at his hair, which is no longer in cornrows, and starts pacing.

He shakes his hands in front of him as he continues pacing, "oh my God, Amarah, I just stood there with my mouth open like a damn fool! What do I do?"

"Pretty sure I looked like a damn fool just from him smiling at me," I laugh. "He's probably used to it."

"Not helping!"

"Ok, ok! Sorry. You text him, obviously. I mean, not like right this second, but yeah, you totally find out what that's all about."

"Oh my God. Ok. Yes, totally. I can do that. Just act normal. No big deal. It's not like I've never dated before. I mean…"

"Emrick!" I grab a hold of his shoulders. "Breathe," I laugh. "It's going to be fine. And you don't have to do anything right now, or ever, if you don't want to."

"Are you high?" He asks. "Have you *seen* the man? Of course, I *want* to."

"Then, whenever you're ready, just be *you*. You're absolutely wonderful and he would be so lucky to get to know you."

"You're right. I'm fucking fabulous and I need to remember that."

"Damn right! Now who is the coach?" I tease. "You've got this, no doubt in my mind, but…" I look up at the darkening sky, "we do need to get back so I can meet with Kordeuv. I can't miss my chance to meet with him and find out what he has to say."

"Yes, of course. Let's get you back."

"But when all this is over, you're telling me everything!"

"Duh."

I smile as I climb into his Tacoma. I haven't known Emrick for long but it feels like we've been friends forever. And even with everything crazy going on around us, my life being a hot mess and, potentially in danger, I can't help but love this moment. I'm so grateful I have someone in this new world that I can share life with. That I can be myself with, with no fear of judgement. And nothing makes me happier than seeing my friends happy.

I'm determined more than ever to end this madness and keep Emrick safe so that he can have his happy ending. Or happy journey to his next stop at least. I may not be able to have my happy ending, but that doesn't mean I'm going to give up on everything. I did that for a month and it did nothing but hurt me.

No, this is beautiful. A beautiful moment given to us in a chaotic, hectic, and otherwise ugly, world. And that's what's important, isn't it? To live life and appreciate life in every moment. Because life is never going to slow down or become easy all of a sudden. As a wise friend once told me, we have to learn to dance in the rain. Something inside of me stirs.

This moment feels like a Blessing.

Two people coming together. The possibility of love, or friendship, Hell, even the possibility of just a lesson. The absolute fact that either way, this is meant to be. We're brought into people lives, and others are brought into ours, for a reason. We just have to slow down and see it.

I haven't had my Faith in a while, but I feel it stirring again, and I'm looking forward with a cautious, but hopeful, heart.

Amarah: Well That Backfired

Get Out Alive by Three Days Grace

The casino is busy tonight. I people watch from a table at the bar on the outskirts of the playing floor. The whiskey and coke I ordered sits untouched, seeping condensation into the drink napkin and my hand, as I hold the full glass in an attempt to seem like I plan on drinking it. I don't. I wipe my palm on my jeans, my leg anxiously jumping up and down as I wait.

Valmont agreed, reluctantly, to extend the private invitation to Viveka. I have no way of knowing if she accepted his offer other than to wait. I also have no way of finding Kordeuv. He said that he would find me so, I'm making myself visible and available. I keep scanning the casino floor, hoping to spot the eighties rocker *somewhere*, but so far, no luck. I tap on my cell phone screen, bringing it to life, so I can check the time for the hundredth time. 12:39 a.m. I blow out an exasperated breath.

"Is this seat taken," a slightly familiar voice makes me jump.

I look up to see Alistair standing next to my table. I squint my eyes, trying to see any clue that might indicate he *isn't* Alistair, but I can't see anything out of place.

"Alistair?" I question.

He smiles and pulls out the chair across from me and slides into it. "You tell me."

That response alone should be my answer, but I use my power to verify the truth either way. I pull my power out and caress against his aura, his energy. Not Vampire. I don't take away his illusion, he must be in disguise for a reason.

"I wasn't sure if our planned worked," I say, as I lean in, placing my arms on the table.

"It did indeed. I'm glad Valmont agreed to this, otherwise, we'd never have this opportunity. Viveka is obsessed with Valmont for reasons I can't even fathom. I think his recent rejection of her has only added to her determination. It's been like a game to her," he rolls his eyes. "A challenge."

I try and *not* think of what she could possibly be doing to Valmont at this very moment. The thought makes me nauseous. "You seem annoyed by her and by her actions. Why are you with her?"

"Like most of her companions over the years, I don't have a choice. Has Valmont told you anything about her at all?"

"Some. He told me how she tricked him into thinking she was a Goddess, and then she killed him. Well, turned him. But she hasn't turned you. You're not a Vampire or a human. Your energy isn't like anything else I've felt before. What are you?"

"You're full of questions, aren't you?" He chuckles. "I don't blame you. I'll try to explain the best, and fastest, way that I can. I can't imagine we have much time."

"No, Valmont was not happy about doing this. I think he'll end it as soon as absolutely possible."

"Viveka found me, well, actually I found her, about four hundred years ago," he sighs, and runs both hands through his hair, well, through Alistair's hair. It looks like it's a gesture he's used to doing with his own long hair.

"I was in Tokyo, living my best life. See, I thrive around

people. The more people, the better. To be specific, I thrive and survive off of sex and sexual energy."

"I've heard of this. I mean, like in fictional human stories and whatever, but I think it was called a…Succubus? Is that right?"

"Close, that's the female version of me, yes. The name for what I am is, Incubus, but that's just half of what I am. That part, of course, came from my father. The other half of what I am, is a Kitsune."

"Ok, I'm familiar with an Incubus, but what is a…Kitsoonay?"

"A Kitsune is a fox," he smirks, "a trickster. This is the side of me that allows me to do this," he gestures to his stolen appearance. "I can mimic any human being as long as I've seen them. The longer I've spent time with them, the better and stronger my illusion becomes. The hardest thing to get right, which you've noticed, is the voice."

"Whoa, no wonder I couldn't figure out what you are. So that's your power? You mimic and feed off of sex?"

He shakes his head, "not all. I also have control over electricity." He closes his eyes and all of the lights in the bar flicker. "And I'm somewhat of a Seer. I can see and hear things happening anywhere in the world, as long as I focus on something, or someone in that specific area."

I lean back in my chair, "what in the actual Hell? How is that even possible? How can you have so many different abilities? That's insane, and completely not fair."

"Coming from an Angel who has no idea what her power is even capable of?" He cocks his eyebrow at me.

I swallow down my shock and fear, my heart is suddenly racing and I glance around, looking for an immediate exit in case I need one. I'm grateful we're sitting in a very public place because I don't think he'll cause a scene here. Then again, like Valmont said several times, I don't know him.

"Don't worry, Amarah, I'm not going to hurt you, and Viveka doesn't know."

"How do *you* know? Only a handful of people know the truth about what I am. How did you find out?"

"I just told you. I can see and hear things around the world. One of the reasons Viveka keeps me and uses me. The story of what you did to all those demons a few months back, travelled far and wide, Amarah. The Unseen is a small, connected world. Something like that would never remain quiet. So, once I heard about what you did, I started to spy on you, so to speak. That's how I found out and that's why I believe you can help me."

"This is insane," I rub my forehead in distress. "This is unsettling and just plain fucking creepy in the worst possible way. You can basically spy on anyone, like a fucking ghost! Is that what you're saying?"

"I hadn't thought of it that way but, yes, I guess I am like a ghost in that aspect."

"So, there's no hiding from you, or others out there like you? That's terrifying. How do we protect ourselves from that?"

"There actually is something you can do to protect yourself from our powers."

I stare at him from across the table, wide-eyed and scared out of my mind at what he's just told me. I wait for him to tell me how I can protect myself, and those around me, but he just clasps his hands together and leans on the table, staring at me.

"And you're not going to tell me unless I agree to help you."

"Close, again. I'll tell you, but only *after* we're successful in freeing me from Viveka."

I blow out a breath and run my hands down my face, "I can't believe this. Any of this. If you're so powerful, how did you get trapped by Viveka? You said you found her in Tokyo? What happened from there?"

He nods, "yes. I was there, again, to be surrounded by people so I could feed off of their sexual energy. You'd be shocked if you knew how many people think about, and exude sex, on a daily basis. In fact, it's pretty heavy in this bar right now," he glances around.

"Alright, I did *not* need to know that bit of information."

He chuckles again, "sorry. I see it on them as clearly as you see their outfit. Well, Viveka was like a floodlight against all the other insignificant flashlights. Her sexual energy is a hundred times that of the normal person. I was drawn to her like a moth to a flame. I had no idea that if I flew to close, I'd burn."

"Sounds familiar to what Valmont's told me. So, why don't you just leave?"

A look of pure aggression flashes across his, or rather, Alistair's face, "I can't."

"She's found a way to control you, hasn't she?"

He nods in confirmation, "while I was busy losing myself in sex with Viveka, I became one thousand years old. This is a sacred year for a Kitsune. It's the year we finally earn our ninth and final tail."

"Tail?" I ask, in confusion.

"Yes, in fox form, I have nine tails. A fox's tails are a clear indication of their age and power. It's kind of like....ummmm, think of a tree. If you cut a tree down, you can see rings in the trunk, are you familiar with this?"

"Of course, each ring in the trunk signifies another year the tree has lived."

"Exactly! A fox's tails are the same, except, it takes many, many years to gain each one. A thousand years to finally gain the ninth and final tail. In addition to the ninth tail, I also gained my hoshi no tama."

"You're gonna have to explain that one to me because I have no idea what you just said."

"That roughly translates to, star ball, in English. It's basically my power in physical form. In the shape and size of a marble. "

"Let me guess, Viveka found this out and she now has this star ball in her possession?"

"Yes," he sighs, heavily. "She has my power in the palm of her cold, dead, vicious hand. If it gets broken or destroyed, I'll be stuck in my human form forever. I will no longer be able to access my fox. I will no longer be a Kitsune. And If I'm separated from my star ball for too long, I'll slowly grow weak and die. That's why I stay close to Viveka. She's also extremely selfish and doesn't allow me to feed off of sex with anyone else but her, or with her. She keeps me satiated just enough that I don't go insane, but not being able to feed on what I need, plus not being in possession of my star ball, keeps me weak. I can't fight her and survive."

"And this is why you need my help. You need me to help you get your power back."

"It's not just about my power, Amarah, it's my freedom. Not only my freedom from Viveka but my freedom from this world, this life."

"What do you mean?"

"My star ball is the only way I get to become Tenko. It's my only way into the Heavens, to become a part of the Universe, forever. It's my destiny and my happy ending. I'm not meant to be on this Earth past one thousand years. I shouldn't be here but she's holding me here against my will."

"Shit, that really sucks, Kordeuv, I'm so sorry. I couldn't imagine being held somewhere against my will for years." I think about my insignificant five days of being held captive and shiver. Five days was excruciating, I can't imagine *years*.

"Two hundred and fifty years. She's held me captive, for two hundred and fifty years, and she doesn't appear to be tiring of me any time soon. Not to mention, she could destroy my star ball and trap me here, forever. That's why I do whatever she wants, whatever she asks of me, because I have no choice."

"And why are you guys here, now? In Valmont's territory. What does she want with him?"

He shakes his head, "she doesn't want Valmont, Amarah, she wants you."

My heart starts to race again at his words. Valmont was right all along. "I thought you said she doesn't know about me?"

"She doesn't. Not exactly. She knows that someone here, in Valmont's territory, is responsible for a massive amount of power, but she doesn't know who. She doesn't know it's you but she wants that power, your power, under her control. That's why she made me attack your Queen."

"Wait, what? What did you just say?"

He shakes his head and a look of guilt settles into Alistair's features. "It was me, in disguise, that attacked your Queen. Viveka thought it would be a good way to get you to show yourself. To use your power, so she could find you."

"What the fuck," I sink back in my chair, trying to digest this new bit of information.

"So, it was never Aralyn at all. That's why there was no trace of her, because she was never even fucking here," I say more to myself.

He shakes his head, "I used her, and the history surrounding her, to stage the attack. Then, I changed my appearance and walked right out the front door."

"This is all so fucked up."

"I know it is. I'm sorry for the trickery, it's who I am," he shrugs. "But I do wish I could have informed you sooner."

"How can I believe you? You know what I am, and you're forced to be loyal to Viveka, why should I believe that you didn't tell her about me? After all, it's your life at stake."

"I didn't tell her because of one simple thing. Hope. I hope that you're good enough, and strong enough to help me. To free me from her control."

"Fuck," I let out a heavy breath. I feel like another ton of bricks has just been added to my already overwhelmed shoulders. "If she finds out that you lied, and are continuing to lie to her..."

"I know," he whispers.

We sit in silence for a few minutes, both of us contemplating the severity of our situations. Kordeuv is stuck with Viveka, bound to her in the worst way, and I'm next on her list of powers that she wants to control. He's taking a huge risk lying to her about me and coming to me directly like this. How can I deny him help if I'm able? And how can I get to her without his help? What other choice do we have but to work together?

"So, Amarah Rey Andrews, will you help me?

"It looks like we're going to be helping each other," I clarify. "I'm going to need to tell Valmont, and probably a few others. We're not going to be able to do all of this on our own or behind their backs."

"Alright. I don't love the idea, but I'm a bit at your mercy so, I'll go with whatever you think is best."

"Good. And I'll need a way to communicate with you."

"No," he shakes his head, "too risky. If Viveka found out we were talking, it would be bad. Worse than bad," he stands up to leave.

"Wait! How else are we going to plan and continue to stay on the same page?"

"I'll keep seeking you out every chance I get. Stay available as much as possible."

I nod, "this isn't going to be easy."

"You have no idea. I have to go. We've already lingered longer than I'd like. Stay alert and stay inconspicuous."

"You too," I say, to his retreating back. "Fuck," I grab my drink and finish it in three large gulps.

I'm going to need more alcohol than that to face Valmont. To tell him he was right. She's here for *me*. This new information isn't going to sit well with him. Not to mention, he clearly kept Viveka distracted and I know he's not going to be in a good mood because of that as it is. The thought of him sleeping with her stirs something in my chest too. Or maybe that's the whiskey going to work.

I shake my head and get to my feet. I need to head back to the Penthouse where Valmont and I planned to meet to discuss everything right away.

The real Alistair joins me on my walk towards the private elevator, "that was quite interesting to see."

I scoff, "you think? It's fucking creepy that he can steal people's faces and bodies. I couldn't imagine seeing my own and knowing it wasn't me."

"It's very creepy," he shivers. "Was he helpful? Did you get the information you needed?"

"Yes, I did. Please send Valmont up as soon as you can."

He nods, does a quick sweep of the Penthouse, and then leaves me to wait for Valmont.

I'm pacing the living room, in front of the elevator, waiting for Valmont to come up. I've already poured a glass of his honey flavored diesel fuel. I figure one glass of this shit should have me prepared to handle just about anything. The only problem is getting it down.

"Man, this shit is potent," I say to myself, as I pace.

I glance at my cell phone for the fiftieth time in the last five minutes.

1:56 a.m.

I told Valmont that we would only need about an hour, it's been longer than that now by seventeen minutes, but hey, who's counting? I can't imagine him wanting to spend more time than necessary with Viveka. No, I should expect him to come through those elevator doors any minute now.

2:23 a.m.

I'm still pacing, though more agitated now. I've had about half of the mead I poured and I feel it slithering through my veins like a live wire. The feeling is not helping to calm me down, but instead, adds to my anxiety.

Where in the Hell is he? Why is he keeping me waiting when he knows how important this is. Wait, what if she's not letting him leave? What if she's determined to have her way with him for as long as she can? What if he's suffering at her hands...because of me?

"Oh, fuck this!"

I unlock my cell phone and dial Alistair. I decide to Hell with it all and down the rest of my mead in one swig. Not one of my better ideas. I choke on the thickness and strength of the alcohol as it rushes down my throat.

"Amarah, are you alright?" I hear Alistair's worried voice on the other line. "What's wrong?"

"Son of a bitch!" I say, through my coughing fits. "How in the Hell does he drink this shit for pleasure?"

"What?" He asks, confused.

"Nothing, never mind. Alistair, where is Valmont? He hasn't showed up to the Penthouse yet."

"Haven't seen him. As far as I know he's still in his office with...her."

The mead settles in my stomach, lighting a fire in my gut, and I can't stay put any longer. "Come and get me," I demand.

"Yeah, I'll be right there."

Three excruciatingly long minutes later, the elevator doors slide open, revealing Alistair on the other side. I don't give him a chance to step out before I'm racing inside.

"Let's go."

He doesn't question me or stall. He just enters the code and gets us heading to the main casino floor, right next to Valmont's office. As soon as the doors open, I'm bursting out of them, rushing towards the steps that lead up to Valmont's office.

Pierce isn't at his usual post, outside of the door. Any time Valmont is in his office, Pierce is here, guarding him. Why isn't he here? I don't have time to think about it before I'm pounding on the door.

"Valmont! It's me. Stop whatever you're doing because I'm coming in, and I *really* don't want to see anything you might be doing!"

I wait for a few seconds, expecting to hear Valmont's response, but nothing comes. What if he's tied up and gagged? What if I walk in on Viveka riding him. I really don't want to see him having sex with her. I already had to witness Logan, naked, in bed with another woman. I really don't think I can handle seeing Valmont fucking Viveka.

The mead is running through my veins, making me feel a bit tingly, and my heart is pounding in my chest and thundering in my ears. I reach for the handle and it's unlocked.

"I'm coming in!" I yell, probably way louder than I need to.

I push the door open and practically run inside, steeling myself for what I'm about to see, but nothing prepares me for this.

It's empty.

I slowly walk further into the office, examining every inch, but nothing seems out of place. Everything is exactly like it usually is. I spin around and that's when I notice the drink glasses at his minibar.

Two.

Two used and dirty glasses. One, with traces of black lipstick on it.

"Amarah, what are you doing?" Alistair's voice sounds from the open doorway.

"Where is he, Alistair? Is he down in the club?"

"I don't know where he is, I've been monitoring you tonight, like every night, because that's what he ordered me to do."

"I'm going down to the club, maybe he's there."

"Amarah, I'm sure he's fine. Wherever he is. Just calm down."

"I'll calm down as soon as I find him. He didn't want to even do this tonight, Alistair, I *made* him. I need to make sure he's ok. I need him to know that it's ok if he had to…if he had to do whatever he had to do. I just need to tell him it's ok."

I push past Alistair, jog down the steps, and quickly round the corner to the entrance of the club. I'm relieved to see Pierce at the entrance.

"Pierce!" I yell, as I jog towards him. "Is Valmont inside?"

He nods, "he's in his VIP section."

"Is he with…her?"

He nods again, "last I checked."

"I need to see him," I demand.

He unhooks the red velvet barrier, "you know the way."

"Thank you, Pierce." I say, as I practically run past him into the club.

"Amarah, wait!" Alistair follows me. "What if he doesn't want to be disturbed?"

"Too fucking bad!" I yell over the pounding music, then I focus on weaving and pushing through bodies, as I head to the VIP section.

I climb the steps onto the VIP platform and walk with purpose to the back of the room. I scan to the left and right of me, desperate to spot his silver-white hair somewhere amongst the bodies scattered throughout the room. I make my way to the back, to the couch he usually occupies, but he isn't here. I turn around, my eyes scanning frantically. Alistair is a step behind me.

"Where is he? Did you see him?" I ask, as I continue looking for him.

"He's not here. He's my Maker, I would be able to sense him, but I don't," Alistair confirms.

It's not like him to just run off on his own. Especially without informing Pierce. Pierce is his right-hand man and his back-up if anything were to ever happen that Valmont needs back-up for. Pierce thought he was here, in the VIP, but he isn't. Maybe he just wanted to take Viveka to a more private place? There has to be a reasonable explanation.

"Maybe he's underground?" I ask, hopefully, trying to keep my panic at bay.

"Let's go check," Alistair turns to head out of the VIP section without even making sure I'm following.

Of course I am. I'm on his heels, not wanting to lose him or be left behind. We push through dancing and grinding bodies again, and rush out of the club, on a mission to find our Master Vampire.

Pierce must see the concern on our faces, "what's wrong?" He asks, his deep voice sounds even deeper with his authoratative tone in full effect.

"He's not in there. We're headed underground to see if he's there."

"What do you mean he's not in there? Of course he is. He would have told me if he was headed elsewhere."

I stop and turn towards the Vampire, my impatience and worry getting the best of me. "Then go fucking find him yourself! I'm telling you he isn't in there, but if you don't believe me and want to waste your time second guessing me, then by all means!"

I don't wait to hear his response or to see what he's going to do. Alistair is already around the corner and out of sight. I run to catch up to him at the elevator. I can barely stand still as I wait for the elevator to stop and let us out. Then I have to wait again as Alistair opens the large gate into the common area. It's full-on night and there are Vampires everywhere. They all seem to stop what they're doing and look at us as we enter the room. I have to swallow my fear down and remind myself that Valmont has claimed me, he's ordered his Vampires not to touch me, I'm safe. My fear is quickly overpowered by my concern for Valmont. We need to find him.

"You look in here, I'll take the private rooms. Stay in the common rooms, Amarah, don't venture into the tunnels," he warns.

I nod and head straight into the room of Vampires. I start asking everyone I encounter if they've seen Valmont. I'm tring to keep my desperation hidden. I don't know what will happen if the Vampires think Valmont is missing. I remember him saying that he has to keep them in line, and I also remember him saying that not all of his Vampires are compliant. Some have their own ambitions for power. Their Master going MIA may enbolden them to act on those ambitious desires. The best I can hope for, is that I come off as a jealous girlfriend, just trying to find a cheating boyfriend.

I meet Alistair back at the gate. One look at his face and I know the answer to my question, but I need to ask it anyway. "Did you find him?"

He shakes his head and we exit the common rooms, gaining more privacy. I still don't feel comfortable discussing the situation so close to Vampire ears so, I keep my concerns locked up inside. The pressure of not voicing my concerns feels like my chest is going to explode. Or maybe that's just my heart beating wildly.

We ride the elevator up to the main floor and Pierce is waiting for us. We take a seond to look at one another and it's plainly obvious. Valmont is missing.

"This is my fault," my voice comes out shaky, in a mixture of panic and guilt. "She must have realized it was a ploy. She knew he was using her and she's done something to him."

"Amarah, calm down. We don't know anything for certain, and it does us no good to speculate," Alistair says, logically.

I can't help the tears that fill up my eyes, as I stand here, listening to Pierce and Alistair discuss our next steps. I hear their voices but I don't hear their words.

I'm flooded with the memories of my last night with Valmont. His adamant refusal to agree to my plan, and the concern that was clearly written on his face. Then the love he proclaimed and showed me, over and over. I used his love for me to get him to agree to this, and he did, even though he knew the danger. He did because of me. For me. Because I asked him to. And now, he's been taken by her and I have no idea how to find him. How to save him. Or even if he can be saved.

"Amarah," his voice strikes me right in the center of my heart.

I turn around and the tears just pour harder down my face. He immediately moves towards me, but then hesitates. I hate that he hesitates. I hate that I did this to him. I hate that I want to run into his arms but I can't seem to get my feet to move.

I barely recognize my own voice as I say, "he's gone. Valmont's missing and it's all my fault."

I see a flurry of emotions run through his body, but he settles on a look of determination. He walks towards me with confident, purposeful strides. The next thing I know, I'm wrapped up in his strong arms, clinging to him tighter than I ever have, crying into his chest."

"Shhhh, it's ok, Angel, it's not your fault. Don't do this to yourself again. We'll find him, ok? I'll help you find him."

I cry harder at his words. At the goodness of him. I'm crying over another man and he's offering to help me find him. Not because he cares if Valmont is safe, but because he knows I can't lose anyone else. Because his love for *me* is that deep. Because he saves me, over and over again, even when I don't deserve it.

In this moment, I don't think about him in bed with another woman. I don't think about being addicted to Valmont's bite. I just revel in Logan's strong arms holding me. Keeping me safe. His voice, soft but firm, soothing my worries. His love is a physical force I can feel as he holds me tightly to him.

And I feel the barrier I've put up between our link shake.

And

    Then

        Start

            To

                Crack.

Amarah: Untimely Epiphany

Wicked Game by Grace Carter

We're sitting in Valmont's office. Emrick has joined us and it's him who I'm sitting next to on the couch. Logan is on the other side of him but I swear, I feel his energy all around me, as if he was right next to me. It took me way longer than I'd like to admit to pry myself from his arms. I could tell that he didn't want to let me go either, but this situation he walked into, isn't the right time to persue his wants. He's always been so level headed and perfect. God, he's perfect.

And what the Hell kind of fucked up person am I, that I can't stop thinking about Logan being three feet away from me, while we're all here to discuss Valmont going missing? A piece of shit. That's what this makes me.

"Amarah?" Emrick's voice pulls me out of my self-deprecating thoughts.

I clear my throat, "what's that?" I ask, completely lost in the conversation that's happening around me.

"Did Kordeuv tell you anything that might indicate where Viveka could have gone? Anything at all?"

"No," I shake my head.

"Are you sure?" Pierce's deep voice rumbles through his

chest.

I look up to where he sits across from me. "I'm sure," I say, through clenched teeth. "You're the one who let him slip away right from under your nose so, why don't you..."

"Now is not the time to point fingers," Alistair interrupts. "No one here is at fault for what happened. There's one person, and one person alone to blame for this, Viveka. Period. So let's all stay on task, shall we?"

I stare at Pierce, refusing to concede, but keeping my mouth shut nontheless. Alistair is right, we can't spend this time arguing amongst ourselves, and we only have a couple of hours left of moonlight to figure out a plan before the Vampires have to go underground for the day.

"You guys have been following them since they arrived, right? Do you have any leads as to where they might have gone?" Emrick asks.

Alistair shakes his head, "we've gotten no information or clues from following them. They've done nothing suspicious and haven't visited any places outside of clubs Downtown."

"There has to be *something*. Viveka hasn't been here just idily fucking around. She has a goal and that's not to shake her ass at every club in town." I say, angrily.

"Well, if you have any ideas, by all means," Pierce opens his arms, giving me the floor to speak, expecting I'll come up empty.

I lift my chin up in stubborn defiance. I hate when people underestimate me. "Logan is our best bet to find him. He can track him, his scent."

As much as it pains me to put this on Logan, it's true, he's our only hope at this point. He's the only Werewolf that has complete control over his wolf. He can turn, and track Valmont, regardless of the phase of the moon. And I feel like an even bigger piece of shit, asking him to do this and putting this on him, considering everything that's happened between us in the past two months. But what other choice do I have? Wait around in the hopes that Kordeuv will be able to get away and tell me where Valmont is? He may be able to, and I still hope he will, but it's not likely. If Viveka knew what we were up to all along, Kordeuv may not be safe either.

"I agree with Amarah. I can try and track him. The sooner I get out there, the better chance I have that his scent is still strong enough to track."

"But what do we do if you do find him? We need a plan. We can't just go in blind. Valmont is scared of Viveka. That says a lot. Shes dangerous, and powerful, and we can't underestimate her," I lecture.

"She is very powerful, but so is Valmont. I don't think he's completely at her mercy," Pierce says. "The only difference is that Viveka doesn't have a line she won't cross, either with other Vampires or humans. She's unpredictable and extrememly dangerous because of it. Whatever we do, we need to make sure she's isolated as much as possible."

"Ok, so the less people involved the better, but we still need strong numbers. Logan you can't go searching for them on your own, we'll be right behnd you, and we should have a few more Werewolves join us for back-up," I order.

The thought of Logan walking into a trap, and being helpless against Viveka, scares the shit out of me. I don't want him to go at all, but Viveka is the most powerful Vampire out there, we need the most powerful Werewolf too. And that's Logan. Plus, I'll be there and I'll be damned if I let anything happen to him on my watch. I didn't push him away, to keep him safe, only to have him walk right into danger alone. No, once we locate Valmont, I'm taking the lead and I make sure that's clear.

"Alright, so we get a small group together, Logan and few Werewolves, plus myself and Emrick. I think we should track him as soon as possible but attack during the day. Won't she be underground and asleep during the day?"

Pierce looks nervous, "not necessarily. Stronger and older Vampires aren't as controlled by the moon and sun, just like Logan isn't as much at the mercy of the moon as younger Werewolves."

"What does that mean? What are you saying?" I ask, confused.

"Valmont doesn't have to be underground during the day. That's why he sleeps in the Penthouse. He can't come into direct contact with sunlight, but it doesn't weaken him as much as it does the rest of us. I'm sure the same can be said for Viveka."

"So you're saying she could very well be up and walking around during the day?"

"Yes," Pierce nods his head. "She will be weaker during the day than at night, but by how much," he spreads his hands and shrugs.

"Fuck! Ok, so do you think it would be best to wait until nightfall again to have you and some other Vampires with us?"

"No, she'll for sure be too strong at night. I still think our best bet is to attack during the day, but just be aware that she won't just be asleep, waiting for you to kill her. Emmerson will be able to go with you during the day. He's a good asset to have in your corner on this, Amarah. He knows Vampires."

I run my hands down my face, "alright, so the three of us, some other Werewolves, and Emmerson. That's at leat six to their two. Plus, Kordeuv isn't technically on her side. I know he's a wildcard, but he may very well be able to help us too."

"Don't count on it," Logan says. "We go in with the knowledge we have. He's here with her, loyal to her, regardless of the reasons. He's our enemy unless he truly proves otherwise."

I don't like it. I know Kordeuv is tied to her unwillingly, but his life and freedom is at stake. He won't chance anything if it risks his power being destroyed, tethering him to this Earth and his human body forever. I feel bad for him, but Logan is right, we can't go in there with the intent to save anyone besides Valmont.

"Agreed," I finally say. "What else are we missing? What else can we plan for?"

"We can't do much else until we find them, *if* we find them. Then, we'll have to plan the details of our actual attack, once we know the terain and what we're up against," Logan explains.

"Ok, well, then I guess there's nothing else to do but prepare," I stand up. "I'll go get ready."

Logan stands up too, seeming to swallow up all the space and air in the office. "I'll make a few calls and get some Wolves here asap."

"I'll inform Emerson and send him up right away," Pierce says, as he stands too.

"We'll meet back here," I say, as I glance around at the men in the room.

They're all warriors in their own right. They've all lived through their own type of Hell, wars, and countless enemies. This isn't the first time they've walked into danger, but no one can seem to hide the overwhelming feeling lingering in the air.

Fear.

Everyone in this room is a little bit scared of Viveka and what we could be walking into, myself included. What if I'm not enough to lead them? What if I'm asking them to follow me to their deaths? Again, that's not something I'll be able to live with, but what other choice do I have? Go alone?

As if he can read my mind, like he always does, Logan steps up to me and pulls my chin up, locking his peridot eyes on mine. "No, Amarah," he shakes his head. "you can't do this alone. I know you want to take on the world, I know you want to keep everyone else out of danger, but that's just not an option. We live here in this world same as you. We have every right to fight for it and protect it. To fight for what and who we love."

I swallow down the thick ball of emotion that's trying to climb out of my chest. It feels like my heart is crawling and scratching its way up my throat to throw itself at Logan. I have to close my eyes, breaking eye contact with him, because I can't handle what I see so clearly in his eyes. I feel it in the simple touch of his fingers on my skin. He radiates love, and it's directed at *me*.

It's a love I don't deserve. It's also a love I don't understand. How can he love me with so much force, yet bed another woman within weeks of me breaking up with him?

I take a small step away from him, out of his grasp, and open my eyes. "As much as I hate to admit it, I know I can't do this alone, and I won't take your choice away. Again," I whisper.

I try to tell him with those words that I understand. I try to tell him that I know I made a mistake by taking away his choice to be with me, regardless of the danger or consequences. Standing in front of him right now, is the first time that I really feel the weight of my decision to leave him. My mistake. But I don't think I can make amends. I don't think we can go back to what we used to be. Too much has happened in such a short time. My heart is broken and it feels like it's beyond repair.

I feel my heart's persistent attempt at escape, I feel those fractures in my walls spreading further and further, weakening my resolve, and tears are suddenly filling up my eyes. I turn and walk out of the office before they can fall. I need to get my head on straight and focus on what's important right now.

Finding Valmont.

Killing Viveka.

We're standing outside, next to Valmont's stretch Escalade, waiting for the Werewolves to join us. It's snowing again and the wind chill is piercing. It stings where it blows across my exposed face, my nose and ears are no doubt red from the cold assault. I know I should probably be colder than I am, considering I'm not wearing a jacket, but I need to be able to move as freely as possible, and the adrenaline and my singular focus have my mind pre-occupied.

I'm dressed in black jeans, black sneakers and a long-sleeve black shirt. I'm ready to blend in with the shadows as much as possible. I'll strap my weapons on in the vehicle but there's no reason to alarm any unsuspecting humans at the moment. As of right now, we look like a regular group of friends, waiting to pile into this fancy SUV, and head out on the town. Although, the sun is starting to push the darkness away, slowly but surely, so I'm not sure where we would be headed at this time of the day. Luckily, there's not much traffic through the casino at this time.

"Logan," a male's voice reaches us on the wind.

I turn and see a man walking towards us. He looks young and not at all like what I was expecting. I was expecting to see someone like Logan or Ethan, Hell, even someone like Emerson, a tough as nails, intimidating presence. Instead, I see a fairly average, unsuspecting guy, walking towards us.

And next to him, the last person on this Earth that I want to see. I'd rather see Aralyn right now, or a demon, instead of...*her*. She strides confidently next to the young man, her thick, red hair, still manages to hang beautifully over her shoulder, in a tight braid. Her head is held high, shoulders back, and her blue eyes catch mine before they find Logan.

I'm instantly burning up, my skin feels like it's on fire, and my hands are itching for my daggers. How dare she show up here! And why is she here? Did Logan specifically ask for her? Or was she sent by Ethan? Ethan is the Alpha, the one who makes all the decisions for the Pack so, maybe he sent her? And he doesn't know the personal issues we have going on. Why would he?

I pull my eyes away from her and find Logan. He's already watching me. I know he sees the fire in my eyes, the hatred I don't even try to hide, and he shakes his head. Barely perceptiple, but he he's telling me, *no, don't do anything stupid*. His eyes are pleading with me and I hate him in this moment. I hate her and I don't even know her. And most importantly, I hate myself. I did this. This is the consequence of my decision walking straight towards the man I love.

Emrick steps in front of me, blocking my view, "Amarah, hey, I need you to focus on me right now, ok?"

My jaw is aching from how hard I'm clenching my teeth and I feel my fingernails digging into the palms of my hands. Emrick snaps his fingers in front of my face and I blink, finally focusing on him.

"I'm gonna need you to put the flames away, Sleeping Beauty. It's time to play nice with the other children."

I look down at my hands and my white flames are flicking up my arms. I immediately pull my power back in and take a deep breath.

"Then keep her away from me," I say, heatedly.

"That's going to be a little hard to do considering we're all about to climb into this SUV in a second. Hey," he grabs my arms and gives me a firm shake. "We're not doing this, Amarah. Tonight is not about your personal issues. It's about finding Valmont and keeping him safe. You know, the other man that loves you and put himself in this position for you. You need to woman up, put your big girl panties on and focus."

I let his words sink in. He's right, like always. This is about

Valmont. Focus on the mission. Get Valmont safe. Kill Viveka. Then deal with whatever fallout happens afterwards. One problem at a time.

I give Emrick my entire focus. "I'm good," I say, confidently.

"You sure, Sleeping Beauty?"

"I'm sure, Coach," I manage a small smile.

He doesn't seem convinced but he lets go of my arms and climbs into the SUV. I follow. I sit on the back seat, next to the side of the vehicle, Emrick slides in next to me so I don't have to sit next to anyone else. The young man is next, he sits next to Emrick, then the woman enters and sits across from me. This is not a better option, I realize, as I glare daggers at her. She calmly stares back at me, refusing to back down or show any sign of weakness. If it was any other woman, or any other situation, I would respect her more for it, but it just pisses me off. Logan is the last in and closes the door behind him.

The air inside the SUV is barely even breathable. It's toxic and heavy. I finally pull my eyes away from the woman to focus on strapping on my daggers that are laying on the floor in front of me.

"This is Kaedon, Ethan's son, and one Hell of a Wolf and fighter. This is Atreya, new to the Pack, and also one Hell of a fighter. They're the best of the Pack."

I don't bother addressing the woman, Atreya, I now know her name, but I do extend a greeting to Kaedon.

"Nice to meet you, Kaedon, I'm Amarah. Thank you for coming."

"It's my pleasure," he says, with a warm smile that eases something inside of me, just a little. "Anything for my man, Logan."

I glance at Logan, and he's once again already watching me. I don't know what he's expecting to see but all I have is anger inside of me. Ok, and maybe jealousy, but mostly the hottest, ugliest anger I've ever felt.

I hear Emrick exchange pleasantries with both of them as I continue to arm myself. The SUV slows and then comes to a stop. The privacy partition slides down revealing Emerson.

"Here," he says, coldly.

We're just outside of the casino grounds, where the security lights don't reach. This is where Logan is going to get out, transform into his Wolf and try to pick up the trail on Valmont. We maybe have forty minutes before the sun is going to take away all of the darkness and shadows Logan has to hide in. We need to hurry.

"Are you ready, Amarah?" Logan asks, no emotion in his voice.

Since he's going to be in Wolf form as he tracks Valmont, and we need a way to communicate, I have to lower my walls and let him inside of my head. And I'm terrified. I'm not sure I can control the barrier I've built enough to only let him in my mind and not open up our link completely. I can't afford to be overwhelmed by his feelings and emotions right now, and I don't have time to second guess my abilities. The sun is racing agaisnt us and time is ticking for Valmont.

I sigh and close my eyes, I visually imiagine my wall like the big steel gate in the Vamppire's underground compound. I imagine my gate lowering, ever so slightly, from the top. Just enough room to let Logan slip into my mind but not enough for him to get all the way through.

When I'm ready, when I think I have my walls where I need them to be, I nod. Logan doesn't waste any time slipping into my mind.

Amarah, can you hear me?

His voice inside of my head hurts. Not physically, but emotionally. It's one of the ways we're connected and it feels like coming home. Or at least pulling into the driveway. It makes me want to drop all of my walls, all of my self-protection, and just let him flood into me completely. Let him consume me and bring me all the way home. It takes all of my strength to hold myself together. I'm squeezing my eyes shut, fortifying myself. My walls.

Yes, I finally respond back and open my eyes to look at him.

Hi, he says, softly. Sweetly.

Hi, I reply.

And that one simple word, crushes me. The look of longing in his eyes destroys me. I'm close to crying, close to breaking, close to losing any control I have. Because they way he just said that one simple word, like he's been waiting an eternity to say it. Waiting an eternity for me to see him. To notice him again. To let him in.

Doesn't he know he's all I see? Doesn't he know he's all I want? Doesn't he know how much I love him? Enough to let him go. To keep him safe. Away from me. But none of that love matters in this moment as he sits next to the woman he's fucking.

I know this is hard for you, Amarah, it's hard for me too. But we're gonna get through this. You'll see.

And then he's out the door. The air in the SUV immediately thins without him in it. I close my eyes and draw in a deep breath. When I open my eyes, they immediately lock with Atreya's. She's studying me, her head slightly tilted, her eyes sharp and focused.

"You're still in love him," she says, matter-of-factly. There's

No anger, jealousy or possession in her tone.

Her words are not what I was expecting and I'm thrown off my game a bit. I don't know what to say. Am I supposed to deny it? Tell her she has nothing to worry about? Tell her I've moved on? I finally settle on the truth.

"It doesn't matter."

I've picked up his scent. It's faint but I'm on it. Logan's voice echoes loud and clear in my mind.

"Logan has his scent," I announce to the group.

"I'm following him. I'll let you know if I lose sight and need to know which way to go," Emerson calls from his seat up front.

"Of course it matters," Atreya continues.

"Look, I don't know who you think you are, but I'm not having this conversation with you," I seethe.

"Me?" She touches her own chest, in an innocent gesture. "I'm just a concerned friend who wants what's best for Logan"

I scoff, "and I'm assuming you're going to say that's you?"

"Not at all actually."

I look at her, more confused than ever. She's not looking at me like a judgemental new lover. She's not acting like a jealous or possessive woman. Maybe that's what Logan likes about her? She's level-headed like he is. I'm still staring at her, trying to understand this fucked up situation I'm in when she throws a grenade into the SUV.

"I know you think you know what you saw, but I'm not sleeping with Logan."

Her words hit me with the force of that grenade. I feel like my chest has been blown up from the inside and pieces of shrapnel are embedded in my heart. Doubt starts creeping into my mind. Why would she say that? Why would she deny sleeping with Logan? Why lie?

"I know what I saw," I say, steadily, trying to hold on to my anger.

"I almost died, Amarah. Logan's power almost killed me. You have no idea what he's been going through since you walked away from him. He's not ok. He holds himself together better than anyone I know, but he's not ok. He's losing control, and the only thing that's keeping him sane right now, is the hope of getting through to *you*. That your love for each other will perservere. And it's a thin thread that's about to snap. The fact that he's even here, right now, helping you find this Vampire, is a testament to his strength. And his love for you."

My head is spinning with her words. Logan's power almost *killed* her? How? I had no idea his power was capable of that. How did it happen? I have so many questions. And how does she know how much he loves me? Can she see it? Did he tell her? Why would he tell the woman he's sleeping with that he loves someone else? Unless she's telling the truth and they *aren't* sleeping together.

I shake my head, trying to focus on the truth. "My eyes didn't make up what I saw. Why are you saying all of this when I saw you! Naked! In bed with him!" I raise my voice, trying to drown out all the questions and rising doubt.

She scoffs, "you've learned nothing about who Logan is. You claim to love him but you have no idea who he is. What he needs. He's a Werewolf, Amarah. A Võltsimatu. As am I. When I was close to death, I needed to heal. I needed Pack comfort, Wolf comfort. Werewolves are physical beings. We use touch as much, if not more, than words. Logan being in bed with me had absolutley nothing to do with sex and everything to do with healing. He saved my life."

I'm so taken aback by her words, I can barely process them, much less try and articulate a response.

"He's been a Lone Wolf for so long he's almost forgotten what it even means to be a Wolf. He can't live like that and truly be happy. He needs Pack life, and if not Pack life, then he needs his mate. He needs *you*, Amarah. He's never given up on you. He's never betrayed you. He's never dishonored your love."

I feel wetness drip onto my hands. I didn't even realize I started crying. Her words have pierced through all of my walls, increasing the fractures in my foundation. My foundation built on nothing but my own mistakes. Guilt, sorrow, and shame are pouring down my cheeks in equal measure. What have I done? What have I caused?

"And just to make sure you truly understand me, you truly hear what I'm saying, in normal circumstances, I'd be more attracted to you than Logan. You're beautiful, Amarah, but what you've done to Logan, how you've acted, is beyond ugly. I understand your desire to protect him, but you had no right to take his choice away. He's an Alpha Wolf. He's built to lead and to protect. He's only ever conceded his dominance to *you* and you threw his love and respect away because you're selfish."

I can't help the sob that escapes my throat. I feel every truth she's throwing my way like a dagger to the heart. One stab after another after another.

"I know," I choke out.

I know, I'm selfish. The decision to leave him, selfish. The decision to ignore him and not *hear* what he was saying, selfish. The choice to sleep with Valmont at an attempt to ease my pain, selfish. I've been carelessly collecting hearts and destroying them along the way because I needed to feel loved. Selfish. I needed attention. Selfish. And all this time, I've had the only thing I'll ever need or want in this life.

Logan. Logan's unconditional love.

And I've thrown it away. And I don't know if I can ever get it back. I definitely don't deserve to get it back.

Emrick and Kaedon have been extrememly quiet and still, as

if they don't want to intrude on what's happening in this SUV. I don't blame them. I'd want to go unnoticed too if I was the one witnessing this mess.

Atreya sighs, "I don't think you're a bad person, Amarah. Not from what Ive heard about you, from Logan and from others. I just think you've made some pretty ginormous mistakes, and I hope you learn from them. I hope you come to your senses and do what's right. Logan has become like a brother to me and, like I said, I want what's best for him. I still think that's you."

And I still don't have words to say so, I just nod, wiping the tears off my face and trying to regain some self-respect.

"I didn't mean to throw all of this at you now, I know it's not the best time, but I didn't know when else I'd be able to set the truth straight. For what it's worth, I'm sorry that it had to happen now, but hopefully this means we can work together on this mission and I don't have to worry about you stabbing me?"

I manage a half laugh, half scoff, at her attempt to disarm this loaded situation. I'm seeimg her in a whole new light now and I hate that I actually like her a little bit. I can see why Logan likes her too.

I extend my hand out to her, "It's nice to officially meet you, Atreya. I promise, no stabbing will come from me. Thank you for being here."

She shoots me a wide, genuine smile, and takes my hand, "Atreya Stone, happy to be of service and to fight alongside the Võitleja."

"Thank God," Emrick exhales a long-relieved breath. "Women are so dramatic."

"Ain't that the truth," Kaedon agrees.

I elbow Emmrick in the side, "hey! You're one to talk!"

"I don't know what you're talking about, Sleeping Beauty. And although we are definitely discussing all of this," he makes small circles in the air between us, "we need to focus on the mission and what we're about to do. So pull it together and put all of this aside for now."

I nod, "I'm good. I'm focused."

Just then, Logan's voice echoes in my mind. *I think I've found their location. Tell Emerson to cut the lights and hang back. I'm giong to inspect and confirm.*

"Emerson, cut the lights and hang back. Logan thinks he found their location. He's going to confirm," I repeat, out loud.

"Copy," Emerson cuts the lights and pulls off to the side of the road, killing the engine.

Be careful, Logan. Inspect only, I reiterate.

I finally look out the window and observe our surroundings. The sun is barely breaking the horizon, and the storm clouds make the light gloomy. The snow has stopped, but it covers the ground around us in a thick white blanket. We're Downtown, but in an empty, deserted area. It looks like an old train station that's been shut down and abandoned.

"Do you see anything up there, Emerson?" I ask, as I scan my side of the street.

"Just abandoned buildings, old train cars, and a few broken down old vehicles. I don't see anyone or any sign of activity."

We all wait in charged silence for Logan to give an update or come back. It feels like hours have passed before the SUV door opens, but the sun is still trying to pull clear of the horizon, so it hasn't been long at all.

Logan is back in his human form and hides behind the door. Only his head and shoulder peek around the door.

"My clothes, please," he reaches a hand inside the SUV and Atreya hands him a pile of clothes. I hadn't even noticed the clothes sitting next to her this entire time.

A few minutes later Logan fully emerges and climbs back into the SUV, fully clothed in jeans, boots, and a regular v-neck t-shirt. His go-to. It sits tightly across his chest and arms, his biceps and forearms are left bare. The veins running up his arms draw my eyes like a kid in a candy store. My mouth waters and I'm suddenly starving for a taste of him. My eyes travel up to his mouth and his generous, full lips. Lips that *haven't* kissed another woman since me.

Angel, you either need to stop looking at me like that or I'm kicking everyone out of this SUV and taking you right now. And, unfortunately now really isn't the best time.

My eyes snap up to his eyes and I see his desire, and also his confidence. He gives me that damn half-smile that I've come to love on him so much. He knows he still affects me and he's reveling in it. Heat creeps up my face as I quickly look away from Logan.

"Sweet Jesus," Emrick says, as he fans himself with his hands. "Why do I feel like I just saw you two fucking and all you did was look at each other? Are you guys going to be able to handle this?"

"I'm fine."

"Of course."

Logan and I speak at the same time.

"Valmont's scent ends here. They definitely went into the old train station. There are several entry points and I'm sure several rooms within and plenty of space to hide or lay traps. We need to be alert and communicate with each other every second possible. We're going to need to move seperately but together."

Emerson is reaching into the back, "here are the comms. Let's get them on and tested before we head out."

We all put our ear pieces in and attach our microphones, while Emerson sets up the communication hub, then we take turns speaking to each other.

When there's nothing left to do, we all look around at each other. I see determination set in each face. They're all battle ready, and unlike earlier, there's no trace of fear. I'm in the midst of fearless soldiers, ready to walk into battle.

"Ready?" Emerson asks?

We all nod and quietly exit the SUV. Emerson, Kaedon, Atreya, Emrick and I are strapped with weapons. Logan looks nakedly unarmed, but I have to remember that he *is* the weapon. Now is not the time to worry about anyone. Everyone here is capable of handling and protecting themselves.

Just as we're about to head out, towards the building Logan identified, Logan whispers, "someone's approaching."

I turn to face the direction Logan is and the others fan out into a tight circle, watching and protecting each direction in case someone tries to take us by surprise from behind.

We wait quietly, our senses on full alert, my hands are resting on my dagger hilts, ready to draw them if necessary.

"There," Logan's Wolf eyes make out the body walking towards us before I do.

A few seconds later, I recognize Kordeuv walking towards us with his hands up. As far as I can tell, he's unarmed. I relax a little bit, knowing Kordeuv really isn't Viveka's ally, but not letting my guard down either.

"Amarah," he addresses me. "I'm sorry," he shakes his head. "She suspected Valmont was up to something and took him. I don't know how much she knows but as far as I know, she doesn't know that you and I met. She still doesn't *know* about you but she suspects," he says, cryptically. I understand what he's trying to say without saying it.

"But she knows we're here?" I ask.

He shakes his head, "no, she was sending me to go and get you. She suspects you mean more to Valmont than he let on. She's planning on using you to get him to talk. She doesn't know all of you are here. I didn''t know either until I came out. We can use this to our advantage."

"How do we know we can trust you?" Logan asks, suspiciously.

He shrugs, "I know it's not ideal but you're just going to have to trust me."

"What's your plan?"

"I can walk in with Amarah, keep her focused on us and distracted, as far as I know, she doesn't suspect me. The rest of you can enter from a different direction. You can attack unseen and catch her off guard when the moment is right. It's the best option we have, but we don't have much time. Valmont does't have much time."

His words send my heart racing. Valmont is ok for now but for how long? We need to get in there now and assess the situation quickly. We need to take control of the situation, get him safe, and illiminate Viveka.

"We don't really have a choice, Logan, we need to trust him. It's the best plan we have."

Logan looks at Emerson, he nods, in agreement with the plan. Logan blows out a frustrated breath. I know he doesn't want me walking in there alone, but he's also trusting me and my abialities.

"Alright," he agrees.

"You're going to need to leave your weapons, Amarah."

"What? Why?"

"She doesn't know who you are. Walking in strapped with

weapons is going to tip her off. As of right now, she just thinks you're a girl Valmont cares about and wants to keep safe. You have your power and she doesn't know about it. She'll underestimate you, Amarah, let her."

"Fuck," I say, irritated. "Alright."

I start unstrapping my weapons. I'm not happy about leaving my Divine weapons behind. What if they're the only thing that can kill her?

I hand one of my daggers to Atreya, "take one inside for me."

She takes it without hesitation and straps it to her thigh.

"Ok, let's go," I start to walk to Kordeuv.

Logan grabs my arm and stops me. We stand here, facing each other. All of the things left unsaid hang heavily between us. I have the urge to kiss him. What if this is the last time I see him? What if this is my last chance to say I'm sorry? To make amends?

I see all the same thoughts flit across his face too, but all he says when he finally speaks is, "be careful."

"I will," I swallow down the rest of my emotions.

We both know now is not the time. We don't have enough time to say all the things we want to say. He slowly lets go of my arm, I turn away from him, and walk towards Kordeuv. I feel like I'm waking away from the rest of my life and I have no choice but to put one foot in front of the other, walking further and further away from the center of my world.

I hold my head up high, pull my shoulders back and push all my emotions down deep. I've had practice locking my emotions away and it comes in handy now.

I'm walking into this situation as the Võitleja, Fey Warrior, ready to fight.

Amarah: Fears Come True

Lifetime by Three Days Grace

The large abandoned building looms up in front of us as we approach. The sun has pierced through the clouds and reflects off of thousands of small green and gold windows. The beauty is marred by broken and missing pieces of glass throughout the structure. I can only imagine how stunning this building was in its prime. It's such a shame, that something someone took so much time and care in designing and building, is left to rot.

Kordeuv leads the way, walking straight down the center of old train tracks that run under a massive open arch. I scan as much of the enormous open space as I can, searching the shadows for any sign of Viveka or Valmont. It takes my eyes a second to process what they're seeing. Up ahead, I spot the shimmer of silver-white, laying on the ground.

All thoughts of my safety flee as I race towards the body that's quickly taking shape in front of. I throw myself down on the ground next to him. He's chained across the train tracks and rays of sunshine are slowly inching toward his trapped body through the broken pieces of glass. If he doesn't move, and soon, the rays are going to stretch across his body.

"Valmont!"

His eyes are closed and he's paler than I've ever seen him. I lift his head up and pat his cheek. "Valmont, I'm here. You're going to be ok. Wake up!" I plead.

He slowly opens his eyes, his eyelids look like they weigh a thousand pounds, as he struggles to keep them open. His normally sparkling turquoise eyes are dull and almost lifeless.

I inspect the chains holding his body down, they're massive and they're locked around the rails. There's no way that I can break him free.

"Valmont, come on, stay with me. You need to break these chains and get free, ok? You don't have much time."

"He can't, Amarah," Kordeuv's voice says, from somewhere behind me. "She's drained him of almost all of his blood. He's weaker than a human right now, barely alive."

I reach for my dagger, to cut my arm and give him my blood, but I don't have my weapons.

"Shit," I frantically look around me.

I get up and run towards the side of the building and pick up the first piece of broken glass I see. I run back to Valmont and slice the glass across my forearm. I wince as the jagged edge pulls at my skin. I carefully hold my dripping arm above his lips, I can't risk him biting me and leaving me incapable of defending myself, but I just hope the drips of my blood falling into his mouth is enough. I hope he's strong enough to swallow it down.

"Kordeuv, what are you doing?" Viveka's voice sounds angry as she approaches us but I keep my attention on Valmont. "Stop her!" She orders.

I feel Kordeuv's arms wrap around me and pull me away, "I'm sorry my Queen, she grabbed a piece of glass before I knew what she was doing. He didn't get enough blood to make a difference," he ensures.

"Bring her to me," she demands.

I fight against Kordeuv's hold but it's no use, he's too strong, and he has no choice but to do as she says. He can't out himself as a traitor to her or risk losing his freedom, or worse.

She's staying hidden in the shadows, avoiding the rays of sun filtering in through all the broken windows. I want to look back at Valmont and see if he's at least stirring, trying to break free, but I keep my focus on Viveka. Once Kordeuv has me standing in front of her, I plant my feet and tip up my chin, meeting her black, dead gaze with my own.

I want to pull out my power and engulf her in my white flames, see if she can survive that, but I don't know if she *will* survive, and as of right now, she doesn't know who I am. I need to give Logan and the others time to get here.

"What do you want?" I ask, pretending not to know she's looking for me. "Why did you do this to Valmont?"

"Don't play coy, Amarah, you and Valmont both know *exactly* why I'm here."

"I swear, I don't know anything! I'm just here for Valmont, Kordeuv told me..."

"Cut the helpless act," she snaps. "Valmont tried to hide you in plain sight. I must admit, he did a good job of pretending you were insignificant, and you played your role well. The hurt and jilted lover," she claps her hands. "Bravo, my dear, bravo."

"I don't know what you're talking about," my voice comes out solid and strong but her words are sinking into me, stoking my doubt. What if we didn't fool her?

"Has anyone told you that you shouldn't lie to a Vampire? We can sense all of your tells when you lie. That's why I was so impressed with your act each time I met you. Although, it wasn't all an act, was it? You really thought Valmont used you."

I don't give her a response, and I figure the less I say, the better. Apparently, she doesn't need a response though.

"You did play your part well enough, but I'm afraid I saw right through Valmont. You see, I knew exactly who you were the very first time I met you, and the way Valmont was blatantly trying to talk you down. No, he tried too hard to make you insignificant, that's how I knew you also meant something to him. He's never been able to lie to me, look like becoming a Master didn't change that."

Kordeuv shuffles his feet and I can't help but wonder what's going through his mind right now. We both seem blindsided by what Viveka knows.

"I knew it was you all along who has this *amazing power* I've heard so much about. Would you like to know how I knew?"

"Does it matter?" I ask, sarcastically.

"You looked me right in the eyes. Even in your impaired state, you looked right into my eyes with no fear. No other being dares look us Vampires in the eyes, especially one as old as me. Yet, you did. And I knew, right there, you were the one I was looking for."

My heart is pounding in my chest, my body is in fight or flight mode, and I can't run. I can't leave Valmont and I can't leave the others. That only gives me one option. I need to fight.

A Wolf howl echoes in the massive space around us and I scan the room, trying to see any signs of Logan and the others. I have no idea which way the howl came from.

Logan! I reach out through our bond.

"Ahhhh, it looks like your friends have encountered my newest additions to the family. You see, I've been busy down here in your beautiful Downtown area. So many unwanted and forgot human beings. Don't worry, I've kept them unfed precisely for an occasion such as this, and I can just imagine how thirsty they are," she laughs, maniacally.

"This was a trap all along," I fight against Kordeuv's hold. He lied to me! He betrayed us and I led everyone right into the arms of the enemy.

"Of course, it's a trap. You think I've lived to be over a three thousand years old by being naïve? I know all the plays you might make before you even think of them," she taunts. "And I know when I'm being lied to the second it happens," she's suddenly holding a glowing golden orb between her fingers.

I never even saw her move and have no idea where the orb came from. I feel Kordeuv's body stiffen next to me, his hold on me becomes bruising, and I suddenly realize what she's holding. His star ball. His power.

"Now, the question is, what am I going to do with the two of you?" She asks, nonchalantly, as she stares at the golden orb in her hand.

"Viveka, please," Kordeuv begs. "I just want my freedom, I'll do whatever you want, please, just…"

"Be quiet!" She yells. "You *will* do whatever I want or I will break this ball, right here, right now. Do you understand?"

"Yes, my Queen."

And in this moment, I know I've lost him. Kordeuv is no longer on my side, not even a little bit. He's going to do whatever it takes to save himself. Well, then, so am I. I feel the comfortable tingle of my power along my skin as I pull it forth. The feeling of my flames flickering through my fingers, calms me and comforts me. I'm not helpless.

"Ah, ah, ah," Viveka tsks. "I wouldn't do that if I were you? Not if you care about the rest of your family and the ones you love."

I hesitate, "what do you mean the *rest* of my family?"

"Well, you see, I've been doing my homework while I've been here, biding my time. I've been adding to my little army, both new recruits and some of Valmont's own Vampires that want their own power. I also had to make a pre-emptive strike so that you'll take me seriously. See, you're going to join me, of your own free will, and you're going to let me use this magnificent power of yours however I want."

"Like Hell I will!" I fume.

"What a shame," she shrugs. "I thought you might say that and that's why I've taken it upon myself to kill a certain *Witch*, and place soldiers surveying the other important people in your life. If anything happens to me, they're order is to *kill*."

My mouth goes dry, my heart sinks into my stomach. Iseta. No. No this can't be true. My power fades as I feel the blow of her threat and lose my concentration. There's no way that Iseta is dead. It can't be true. And who else has she uncovered is close to me? Ana? My human mom and sister? My friends?

"I don't believe you," I deny the truth of her words as hard as I can.

"You think I'd leave a powerful Witch alive to potentially come to your rescue? Even if I am stronger, why take that chance? I don't take chances and I don't leave anything to chance either. You will join me, Amarah, or I will destroy everything and everyone that you love."

The next events happen so quickly I can barely keep up. I hear the rattling and breaking of chains as I'm yanked from Koreuv's hold. I'm suddenly in the arms of Viveka, one hand with a death grip on my upper arm and the other around my throat. I can feel her razor-sharp nails slicing into the skin already. Kordeuv has his back to me, facing the new threat, ready to fight.

"Let her go, Viveka," Valmont's cool and calm voice washes over me, just seconds before Logan comes charging into the room.

He's bloody and dirty and comes tearing through the room like a fucking EF5 tornado. I immediately want to ask if he's ok, if the others are ok, but we don't have time. At least he's standing here, in front of me. I blow out a relieve breath, some tension leaving me, as I see that both men are standing in front of me, alive. There's no way she can fight both of them together but, unfortunately, she has all of the bargaining chips in her corner. Me.

"I will gladly let her go just as soon as she agrees to come with me," her voice sounds so soft and sweet. So innocent. Damn if that isn't the biggest fucking con of all.

"I'll never go with you," I hiss.

She tsks again, "wrong answer I'm afraid. I will just have to take everything and everyone you care about away from you, Amarah. Until you have no one left and nothing worth living for. Then, you will come with me. Kordeuv, give Valmont his sword."

What? She brought his sword here? Why on Earth would she willingly arm him? Nothing she says or does is what I expect. I don't know what to do. I don't know how to move forward. I just want to keep them safe. To keep everyone safe. And if her threat is real, I can't kill her. My hands are tied and I'm so confused. I don't know what's real and what's a lie. And just like Viveka said, I can't take the chance.

Valmont looks just as confused as I feel as he takes his sword from Kordeuv.

"Kill the Werewolf," Viveka orders.

"No!" I yell!

Viveka sinks her nails deeper into my throat, cutting off my protests.

I look at Valmont and I plead with everything I have in my eyes. I manage a strangled whisper, "please."

"Kill him, Valmont, or I swear to whatever Gods are listening, I will rip out her throat and then cut out her heart."

I see the fear of her words grip him. He swallows hard, his eyes are locked on mine, and I see the second his fear turns to sorrow.

"I'm sorry, Amarah Rey."

I try and shake my head. I try and fight against her hold, but her grip is like a vice, holding me tightly to her. How can someone so small be so fucking powerful?

"She will kill you if I don't do this. I told you, that I would do anything to keep you safe, even if it kills me. I meant every word," he says, sadly, as he swings his sword and faces Logan.

"I'll come with you," I plead. "I'll come with you!"

"Too late," Viveka laughs.

Logan squares off with the Valmont. His hands lengthen into claws, his eyes bleed to amber, and he focuses in on the new threat. If it was any other time, I might have hope that Logan could win against Valmont. They're both extremely powerful in their own right, and Logan is one of the best fighters anyone has ever seen, but this is no longer a fair fight.

Valmont has my blood in his veins. He's unstoppable.

Logan, I reach out to his mind. *Logan, you can't fight him. He has my blood in his veins, he's too strong.*

I'm not afraid of him and I'm not leaving you, Angel.

Please logan, I plead. *Run, just run! Save yourself, please!*

And then I'm out of his head as they're both a blur of speed colliding with each other. The world around me disappears. Nothing else matters but the two men fighting for life in front of me. I can't make sense of anything.

A glint of steel.

Silver-white.

Claws.

Blood.

They part for a second and they're both covered in blood. I can't tell if it's from cuts they each have or if someone is hurt worse than the other. Then they're back together in a blur of colors.

I can't even hear the sounds of the fight. All I can do is try and follow the movements the best I can but I can't see a damn thing. I'm holding my breath. My heart feels like it's suffocating in my chest. Like a fist is squeezing it, tighter and tighter.

They break away again, Valmont is on his feet, deep claw marks across his arms and chest. Logan is kneeling on one knee, holding an arm tightly across his body. He's clutching a wound I can't see in his side. There's a huge gash in his thigh, blood running freely down his leg, soaking his jeans. His upper body is riddled with cuts and he's gasping for breath. His eyes slowly turn back to their beautiful lime green and they lock with mine.

I hold his gaze, fighting to keep the tears at bay. I don't want to cry and lose sight of him in my tears. I'm still holding my breath, fearing that if I breathe, if I make any sudden movements, I'll break this moment, and my worst fear will come true before my eyes.

"I love you," he says, as he pushes himself up to stand.

The next second, Valmont's sword enters his chest, right through Logan's heart and rips through his back. Valmont pulls the sword free and Logan falls to his knees, and then to his side.

"Noooo!!!!" I try to scream the word, but it comes out a strangled scream because Viveka's hand is still gripped tightly around my throat.

All of my barriers come crashing down and I'm flooded with Logan's emotions…and pain. My knees buckle and I fall to the ground. She must have let go of me, because the next thing I know,

I'm crawling on my hands and knees towards Logan's unmoving body.

I don't register the distance or the time that passes. All I know is that I'm suddenly holding Logan in my arms. I've seen this scene a million times before in my nightmares but it's never been more real than it is now.

"Hang on, Logan. Let your body heal. You can heal this, I know you can," I cry over him.

"Silver," he wheezes.

Of course, the sword is silver. I shake my head, "it doesn't matter, you can heal this. You're the strongest person I know. Please, you have to."

"I've never stopped loving you, Angel," his voice is barely above a whisper.

He coughs on the blood filling up his chest and I feel the warmth of it spatter across my lips and chin.

"No, no, no, no," is all I can say as I rock him in my arms. His eyes are locked on mine, pleading, and I know he's desperate to say a million things he never got to. I'm desperate to say all the things I never got to. But at least we can feel it. We can feel each other.

I can feel his love, I can feel the truth of his words. I know he never betrayed me or lost hope in us. I'm so overwhelmed by his beautiful, unconditional love. All I can do is pour my love back into him too.

"You were supposed to be safe! This w-w-asn't supposed to h-app-pen. I was trying to save you," I try and say everything I need to say through my sobs but I can't find the right words.

His love is radiating through me but I'm pierced just as deeply with his pain. It's like I can feel the whole in my own heart. The stab of the word as it entered my chest and the slice as it was pulled free. I can feel my heartbeat slowing...or is it his? I can feel our link diminishing. I can feel his love, like a punctured tired, seeping out of me.

"I'm sorry, Logan, I'm so sorry. I love you so much! I'm sorry! This wasn't ever supposed to happen! Please don't leave me. Please!" I scream at him through my tears. And then I kiss him. Desperately trying to breath my life into his. "I love you! I need you! Please don't leave me! Logan, please! I need you. I can't survive this life without you. Please don't go."

"Angel," he manages to sputter out as a single tear slips down the side of his face.

I feel the second his life ends. Our bond goes quiet. Empty. Cold. Like his cold, drying blood on my face. There's a gaping, open hole inside of me where he used to be. Even with me blocking our connection, he was always there, always with me. And now I have nothing. Nothing left inside of me. No love. No anger. No emotion of any kind. I'm a hollow husk. An empty shell.

I throw my head back and scream to the Heavens. A scream that shatters the rest of the glass windows as if a hurricane wind blew them out. I don't try and shield myself as shards of glass rain down on me. How could God do this? How could he let this happen? I scream and I scream and I scream as I hold onto Logan's dead body.

"Will someone please shut her up?" I hear Viveka's voice from somewhere far away.

Then everything goes quiet.

A familiar voice finds me in the dark.

"Amarah?" I hear the strike of a lighter before I see the glow of the flame heading my way.

For the first time, Lucifer's face looks evil, in the flickering flame and shadows. He looks like what he is. The Devil. And I can't bring myself to care. Drag me to Hell. Let me burn for Eternity. Nothing else matters anymore.

"Amarah?" He asks again, as he squats down and addresses me where I'm lying on the floor. "Are you having another nightmare?"

I shake my head.

He looks around at the pitch black darkness pushing in all around us. "Then what is this? What are you doing here?"

I shrug.

He sighs, "come on, Amarah, talk to me. Use your words. Maybe I can help. Haven't I always been able to help?"

"You can't fix this," I say, my words void of emotion. Empty.

"Well, we don't know until you tell me what's broken."

"Broken. The world is broken. People are broken. Life is broken."

"Alright," he moves to sit next to me, his hands resting on his knees, his hand still holding the zippo lighter. "Well, I can't fix a broken world I'm afraid. That's not exactly my department," he chuckles.

I don't laugh.

"Ok, this must be really bad. What caused the world to become broken, Amarah? Why are you here?"

"He's gone."

"Who's gone?"

"Logan."

"Ah, I see, you're still broken up about the Wolf."

"No."

"No?" he sounds confused.

"He's…" I can't bring myself to say it out loud.

The silence surrounds us, just as thick and threatening as the darkness, as Lucifer waits for me to elaborate.

"He's what, Amarah?"

"He's dead."

Lucifer sucks in a breath, "I see."

We're quiet for another few minutes as the truth of my words settle around us. I'm still empty. Completely numb. If I thought I was numb before, when Andre died, I was so wrong. I feel absolutely nothing inside of me. I just want to lie here, in the darkness, and let it consume me.

"Well, what if I told you that I *can* fix this?"

That gets my attention, and I'm sitting up, facing him in an instant. "How?"

"There's a short time when the soul...*lingers*, so to speak. I could bring his soul back to his body and heal whatever injury caused his death."

"You can do that?"

"I can. I'm not supposed to interfere, obviously, but it's possible. Besides, what's God going to do to punish me?" He laughs, heartily.

"Do it! Please, do it!"

"Now, now, hang on. Something like this isn't easy. I'm going to need..."

"Whatever you need! Anything. Whatever I have to do, name it."

"Well, I recall a conversation we had not too long ago where you were upset because you're always someone's target. Your power is a target. Your power is why you chose to leave Logan, to keep him safe from yourself. What if you no longer had to worry about your power being an issue?'

"You want my power?" I ask, confused? "But you're Lucifer. You're a full on Angel and I'm only half. Why do you want my power?"

He shrugs, "Oh, I have my reasons. But let's not focus on me, let's focus on you. This is a win-win for you, Amarah. Logan, alive. No power to threaten your happiness."

Lucifer has never asked me for anything before. Why now? Why does he want my power? It's insignificant to his own. It doesn't make sense, and yet, it must be important.

"Tick-tock, Amarah. A soul doesn't hang around for long. If you want this to happen, you need to make a decision quickly."

Every fiber of my being is warning me that this is wrong. The one thing everyone knows, is that you don't make deals with the Devil! But my love for Logan transcends everything else. All reason.

"Ok, yes," I agree. "My power for Logan's life."

Lucifer hold out his hand, "we need to shake to seal the deal. Unless you'd prefer another kiss?" He smirks at me.

I place my hand in his and he grips me tightly. I feel the sensation of something slithering up my arm but nothing's there. Nothing physical anyways. It creeps up my neck and I feel it enter my mouth and slither down my throat. I gag at the sensation but there's nothing actually in my throat.

Then I feel my power stir in my chest. It's the only thing I have left inside of me. I thought I was completely empty, but I was wrong, my power is still there. Now, it's being pulled from me. My initial response is to fight agaianst it. This is my power! It belongs to me!

"You need to give it to me freely, Amarah. Logan's life is at stake."

I hold on for one last second before I let go. I feel my power as it's ripped away from me, and I'm suddenly left feeling cold and alone. Now, I'm empty. There's nothing inside of me but human organs.

Nothing magical.

Nothing Divine.

I'm about to fall back to the floor, close my eyes, and let the darkness take me, when I'm suddenly thrown back into reality. I'm laying on Logan's chest. I lift my head up and look around. I see

Valmont, Kordeuv and Viveka, but they're frozen.

Lucifer's voice makes me turn my head to find him. He's standing in one of the sun rays, his arms held out to the side, his face tuened up towards the light. He takes in a huge breath of air and slowly lets it out.

He laughs, giddily, "oh, it has been too long since I've tasted the air and felt the sun on my skin!"

I glance around and can't tell if I'm still in my dream world or if I'm truly back on Earth.

Lucifer slowly turns around to face me, "well, a deal is a deal. Shall we?"

He starts to walk towards where I'm still thrown over Logan's body, when a blinding white light floods down on us out of nowhere. I throw my arm up, protecting my eyes from the light. I hear a loud thud as something lands heavily on the ground next to Logan's body. Something slowly starts to rise and take shape in front of me.

A body.

Wings.

The light slowly fades and I'm able to see the man standing between us and Lucifer. He's tall and imposing. His body is thick and strong, solid as a mountain. His wings are white as snow, white as the light he just decended from, and they're spread wide, each one twice the size of his body. His body is wrapped in golden armor and a sword sits down the length of his spine and I know exactly who this is.

Archangel Michael.

The real, Archangel Michael. How could I have ever misstaken Lucifer for him? I haven't even seen the Angel's face and there's no comparison. When he finally speaks, his voice moves through the air and Earth as if they're one.

"Don't you fucking touch him."

"My, my, brother, this is a mighty surprise indeed. What has possessed the righteous Archangel Michael to break a precious *golden rule* and come down to Earth? If it's Amarah you're trying to protect, I'm afraid you're too late. She's already given up her birthright, to me, and we both know you can't best me brother."

"I don't need to best you, Luci, you of all people should know you can't mess with destiny no matter how hard you try. *His* plans are still in place." He looks over his shoulder at me, and his face takes my breath away.

His wavy blonde hair hangs down to his shoulders and seems to shine just as brightly as the sun. His eyes are golden yellow, steely and strong as they lock with mine, but also warm and comforting. His face is strong, sharp angles, and yet soft and beautiful. His voice, when he speaks this time, seems to fill me up from the inside out. Giving me something to hang on to, something to feel inside of me.

"All is not lost, Amarah, as long as you keep fighting. As long as you keep Faith and belief in your heart. The fight is not over."

I'm crying and I don't even know why. Because he's so beautiful. Because he's an Angel. Because I feel his Divinity deep in my bones. Because I want to believe more than ever. Because for the first time since Andre's death, I have hope again. Hope that He is out there. That He is listening to me. That I'm not alone. I'm never alone.

"Well, isn't that a wonderful little story of hope. Boring!" Lucifer chides. "If you aren't here to get your hands dirty, then why did you come brother?"

"I'm here for my son."

Author's Note & Acknowledgements

I know, I know! This one ends on a little bit of a cliff hanger...
As much as I'd like to say, "I'm sorry." Well, I'm not! Haha As a
reader, first and foremost myself, I LOVE when books leave me dying
to know what happens and dying to pick up the next book
immediately!

But, I'm afraid, you're just going to have to wait since, well, the final
book hasn't even been started yet. Ooops! But I promise I will work
endlessly to bring you the best book yet! The next book, book 4, will
be the final book in the Amarah Rey, Fey Warrior Series.

Just a reminder to please leave your review and feedback on
Amazon and/or any other social media platforms you use. Reviews
are so very important to us so, please, take a few minutes to write
down your thoughts for others to see. As always, please be kind.
Honest, always, but also kind.

And if you're here, reading this, then I owe you all the thanks, all of
the gratitude that I have in my body. Authors are NOTHING with you,
the reader. I know this and I appreciate you beyond what any words
could ever express.

I want to thank everyone that has been supporting me throughout this
amazing journey. I will give individual recognition in my final author's
note in book 4. Until then, please just know that whether or not I
express it to you personally, I am forever and ever grateful to YOU.
You, the one reading this. Thank you.

Made in the USA
Middletown, DE
30 May 2023

31528831R00250